# These Violent Delights

## A Modern Retelling of Romeo and Juliet

Jeanette Battista

Also by Jeanette Battista

**The Moon Series**
Leopard Moon
Jackal Moon
Hyena Moon
Hunter Moon
Fox Hunt (short story)

Long Black Veil

**The Demon's Gate Series**
The Iron Bells
The Stone Golem
The Demon's Gate

Played

**Books of Aerie**
An Unkindness of Ravens
A Murder of Crows

These Violent Delights

# DEDICATION

To all of my English teachers

# CONTENTS

# ACKNOWLEDGMENTS

A huge thank you to the people who read early versions and pieces
of this book: Molly, Melissa, Amanda, and Heidi.
To Laura, for creating a cover beyond my wildest dreams.
To my dearest LGBTQ+ friends and allies, I hope I did okay.

# ACT ONE

*True, I talk of dreams,*
*Which are the children of an idle brain,*
*Begot of nothing but vain fantasy,*
*Which is as thin as the substance of the air…*

*Romeo and Juliet, Act I, Scene V*

# CHAPTER ONE

Well, here she was.

Julie looked around what was to be her new home for the next nine months and tried not to dissolve into a puddle of anxiety-riddled goo. The walls of her dorm room were an off-white, a completely non-threatening shade of beige that managed to be neither welcoming nor comforting. As she wrestled with her rolling suitcases, camera bag, and laptop case, Julie noticed the chest of drawers, desk, and twin bed that made up the furnishings in the room and breathed a sigh of relief. At least her parents had gotten her a single. She sent off a quick, silent prayer of thanks before dumping her shoulder bags on the bare mattress.

Okay, so this was it. Taking a deep breath in, Julie settled herself. She would unpack. She would go downstairs and get the boxes that her mother had shipped for her full of school and room supplies. She would put up pictures and stuff that reminded her of home. She would make her bed.

She would *not* curl up on it immediately after and cry like an abandoned child lost in a forbidden forest. Even if she felt like one.

Julie had spent her summer in a low-level state of panic. Her parents had dropped the bomb about boarding school when she'd been elbow-deep in dish soapsuds and hot water. When they'd given her the news about changing schools to improve her college chances, she'd almost vomited her dinner back into the stockpot she was scrubbing, managing to stop herself only because it would make more work for her.

They'd told her that Verona Prep was a feeder school for the Ivy Leagues, its rigorous program tops in the country. There hadn't been any talk of her *not* going, even if it was a lot more liberal-leaning than her parents ordinarily supported. The next weeks passed with Julie feeling like she was stuck on one of those horrible rides that took you up fifteen stories only to drop you to the ground at breakneck speed. Her life in Kansas had basically become a walking Tower of Terror.

Her parents were at least excited about her impending move to the East Coast. Or as excited as their busy schedules allowed them to get. Her father devoted much of his time to his upcoming Senate campaign, while her mother decided to make the moral degradation of today's youth her pet project and ended up in a Twitter war with a pop star's followers. A lot of the dinner table talk focused on those two things, which made Julie weirdly glad. If no one talked about her impending move to Verona Prep, Julie could pretend it wasn't going to happen—at least until it came time to pack.

She missed her two older sisters terribly. One was away at college, studying to be a lawyer, and the other was in medical school. The baby of the family, Julie had always been coddled and cooed at, but now that her sisters were absent, she realized how much she missed their support. Especially since her parents had told her to make the right kind of friends and Julie honestly had no idea who those might be. Other Christians? Republicans? Moderates? All she wanted to do was finish high school, join a photography club, go to church, binge watch Supergirl, and eat cheddar pretzels. If she could find people that were down with those things, those were the right kind of friends for her. But she feared her parents meant something entirely different.

Heaving a sigh, Julie returned to the present. She was here now. Time enough for woolgathering later. First things first: unpacking.

Julie made short work of the clothes and shoes in her suitcases, putting things in drawers and closets, and eventually stowing the suitcases beneath her bed. Feeling proud that she was forty-five minutes into it and hadn't cried yet, she then trooped down the stairs to retrieve the rest of her things. The boxes were heavy and awkward, but the RA helped her and by the time all five of those boxes sat on her bedroom floor, Julie ached from exertion.

She'd finally managed to find her bedding and had begun making up her bed when she heard a knock on her half-opened door.

"Hello?" she called to the earnest looking brown-haired girl waiting in the doorway. "Can I help you with something?"

The girl flushed a light pink, shook her head as though losing an argument with herself—something Julie could totally identify with—and then stepped inside Julie's room. "Hi, I'm Tyndall Sutcliffe," she said, offering her hand. "Your mom called my mom . . ."

Julie sort-of remembered her mom saying something about a possible friend of the family being at Verona already, but she'd been so busy packing for, and stressing over, school that she hadn't been paying much attention. Oops.

"Oh, hey," Julie said, shaking Tyndall's hand. "Sorry, I'm still getting used to everything. I'm Julie Cranston."

Tyndall smiled. It did wonders for her face, taking it from mousy and serious to puckish and inviting. Julie smiled back before turning around to deal with her bed linens, feeling her face warm with a flush. "Thanks for coming by," she said as she shoved boxes off her bed so she could make it.

Tyndall reached over and took a corner of the fitted sheet Julie's mother had picked out for her. Her mom had picked out all her dorm supplies: desk set, comforter, bathroom accessories, towels, and anything else that had been on the list Verona provided to incoming students.

"You don't have to do that," Julie told her. "I can get it."

"I don't mind," Tyndall answered, tucking one side of the sheet under the mattress. "Many hands lighten the load."

Julie felt a bout of homesickness hit her like a punch from a prizefighter. Her mother used to say that when she was rousting the kids to do their chores. She swallowed around the sudden lump in her throat. She missed home desperately. "That they do."

Determined not to lose it in front of what amounted to a total stranger, Julie asked, "Where are you from?"

Tyndall shook out a pillowcase. "Dallas. My dad's a pastor with his own church." She reached for one of Julie's pillows and began to stuff it into the case. "He's got one of those syndicated broadcasts that airs his Sunday service all across the state every week."

Julie heard the note of pride in Tyndall's voice and smiled, reminding her how proud she was of her father. "You're a long way from home," she noted. "It must be hard." Lord knew it was hard for Julie. "Do you get to go back often?"

Tyndall deposited the covered pillow on Julie's bed, smoothing down the cotton blend with a nervous hand. When she seemed satisfied with its placement, she turned and picked up a sham and began the process all over again.

"Not really," she said. "My parents are pretty busy with my Dad's work and ministry. I only went home for a week this summer. The rest of the time I spent here."

Julie folded the ends of the sheet into hospital corners and tucked them under the mattress before glancing up at Tyndall. The girl wore a serene expression that didn't quite fit her. Julie knew that she'd have been miserable in Tyndall's place—she couldn't imagine not going home for the summer, especially if she'd already spent nine months at Verona. "That must have been lonely."

"Oh no," Tyndall assured her with forced brightness. "They hold a summer sleep away camp here. There were lots of other people here." She shrugged, dropping the other pillow on the bed. "You might like the students so much you'll decide to stay here for the summer too."

Julie felt something twist in her gut and kept her gaze lowered. Had she done something to make Tyndall think she liked...? No, she couldn't have. Even Julie's parents didn't know about the feelings she sometimes experienced around other girls. There was no way Tyndall could have picked up on it after ten minutes.

Still, it would be a good idea to change the subject. "I don't think so. I'd be crazy homesick if I couldn't go back to Kansas for the summer."

"First time away from home, huh?" Tyndall nodded sagely, as if she'd expected that response. "I think that's why your mom reached out to my mom once she found out you'd been accepted. She figured you'd be lonely and need someone to show you the ropes." Tyndall grinned. "And here I am!"

Julie gave her a half-hearted smile. "Yes, here you are." Something uncomfortable lodged in her chest, a feeling like she'd swallowed a boulder. Julie didn't know what her mother had said to Tyndall's and it made her nervous. "How do our moms know each other?"

Setting another pillow down, Tyndall answered absently. "They met on a Facebook page for Christian wives a few years back. Really hit it off. I think it was my mom who mentioned Verona to her."

Well, at least Julie knew whom to thank for the massive upheaval in her life. But that wasn't something she wanted to think about right now. Best to stay on safe topics.

"So how did you wind up all the way here from Texas?" Julie asked as she smoothed out the butter yellow and grey flowered comforter across her bed.

Tyndall ducked her head, suddenly awkward. "It's a really long and boring story."

Julie knew an evasion when she heard one; she used them enough herself to recognize it. "Okay," she said simply, willing to let it go. She liked Tyndall; she seemed like a nice person. Julie didn't want to cause her any pain. Some things, she knew, were better left unsaid.

"I noticed your camera," Tyndall said, by way of changing the subject. Julie looked at her camera bag sitting on her desk. "What do you like to take pictures of?"

Scrounging through another box filled with desk supplies, Julie shrugged. "Anything really. Whatever catches my eye mostly. I like the control I have when I'm behind the lens. The world can look the way I want it to."

Tyndall nodded emphatically in understanding. "Sometimes it feels like the world doesn't want us to be who we are or to do what's right. Being Christian is hard right now when it feels like everyone is against you. It's got to feel good to take back control."

Julie tilted her head, confused. "Where did that come—," she began to ask, only to be cut off by another knock at her door. Julie called, "Come in!"

Her prefect, a senior named Rinko, pushed open the door, her arms full of flyers. "Hi Julie! Welcome to Verona and Cap Hall!" the prefect said brightly. She spotted the other girl and Julie thought her smile dimmed just a bit. "Oh, hi Tyndall." She turned back to Julie. "I just wanted to drop by to see how you were adjusting, but it looks like you've already found a friend." Rinko smiled. "How's it going?"

"So far, so good," she told Rinko, studying the senior carefully. The prefect was Asian, with dark hair and eyes. Her hair was cut in a short, glossy bob that Julie immediately envied. Her own hair was its usual nest of heavy blond waves and corkscrew curls, puffing out from her head in a thick lion's mane. "Just getting unpacked." She leaned casually against the bedframe. She wanted to come off as cool and confident, not like some needy, scared girl away from home for the first time.

"Awesome," Rinko said. "Glad to hear it. If you need any help with anything or have a question, just come find me. My room's right down the hall." Rinko pointed to her right and Julie peered in that direction, as if she'd be able to make out which closed door was Rinko's. Gosh, she was a dork. She quickly pulled her gaze back to Rinko's pretty face.

"Oh, here," the prefect said, shoving a flyer at her. "There's a mixer tonight for all of the new students. Mostly freshmen, but there will be some new upperclassmen like you there too. And most of the prefects will be there. It should be fun!"

Julie glanced at the piece of paper in her hand. NEW STUDENT MIXER it read, followed by the time and location. Rinko had sketched out a map of campus with Cap Hall circled and a dotted line leading to Merrill Hall, the site of the mixer.

"Oh, um, thanks. Yeah. I'll try to make it." Julie nodded her head, feigning enthusiasm.

"I hear Monet's daughter might be there!" Rinko said in a low voice, carefully eyeing the empty hallway. Julie felt like they were spies passing along coded information. "You've heard she goes here, right? She's a late transfer. I think they put her in Montag Hall."

Julie felt her face flush and looked down at her feet. "No, I hadn't heard. Thanks for the info about the mixer!" She shut the door before she had the chance to say or do something to embarrass herself.

The room was quiet for a few moments. "So are you going to go?" Tyndall asked into the silence.

Julie shook her head and said, "I don't think so. Mixers aren't really my thing." They were so *not* her thing. Like if it were possible to have an anti-thing, mixers would be Julie's. Forced socializing was about as desirable as mucking out a horse stall in the heat of summer. Or a root canal.

"What if I went with you? It could be fun!" Tyndall blinked up at Julie, deploying what amounted to puppy dog eyes.

Julie gave her a dubious look. "You and I have very different ideas of fun, I think," she said, smiling.

Tyndall laugh-snorted. "And I'll be there to look out for you— it won't be *that* bad."

Swallowing back a sigh, the best Julie could give her was a "We'll see."

CHAPTER TWO


Romy Montoya slumped in the backseat of the Maybach her mother had ordered for them and tried not to pout too obviously. She was nearly seventeen, she knew she should be over being petulant when things didn't go her way, but sometimes a good pout was the only thing for it. Today was one of those times.

"I still say this is stupid," she muttered to no one in particular.

"Oh, are you talking to me now?" Her mother, international pop icon Monet, glanced up from her tablet to spear her daughter with a withering glance.

"I talked to you on the plane," Romy protested.

Monet rubbed at her temples. "Grunts and uh huh's do not qualify as speech, Romes."

"In some cultures they do," she huffed.

"I don't want snark to be my last memory of you until I visit on Parents Weekend." Her mother stared at her, eyes shining with unshed tears.

Oh no, if her mother started, Romy would start and that was not what she wanted. "Come on, you'd think I was a pod person if I didn't snark at you a little."

Monet's long-suffering sigh was epic, making Romy feel a touch better. While she'd stopped being mad at her mother earlier that summer when Monet had told her that she'd be going to boarding school on the East Coast, it was still good to know this wasn't an easy decision for her mom to make.

Romy understood that most people who only knew Monet's public persona would be surprised to learn that the music star was an actively involved parent. She insisted on family meals whenever she was home, which tended to be a lot of the time when she wasn't touring. Romy was Monet's only child—the result of a three-year relationship with her nutritionist eighteen years earlier—and her mother took the responsibility of motherhood seriously. Monet had gone to almost every parent/teacher conference, been to Parents' Nights at every one of Romy's schools, and still checked in every day she was away to make sure that Romy was doing okay and didn't need her home.

Monet was a persona, a mask that her mother took on and off like a pair of shoes. At home, she was Romy's Mom and Romy liked it that way.

She knew that the decision to send her to Verona Prep Academy was not made lightly.

Living in L.A. under constant paparazzi surveillance was like being a bug in a bell jar, especially when all of your friends were children of famous people too. Romy hadn't had a wild phase yet, but the press was sure trying to invent one for her. There was always a new picture of her with some random person and a headline touting a new relationship or secret affair. She was thinking of inventing a *Rumors about Romy* Bingo game just to keep things interesting.

It had been a paparazzi video on DZN that had started the whole Verona Prep thing. Monet had just arrived home from one leg of promotion for her new album. Romy had been in her room, texting her best friend, Rosalyn. Roz had just gotten out of rehab for the usual "exhaustion" that most celebrity teens seemed to suffer from, and Romy liked to make sure she was doing okay.

Monet had bellowed up the stairs, using Romy's full name. Whenever her mom busted out 'Romy Teresa Montoya,' Romy knew she was *beyond* pissed off.

"What's up?" she called as she stuck her head into the hall.

"Get your butt down here. Now!"

"Crap," Romy had muttered under her breath and hustled down the stairs. That was the voice of a woman who was not in the mood to wait.

She descended the stairs to find her mother standing in front of the giant television mounted to the wall in the living room. She'd paused the show she'd been watching.

"So, what's this?" Monet held her arms crossed over her ample chest, remote in hand. Her straight dark hair was pulled up in a high ponytail and her face was bare of makeup. She looked nothing like the woman plastered on album covers and magazine spreads. She pointed at the screen with one lacquered nail.

Romy glanced at the image on the television. A picture of Romy lunging at a guy while being held back by three friends was frozen on the massive screen. The pap had caught her in mid-snarl, looking more than a bit feral.

Her gaze skipped back to her mother's face. Monet did not look amused.

Good God, how the hell had DZN even gotten that picture? Seriously, it was like those people teleported in at the first whiff of celebrity shenanigans. If there were an argument to be made for magic existing, they would be Exhibit A.

"It's no big deal," she began. "This guy started hassling me and Rosalyn and the rest of our group because she and I were holding hands. He was drunk and looking to start something."

"Looks to me like he did," her mother observed, gaze flicking to the screen and then back to her daughter's face.

"Mom, he shoved Antimone and said something really racist to Shawna." Romy pointed at the television. "That only shows a small part of what happened when we were out. And that was like over a week ago." She tried not to roll her eyes. It must have been a super slow news cycle to dredge this up.

"I'm well aware that it was over a week ago," Monet said, rubbing at the bridge of her nose. "You know how I know that? Because my lawyers have been dealing with this asshat because he threatened to sue you or have you arrested."

"I didn't touch him!" Romy glared at the guy on the screen.

"It doesn't matter, Romy." Monet sighed. "How many times have I told you that?"

"What did he want?" she had asked, feeling like she was the worst kid in the world. She hated disappointing her mother. Monet had never had to buy her out of trouble before and Romy didn't want her to have to start now.

"You don't need to worry about that. It's been dealt with." Her mother frowned. "This can't happen again, Romy. You have too much to lose to just freak out and attack a guy, kid. You're better than that."

"You just expect me to ignore it when someone abuses one of my friends?" Romy gave her mother a hard look. "You wouldn't have done that—you *don't* do that. I remember the shots of you getting in some guy's face at a rally when he told Uncle Nick that all fags go to hell and he should just catch AIDS and join them. You didn't care about someone taking your picture at the wrong time because what that guy said was wrong and you were protecting a friend."

"We're not talking about me, Romes." Monet shook her head, the ponytail swinging back and forth. "I was older then and already established in my career when I did that. You haven't even grown up."

"I'm sixteen, Mom," she scoffed.

"Yeah, and you don't know anything about what the real world is like at sixteen," Monet told her, voice snapping in anger. "So you are going to listen to me now." She took a deep breath. "You were damned lucky that guy didn't press charges, Romy. What you did was attempted assault! You may only be sixteen but that doesn't mean you get a free pass. Just because I'm your mother doesn't mean you wouldn't—and couldn't—be arrested for something like this."

"I didn't even touch him!" Romy protested again, hands clenched into fists on her hips. "And he touched us first anyway!"

"That's not what the picture shows, Romy. You're coming to the age where you've got to be more careful about this stuff, about the people you hang out with and the people who may be watching." Monet shook her head again, ponytail swinging back and forth like a pendulum. "I've been thinking a lot about this, and I've made a decision. You're going to be attending school at Verona Prep Academy this year."

"What!?" Romy gaped at her mother. "Where the fuck is that even?"

"Language," Monet reminded, before answering the question. "East Coast—Connecticut." Monet's face was fierce when she spoke. She walked closer until she stood in front of Romy. "You need to get out of L.A. for a time, get some perspective. Things are crazy out here, and I don't want you getting a bad reputation because you're followed around by photographers every minute of your day. You need to be able to make mistakes without having them follow you around for the rest of your life."

And thus, it had been decided. Romy would spend her junior and senior year at Verona Prep and try to stay out of trouble. The school had a strict honor code, a social media policy, no tolerance for bullying, and wouldn't allow paparazzi on the grounds. While Romy wasn't thrilled that she had to leave her friends, she couldn't say she was unhappy about not being snapped every time she left the house, especially now that her mother and some wannabe Senator's wife were feuding in the news.

But it didn't mean she couldn't give her mother grief about it. Romy stretched her legs out in the car, still feeling stiff from the flight east, and said, "I'm probably going to die of boredom out here. What do they do for fun? Hay rides? Apple picking?"

Monet pulled her sunglasses down her nose to survey her daughter. "As opposed to sneaking out to clubs underage or getting sent to rehab? How is Rosalyn, by the way?"

Okay, Romy had to admit that was a good burn. "Staying clean so far. That rehab place seems to have worked for her." She was tempted to check her phone for a text from Roz, but knew that her mother would not appreciate it.

"I'm so happy for her." Romy frowned at her mother's obvious sarcasm, but refrained from mouthing off after a warning look from Monet. "She's a perfect example of what I've been trying to tell you about L.A. Where are your friends headed? Do they have any goals besides being famous and posing for pictures? Do they have any idea what they want to do with their lives?" When Romy opened her mouth to answer, Monet shook her head. "I know *you* aren't like that. You want a career in music. You have plans and goals and drive but it is being wasted out here as you squander your time going to clubs and parties."

"I'm not an idiot, Mom." Romy countered.

"Precisely," Monet said briskly, giving her daughter a sly look. "Which is why I am sending you away to *learn*."

Romy frowned. "Huh?"

"Education is important. If you're going to go into the music business, you need to go to school. I'll support you in whatever way you need me to, but first graduate high school and college." Her phone began to buzz, but she ignored it for the time being.

"I don't need to go to college!" Her mother was being so unbelievably unfair. "And by the time I'm done with school, I'll be too old to do anything. I may as well be dead! You didn't go to college!"

"You're not *me*, Romy. I want you to have all the choices available to you, all the opportunities. Staying in L.A. was only going to get you into trouble. You deserve some breathing room, not to have to worry about someone snapping a picture or taking a video of you without you knowing it. Verona Prep will give you that. You can be a normal kid."

Smirking, Romy said, "I hate to tell you, but normal kids don't go to boarding schools across the country."

Monet smiled, reaching out to ruffle Romy's hair. "Well, this one does."

"Ugh, stop! Do you know how long it took me to get it perfectly messed up today?" Romy batted her mother's hands away from her head.

Monet pulled her in for a hug across the seat. "I love you, Romy. I know this is hard for you, but I am trying to protect you."

Romy dug her forehead into her mother's shoulder. She shouldn't still need this kind of support, but she'd be lying if she said it didn't make her feel better. Her arms came up to wrap around her mother. "I know. But I don't need protection."

Monet smiled fondly. "You'll always need protection—and you'll always have it so long as I'm around. You're my baby, Romy. You'll always be the most important thing to me."

Romy made a face. She hated sappy moments like this because it made her feel like she was in kindergarten again, crying over a skinned knee. She didn't like how warm and comfortable statements like that made her. She was almost an adult, for heaven's sake!

Monet glanced down at her phone, reading the text that had come in a few moments ago with a sour expression on her face. Before Romy could ask her about it, their driver turned around and said, "We're here."

# CHAPTER THREE

Romy lugged her duffel bag and laptop case up the stairs while Beverly and one of the bodyguards from the other car followed with the rest of her stuff. There was no elevator, which sucked mightily, but since Montag Hall looked to have been built when dinosaurs still roamed the earth, Romy wasn't surprised. She hit the second floor landing with a grateful sigh and began to scout for room 12.

"Found it!" she called after a few moments. "The pelican has landed. The fat lady walks at midnight and all that other covert code word crap. You can send in the Mom." Monet was waiting in the hired car for the all-clear. Romy appreciated that her mother didn't want to make her move-in day another public appearance. This move was stressful enough as it was.

Beverly Balthazar—Bev—stumbled up to Romy, trying to juggle both Romy's rolling suitcase and her phone, neither particularly successfully. She was Monet's personal assistant and all around Girl Friday of the past five years. She swiped at something on her phone, brow so furrowed that Romy was pretty sure she could plant seeds in her forehead.

"What's going on?" Romy asked her.

Beverly glanced up, scowling in irritation. "It's that Cranston woman again." Kansas state senator David Cranston's wife was taking on Monet for her lyrics, risqué videos, and her charitable foundation for LGBT youth in the court of public opinion, claiming the singer was corrupting today's youth with her moral failings. The senator and his wife were conservative Christians who believed that homosexuality could be cured.

"How bad is it?"

Beverly swiped through a few more screens on her phone before answering. "Looks like it will just be a lot of bluster before it eventually blows over once the election's done. It's like Tipper Gore in the eighties."

Romy nodded, though she really didn't understand why this was even a thing, nor had any idea who Tipper Gore was. Cranston was running for the US Senate on a conservative platform that came down hard on the side of traditional family values and against gay rights. He scared the crap out of Romy, who identified as bisexual, especially with his talk about his support of gay conversion camps. Why his wife had picked a fight with her mother still confused her. She'd have thought he had enough publicity.

"Her husband has taken a hard line about gay marriage being a sin and that sexual orientation is a choice, so she's very vocal about young people being influenced by liberal propaganda like your mother's foundation." She smiled grimly at Romy. "And you should know that she's probably going to bring you—and a few of your exploits—into this mess."

Of course. Romy's very existence was like waving a red flag before a bull. Cranston's wife—what the heck was her name?— wouldn't be able to resist using Romy to make her points about Monet's negative influence. Romy was suddenly glad for the last minute transfer to Verona. She didn't want to give the candidate or his wife any more ammunition.

Romy chose not to think about all that at the moment, instead opening the door to her room. She barely glanced at the young woman seated on the window bench as she trudged in to dump her stuff on the unoccupied bed. When Romy was finally divested of her load, she sized up her roommate.

The girl was tall; even seated, Romy could tell that she looked to be all leg. Her skin was a terra-cotta, reddish brown color, her mahogany hair done up in twists. Her eyes were large, oval, and golden-brown. Romy idly wondered if Verona Prep had decided to put both the brown chicks together. Romy was of average height and lanky, with shiny dark hair, courtesy of her Korean father. Her russet skin and brownish green eyes came courtesy of Monet's Puerto Rican roots.

Romy told herself she was being paranoid. Verona Prep had a reputation for being pretty liberal for a boarding school. She could wait until there was proof they were clumping the more racially "diverse" students together before she got her social justice on.

"Hey," she greeted her roommate, ducking her head in a sudden onset of shyness. "I'm Romy."

Her roommate got up, and yep, she was tall. Like model tall, maybe five foot ten or eleven. She bounded over in a tangle of gangly limbs and said, "Oh my God, I have been waiting for you, like, forever. I'm Mercury. Welcome, roomie!"

"Mercury? Like the planet?" Romy couldn't help asking. Why did this girl's name seem familiar?

Mercury rolled her eyes. "Yeah, I can thank my dad for that. He's an astrophysicist—loves all things planetary. My brother is name Cosmo—you know, after cosmos. And my littlest sister is Ceres."

Astrophysicist? Did that mean . . . "Is your dad Will Tyrell Highbrook?"

Nodding, Mercury sat down on her neatly made bed. "Yeah, that's him. The guy who suddenly made planetary stuff cool again." She shrugged. "He's mostly just a huge geek."

Holy crap. Romy plopped down on her own mattress, sure her eyes were as round as dinner plates. Will Tyrell Highbrook was the shit. She'd watched his whole series on the universe when it had aired on PBS. There was talk that he was going to get a late night talk show on one of the science channels. He was insanely cool.

And she was rooming with his daughter. Hell yes. This year might not suck so badly after all.

Beverly staggered in, dragging one of Romy's giant suitcases. Trev, the bodyguard, wheeled the case he was carrying into the room and stepped back into the dorm's hallway. Romy pulled both cases out of the way as her mother strode into the room.

"This is actually better than I was expecting," Monet said as she entered, turning so she could take in the dorm room from all angles. She wore a creamy white trench coat over a brightly patterned maxi dress. Huge sunglasses held back her black hair. Romy thought her mother looked like she should be on a beach somewhere, sipping a colorful drink with an umbrella in it, not moving her daughter into a stuffy boarding school in the Northeast.

"You—you're," Romy's roommate stammered out, golden brown eyes wide. Mercury looked from mother to daughter and back again. "You're *Monet.*"

"Guilty as charged," Monet said, a friendly smile gracing her perfectly painted red lips. She extended her hand. "And you are Romy's roommate, yes?"

"Definitely yes!" Mercury nodded so enthusiastically, Romy thought her head might fall off her neck in protest at the treatment. "I'm Mercury Highbrook." She shook Monet's hand vigorously.

"A pleasure to meet you, Mercury." Romy's mom took her hand back before turning to her daughter. "Well, what do you think, kiddo? Can you be happy here?"

Romy shrugged, fiddling with the handle of her suitcase. She could be happy anywhere—happiness was a state of being, not a location. Whether this school was a good fit for her, well, that remained to be seen. She was excited that she liked her roommate; in fact, Mercury seemed like a good fit for her.

Monet leaned forward, scanning Romy's face. Romy met her mother's hazel gaze—almost a twin to her own—and held it. "I'll be okay," she told her mom.

Monet pressed a kiss against Romy's forehead. "I'm proud of you, baby."

Shifting from foot to foot, Romy nodded. Her throat was suddenly too tight, like it was hard to breathe. For all of Romy's independence, this would be her first time she was away from home for anything other than a vacation. Even when they'd moved to New York so her mother could perform on Broadway for a limited run, Monet had always been with her. The thought of being truly by herself scared her almost as much as it exhilarated her.

"Thanks, Mom." She had to force the words out around the lump in her throat.

"Okay!" Monet straightened, voice brisk, but her eyes were bright with unshed tears. "So I will leave you to get unpacked, but I'll be back for dinner. Mercury, you want to join us or do you already have plans with your family?"

Romy gave her roommate a smile, letting her know she was welcome. "I got here yesterday, so my parents already left. If you're sure I wouldn't be imposing, I'd love to go."

"Of course we're sure," Romy told her. "It'll be cool."

Monet beamed at them. "Beverly will call with logistics. I'm not sure if we'll need to worry about photographers this far out. I may just send the car, and we'll go from there." She brushed Romy's cheek with the back of her hand before stepping toward the door.

"Did the paparazzi really follow you?" Mercury asked. "Up here?"

"Dump trucks full of a-holes," Romy told her.

"Language," Monet reminded, and then she was out the door.

Romy rolled her eyes, and then began to unpack. Her dorm room was pretty big, but there was two of everything: beds pushed against opposite walls, desks, chairs, and wardrobes, so it felt a little cramped.

"Wow." Mercury perched on the back of her desk chair, feet on the seat. "Your mom is *MONET*." She leaned forward, elbows on her knees. "What is *that* like?"

"Pretty much like everything else. She's my mom." Romy stuffed t-shirts and underwear into one of the empty drawers of her wardrobe. "Your dad's pretty famous—it's probably like that."

Mercury laughed. "Hardly. My dad is fairly new to the fame game. Your mom has been famous for over twenty years! *You've* been in the news since you were a baby. You were on the cover of Vogue in swaddling clothes." She played absently with one of her twists. "Anyway, we don't have photographers chasing us around or journalists digging through our trash. It's mostly tame. Nothing like what you have going on." She cut her eyes at Romy, as if she was debating if she should say what was on her mind. She seemed to come to a decision quickly. "So—and you can totally tell me to butt out and not answer—but what are you doing at Verona? I mean, I'm sure there were plenty of places for you to go to school in Hollywood, right?"

Romy dug out her sheets that Beverly had bought using the list Verona Prep had provided. She ducked out into the hall to find the pillows in the stacks of stuff the bodyguards had piled next to the door.

As she unwrapped the sheets, Romy told Mercury about the agreement she'd made with her mother. "I made a deal with my mom. She's worried I'll get into the business way too young without exploring my options. So I have to finish high school and college before I can even think about releasing any music or signing with a label. Officially, anyway. I have a YouTube channel where I post amateur stuff."

It was more than just amateur stuff, but Romy didn't want to sound arrogant. She posted snippets of her original songs, videos of her playing guitar and piano, and even full versions of some of her more popular covers. She didn't track her numbers much; Romy assumed a good chunk of her followers were fans of her mother's anyway. It was her mother who had told her she had over six million subscribers. Her last upload had gotten over two million hits in less than a day.

Numbers and popularity weren't a huge deal to Romy, not like it was to some of her friends. Rosalyn would go into a deep depression if she ever dropped below a million followers on Twitter. Still, Romy had accused her mother of stalking her YouTube stats. Monet had thrown a grape at her head when she'd said as much.

Romy began to make her bed, surprised when Mercury got up to help. "Anyway, Mom was pretty adamant that I get into a good school and Verona Prep is supposed to be one of the best for getting into an Ivy. Personally, it doesn't matter where I go—I'm pretty sure music is going to be where I end up, one way or another, but I think college is a good idea. Can you grab my comforter from out in the hall?"

"Sure." Mercury was back a few minutes later with a red and black brocade comforter that looked like it belonged on the set of a Dracula biopic rather than in a teenager's room. This was the last time she let Beverly pick out room décor. "But why Connecticut?"

"Thanks." Romy unzipped the plastic covering housing the ridiculous comforter and draped it over the bed before answering. "We lived in New York for a little while. I think Mom prefers the East Coast, to be honest. And it *is* kind of getting crazy in Hollywood. A couple of my friends have already been to rehab, one got married and had it annulled just a few months ago. I think I'm one friend's de facto sober coach. I get stalked by the paps all the time. I'm okay going somewhere with a lot less drama." She looked at Mercury. "What about you? Is this your first year at Verona?"

"Nah," she answered, waving her hand. "I started my freshman year here. It's okay, better than most from what I've heard. And I live in NYC so it isn't that far from home. Not like you." Mercury tilted her head as Romy stepped away from her bed to survey the finished product.

"You've really got an *I'm the heroine in a gothic novel* look going on over there," she observed.

"Yeah, it's not what I would have picked out for myself. Bev— she's my mom's assistant—handled most of the shopping and she did the best she could." Romy shook her head in mock despair.

"Just so long as you keep your fangs on your side of the room, we'll be fine," Mercury joked. "And try not to sparkle too much."

With a snort of laughter, Romy turned to face her roommate. "I'll do my best not to drain your blood or burst into flames at inappropriate times."

"As one should," Mercury said, nodding sagely.

Romy quickly unpacked, dragging more and more items in from the hallway, until everything had found a place in the room and been put away. When she was finished, Mercury showed her the important parts of the dorm—laundry room, trash chute, snack machines, and student lounge—and introduced her to some of her friends on their floor.

They were relaxing on her beds, listening to a few of Romy's original songs that Mercury had asked to hear, when there was a knock on their half-open door.

"Come on in!" Mercury yelled over the music.

A girl, older than Romy, stepped inside. She was white, blond, and pretty in that preppy way Romy associated with boarding schools. She wore a denim skirt and polo shirt and a pair of red Toms. Surprisingly, no pearl necklace adorned her neck, but Romy suspected they might see one once classes started. Then she mentally slapped herself. She hated it when people made judgment calls about her just because she had a visible tattoo, multiple ear piercings, and short hair, and here she was doing it to someone else. Not cool.

"Hi there!" the newcomer said brightly. She turned to Mercury first. "Good to see you again, Mercury. Summer good?" At Mercury's nod, the new girl looked over at Romy. "I'm Olivia, and I'm one of the prefects for Montag Hall. You're Romy, right? I wanted to come over and introduce myself and see how move-in was going. You guys doing okay?"

"Fine," Mercury said.

"It's all good," Romy agreed.

"Terrific!" Olivia chirped. "There's orientation tomorrow and everything you need—your schedule, maps, good to know info—is in that packet on your desk." She pointed to a fat white envelope that Romy hadn't bothered to open. "Tonight we're having a mixer for new students that you might be interested in going to. There will be some freshmen there, but also some of the new upperclassmen too."

She handed Romy a flyer. It had all of the mixer information: location, date, time, even a handy little map. "Thanks," she said, "I'll think about it."

"Okay, sure!" Olivia was one of those people that sounded enthusiastic about everything. She was probably perky even when she was throwing up with the stomach flu. "Hope to see you there." She backed out of the doorway with, "I'm on the first floor if you need anything. And welcome to Verona Prep!"

Once Olivia left, the roommates stared at each other. "There were far too many exclamation points in her speech. Nobody is that excited over orientation *ever*," Romy told her roommate, setting aside the flyer.

"That's why she's a prefect. They tend to pick the really perky people." Mercury cocked her head, observing Romy for a moment. "You wouldn't be interested in coffee, would you?"

"God yes!" Romy bounded to her feet, stretching out a hand to her roommate. "Lead me to the Promised Land and I will be yours forever."

With a laugh, Mercury tucked Romy's hand in her arm and led her out the door.

# CHAPTER FOUR

Julie kept close to the wall of the common room of Merrill Hall, watching the crowd mingle. Most of them were freshmen; she recognized a few of them from move-in day. The girls of Verona seemed trendy and far less conservative than her friends back at home. She wasn't certain how she was supposed to "make connections" with them. A number of them looked like they'd just stepped off a fashion runway, while others looked like they might have slept next to a garbage bin with how artfully ripped and distressed their clothes were.

"You should introduce yourself," Tyndall said. "It's no fun if you don't even try."

Tyndall stood next to Julie's spot at the wall. She was ebullient, friendly, and always seemed outgoing. There were no strangers to her, just friends she hadn't met yet. Julie couldn't help but feel like she was holding the other girl back from socializing. She was more than happy to hold up the wall, but Tyndall jerked and twitched every time a new person walked into the room, as if she held herself back so she didn't abandon Julie.

"You don't have to stay beside me all night," Julie told Tyndall after another aborted step forward nearly made her gnash her teeth. "I'll be fine if you want to go and say hi to people."

Tyndall shook her dark hair from her shoulders. "It's okay, I don't mind waiting with you. I'm not going to abandon you on your first night out here. I promised your mama I'd look after you!"

She'd promised her mother—what did that mean? Julie's inner alarms sprang to life. She didn't need or want someone to shadow her every step and report back to her mother.

Julie waited a few more minutes, noticing how Tyndall smiled and waved at people. Feeling more than a little guilty, she tried again. "Seriously, Tyndall. Go on ahead and talk to people. I'm probably just going to get some punch or something."

Tyndall pursed her lips and for the first time, Julie felt real disapproval roll off her. "You know, you should actually mingle," Tyndall murmured, smiling at a random passing freshman. "Make some new friends. I swear almost everyone here is super nice." She smiled, but Julie heard an undertone of pressure in her words, like a less intense Lady Macbeth. "You could do some real good for some of the students around here."

A commotion at the entrance pulled Julie's attention away from Tyndall before she could ask what she meant. Two newcomers stood in the doorway, surveying the room. One was a tall black girl and the other was… well, Julie wasn't sure what to make of her. She was of average height, thin, and pretty in an androgynous way. She wasn't white, but she wasn't as dark skinned as the girl she'd come with, so maybe biracial? Her hair was short and spiky with red streaks throughout it. A collection of silver rings arched up her ear, and a tattoo winked from the inside of her left wrist. She wore a t-shirt for a band Julie didn't recognize, some ratted out skinny jeans, and a pair of half-unlaced black boots.

"Oh sweet baby Jesus," came Tyndall's whispered exultation. "I can't believe she actually came." The Texan turned to her, concern—and a little bit of glee—sparkling in her eyes. "Are you going to be okay?"

"Why wouldn't I be okay? Who are you talking about?" Julie asked, unable to pull her gaze from the girl in the band shirt. She felt her heart begin to beat faster, a combination of panic and something else she didn't want to name. She remembered the "talk" she'd gotten from her parents when they'd tried the whole sex-ed discussion. *It was Adam and Eve*, her mother had said, *not Ava and Eve or Adam and Steve. Remember that, Julie, and choose your friends accordingly.*

"You have to know who that is, right?" Tyndall asked, inclining her head towards the newcomers at the door. "The one with the spiky hair? Your mom's been fighting with her mom for the last six months!"

"Ummmm?" The girl didn't look like someone she should recognize. Julie didn't follow pop culture all that much.

Tyndall turned to face Julie and took her by the shoulders. "You really don't know? She's *Monet's* daughter, Romy." She cut her eyes over to the young women at the entrance once more. "She's a total party kid, always getting in trouble. I heard she's already been to rehab twice. I bet that's why she's here. Plus she's gay or bi or whatever." Shaking her head, Tyndall continued. "Her mother must have promised them a new building or something to get *her* accepted. She was nearly arrested for starting a brawl outside of one of those clubs her and all of her rich friends go to."

Julie stared. Tyndall seemed to know an awful lot about this young woman. Keeping her thoughts to herself, Julie shifted her gaze back to the young woman in the band shirt. So that was Monet's daughter? She knew about the feud between the pop star and her mother—Monet's music, videos, and interviews were discussed in detail in her house—but Julie hadn't paid attention to anything about Monet's daughter. Her mother hadn't focused much of her energy on the girl and Julie had been too busy hiding secrets of her own to care much about someone else's famous kid.

"I think I'll go over and introduce myself," Tyndall said sweetly, pushing away from the wall.

Julie grabbed her new friend's arm before she could take a step, alarmed at her tone. While she didn't think Tyndall would start anything at the mixer, she didn't like the relish with which her new friend had listed all of Romy's crimes. Julie just wanted a quiet night. She barely even knew Tyndall, as friendly as she was. Julie just wanted to keep her head down, get through her two years at Verona and flee to college.

At Tyndall's suspicious look, Julie felt her stomach twist into knots, but she kept going. "Hey, you're right, let's mingle. I may as well meet some of the other new kids."

Tyndall looked surprised, seemingly confused by Julie's change of heart. "Oh! Sure, Julie." She stared at her for a long moment, and Julie had to fight not to fidget beneath such an assessing gaze. Tyndall was mostly sweetness and light, but she could be downright scary when the situation called for it. Or maybe Julie was just a giant chicken who hated conflict of any kind.

It was probably that.

Putting her hand on Julie's arm, Tyndall drew her closer. Julie felt uncomfortable sweat break out on the back of her neck. "I can introduce you to the right people." She paused, as though carefully choosing her words before she spoke again. "Girls who think like we do. It can be hard finding each other in a school like this."

"Girls like us?" Now Julie was completely confused. Tyndall didn't mean what *that* sounded like—there was no way. Julie held herself still, afraid to move or speak. "I don't understand."

Leaning in closer, Tyndall whispered, "You know." She glanced around. "Christians."

Julie breathed a sigh of relief. "I don't think it's that big of a deal if we're Christians," she told her.

Tyndall gave her a long-suffering look. "You haven't been here long enough, but trust me, it is. Most of these girls wouldn't know the Bible if it smacked them upside the head." She grinned suddenly. "But when I heard you were coming to Verona, I knew it was a sign. Did you know there's a chapel on campus that isn't used? We could change that!"

Julie swallowed nervously. "Is that why you think I'm here?" She wasn't comfortable with any of this.

"I know it is," Tyndall said confidently.

Julie glanced back toward the door, but saw that Monet's daughter and the girl she'd come with had already moved deeper into the crowd of people. Her gaze swept the crowd, but Julie couldn't find Romy in the large group of people. Her stomach sank in disappointment, but it was probably for the best. She didn't need to tempt fate by running into Monet's daughter.

Taking a calming breath, Julie turned back to Tyndall and managed a small smile. "Look, seriously, go mingle. I'm just going to get something to drink and I'll catch up with you," Julie urged, needing some space to herself. Tyndall's intensity became overwhelming after a while. "Okay?"

Tyndall stared at her again, and Julie felt the girl sizing her up. She didn't like it, but she held her ground. Finally, Tyndall looked away at the room full of people. "Sure." She paused, then turned on a megawatt smile, suddenly that luminous and engaging person from before. "I'll find some people to introduce you to. See you in a bit." With a flounce of her hair, she sauntered over to a knot of new students, wide and fake grin firmly in place.

Leaning back against the wall, Julie breathed out a sigh of relief. Thank goodness. Tyndall was very... zealous. Julie had encountered that a lot in recent years—ever since her family had changed churches and her father had gone even further right in his political rhetoric. It still made her uncomfortable several years later, like a scratchy sweater that didn't fit right. Tyndall meant well, Julie was sure, but she just came on a bit strong. She knew she was lucky to have found someone willing to show her the ropes of Verona, and she couldn't afford to alienate Tyndall.

Okay, she was just going to go get a cup of punch, maybe a cookie or fifteen, and then tell Tyndall she had a stomachache. It wasn't a lie; her stomach was unsettled from their conversation and from being around all these strangers. Julie wanted to abscond back to her room. She'd made an appearance. She had tried. She'd make more of an effort to meet people in her classes or in clubs, but this mixer was pretty much over for her.

Julie's gaze searched the room one last time, but what—or who—she was looking for she wasn't sure.

♪ ♪ ♪

Romy had tried, she really had. Mercury was great, and Romy really appreciated her roommate coming to a mixer she basically had no reason to attend, but there was only so much interference Mercury could run between Romy and the other students who recognized her. At first it wasn't a big deal: a surprised glance here, some intense staring there, a shyly muttered, "Are you really Monet's daughter?" or the odd excited squeal and stolen touch. But once word spread that Monet's daughter was at the mixer, things got more complicated.

One student had asked her about the picture of her and Rosalyn—something Romy had forgotten about. It had been one of those ubiquitous DZN articles with a headline that read, *Lesbian Daughter of Monet Has Wild Night with New Love,* complete with a picture of Rosalyn laying a big smacking kiss on Romy's lips.

Romy remembered that 'wild' night and the moment when the picture was taken. Roz was shorter than Romy was, and blessed with a metabolism that ensured she'd never have to diet while providing her with an ass that would do one of Monet's backup dancers proud. She wore her blond hair in a constant cloud around her face, the ends tinted teal. It hadn't been a terrible picture, although Romy hadn't really given the camera her best side.

Romy had given the freshman who asked about the picture and the kiss the usual answer: they'd just been messing around. It had been a stupid idea, something Rosalyn had suggested as a way to act out and gain some attention from Roz's otherwise uninterested parents. Romy had gone along with it for...no real reason, now that she thought about it. She'd wanted to see what Rosalyn would do if she didn't stop her.

The kiss had been nice. Nothing earth-shattering or life-changing. Just nice. It worried Romy a bit—she'd had a crush on Rosalyn for such a long time. She'd thought that the kiss would feel…different. Better maybe. She'd expected the feeling of lights flashing all around her, the buoyance of her heart making her insides float.

She'd gotten *nice* instead.

It was not something she wanted to discuss with nosy strangers who felt she owed them insight into her most intimate thoughts just because they followed her on Twitter.

Romy stepped away from yet another knot of people to move around the room. She'd had to turn her phone off as it blew up with Twitter and Instagram notifications. She sounded like a belled cat with her phone's nonstop chiming. Romy knew most, if not all of them, would be along the lines of "OMG, met Monet's daughter!" or horrible pictures of her from a sneaky camera phone click.

Romy pushed through the press of new students, now gathered in an amorphous circle in the center of the room, and made her way to the table along one wall where drinks were set out. She was ready to bail—had been ready about five minutes after she'd walked into the mixer—but first she needed some water.

There was a girl standing in front of several trays of cookies. She was about Romy's height, with a magnificent head of wheat-colored hair that fell down her back in tight curls and waves. Romy quietly stepped up beside her, surveying the drinks on offer.

"They have anything other than soda here?" Romy asked, turning bottles around to check labels.

The girl at the table jerked in surprise, hands freezing on the cookies she was squirreling away inside a few napkins. She glanced over at Romy and her face went through a series of expressions, only some of which Romy could identify. She caught surprise, distaste, and nervousness, but there were couple of others that eluded her. Romy marveled at the mobility of the girl's pretty face and how she managed to seem guarded and open at the same time.

"Hoping for something stronger?" the girl replied, lips drawn down in a tight frown, gaze still on the plate of cookies in front of her.

*Ohhhh-kay.* That seemed somewhat pointed even though Romy had never seen this person before in her life. Still, she had plenty of practice letting stupid comments roll off her, even if this chick was someone she'd normally be attracted to.

"More like hoping for something without high fructose corn syrup and a shitload of chemicals in it," Romy answered mildly. She saw the girl's eyes widen in surprise. The beginnings of a smile twitched at the corners of her mouth before she stopped it.

Romy raised an eyebrow and continued. "I mean, what? Not even a bottle of water?"

"You might be the only high school student in the history of the United States to not appreciate free caffeine and sugary goodness," the stranger told her, sounding a teensy bit friendlier.

"I'm Romy." She started to offer her hand, but thought better of it. Instead, she nodded at the girl with the cookies in her fists.

The girl's eyes darted around the room, almost as if she was checking to make sure no one heard her talk to Romy. Romy's gaze followed hers, trying to figure out what exactly she was looking for, but she couldn't find anyone or anything that jumped out.

She finally turned her head so Romy could get a good look at her face. Serious blue eyes regarded her from a round face flushed from the heat of the room. Peachy skin highlighted in ivory where the overhead lights struck brow, chin, and cheekbones, Cupid's bow lips cast in shadow, and a body wrapped in J. Crew clothes. One of those *good* girls, every inch of her. She probably had pearls that she wore on special occasions. But man, she was pretty.

Romy paused, arrested by her thoughts. What was wrong with her? Had there been something in the Icelandic water she'd had at dinner? Why was she having such flights of fancy now? Sure, she was cute, but Romy was going to embarrass herself if she kept on staring.

"Julie," the girl said, voice pitched low so only the two of them could hear. "Julie Cranston."

The name pinged something in Romy's head, some kind of recognition. She'd heard that name somewhere before. She'd almost placed it when someone announced the mixer was officially getting started.

"Who's ready for some icebreakers!" one of the prefects called out to the large group of students milling around.

"Oh, no freakin' way." Romy caught Mercury's attention and gave her the signal that she was getting the hell out of there before she was forced to join in some time-honored, horrible getting to know you game.

"Right behind you," she heard Julie mutter behind her as she walked quickly to the door, out into the hallway, and outside the building.

The night was clear, the temperature dipping into *cool enough for long sleeves* conditions. Romy crossed her arms over her skinny chest in an effort to keep warm in her thin t-shirt. She'd left her hoodie back at her room in Montag. She tilted her chin up to take a look at the stars, so much brighter on this coast than back home. Must be a lack of smog.

"So you felt the need to sneak out too, huh?" she asked Julie as the two of them walked into the night.

Julie didn't say anything, but she didn't leave either. Romy continued. "You got something against icebreakers?"

"No, just against being required to participate in awkward situations made more so by forced intimacy," she said tightly, serious.

Romy burst out laughing. "So why were you at that mixer anyway, aside from a need to thieve as many cookies as humanly possible?"

She caught sight of Julie's blush before the other girl ducked her head. "Someone who lives on my floor sort of forced me to go and be social. Said I should meet some of the students before classes begin." She shrugged, hands full of napkins and baked goods contraband. "I don't know what I was expecting. Mostly it was just freshmen and they seemed to all know each other already." She glanced over at Romy. "What were you doing there?"

Tucking her hands into the pockets of her skinny jeans, Romy glanced behind her at Merrill Hall. "Honestly? I have no idea." It was her turn to shrug. "My mom found out about it at dinner and thought it would be a good idea if I went. Make new friends, that sort of thing, since I'm a junior and kind of missed hooking up with all the other kids in my year." She grinned. "I kind of forced my roommate to come along with me."

"Your mother was here?" Julie sounded a little jealous. "She actually came out here with you?"

Nodding, Romy glanced over at the pretty young woman walking beside her. "Yours didn't?" She saw Julie flinch, and then backtracked. "I mean, yeah, my mom did. She flew back out after dinner."

"She got a flight out that late?"

Now Romy fidgeted, clearing her throat awkwardly. She hated when she had to out who her mother was, but she wasn't ashamed of Monet or her success. Romy wasn't going to lie about where she came from or who she was. "She has a private plane."

She stopped walking and looked at Julie—they were of a height and Romy was happy not to have to crane her neck to look into her face. "My mom is Monet." She toed the grass beneath her boots. "You know, the singer."

"Oh." Julie's voice was quiet, but not surprised. She didn't flip out either—most people who found out who Romy's mother was usually reacted like Mercury, or worse. Julie just seemed to…deflate.

"Hey, can I have a cookie?" Romy asked just to have something to say. She didn't like to eat processed foods. She felt better when she ate foods closer to their natural state, but there was a weird undercurrent of tension between them that hadn't been there before. "Or are you holding them all to sell on the baked goods black market later?"

Julie glanced over at her, startled, and then grinned. Unwrapping one of the napkins she had in her hands, she held out a fistful of Oreos. Romy took one, eyeing it with distrust. "They couldn't even spring for Double Stuf? Misers."

A giggle. It was the cutest sound Romy had heard all day. Maybe all week. She smiled, cutting a glance out of the corner of her eyes and stood still, stopped by the unfettered smile on Julie's face. She'd looked strained all evening—at least since Romy had been watching her—and to see her like this was like seeing the clear blue sky after a hurricane.

"I like it when you laugh," Romy said, before she could stop herself. She felt the flush heat her face. *Smooth, Romy, really freaking smooth*. She didn't even know if Julie swung that way and she was already flirting with her.

Maybe she should invest in a Beverly, like her mom had—an assistant that was really there to stop her before she made a gigantic ass of herself. She wondered if Mercury might be interested in the job. Romy was usually the designated NO-friend; it might be nice to have one of her own.

Romy began to walk again, letting out a quiet, relieved breath when she heard Julie moving along with her. "What dorm are you in? I haven't seen you in Montag." She smiled at Julie, hoping to get the girl to smile back at her.

"I got put in Cap. I asked for a single." Julie stopped walking, so Romy did as well. "There's probably something I should confess before we go any further."

Romy grinned nervously. Oh, they were going further? That sounded promising. She resisted the impulse to say it though—even she couldn't spout a line *that* cheesy. The confession part sounded less so. She confined herself to a curious, "Oh?"

Julie bit her lower lip, not meeting Romy's eyes. "My mom hates your mom," she blurted out.

"Huh?" *Wow, that was erudite. Good job, Romy, well done.*

"My mom. My dad's running for Senate and my mom has been arguing with yours about her terrible influence over her fans."

Romy's mouth opened and closed, confused for a few precious seconds. Then it dawned on her. *Cranston.* That's where she'd heard that name before. All the news stations were running with the feud between the future senator's wife and the pop star. Romy had ignored most of it—this wasn't the first time someone had gone after her mother after all.

Still, anger flared inside of her. Romy barely knew this girl and she was supposed to listen to her insult her mother? No.

"A terrible influence over her fans? You make her sound like a mind-controlling she-hag." Romy tilted her head, staring at her intently for a few moments. Julie, surprisingly, met her gaze with an unapologetic one of her own. "Also, why would you basically begin a conversation like that? You don't think that was maybe just a little bit rude?"

Julie's eyes widened and Romy had to bite the inside of her cheek to keep her righteous anger from dissolving under a flood of hormones. Julie looked so cute—all big blue eyes, snub nose, and raised eyebrows winging up to hide in the mane of hair that framed her face.

*You got it bad, Montoya. You don't even know this chick.*

Didn't mean she didn't want to get to know her, though.

*NO. No no no.* Bad Romy, no cookie, not that she ate the things anyway.

"I just thought it would be the right thing to do to tell you who I am," Julie began, taking a step backwards, as if she were frightened of Romy. "You know, so there's no confusion. And no, I don't think it was rude."

Romy stared at her. Julie was something else, though what that something was remained to be seen. "Confusion about what? Your mom attacked my mom for standing up for LGBTQA youth. Your mom is *wrong.* End of story. Not seeing what there is to be confused about."

She saw Julie inhale, her chest rising and falling beneath her sweater. Her blue eyes narrowed, and Romy braced herself for a verbal smackdown from a cute but woefully uninformed girl.

What she got was, "Oh, yeah?"

Romy blinked, waiting. Nothing else came. Julie turned pink, scowling, staring down at her feet. Even that was rather adorable. Romy gave herself a mental smack. *Not helping, hormones. So very not helping.*

She tried not to laugh. This was completely ridiculous. "Yeah," she said, trying to recapture her anger only to find it ebbing away. In its place all she felt was a kind of bone-deep weariness that came from having to explain to people that being gay wasn't a sin or a mistake or a choice. She shouldn't have to do this. And yet here she was. Again. Fuck this noise.

"You know what? Whatever." Romy tucked her hands in her pocket, the Oreo crushed to crumbs. "You're going to believe whatever you want to anyway, and I'm really over having to explain to people like you and your mom why I should be allowed the same rights as everybody else." She took a deep breath, feeling an ache in her chest that hadn't been there moments ago. "So how about you stay out of my way, and I'll stay out of yours. That way there's no *confusion*."

Julie actually looked hurt when she said this, but Romy didn't care. Well, maybe a little, but it was lost in the blanket of irritation she was currently smothering beneath.

"I didn't mean to offend—," Julie began.

Romy cut her off. She was not interested in apologies now, no matter how cute the mouth they spilled from. "And yet, you did." She shrugged one shoulder, turning around.

"I just thought you should know who I was! You didn't seem to recognize my name!"

Romy kept walking, intending to just go back to Tag Hall and scream into her pillow. Or maybe write an angry response song. She couldn't decide. Then she thought better of it and stopped. She turned. Julie stood behind her, some distance away, hands full of cookies. Romy stared at her, honeyed hair gilded by the light of the rising moon.

"Or maybe I didn't care *what* your name was. Did you ever consider that?"

Julie put her hand to her throat, shock plain on her face. "You'd want to be friends?"

Romy steeled herself. She wasn't going to beg for friendship—or anything else. "Guess we'll never know." Taking a step back, Romy gave Julie a penetrating look. "See you around, Julie." Without waiting for a response, she turned her back on the Cranston girl and headed back to her dorm. She didn't look back.

## CHAPTER FIVE

Throwing herself on her bed, Romy snagged the pillow and buried her face in it. Then she screamed. This night had been a waste of infinite proportions. First that stupid mixer and then meeting Julie Cranston. She screamed into the pillow once again before throwing it across the room in anger.

Unbidden, her gaze went to the slightly crumbling Oreo cookie that sat on a tissue on her desk. It mocked her, that cookie, sitting there in sugary judginess at her idiocy. With a groan, Romy leaned over and swept the cookie into the trash can. Stupid cookie. Evil cookie. Death to the cookie. She debated about getting it back out, crushing it to smithereens and *then* throwing it away again, but restrained herself. She was not petty.

Oh, who was she kidding? Yes she was.

Mercury walked in when she was pounding the tissue-wrapped cookie beneath her fist. She closed the door behind her with an amused smirk on her face.

"Did the cookie do something particularly heinous to deserve such treatment or is it just displeasure with Oreos in general?"

Romy swept the mess into the trashcan. Again. "Just frustrated."

"Hey, thanks for leaving without me," Mercury said mildly, sitting on her bed and flinging Romy's pillow back over to her.

Romy caught it and tucked it against her chest. "Sorry," she said, head hung low. "It was stupid."

"Where'd you go?" Mercury leaned her back against the wall, tucking a bare foot up onto her bed and wrapping her arms around her bent knee. "I mean, I don't blame you for skipping out on the icebreakers—what do they have against us socializing without outside help?—but you could have come and got me instead of just giving me a high sign."

"I know, I know. I suck." She fell backwards, shoving the pillow over her face once more. "Who's the worst roommate? Me."

"Who was that girl you were talking to?"

Romy groaned into the pillow. "I'm an idiot. Fight me."

"Didn't go well?"

Dropping the pillow behind her head, Romy glanced over at her roommate. "She's David and Jeanine Cranston's daughter. You know, the nice lady talking smack about my mom all over the news."

"WHAT?!" Mercury dropped her feet to the floor again. "You were macking on your mother's arch nemesis' daughter?" She threw her arms in the air in desperation. "Girl, that is not what I would call making good decisions!"

Romy sat up suddenly and shouted, "I did not make out with her!"

"But you wanted to?" her roommate asked, giving her a surprised look.

Staring at her hands, Romy admitted. "Yeah." She sighed. "It's dumb. Hormones, that's all it is. I don't even know if she'd be interested."

"I doubt it. I mean, isn't her dad some bigwig in the right wing Christian faction? I don't think he'd be okay having a daughter who kissed chicks, just sayin'."

Romy slumped. Mercury was right. There was no way someone like Julie was gay or bi, no way that she'd be anything but straight as an arrow.

No way would Julie be interested in someone like Romy.

So why was she getting all hung up over her pretty face? There were lots of pretty faces. Mercury, for instance, was gorgeous, but Romy didn't want to ruin a good roommate situation.

"You're right. Totally right. I get it." Romy pushed herself backwards on her bed until her back rested against the wall. "I don't know why I care."

"So what happened?"

Shrugging, Romy began. "We were having a pleasant chat—she insinuated that I was looking for alcohol, I might have accused her of engineering a cookie shortage to manipulate the school's secret baked goods black market—then we escaped the hell that was forced intimacy in a room full of total strangers. We *bonded*. We were getting to know each through the magic of pilfered Oreos when she busted out the "my mom hates your mom" card."

Mercury grinned. "A magical night then?"

"Like a David Blaine Vegas show."

"How'd you leave it? I mean, I feel it's pretty safe to assume you guys aren't going to be picking out china patterns any time soon, but…" Mercury trailed off, allowing Romy to fill in the blank.

Romy scowled. "She said, and I quote, 'I don't want there to be any confusion between us', which pretty much killed the mood. You feel me?"

"Ouch." Mercury leaned forward, gaze open and earnest. "A conversation like this requires ice cream or junk food or something."

"I just pulverized the only bit of junk food I had. Unless you're partial to snorting Oreo dust, in which case, tonight is your lucky night." Romy pushed herself to her feet, walking over to her wardrobe to get her toiletries. "I think I'm just going to go to bed if it's all the same to you. I'm beat."

"Sleep is best to mend a broken heart. Sleep knits up the raveled sleeve of care."

"Are you going to quote Shakespeare every time you're deprived of late night snackage?" Romy nabbed her towel and walked to the door.

"Who says I'm deprived?" Mercury reached over to her desk, pulling open the middle drawer. Snack cakes, candy, and brightly wrapped cookies lay nestled inside.

"So can I ask you something? I mean, you already kind of answered it, but I want to not assume anything." Mercury waited for Romy's nod before continuing. "Are you really a lesbian or is that just stuff the reporters say to sell papers? I don't really care one way or the other. I just wanted to know so I don't offend you by saying something stupid."

Romy looked over at her roommate, exhaustion hitting her like a subway train. "I'm not a lesbian. I'm bisexual but that doesn't make for the same headline bait as me being a big ol' lezzie. And most everyone lumps us bis in as gay anyway. People assume that bisexuals are just people with lifestyle commitment issues," she said mildly. Sometimes she was really sick of living in America where everyone seemed obsessed with a binary system: two political parties, two genders, two sexualities. Ugh.

She continued. "Is me being bi going to make you feel uncomfortable?"

Mercury waved her hand. "Nah. It's cool. Just let me know if I do something thoughtless."

"Sure." Finished gathering her toiletries, Romy stepped to the door. "I expect you to be passed out in a sugar coma when I get back from the bathroom."

"Aye aye, captain," Mercury said, saluting her retreating back.

The communal bathroom was blissfully empty when Romy walked in. Classes didn't start for another day, so she suspected the girls on this floor weren't keeping to set schedules until they absolutely had to. She quickly washed her face and brushed her teeth, watching her reflection in the mirror and thinking about what Julie was doing at the moment. She thought about what she might say if she ran into Julie again: the made up conversations, the imagined dates like hayrides and fall fairs. Apple picking, maybe. Something suitably New England-y that didn't involve subjugating the indigenous populace. As she rinsed her mouth of toothpaste, Romy shook her head. She was being stupid—massively, unthinkably stupid. Crushing on Julie Cranston was a mistake of galactic proportions.

Gathering up her toiletries in her plastic carry-all, Romy returned to her room. Mercury had opened up a box of Devil Cremes and was in the process of shoving almost the entire snack cake in her mouth. A host of empty cellophane wrappers littered the floor surrounding her bed.

"Sure you don't want any?" Mercury asked around a mouthful of cake so it came out more like muffled hooting. Romy got the gist, especially since her roommate was waving a plastic wrapped cake at her.

"I'm good." She pulled out her pajamas: a Gir t-shirt and matching Invader Zim sleep pants. No matter where she might end up, these clothes always felt like home to her.

"Cute!" Mercury enthused, as she sipped from a can of diet soda.

"Thanks." Romy climbed into her bed, snuggling down beneath the vampire comforter. "I feel like one of Dracula's Brides in this stuff."

Mercury grabbed her phone. "You have got to let me take a picture of you." She raised the phone to capture the entire length of the bed. "Okay, make your best vampire face!"

"I vant to suck your blood," Romy said, mouth open wide to reveal fangs she didn't have. She hooked her fingers into claws too, just for verisimilitude. She held the pose until she heard the tell-tale shutter sound of the phone's camera, then flopped back down.

"Awesome," Mercury said, raising her phone so Romy could see the picture. "Can I post to Instagram?"

"Sure, knock yourself out." She fumbled for her own phone. "So long as I get to take a picture of your Hostess snack cake debauchery."

Mercury posed with all of her discarded wrappers, half a snack cake in each fist. Romy took the photo, smiling at her roommate's antics. Merc really did remind her of Rosalyn, without the pesky drinking problem. She could see herself digging Verona Prep. This place wasn't so bad if she got Mercury as a roommate.

She uploaded the pic to her Instagram account with the caption, "Junk food zombie!" Mercury laughed when Romy read it aloud, then hopped off her bed to dispose of the wrappers. Romy snuggled down into her bed, surprised at how comfortable it was. It wasn't as big as her bed back home, but it wasn't a lumpy monstrosity that was the stuff of nightmares either.

"You mind if I read for a bit?" Mercury asked as she bounced back to her bed.

"Go right ahead." Romy yawned. "Not gonna bother me at all."

"Night, Roomy," Mercury said with a chuckle. "Roomy Romy." At Romy's eye roll, she said, "Watch out for Mr. Sandman."

Propping herself up on her elbow, Romy asked, "What, like the *bring me a dream* guy or the Endless one?"

Mercury shook her head before tying up her twists in a silk kerchief. "No, like the guy who decides if you have good, happy dreams or horrible nightmares." Her roommate leaned back, hands behind her head. "Will you dream of your pretty Julie, maybe kissing her in a canoe in the middle of a moonlight dappled lake, or will you dream of a disgusting walker that's going to eat your brain? Will you dream of winning five Grammys or will you dream of being shot out of a cannon to smash into Mount Rushmore? Will you dream of fluffy kittens giving you sweet head rubs or will you dream of a werewolf drooling while it eats your intestines?"

"Okay, those were fairly specific fears, although none of them are mine. Those things don't scare me."

"Fine, some of those may have been a tad personal." Mercury frowned, thinking. "Okay, then maybe you'll dream of loudmouthed senators' wives who are suing your mom and the daughters that you're in desperate love with?"

Romy's pillow caught her square in the face.

# CHAPTER SIX

The walk back to Cap felt colder than it should have. Julie trudged up the stairs to her room, her heart and mind as heavy as her feet. She shouldn't have left the mixer. Actually, she shouldn't have left her room. It was a mistake, and it had just led to more mistakes— like talking to Romy Montoya. Alone. Just the two of them.

Letting herself into her dorm room, Julie closed the door and leaned her back against it. A time machine. She needed a time machine. Somebody needed to get on inventing that.

Julie pressed her cold hands against her flaming face. Her fair skin held her blushes for far too long. It was humiliating.

Walking over to her bed, she plopped onto it face-first, stifling the groan that escaped her lips. She wanted to call her sister just to hear a friendly voice, to listen to some encouraging words that would assure her she wasn't a social pariah, but knew her sister had more important things to worry about than Julie's mental breakdown and descent into social leprosy. Julie thought about calling her mother, but realized things would only get more complicated if her mom got involved. Her mother would want to know if everything was okay, and she'd be able to sniff out Julie's failure like a hound tracking a scent. Julie definitely didn't want to talk about or examine her feelings about Romy Montoya with her mother.

Shoving her hair out of her face, Julie pushed herself up. Sitting on her desk, looking like a gift sent by angels, was her camera bag. Scrambling out of bed, Julie reached for it and pulled it onto her lap. Carefully, she pulled out her Nikon and checked it over to make sure nothing had happened to it on the plane trip. She loved this camera the same way other girls loved shoes or their pets— Julie had saved up all of her babysitting money for almost a year to be able to afford it and the lenses that went with it. Her parents believed that their kids should have to pay for the high-end items they really wanted so they'd appreciate them more.

She turned it on and looked through the viewfinder. After taking a few experimental shots of her room, Julie moved over to her desk. The window just above it looked out over the quad. A massive maple stood sentinel right outside, branches nearly touching the pane of glass. Pushing her desk to the side, Julie wrestled open the window and tucked herself against the sill.

A hush had fallen over Verona. The sun had set, and darkness had settled like a net over the campus, broken only by the light of stars glimmering overhead. The moon, a crescent sickle, rose in the sky. The maple hadn't shed its leaves yet, and its clothed arms stretched out like it wanted to catch the moon and wear it as a necklace.

Julie leaned out, camera pressed to her face. She sighted, breathed out, and hit the button. The faint snap of the shutter settled something inside of her, soothing her rattled nerves. Taking a few more shots of the night-dimmed campus, Julie let the magic of the camera do its work. Her stomach unknotted, her shoulders relaxed as she changed position to lean farther out to get a better view of the front of the building from her window.

A girlish laugh broke the stillness. A group of four students crossed the quad, chattering like birds. Julie watched them as they walked, using the long lens of her camera to get a better look. None of them was Romy Montoya.

Julie ducked back inside, nearly banging her head on the sash in her haste. What was she thinking? Why had Monet's daughter even popped into her head like that? She shook her head, as though that could erase the traitorous thoughts from her mind. She just felt bad that she'd embarrassed herself in front of Romy, that was all. Julie should have stood up for herself, should have said that her mother was trying to protect vulnerable young people who might be swayed by Monet's music or her liberal agenda. That would have shut Romy up.

Why hadn't she said any of that?

Because Romy had left her tongue-tied, floundering like a fish out of water. Julie had never been quick with comebacks and she hated arguing. Romy had confidence and an easy way with words—things that Julie dreamt of attaining. Julie bet Romy was never struck dumb at the thought of talking to another person. She probably always had an answer for every question and a thousand comebacks to every insult.

Julie felt like she'd swallowed hot coals. Her stomach *burned*. How dare she? How dare Romy be so comfortable in her own skin? How dare she be proud of who she was? She was gay! There was nothing to be proud of in that. Julie's mother and father said that homosexuality was a choice, that it was a sin. It said so in the Bible. Julie had been raised on that fact. To see Romy, so unapologetic about who she was, to see her taking up space instead of trying to make herself small enough so that she disappeared, made Julie want to smash something.

She prowled the room, feeling like the walls were closing in on her. How dare Romy Montoya, the daughter of a talentless hack of a woman who'd only gotten where she was by selling her sex appeal and making a disgusting public spectacle of herself, criticize Julie's mother? Romy had no room to talk about Julie's mother! She had no room to talk about *anything*.

With shaking hands, Julie managed to put her camera back in its padded bag. Her fury scalded her, made her feel righteous and unafraid. She wanted to run out and track down Romy Montoya and tell her all of things she'd just thought and see what she had to say then. Julie wanted to see the abashed look on Romy's face.

She wanted to see Romy and…

Julie's hands fisted in the straps of her camera bag. What on earth was she thinking? She did *not* want to see Romy, in any capacity. She certainly did not want to talk to the girl ever again. Julie had other things she should be thinking about, things like school and making her parents proud and classes and making friends. Girls like Tyndall were the ones she should be thinking about, not *thinking* thinking about, but—

"Sweet dancing Moses!" she cursed aloud as her thoughts began to spiral into a never-ending whirlpool of stupidity. "Shut up, brain!"

♪ ♪ ♪

Julie awoke on the morning of the first day of classes with a lump in her throat, a knot in her stomach, and the nearly overwhelming need to crawl underneath her bed and not come out unless the fire department threatened to break out the Jaws of Life. But then she decided that she wouldn't fit under there along with her suitcases and it would be too much work to move them so she might as well shower and get ready for her first real day at Verona Prep.

She was grateful to see Tyndall waiting for her outside of her door. They'd compared schedules and wound up having their first class—English—together. The knot in her gut untangled a little at the thought of knowing at least one person in one of her classes. They stopped by the cafeteria for breakfast before class, where Tyndall introduced her to three other students—one freshman and two sophomores. Clarice, the freshman, stared at everyone with wide, fear-filled-eyes. It was like watching a field mouse tracking the flight of a barn owl. Julie's heart went out to her and she made a point to sit next to her.

The sophomores, Trisha and Grace, were far more relaxed. They greeted Julie warmly when she sat down. Tyndall made introductions all around.

"Trisha and Grace are members of the Bible study group I started the first year I got here. Clarice lives on their floor."

"Are you guys in Cap?" Julie asked.

Grace shook her head, red curls bouncing. "No, Montag. First floor."

"That's where Romy Montoya lives," Julie's mouth said before her brain engaged. She forced thoughts of Romy out of her head and focused on her parents and how disappointed they'd be with her if they knew what she was thinking.

She wanted to be good for them, to win their approval. She told herself that they only wanted what was best for her, like parents everywhere. Julie knew what they expected, and she was determined to give it to them. This was her first real trip away from home and she wasn't going to ruin it by betraying everything her parents stood for. Just because she was…different, well, that didn't mean she had to give in to it.

"Yeah, she's on the second floor. She rooms with Will Tyrell Highbrook's kid." Trisha sniffed. "I haven't met her yet."

"Who's Will Tyrell Highbrook?" Julie asked, nibbling at the corner of a piece of buttered toast. The name sounded somewhat familiar.

"He's that scientist who is all jazzed about space." Grace waved her hand dismissively. "His daughter is a junior. She's been going here since she was a freshman, so you'll see him around on parents' weekend."

Julie raised her eyebrows. "Is he famous?"

Tyndall shrugged. "I guess you could say that. Not someone you'd want to associate with though, and neither is his daughter." She made a disgusted face. Grace laughed, a bright chiming sound.

Heat prickled the back of Julie's neck. She felt like she had missed something important, like there was an inside joke here that she hadn't been clued-in on, but that she was expected to get just the same. It made her uncomfortable. There was something mean in Grace's expression when she laughed. Glancing at Clarice to see what she thought of the conversation so far, Julie noticed that the freshman kept her head down, communing with her oatmeal rather than joining in the banter.

"Where are you from?" Julie asked her, smiling when Clarice's head jerked in surprise.

The girl looked around, as though making sure that Julie was really speaking to her before answering. Pulling her light brown hair over her shoulder, she said, "Just outside of Charlotte in North Carolina."

"First time away from home?"

Clarice nodded, brown eyes wide. Julie smiled encouragingly. "Aside from summer camps, me too."

"My parents are getting a divorce," Clarice whispered, gaze darting to where Tyndall and the others sat. "I think they sent me here to get me out of the way while they figure everything out." She lowered her voice even more. "I don't like it here."

Julie reached across the table, touching Clarice lightly on the wrist. "I'm not completely sold on it either," she whispered back.

Clarice's smile was radiant. Julie stared for a brief moment, struck dumb by how pretty Clarice was when she didn't look scared out of her mind. Then she returned the grin. "If you ever need to talk, I'm in Cap Hall. Room 212."

"Thanks." Clarice took a bite of her oatmeal.

"You're coming to our Bible study, right Julie?"

She turned her head to look at Tyndall. "When is it?" Julie didn't want to commit herself to too many activities just yet, especially since she didn't know how much work her classes were going to be. Plus, she hoped there was a photography club on campus that she could join.

"Wednesday nights. Since there's not a service on campus, we do the best we can."

Picking at the edge of her toast triangle, Julie hedged, "Well, if I don't have too much homework. My parents expect me to make the honor roll…"

"Oh, we'll all help you study," Tyndall enthused, rolling right over Julie's response. She beamed. "See, it's like it was meant to be!"

"That's terrific!" Trisha said, adding, "Bible study is really fun. You'll love it."

"Yeah, okay." Julie gave each of them a tremulous smile, still not ready to agree outright. "I'll see what my schedule looks like."

"Grace, will you take a picture of us?" Tyndall asked, handing her phone to the other girl. "I want to document the first day of Verona Prep with Julie Cranston!" She slung her arm around Julie's shoulders and smiled widely.

Julie went stiff, a rictus of a smile plastered across her face as the phone's camera flashed. She hated photos being taken of her, especially when she hadn't agreed to them. She wanted to pull away but she didn't want to seem rude, and Tyndall had been very nice and helpful to her, if a little bit pushy lately. When Grace showed them the picture, Julie hid a wince. Tyndall looked good—she'd obviously practiced her duck lips—but Julie looked like Satan was right behind her and she was afraid to turn around.

"Poop!" Tyndall exclaimed as she checked out the photo. "We've got to go or we'll be late."

Julie gave Clarice an encouraging smile as she gathered up her things, almost happy to be going to class if it meant no more horrible photos.

CHAPTER SEVEN


First day of class. Okay. No prob. She got this.

Romy styled herself carefully: khakis, white button down, blue vest, black skinny tie, and combat boots. All within the parameters of the school uniform but with a bit of added Romy flair. Spiky hair. No makeup, not that she ever wore much anyway. Vegan leather wristband. Checking herself out in the mirror, Romy nodded once. Acceptable. Mercury laughed at her as she fussed with her hair one last time before following her roommate down the stairs and out the main doors.

They headed to the building that housed their English class. Romy wished English had come later; it would be hard to stay awake in one of her less favorite subjects. Science and history had always been her favorites—after music, of course. English was something she was good at, but not a subject in which she cared to push herself.

Grabbing seats next to each other, Mercury and Romy watched the rest of the class file in and take their seats. Romy perked up a bit when Julie Cranston trotted into the room, her massive waves of clover-honey hair pulled back in a ponytail. Then she remembered the conversation from two nights ago and slumped back down in her seat. Julie might be pretty but she was a definite no-fly zone.

The teacher, a Mrs. Escalus, stepped in shortly after Julie took a seat. Romy sat up a bit straighter and tried not to yawn. She'd need to work in time to grab a soy latte or something with caffeine to have coherent literary discussions before ten a.m.

"Good morning class," Mrs. Escalus began, and broke the ice with a brief introduction. Then she ran down the class list, making note of each student's preferred nickname. Romy felt her hands grow damp as the teacher got closer and closer to her name on the list, although she did pull out of her growing nervousness long enough to notice that Julie wasn't short for anything and that she looked really pretty in the sky blue oxford button down she was wearing.

"Romy Montoya?"

Students turned around in their chairs to gape at her. Romy hated this part of a new school. Most everyone in Montag had heard she was at Verona and knew whose daughter she was, but those in the other residence halls had not, or had put it down to a rumor. Now they were getting their first look at her. Despite all of the paparazzi attention she got out in Hell-A, she still hated being stared at like some kind of zoo exhibit. *And here we have the wild musician's child in her natural habit. Note the designer sunglasses that cover up the dark circles from a nightlife filled with underage drinking and debauchery. No, no, don't take pictures, it just upsets her.*

"Present. I go by Romy." She saw several heads lean closer together as girls began to whisper, and a couple of people getting out their phones. "And yes, I am *that* Romy Montoya," she added to head off any questions or speculation. God only knew what these people had heard about her.

"Ladies." Mrs. Escalus spoke over the growing whispers of the class. "Do I need to remind you of the Verona code of conduct and respecting your fellow students' privacy?"

Silence. Romy swore she heard crickets chirping. Possibly the polar ice caps melted as she waited in the silence. Awesome. Brilliant. A-*fucking*-plus. She wanted the ground to open up and swallow her whole as a few of the girls continued to stare at her like she was from freaking Jupiter. Yay. In L.A., she was used to this; she expected it. Here, in a place that looked like a Land's End catalog, she felt unprepared.

Determined not to be intimidated, Romy kept her head up, staring around the room. Her gaze fell on Julie, only catching her mass of hair and a little of the side of her face, but there was a flush on her cheek. The girl beside Julie had leaned over to whisper in her ear. Romy could only imagine what she was saying to Julie. Or what Julie might be thinking.

A few giggles started, but were quelled when Mrs. Escalus spoke. "Thank you, Romy." The teacher moved on to the next student on the class list.

Romy noticed a few furtive glances, most especially from the girl that came in with Julie. Her name—when the teacher finally got to her—was Tyndall Sutcliffe. She wore a sneer on her face so comfortably Romy wondered if it had been there since birth. She almost felt bad for Julie having to sit next to her, but then she remembered what Julie had said the night they met and the feeling withered. Maybe they deserved each other.

"What is Tyndall's problem with you?" Mercury muttered, cutting her eyes at Tyndall.

Romy shrugged, refusing to look. Chicky-poo was going to have to try harder than a few glares to make Romy cringe. If that was the worst she could do, Romy felt sorry for her.

"If she keeps turning her head around like that to stare at you, she should get a swivel installed in her neck," Mercury murmured. "Before she breaks something."

Romy hid a smile by tucking her face against her shoulder. She really loved her roommate.

As Mrs. Escalus passed out the syllabus and went over the papers and tests for the year. Romy propped her cheek on her fist and did her best to stay conscious. The assignments ran together. She only perked up when her teacher mentioned a group project.

"We're studying the Americans this year as you all know. I expect you have completed your summer reading and essays. You can drop those off at my desk on your way out. Now, because we have such a heavy reading load, we're going to have different groups lead the discussions of some of the novels. Everyone will have to do the reading—it is required, of course—but the focus of each group will be to fill in the narrative and historical gaps along with leading the discussion of the texts. In that way, we'll be able to enjoy a richer understanding of the short stories or novels of that particular period, as well as grounding it in the time period of its creation."

Romy saw Tyndall raise her hand "Do we get to choose our group and author?" The girl glanced at Julie as she asked. Romy's back stiffened, a burn of jealousy flaring in her chest, before she could stop her reaction. She had no reason, no reason *at all*, to be even the slightest bit jealous. Julie could barely stand her and Romy felt the same.

While Romy was busy having her emotional crisis, Mrs. Escalus shook her head. "No, Miss Sutcliffe, I have already assigned both the groups and their respective authors. Most of you have been at Verona for several years and I think it is important to mix our newer faces in with those who have been here a while. And no trading of groups! Any other questions?"

Romy smothered another smug smile, the fire of satisfaction now alive in her chest. It was obvious that Tyndall had hoped to be in the same group with Julie—and she still might be, depending on how Mrs. Escalus divided the class—but Romy couldn't help but be pleased that Tyndall's plans were thwarted.

When no one else raised their hand, Mrs. Escalus continued. "Excellent. I'm going to call out the groups now." Romy perked up, alert for her name and the author she'd been assigned.

Mercury was put in the Nathanial Hawthorne group with Tyndall and two girls named Ayda and Sherilynn. "Julie Cranston,

Romy Montoya, Gabrielle diSpirito and Bonnie Randallman," Mrs. Escalus said, "you have Edgar Allen Poe."

Romy glanced across the room to see Julie's wide, shocked blue eyes staring back at her.

Oh crap.

♪ ♪ ♪

When Mrs. Escalus finally dismissed class, Romy sat in her chair for a few seconds, sharing a bemused look with Mercury. "Those groups are certainly interesting," was all her roommate got to say before Gabrielle and Bonnie descended upon them.

They seemed like perfectly nice people, but Romy only had eyes for Julie. She and Tyndall walked over to join them, Julie's expression taut with worry. She kept glancing at Tyndall like the girl was a loaded gun. Romy felt her shoulders tense as they stopped in front of her desk.

Gabrielle paused in gushing about Monet's latest single and how she'd loved the woman's music for years as the others joined them. "Hi Tyndall."

Tyndall gave Gabrielle a perfunctory nod before turning her full attention on Romy. Romy felt a bit like she'd been caught in a floodlight, her every flaw exposed. Tyndall wore an unfriendly expression, her green eyes hard like chips of jade, her lips twisted in a slight sneer. Romy wondered who this chick was and why she already disliked her so much. It usually took Romy at least a couple of days to thoroughly work someone's nerves.

"So is it true you got sent here instead of going to rehab?" Tyndall asked in a snide voice.

Romy blinked, caught off guard. She was used to fielding questions from the paps and reporters out in L.A.; she hadn't expected such an in-your-face reaction out here. It shouldn't have surprised her, but it did. She'd gotten lulled into a false feeling of safety by how friendly most everyone was. She'd made a mistake.

"What is wrong with you? Rude!" Mercury snapped, rising out of her chair.

Romy stared at Julie, unable to look away from her. The girl chewed at her lower lip, the plump pink flesh caught between pearly teeth. Julie looked torn, as if she didn't know whether to denounce her friend or support her.

"I'm sure Romy's heard much worse," Tyndall said, smiling sweetly. She turned back to Romy. "Isn't that right?"

Ah, so here it was. A local mean girl, ready to teach Romy the pecking order. How utterly predictable. How colossally boring.

Too bad for her Romy didn't give a shit.

Bonnie and Gabrielle stared curiously, as though watching a bloodless boxing match. No help would be forthcoming from them, not that Romy expected it. She was used to being viewed like some kind of train wreck; she just hadn't thought it would be at Verona, or at least not in the first class of the day. Maybe she'd believed her mother's words a little too much, that this would be a fresh start for her. She should have known better.

Drawing her attitude on like armor, Romy stood, wearing her coldest expression. Tyndall would not get to her and she would not feel bad for who she was or where she came from. She had nothing to be ashamed of and she'd be damned if some boarding school bully was going to try to make her feel bad just for existing.

"Awww, that's so sweet of you to care," Romy said in her brightest, most Disney princess voice, knowing it was at odds with her expression, "but guess what?" She dropped to her lowest register, voice now nearly a growl. "It's none of your damn business why I'm here." Then, just to confuse the girl more, she gave Tyndall a blinding smile before sliding around her and making her way to the door, Mercury already moving to her left. She heard Tyndall's choked sound of surprise and Gabrielle and Bonnie's muffled laughter, but Romy didn't look back.

Julie hadn't made a sound.

She'd almost made it down the hall and to the front door before she heard a breathless voice calling after her. Romy turned her head to see Julie running after her, peach-pale face flushed with the exertion and the heat of the building.

"Wait!" Julie called.

Mercury raised one elegantly threaded eyebrow when Romy stopped. She waved Mercury on ahead, unsure of what Julie might say. Romy was sure she could take Julie on by herself with no problem. Romy had on combat boots; Julie wore ballet flats. It was a mindset thing.

Romy rested her hand on one cocked hip and watched as Julie approached. Her pace slowed as she neared. Romy observed her closely, trying to get an idea of what Julie wanted by the expression on her face. Julie appeared cute, but constipated. Romy sighed. Even that looked good on her. It wasn't fair.

Julie stopped when she was still some feet away. "I, uh, wanted to talk to you."

"Yes?" Romy kept her expression carefully neutral.

"I was wondering," Julie flushed and looked down at her navy ballet flats, "if you were free to meet up. Maybe Thursday afternoon?" Julie glanced up, hopeful.

Romy blinked rapidly, unsure that she'd heard Julie correctly. What was going on here? "You want to meet? With me?"

Julie nodded quickly. "Well, yes, I mean we're all going to need to get together to talk about the project."

Romy felt something deflate inside of her. "The project. Right." She shook her head, bangs falling into her eyes. She couldn't believe how stupid she was. Of course Julie wasn't interested in talking to her outside of class. As she attempted to recover her chill, Romy babbled, "Uh, yeah, Thursday should be fine, I guess. After classes are done for the day. Sure, why not?"

Julie smiled unconsciously with relief and that simple expression made Romy's heart beat faster in her chest. Yeah, this nonsense needed to stop. She was not crushing on a straight girl. Nothing good ever came from something like that. "Okay," Julie said, letting out her held breath. She looked uncomfortable, like she didn't know whether to be pleased or angry. "Meet in the Cap Hall lounge. Let's say 3:30?"

Romy nodded, desperate to be gone, especially when she saw Tyndall glaring at her from the doorway of Mrs. Escalus' classroom. Turning to follow Mercury, Romy tossed a, "Yeah, sure," over her shoulder.

She felt Tyndall's eyes on her back the entire way down the hall.

## CHAPTER EIGHT

Julie hit the keypad on her cell phone to dial her older sister with shaking fingers. Romy Montoya was in three of her classes. Three! They'd been paired on a group project together in English class. She had to work with her—her grade depended on it! How was she supposed to handle this? Someone who stood in front of the class and owned who she was unapologetically, as if she had a right to be seen and heard just like everybody else. How could Romy live like that?

Her sister picked up after the fourth ring. "What's going on, Julie?" Karen asked in a sleepy voice.

"Oh gosh, I woke you up. I'm so sorry, Kar. I can call back later!"

Her sister soothed her. "Nah, don't worry about it. I was just taking a nap before afternoon labs." Julie heard her bite back a yawn. "What's up?"

Plopping on her bed, Julie attempted to make sense of the riot of thoughts in her head. "You won't believe who's in my class."

Karen murmured to someone where she was, then asked, "Who?"

"Romy Montoya."

A pause. "Who's that?"

Julie gaped at her phone. "Who's that?" she spluttered after a moment of rebooting her brain. "Who's *that?*"

"I'm trying to figure out how to cure infectious diseases over here," Karen sighed. "I don't keep up with every new girl group that comes along."

"She's not in a girl group!" Julie practically shouted, before reining in her temper. "She's Monet's daughter! You know, the not-so-nice lady our mother is currently fighting in the news for being a public menace to the morality of young people?"

"So?" Karen sounded bored.

"What do you mean, so? I'm in a study group with her!" Julie felt her heartbeat rise. Her sister was not reacting in any expected way. She felt like she was flailing around in water out of her depth.

Julie could practically see Karen's shrug through the phone. "I'll say it again—so?" When Julie didn't immediately respond, her sister continued. "You just work with her until you get your grade and then you go back to ignoring her. Problem solved."

Problem *not* solved. Gritting her teeth, she snapped, "It's not that easy, Kar."

Her sister went quiet, as though she were choosing her words with care. When she began to speak, her voice was low and serious, the whispered sharing of a secret just between the two of them. "I forget how young you were when Dad made the switch. You probably don't remember much."

Julie furrowed her brow. "What are you talking about?"

"You were, I don't know, maybe seven?" Karen stopped, responded to a question from her roommate, and continued. "Dad had lost his bid for governor and he wasn't doing so well with it. He took a lot of the polls to heart. He ended up firing almost all of his old staffers and hiring new people who told him to go neo-con. Don't you remember leaving our old church and going to the one we do now?"

Playing with a rough thread on her jeans, Julie thought back to her childhood. She remembered the old church they'd attended—a bright yellow house of worship that always seemed filled with music. She'd gone to Sunday school there, and the pastor had been really kind. She dimly remembered crying when she'd found out they wouldn't be going there anymore, not understanding why.

"Yes," she said reluctantly. Julie hadn't liked the new church and she still didn't care for it, but she'd been going there for eight years. She'd managed to get used to it.

"Well, Dad had to find a church that better fit in with his new outlook. We've always been Christians, but he needed to find us a place that preached about what his new base of supporters cared about."

"That sounds kind of . . .," Julie trailed off when she couldn't think of a word that didn't sound insulting.

"Pastor Will doesn't preach anything we didn't already believe in. He's just a little more, um, strident in his views about it."

"What does this have to do with Romy being in my class though?" Julie asked, adrift in the conversation. She wasn't sure what her sister was trying to tell her and she didn't really understand how they'd gotten on this topic. She cared about how to deal with Romy without getting into trouble.

"I'm telling you, you don't have to do anything about Romy! There are many different people in the world. You aren't always going to like all of them and you certainly don't have to get along with them, but you don't have to make the interaction harder for yourself." Karen said, sounding exasperated. "Just do the project and forget about her. Do you know why Mom and Dad sent you there?"

Julie swallowed hard. "Yeah. I'm supposed to make friends with some of the daughters of the East Coast Republicans that go here. I mean, that's not the only reason, but Mom told me I should try." It bothered her to say that out loud; she didn't like socializing and she certainly didn't like socializing when she felt like there was an agenda behind it. Did other girls feel the same way? Were other girls asked to do this for their parents?

"So focus on that and on making it through your studies. Are you still taking pictures?"

"Yeah." Going out for walks with her camera calmed her down, gave her an outlet for all of her anxiety and nervousness. She was in control of the shot—she could make it look however she wanted. It was her eye in the viewfinder, her brain working behind the lens.

"You know that helps you stay focused." Julie heard the smile in her sister's voice. "All you have to do is get through this one group project. That's all. Then you can forget all about the girl."

"Romy's bisexual though," Julie whispered, feeling like just speaking it was a sin. Just saying it aloud made her feel too vulnerable.

Another pause on the other end of the phone as Karen thought about her response. She spoke slowly, still working out her thoughts. "And?"

Now it was Julie's turn to shrug. "I don't know."

The silence on her sister's end felt weighted. "I think going to Verona might do you some good, Julie," Karen said at last. "Open you up to new things. You're going to meet all kinds of different people. Some of them think differently than we do, worship differently than we do. That doesn't mean they're horrible people. It took me leaving home to realize that."

"How do you, I don't know, reconcile it? I mean, some things are just wrong, you know?"

Karen chuckled. It made Julie feel warm and safe. Like she was home in her sister's bedroom, talking late into the night instead of hundreds of miles away from her. "I'm a studying to be a scientist. You can still be a good Christian and follow your heart, Julie."

Julie gave a weak laugh because she wasn't sure what else to do. Her heart plummeted to her feet. *Yeah, follow her heart. Right. Maybe off a cliff.* "Yeah, okay. How's med school?"

Thankfully, the subject change worked and all Julie had to do was listen to her sister as she rattled on about which disease's effects they were studying in which lab and how the techs had assigned a sliding 'creepy' scale for the way the cells looked under the microscopes. Julie listened with half an ear, content to let her sister ramble. Her mind was back on Karen's question.

She could be civil to Romy Montoya. Just because she was paired with her didn't mean she didn't believe in the things her father championed. She was pro-life, she did believe in abstinence education, and she was most certainly a Christian. Jesus had loved everyone, had told his disciples to treat people the way they would want to be treated. She could treat Romy with respect, just as Jesus would have done, and leave it at that. She could be a Christian and not give into her unnatural feelings.

By the time Karen said goodbye, Julie felt better about her choice. She would do the project with Romy—she would not ask to be moved to another group. Just because Monet's daughter made her uncomfortable didn't mean she had to give in to it. Public speaking made her uncomfortable but she did that too. She could handle it.

She would just imagine what Jesus would do and go from there.

🎼 🎼 🎼

Julie jiggled her leg as she sat in her desk chair and looked out over the quad. It was Wednesday afternoon. Classes were done for the day, and she had no desire to work on the homework for the next. She was slowly getting into the swing of things, her life settling into a routine centered around her classes and the few social activities she wanted to attempt, but there was one thing that was missing: church.

She hadn't had a chance to go into town and see if she could find a place of worship to her liking—she didn't have a car, although Julie guessed she could always Uber a ride. Tyndall had been hinting heavily that she should come to her Wednesday night Bible study, but Julie wanted to keep her options open. She had a feeling that once she showed up to that group, she would need grease and crowbar to get out again.

That wasn't fair though. Julie truly believed that Tyndall meant well; she was just very pushy in expressing her good intentions. Julie knew she'd get a knock on her door before the group met—Tyndall would want one last chance to try to get Julie to come with her. Julie didn't want to be in her room when that happened.

There was a small chapel on campus. Julie knew it wasn't her denomination; instead it was Unitarian or something equally non-threatening to the wealth of liberals (and their parents) attending. But Julie felt desperate, so she grabbed her camera bag, slid it over her shoulder, and headed out to see if prayer in the chapel would help soothe her distress.

Her distress had a name: Romy Montoya. Julie didn't see the girl outside of the three classes they shared, but that didn't stop her from popping up in Julie's mind at all hours of the day. Julie knew she had to see her and be nice to her for their group project meeting tomorrow. She already dreaded it.

Romy's hands. Julie couldn't stop thinking about Romy's hands. Those long fingers, perfectly designed for stroking the strings of a guitar or striking the ivory bones of a piano. The ragged cuticles that looked ready to snag on something and the unevenness of her fingernails. The slight purpled veins that stood out like a faint treasure map on the back of her brown hands.

Julie thought about how those hands would feel holding her own. How they'd feel tangled in her hair or resting against her cheeks as she tilted Julie's head up to k—

Those thoughts terrified her. She wished they weren't a part of her. They absolutely could not be.

And yet, they were.

She'd had strong feelings for a female friend before—something Julie thought was normal between best friends. You were supposed to love and support each other. That's what friends did. But Julie's mother had taken her aside and said that perhaps the friendship was getting too intense. She'd told Julie to back off for a bit. Julie had done so, not really understanding what her mother meant, and focused on other friendships.

Had her mother suspected Julie was gay then? Might she still?

Nearly blind with a dull, relentless panic, Julie crossed the grounds, barely noticing where she was going. It wasn't until she stopped at the doors to the stone chapel on the west side of campus that she woke from her fugue state.

She expected the doors to be locked, so she was surprised when they opened beneath her hand. She crossed the threshold, waiting for that sense of calm to wash over her, the way it did when she was home. Not in her regular church, but her old one, the one she'd been baptized in, the one she held in her earliest memories. The one that had a lot more 'Shalts' than 'Shalt Nots' in the pastor's sermons. She'd stopped by that church before she left to head east, needing to see it one last time. She'd even gotten to say hello to her old minister, who still expressed regret at not being able to hear her sing every Sunday.

By contrast, this place felt old and sterile. Cold. Julie didn't like it, but she walked forward anyway. What else was she going to do? She needed to stay out of her room, she wanted to pray, and she'd already walked halfway across the campus to get here. It was stupid not to go in.

A few candles were lit. Sunlight streamed through the stained glass windows, painting the wooden floor in geometric patterns of colored light. Julie moved through them, blue and green and red playing across her face. The church was quiet, except for the faint sounds of movement near the altar. Julie breathed in deeply, taking in the faint scent of wax and furniture polish, of wilting flowers, and that weird vestment smell that she associated only with churches.

She wanted comfort. She wanted to feel safe. But the things she felt inside of herself were anything but comfortable. Had her thoughts of…girls gained strength by her coming here? If she'd stayed home, would she have been able to keep pretending she didn't feel the things she felt? These horrible feelings would have lain dormant, wouldn't they?

Just one more reason to hate Verona Prep.

"Can I help you?" came a man's voice from the front of the church.

Julie glanced over her shoulder to make sure there wasn't someone else present that he could be talking to. When she turned back around, the man stepped out from behind the altar, a welcoming smile on his face. "I'm Pastor Laurence. Can I help you with something?"

"I'm Julie," she said, not wanting to be rude. "I just came here to pray."

He nodded, his smile morphing into a delighted grin. "Please, make yourself comfortable then. I must say, I don't see many students here unless it is for an actual Sunday service. It's a pleasant change."

"I was sort of hoping you'd have a Wednesday evening one," she went on, walking down the center aisle to find a place toward the front of the chapel. "I always went to the one at my home church."

"Unfortunately, I can only offer proper Sunday services," Pastor Laurence told her, as he bustled about with the cleaning, "but you are always welcome here for prayer and reflection."

"Thank you."

Julie lowered her head and closed her eyes, but her mind refused to settle. She shifted in the hard pew and tried to calm her whirling thoughts. Images of Romy assaulted her brain—the way she nibbled on the cap of her pen, the red streaks in her hair turning to flames when the sun caught them just so, the glittering dart of her eyes when she would glance over at Julie. Romy's scent—like limes and amber—when she stood close to Julie that day in the hall.

Stifling a frustrated groan, Julie rubbed at her eyes. This was not helping. In fact, it was the *opposite* of helping. She wanted to reach in through her eyes and claw out the parts of her brain that were being so magnificently unhelpful. She couldn't remember the third angle theorem in Geometry, but by God, she could remember how amazing Romy Montoya looked in skinny pants and a man's vest.

It wasn't fair.

"Forgive me for intruding," Pastor Laurence's voice interrupted her self-flagellation, "but it might help to talk about whatever it is that's bothering you instead of grinding your molars into oblivion." When Julie looked up at him, startled, he shrugged and added, "Just a thought."

Letting out a heavy sigh, Julie slumped back in the pew. "I'm not sure how it could get worse," she mumbled by way of accepting.

Laurence laughed. "Well that's one heckuva recommendation." When Julie began sputtering out an embarrassed apology, he waved her words away. "I was trying to be funny and missing the mark." His expression turned serious. "Now, what is troubling you?"

Julie glanced around again, the feelings of homesickness and insecurity rising like bile in the back of her throat. She'd been gone barely a week and already she missed her family terribly. She missed her dog, Fluffles, and her room, and her friends from her old school. She missed the familiar faces and places that she'd grown up with, the comforting routine of the known and the accepted. Verona Prep was none of these things.

Verona Prep was change, discomfort, and strangeness wrapped up in one autumnally decorated package.

She thought about the disappointment on her parents' faces. She wondered why this was happening to her, and why it had to be now. But thoughts of Romy wouldn't leave her be—and she hardly knew her. This was big, bigger than she was, bigger than Verona, bigger than her family. She felt poised on the edge of a knife, willing to cling to it despite it slicing her hands to ribbons because it didn't matter which side she fell from because the fall was all that mattered.

As if he knew the reason behind her hesitation, Pastor Laurence told her, "Nothing you say goes beyond these walls. Whatever you tell me is in confidence, just between the two of us." He settled next to her.

"You promise?"

"My word as a minister." He raised his hand as if he were being sworn in on the Bible.

Julie took a deep breath. It would have to be enough. She couldn't go the whole semester questioning everything she knew as she'd done this past week. She'd go mad. "How do you feel about gay people?"

CHAPTER NINE

Romy sat in one of the trees at the western edge of campus, right behind the music building, sipping bottled water and eating an apple. The day had been a blaze of sunny warmth, though it was still cool to her SoCal-thin blood. Once she'd finished her classes and homework, she'd decided to take a walk around the grounds while Mercury was meeting with the Model UN group. They'd meet up for dinner with some of the other students on their floor later. Meanwhile, Romy was at loose ends.

She'd been blocked since she arrived. The music she relied on to keep her grounded wasn't happening for her. Romy blamed the constant noise and distraction of settling into the routine that was now her life at Verona, but she knew that was only part of it. She'd had way more distractions in L.A. and had no problem writing songs.

Her phone pinged. Biting down on her apple, she fished it out of the pocket of her pants. Roz was texting her. The sudden icy wash of homesickness crashed over her, momentarily taking her breath away. Suddenly the memory of the kiss with Roz—the incident that started all of this crap—swallowed her.

The kiss meant nothing to Roz; just another way to end up in the gossip rags and on the entertainment news cycles. Romy had kept her disappointment to herself.

Heaving a resigned sigh, Romy tucked herself closer to the tree's trunk and unlocked her phone. Roz's text had just come in.

**R0z: Have you seen Twitter?**

Taking another bite of her apple, Romy texted back.

**RM: No. Why?**

It took a few minutes for Rosalyn to text back. In that time, Romy finished her apple and threw the scant remnants of the core to the ground. She licked her fingers free of juice and waited. Roz's response was a link. Romy clicked it.

She immediately wished she hadn't.

Romy liked to think she developed a pretty thick skin against the internet comments that attacked her and her mother. That didn't mean they didn't bother her on some level, but Romy had learned to push those hateful tweets and YouTube comments to the back of her mind, mostly because there were so many other voices—supportive voices—that drowned them out.

This was different.

The tweet was a close up picture of her and Roz's kiss. The comment below it read: **Do you want *this* going to school with your children? #stopthegayagenda**

The tweeter's handle was @jesussez.

Romy's stomach did a nasty flip-flop. The replies to the tweet were sickening; the voices of dissent drowned out in a sea of hate. There were other tweets in the @jesussez feed, but Romy couldn't bear to look at them.

**R0z: You okay?** 😣

Swallowing around the giant lump in her throat, Romy shut the app.

**RM: No.**

If it was possible for a text to sound subdued, Rosalyn's next one did. Or at least that's how Romy read it.

**R0z: There's a pic of u @ school.**

RM: **Verona?**

R0z: **Yep.**

RM: **I'm not looking at it**.

She couldn't. Not that she didn't want to. She *couldn't*. Romy desperately wanted to believe that Verona Prep was a safe place for her, to believe that such hatred couldn't happen here, in school. Among her peers. She knew she'd grown up privileged—other kids with brown skin didn't come out nearly so fortunate. She'd been raised in a liberal and wealthy area of the country by a world-famous superstar. L.A. had been her chrysalis.

R0z: **Smart. Fwiw, Namina's keeping an eye on it. All sjw.**

R0z: **oh burn! She's reporting it to admins as hate speech!!!**

Romy had to smile at her friend's enthusiasm even if it saddened her at the same time. Roz was always up for challenging the establishment in the short term, and she was a lot of fun and energy, but inevitably she grew bored and wandered off to do something more interesting. Causes didn't last long with Roz. Namina, though, was ruthless about calling out injustice wherever she saw it.

RM: **Nam's got a cause. Watch out!**

R0z: **U think they'll shut it down?**

Taking another sip of water, Romy thought about it. Shutting those comments down was important—you couldn't let vitriol like that stand. But what bothered her more was the fact that there was a picture taken of her *here*, at Verona. A place where, supposedly, the paps couldn't get to her. So it had to be another student or—God forbid—a teacher. Where did that leave Romy? She glanced around, wondering who might be watching her right now.

After a few moments of engaging in her paranoia, Romy texted back.

RM: **Prolly not.**

R0z: **U ok?**

RM: **ya. How r u?**

R0z: **Sober. It sux.**

RM: **Does not. :P**

**R0z: only because you've never tried, Miss Straightedge.**
**RM: imagine me giving you the finger.**
**R0z: such a rude imaginary gesture from such a nice girl.**

Their texting went on and Romy felt the knot in her chest begin to loosen. The situation still wasn't great, but she could deal with it. She'd get in touch with Bev and her mom to give them a heads up, but she could deal with someone spewing anonymous hate on the internet. She'd just be cautious in who she chose for friends around here. If there were someone stalking her, she'd need to be wary.

The crunch of leaves some distance away drew Romy's attention from her phone. Glancing up, she went still, one hand gripping the tree branch tightly. Julie Cranston squatted with a digital SLR camera to her eye, taking a picture of the old student chapel. As Romy watched, Julie shifted to a different angle and took another shot.

Julie moved down and away from the paved path, stopping in her walk every so often to snap an image that struck her fancy. Sometimes it looked like she was taking pictures of her shoes surrounded by leaves just barely beginning to change color, sometimes it was the sky itself. Romy stayed still, watching as Julie moved closer and closer to her until she began to feel a little like a stalker herself.

She decided she should probably say something while Julie still had the chance to turn and walk away. "Whatcha doing?" she called from her perch in the tree.

*Smooth, Romy.* Her inner self rolled her eyes. *Real original.*

Julie looked up, startled, her blue eyes scanning her surroundings. Her body seemed to relax when she spied Romy nestled in the 'v' of two branches. Cocking her head, she asked, "Why are you in a tree?"

"I think the bigger question is, why aren't you?" Romy grinned. It faltered when she noticed how unhappy Julie looked. Maybe it would have been better if she'd kept quiet and let Julie go on her way. She probably wouldn't have even noticed Romy.

"Can I take your picture?" Julie asked, surprising Romy. She sounded almost angry, sort of defensive and challenging.

Romy jerked her head back, nearly braining herself on a tree limb. "What? Why?"

Tilting her head so she didn't have to squint, Julie replied, "I like the composition of this shot. Just sit there and check your phone or whatever it was you were doing."

Giving her a dubious look, Romy decided to go with it. People were already taking pictures of her at school and whoever it was, wasn't being nearly so obvious about it. And Julie seemed too nice and polite to do something awful. If the picture did show up on the internet, at least Romy would know whom to blame for it. What could it hurt? Pulling out her phone, she began to scroll through her Tumblr feed. Once in a while, she risked a glance over at Julie who moved around beneath the tree, taking shots from all different angles.

"Did you come from church?" Romy finally asked when the silence got too much for her. She lifted her chin towards the stone building in the distance.

"Uh huh," Julie answered, working her way around the trunk, camera up to her face once more.

"What were you doing?" It seemed strange to go to a church on a Wednesday afternoon. Granted, Romy didn't have a lot of experience with churches; she'd gone to the Enlightenment Center with her mother until she'd decided to figure out religion on her own.

A pause in the rustling beneath her. Then, "Playing mah jongg."

Romy blinked. "Was that sass?" she asked, a delighted smirk quirking her lips. Who knew? "I'm pretty sure that was sass."

"Maybe."

She thought Julie's voice held the faintest hint of laughter. Romy was seized with the urge to hear what a real laugh from Julie sounded like now that they each knew who the other was. It felt important, more important than anything else in Romy's life at the moment. This was a whole different side of Julie—far more appealing than the student in her English class and even more alluring than the stranger at the mixer.

Julie moved away from the tree, apparently satisfied. "See you tomorrow," she called over her shoulder as she walked away, head lowered as if some great weight pressed down on her.

Romy wanted to follow, felt the itch of it in her feet. But something told her to let Julie go, that whatever had caused this détente was a fragile thing. Pushing for more would only make things worse. Romy knew she didn't want that. She honestly wasn't sure what she wanted when it came to Julie, but she couldn't deny that the brief five minutes they'd just spent not actively loathing each other had been…nice.

So she whispered, "Yeah, see ya around," and kept to her spot in the tree.

# CHAPTER TEN

Jesus would not smack the taste out of someone's mouth. Jesus would not smack the taste out of someone's mouth. He would *not* smack the taste out of someone's mouth. He. Would. Not.

Julie kept her sigh to herself. The first group project meeting was not working out well at all.

Romy was naturally vivacious. She drew eyes to her as easily as Julie drew breath. Everyone wanted to talk to her, to sit next to her, to hear what she had to say, to find out what brand of jeans she wore. Every time their little group managed to make any headway on what they were going to do on the project, somebody would ask a question about L.A. or Romy's mother or her music.

Julie knew she couldn't blame Romy. The girl actually seemed embarrassed and a little uncomfortable with the attention. Romy did her best to answer politely, but as the group meeting went on, Julie saw the twitch at the corner of her eye whenever the over-eager Gabrielle asked another question that derailed group discussion. Julie recognized the expression because she'd worn one similar often enough when her father was on the campaign trail. Julie knew how it felt to be a butterfly under glass.

Romy had to be used to it by now though. She'd been catnip for paparazzi since she was born.

Julie squashed the flare of sympathy. Romy's childhood hardships were so not her problem. Bad enough that she'd weakened after her talk with Pastor Laurence to talk with the girl. She couldn't relent any further.

"If we could get back to the theme of Poe's works," Julie snapped, finally losing her patience, "before the ice caps melt, that would be terrific." She glared at Gabrielle and Romy.

Gabrielle had the good grace to look abashed. Romy stared at Julie with her mouth half-open in shock. She closed it, then leaned back on the couch, a thoughtful expression on her face. Julie tried not to wonder what Romy was thinking. It didn't matter.

With everyone finally back on track, Julie said, "I think we should focus on the themes of darkness and death in Poe's stories and poems. That should give us plenty to work with, especially since Mrs. Escalus wants us to incorporate details of his life into what he wrote. There's a lot we can use there."

Gabrielle and Bonnie nodded their heads, willing to go along with her plan. Good. "So I think we should—"

"There's plenty to use but all of it has been done to death, pardon the pun," Romy said, finally leaning forward from her slouch against the back of the couch. "Why don't we focus on his detective fiction—see how his life played into the stuff he put in his detective stories?"

Now it was Julie's turn to stare, slack-jawed. That was…actually a good idea. She clenched her teeth around that sentence before it made it out of her mouth. She sucked a deep breath in. It lodged in her throat halfway through and she ended up in a coughing fit.

*Nice, Julie. Really nice.*

She bent over, unable to stop hacking. She covered her mouth with one hand and tried to control whatever was going on with her lungs. Someone rapped on her back with the flat of their palm, just hard enough to soothe. Finally, Julie managed to drag a bit of air into her chest and straightened.

And stared right into the gold-green-brown eyes of one Miss Romy Montoya.

*Rats.*

She had *really* pretty eyes.

Those eyes watched Julie with guarded concern, dark brows furrowed. Julie jerked away from Romy's touch as though she carried the Black Plague, waving her off as she did so.

"Are you okay?" Romy asked, taking a step closer to her.

Julie nodded vigorously, setting off another round of gentle coughing. Swallowing it down, Julie walked over to her book bag, putting a chair between her and Romy. When she felt like she could talk without setting off another round of black lung, Julie faced the others in the group. Romy sat perched on the arm of the couch, watching Julie curiously. Julie ignored her.

"Who's in favor of death imagery?" She was the only one who raised her hand. Julie felt the frown form on her lips and made a conscious effort to smile instead. "And detective?" Romy, Gabrielle, and Bonnie raised theirs. "Well, I guess that settles it." She did her best to sound perky. She probably sounded dangerously unhinged.

"Hang on," Romy said, hand still raised. "Why can't we do both?"

"Both?"

Romy nodded, short black bangs falling into her face. She pushed them away with an almost adorable little huff. Julie felt her lips twitch and banished the smile back to the ether where it belonged. "Yeah, I mean, people are pretty complicated, right? So why can't we do this like a comparison sort of thing. Here's this analytical kind of guy who writes about solving violent crimes and here's this part of him that likes talking to ravens that represent the great unknowable of death, as well as this guy who seems like a lovesick tool sometimes. He kind of encompasses the entire human condition."

Now Julie did gape. So did the two other girls. Who knew Romy was actually smart? Julie gave herself a mental smack—that wasn't fair. Romy shifted uncomfortably on her perch. She looked down, mumbling, "Or something like that."

"That's a really good idea," Julie said before she could stop herself. What was she thinking? It may be smart, but it also meant extra work for the group—this was going above and beyond what Mrs. Escalus required.

"I love it!" squealed Gabrielle. "We should divvy up stuff so that everyone doesn't have to do all the reading."

Bonnie nodded. "I'll take his death poems!"

"I call short stories," Gabrielle said.

"Romy, do want his detective stories?" Bonnie asked. When Romy nodded, the girl turned to Julie. "Which leaves you with the love stuff."

"Is that cool?" Romy glanced at her, uncertain. "I'm happy to switch."

Oh, there was a joke there, and Romy knew it too—Julie could see it in the way she stiffened after the words left her mouth. But Julie had said she was going to be like Jesus. And Jesus did not go for the low-hanging humor fruit.

"No, it's fine," she answered, trying to keep the irritation from her voice and feeling like she mostly succeeded. "I'll take his weird 'I'm in love with death and my cousin' stuff."

"Some of it overlaps, so we can talk about that too," Romy offered. "And you guys," she pointed at Bonnie and Julie, "can work it out so you don't double up on the same stuff. Saves you some work."

"Sounds good to me," Bonnie said, beginning to gather up her belongings.

Julie checked her phone. They were just about out of time. Clearing her throat, still raw from her coughing fit, she asked, "Is everyone okay meeting back here next week? Same time, same place? I can organize the reading lists if you all will give me your email addys." She ripped out a piece of paper from one of her notebooks and passed it around the group.

Each of them said their goodbyes and left after adding their email addresses and phone numbers to the page. Julie busied herself putting her things away since she didn't have far to go. Romy waved Gabrielle to go on without her as she shoved her laptop into her satchel. Soon it was just the two of them in the lounge.

Romy scribbled her email on the page and then passed it over to her. Julie took the paper, shoving it into her bag without looking at it. Romy's face changed—disappointment flashing across it like summer heat lightning—and then she was back to smiling.

"Didn't mean to distract from the group," she apologized, surprising Julie. Even if Romy didn't like it, Julie never expected her to be self-aware enough to apologize for the way her fame might inconvenience other people. "It won't happen again—once people get used to me, the curiosity usually goes away. Turns out, I'm remarkably boring."

Julie clutched the straps of her book bag tightly, almost desperate in her desire to get away. This wasn't how this was supposed to go at all. All of her interactions with Romy always went worse—or better, depending on how she looked at it—than Julie expected.

"That's okay," she managed to get out in a normal-sounding voice. "I bet it gets tiring."

Romy shrugged one shoulder. Julie found her eyes following the movement, tracing the line of Romy's shoulder to her neck, then up the hinge of her jaw, to rest on the jut of her cheekbone. Julie stared, mesmerized at the play of light over dusky skin, the way the overhead fluorescents threw the planes and angles of Romy's face into highlights and shadows.

"A little, I guess. I imagine it must be the same for you." Romy's husky voice jerked Julie out of her reverie. What was she even doing? Julie needed to get out of there now. Like five minutes ago.

"Why would you think that?" Julie wound up asking, even though her inner voice was screeching, *Shut up and leave!* That voice was super-annoying.

Another half-shrug. Julie swallowed as she saw the outline of Romy's collarbone through her v-neck shirt. Romy said, "Just thought you might get some of the same with your parents being who they are. Can't be easy being a politician's kid."

The reminder of her parents, especially coming from Romy's lips, threw her. Julie blinked, coming back to herself with a lurch. "I've gotta go," she mumbled, before scrambling for the safety of her room.

♮ ♮ ♮

Julie slowly settled into a routine at Verona. Wake up, shower and dress, hit the cafeteria for breakfast with Tyndall and the others, and then head off to class. There was time for studying in the afternoon, a photography club meeting, and then it was dinnertime, again with Tyndall and a few of the girls from Cap Hall. Julie would have liked to branch out more on her own, but Tyndall always seemed to appear out of nowhere to collect her. Julie was beginning to wonder if the girl had lojacked her while she slept. She felt smothered, especially as Tyndall's attempts to get her to go to her Bible study group became more intense. She visited with Pastor Laurence almost every Wednesday, to talk about small things and those of greater import.

The strain of trying to cope with the sudden eruption of feelings for Romy, and the worry that anyone would find out about them, gave her plenty of fodder for her conversations with the minister. She hadn't told him who was causing her such distress, but she suspected he knew, or would figure it out shortly. She had no reason to trust him except that he reminded her of the minister at her old church. It was dangerously stupid, she knew, to trust a total stranger, but she chose to listen to her gut and take the risk.

Distance and absence certainly didn't seem to be helping Julie reach any kind clarity. She stared at the photos in her camera's memory, hoping for an epiphany. She'd memorized the curves of Romy's face, the shade of green-brown of her eyes, the thickness of her eyebrows, the exact placement of the red streaks in her black hair. Julie suspected she knew Romy's face better than she knew her own.

Julie had called her other older sister, Donna, and her mother, a few times just to talk. Her mom had filled her in on what was going on at home: school and church updates, campaign stuff, her latest obsession with eradicating the voles in their yard. Julie missed her old life something fierce, especially when her mother spoke of Julie's friends still going to her old school. She ached with it, like she'd had a part of her body hacked away. When Julie had talked to Donna, she'd nearly come clean about her growing interest in Romy, but stopped herself. Still her sister could tell something was bothering her.

"Look, Jules, just keep your head down and hang in there, okay?"

"I'm doing my best. Did I tell you that Monet's daughter goes to school here?"

Donna went quiet. "Do Mom and Dad know?"

"I haven't told them yet. We don't talk much." Julie bit her lip. Maybe she shouldn't have told Donna.

"Mom and Dad or Monet's daughter?" There was something in Donna's voice that put Julie on edge.

"Both. Either." Julie felt her stomach twist. She wasn't ready to have this conversation.

"I know you're not happy, Julie," Donna said. "But sometimes you have to make sacrifices for the family."

"I know that." Julie had gotten off the phone quickly after that and fled to the library

The library was where she ended up spending most of her time when she wasn't in class or her room. She liked the library—there were residence rooms in a wing connected to the building. Julie hoped to score a room there for herself next year. The library was a massive squat white building with formal, Greek Revival columns in front. Inside, wide tables were interspersed among the stacks as well as in specified study locations throughout the three floors of the place. The low hum of student voices and the shuffle of feet against the stone floors were a pleasant background noise that made studying easier.

This afternoon, there were a lot of students present, many more than usual. Julie suspected it was because the first tests approached; she had one in math on Thursday. But today she needed to get an article and some background reading done for her group project in English. She'd already blitzed through the standard collection of Poe's poetry while her class was reading The House of Seven Gables. She needed some history of the period and biographical notes to round out her part of the presentation.

Julie looked up at the solid thunk of a pile of books being dumped onto the wooden library table. She froze when she saw the person who had just deposited said books. Romy Montoya, looking ridiculously cute in a purple and yellow flannel shirt over a black tank top with little skulls all over it, stood there with a sheepish smile.

"Sorry," she said. "All of the other tables are full."

Julie looked around at that. What Romy said was true; all of the tables in the immediate area were occupied or else had no space to put down even a notebook. It was just Julie sitting at this table and there was plenty of room to spread out.

She felt a brace of butterflies flutter in her stomach; she could share space with Romy, she could get through this. "It's no problem," Julie said and returned to the required reading for her English assignment, determined to ignore Romy's presence as best she could.

God was testing her. She was sure of it. Swallowing, Julie gripped her pen tighter. She would pass this one.

Romy sat down, neatly stacking the array of books into two piles, before pulling out a notebook and pen from her messenger bag. With a sigh, she pulled the first book open and began to flip through it until she found the chapter she needed.

Julie couldn't help but notice everything Romy did. She ended up reading the start of the same paragraph five times as she tried *not* to notice the way Romy's brows pulled down in concentration or the way her nose wrinkled when she clearly didn't like what she was reading. With a jolt, she realized she was staring and that Romy was staring back at her, wearing a quizzical expression.

"Do I have something on my face?" Romy asked.

Covering, Julie said, "I think it's ink. Next to your nose." Julie gestured to the imaginary mark, watching as Romy took her sleeve and scrubbed at her cheek. "You got it."

Romy ducked her head, smiling. "Thanks."

Julie resumed reading, more determined than ever that nothing else would distract her from her studies. So when Romy cursed and began rooting through her bag, Julie didn't even look up. She still had no idea what the paragraph's content was, but at least she'd finished reading it this time.

"Hey, can I borrow a pen?" came Romy's furtive whisper. "Mine just ran out and I apparently didn't pack another."

"Sure." Julie reached into the front pocket of her bag where she kept pens, lip gloss, and other assorted items for quick access. Her fingers found a cylindrical shape and she pulled it out without even bothering to look, passing it across the table to Romy. She didn't take her eyes from her reading.

It was silent for several moments and then Romy's chuckle broke the stillness. Julie frowned, determined not to look up again, but when Romy dropped her head to the top of the table and her laughter shook its surface, Julie had no choice but to pay attention to what was ailing her tablemate.

"What is wrong with you?" Julie whispered, horrified at the looks they were getting from nearby students.

Her eyes went round as Romy held up a white cylinder between her index finger and thumb. Julie felt her cheeks grow hot and she was certain her head was going to burst into flames at any moment.

"I don't think I'm going to be able to get much work done with this," Romy chortled. "Maybe pens mean something different in Kansas?"

Julie had just handed Romy a tampon instead of a pen.

"Sweet dancing Moses," Julie cursed, snatching the feminine hygiene product from Romy's unresisting hand. "I . . . um . . . oh wow. I have to go. Like now."

She was mortified. She had to get out of the library immediately. Flee the country. Seek asylum in a foreign land for reasons of utter and complete humiliation. How did one get falsified documents anyway? Julie swept her things into her bag haphazardly, not caring if her notes got crumpled. Leaving her library books behind, she fled the study space as quickly as her legs could carry her, despite Romy's loud whisper for her to come back.

There was no way she could ever look Romy Montoya in the face again.

Well, at least that was one problem solved.

🎼 🎼 🎼

Julie rolled over onto her back and stared at the ceiling. She'd been trying to go to sleep for the past hour with no luck. Her mind refused to shut off, her thoughts racing around like barrel riders in a rodeo. With an exasperated sigh, she shoved the pillow over her face and let out a tired scream, muffled against the padding.

Romy. That was her problem. Julie could not stop thinking about Romy—the way her crooked smile made Julie's heart stumble in its rhythm. The way Romy's eyes seemed to shine a light on the parts of her that Julie had kept hidden for so long she'd almost forgotten they were there. The way Romy draped herself casually over any available surface—including vertical ones—with a long-limbed grace that made Julie's face heat. Nobody should be that attractive. Julie wondered why no one else seemed to notice. Or maybe it was just that Julie was so tuned into the things that made Romy so...Romy...that it didn't matter if anyone else noticed. Julie noticed enough for five people.

She tucked the pillow back under her head. Her feelings were not going away; far from it. It was getting worse. Julie had tried avoiding Romy outside of class and that hadn't worked; Romy still crossed her path regardless of how Julie tried to keep out of her way. The problem was the more time Julie spent around Romy, the more time she *wanted* to spend with her. Even Tyndall had asked about it. Julie had played if off as just the group project, but it was a reminder to be more careful. Tyndall took an unhealthy interest in how Julie spent her free time and it was beginning to get on her nerves.

Growling, Julie pushed herself up. She wasn't getting any sleep now, that was for sure. She looked around the room, able to make out the shape of things in the darkness broken only by the moonlight that crept in through the cracks in the blinds. It was lights-out, so it wasn't like she could read, and students weren't allowed televisions in their rooms.

Snagging her laptop, Julie plopped back down in bed, her back against the wall. Maybe editing some of her photos for the club would help her fall asleep.

She pulled up Photoshop Elements—the program had come free with her Mac—and selected the album where she wanted to work. It was the one that contained the pictures of Romy. Julie intended to edit the photos she'd taken of the church and the trees around it, just beginning to step into their autumn finery.

Her fingers betrayed her, selecting Julie's favorite image of Romy. She'd caught Romy in an unguarded moment. The girl had been checking her phone, an amused expression on her face, her lowered lashes sweeping the apples of her cheeks as she looked down. She looked like she'd forgotten Julie was even there with a camera. She crouched in her tree, set between the v of two branches, the dying sun dropping into its coffin behind her. The tips of her hair were lit up like stars.

Julie reached out, touching the screen with her fingertips, tracing the full line of Romy's lips. She wondered how soft or chapped they were, what they might feel like pressed against her own. How warm would they be? How rough? What would her mouth taste like? How soft would her skin be beneath Julie's palms?

She remembered a sleepover at Brianna Tate's house two years before. The girls had been playing the time-honored sleepover game of Truth or Dare, and Julie had been dared to kiss Helena Markham. It hadn't been the dare that had made her burst into tears, but the realization that she'd wanted to kiss Helena so badly even without the dare.

As much as she hated it, as much as she didn't want to admit it, there *was* something wrong with her. Her parents, her new church, all of them said that homosexuality was a choice. She should be able to choose *not* to be like this. Homosexuality was fine for someone like Romy, someone with options and possibilities, but Julie wasn't Romy.

What she felt was sinful, an affront to God, a mistake. She'd go to Hell if she ever engaged in such wrongness. Julie had tried her best to stamp out those feelings, had prayed and prayed, had even tried bargaining with God, all "If you could just make it so I like boys, I'll tithe you all of my American Girl dolls and I'll always eat my asparagus without complaint." Like that would do any good.

And yet, when she'd spoken to Pastor Laurence on that first Wednesday of classes, he'd assured her that there was nothing wrong with her, that being gay was completely normal.

It was the first time anyone had ever said that to her. And now she couldn't get the words out of her head or the hope out of her heart. What would it mean if this was *her* normal? Could it possibly be okay, acceptable even, to be with Romy? Was there really nothing wrong with her?

Julie fell onto her side, the laptop sliding to land on the bed beside to her. What was she even doing anymore? Her eyes felt heavy and gummy. Maybe she could fall asleep now. She shut the lid of her computer before dropping it down to the floor beside her bed. She still didn't have answers to any of the things bothering her, but maybe she'd never have answers.

Maybe there weren't any answers to be had at all. Maybe she'd just have to make up her own.

Fluffing up her pillow, Julie rolled on her side to face the wall and curled up in a ball. For a few minutes she listened to the quiet of the dorm, the distant hum of the night sounds outside her window, and then she was falling into a sleep wherein she dreamed of masks she hated wearing because they didn't fit her.

# CHAPTER ELEVEN

Romy sat in one of the music practice rooms, hands resting on the piano keys. She was taking Vocal and Music Instruction and Music Production, as well as Music Theory, and she still felt like she still wasn't doing enough with her music. She hadn't written a song or a lyric in days. Could Verona have stolen her inspiration, her creative spirit? God, that was depressing.

Her fingers roamed across the keys, plunking out notes here and there, as she hoped for a lightning strike of…something. Ugh. She wanted to smash her head against the gleaming black of the piano. Maybe a concussion would shake things loose.

With a sigh, Romy closed her eyes and noodled. That's what she called it when she just let go, not caring if she came up with anything worthwhile. Notes flew into the air, floating above her head as she lost herself in melody, in the crest of the high notes and the troughs of the lows. As she played, her mind jumped from people to places to experiences, letting them flood through and then out of her through the notes of the piano.

Julie's face appeared in her memory. It was so unexpected that Romy's hands momentarily stilled. And then, just that simply, the music poured out of her, her fingers flying over the piano keys like birds taking wing. She thought of Julie, of her face, her form, her sweetness, and crafted an ode to everything that Julie was, that she represented.

It should have felt strange. Romy didn't know Julie, barely knew her at all, and yet, there was a feeling there, like Romy had known her all her life. Maybe not known Julie, that wasn't right, but known *of* her. Romy fed those feelings of familiarity into her playing and conjured musical magic: a picture of the girl in notes and sounds. Shoulders hunched, foot tapping on the pedal, Romy played everything she knew she wanted into being.

As her fingers slowed and eventually stopped, Romy finally opened her eyes. She felt lighter, freer than she had when she sat down. She and Julie didn't run in the same circles so they hadn't had many interactions. The way Tyndall hounded Julie's steps, Romy had a feeling there wouldn't be any in future either. There was a part of her that told her to let her crazy fixation on Julie go, that she was pushing for something more with a straight girl who could never give her what she wanted. Romy wished she could listen to that part.

Why couldn't she get Julie out of her head? She'd never obsessed over someone like this before; not with Whit, her first boyfriend, not even with Roz who she'd crushed on for years. Was it because Julie Cranston was forbidden fruit? A challenge? Looked like she was in desperate need of a friend?

Julie was straight and this line of thought was dangerous. What if she did somehow become friends with Julie? Would Romy be able to handle just friendship?

Romy hit playback on her phone; she recorded her session as she always did in case she came up with some nugget of brilliance. She couldn't compose on paper like other musicians. She had to fumble around with sound before it finally clicked in her head. Much of what she did was on her computer anyway.

As Romy listened to the playback, she could hear the moment she'd begun to think of Julie—a progression of notes began to appear that repeated throughout the rest of the song. Romy jotted them down in a notebook and turned back to the piano. Fingers sliding over the keys, she began again, this time beginning with those notes, mind and ears full of Julie.

If music classes were her salvation, then the Twitter gifs were Romy's penance for all of the horrible things she must have done as a child. Things had escalated—new memes and gifs sprung up every day, taking on a life of their own. @jesussez posted something new once a week, usually a Bible verse slapped onto a picture of Romy taken somewhere on campus. Roz had taken to notifying Romy whenever a new one popped up.

Romy would have been happier not knowing.

Mercury advised Romy to go to the Dean since this probably qualified as some kind of cyber bullying, especially since the pictures were obviously taken at Verona, but Romy held off. She did tell Bev and her mother though.

At first Romy wondered if Julie was behind the photos, especially when Mama Cranston's legion of followers started sharing them all over social media. Monet had called, frantically worried. She'd mentioned hiring a bodyguard, which Romy shot down—she was not going to look like she was scared. Her mother then insisted she speak with a counselor, something Romy also nixed.

She quickly eliminated Julie from her roster of suspects. None of the pictures Julie had taken with her permission had been used in the memes. She hardly ever had her phone out, and these pics were clearly taken with a phone's camera. Namina reported every instance to the social media in question, but so far had no luck in getting the handle suspended.

It was just one more unpleasant thing she was learning to live with. The first being Tyndall Sutcliffe.

Romy had no clue what she'd done to piss Tyndall off, besides being born, but Romy was getting pretty sick of the shade she kept trying to throw. Snide comments in class, more pointed ones outside of them, talk of protecting impressionable young minds from "unclean" influences made Romy grind her teeth to stop the retorts she wanted to make. They only shared two classes, thankfully, otherwise Romy would have been forced to muzzle the girl for Tyndall's own protection.

After a particularly unpleasant day, Romy, Mercury, a senior named Summer, and another junior called Katelyn, walked into the dining hall for dinner. Immediately Romy noticed a small knot of people toward the back of the hall beside a bank of tables, but lost interest when Mercury dragged her to the cafeteria line. It was Taco Tuesday and Romy did enjoy a vegetarian taco salad.

They'd all gathered at their usual table and had begun eating when a sophomore student Romy recognized as being one of Tyndall's crew came to the other side of the table. "Sign the petition?" The girl stuck a clipboard under Summer's nose as she tried to eat her burrito.

"Petition for what?" Katelyn asked, peering over Summer's shoulder at the forms on the clipboard.

"The fall dance is coming up and concerned students want to make sure the musical choices reflect the upstanding morals of Verona Prep." She smiled cheekily.

Mercury leaned over, plucking the clipboard from the girl's hands. Her bronze eyes swept over the page as she skimmed the contents. "It's a list of songs they feel should be banned from the dance."

Romy and Mercury turned in unison and found Tyndall Sutcliffe at the tables toward the back, directing her clipboard-toting minions to various tables around the room. Romy rolled her eyes. *Of course.*

Mercury turned back to the sheet. "Who chose the songs on this list?"

Romy saw the girl's gaze flicker over to Tyndall before she looked back at Mercury. In a nervous voice, she answered, "It was a joint effort by everyone in our Bible study group."

"Uh huh," Mercury scoffed. She pursed her lips and gave the sophomore a disbelieving look. Handing the clipboard back, she continued. "Hey Romy, guess whose songs are on that list?"

Romy grabbed at the clipboard, snatching it roughly from the girl's hands. "You have got to be shitting me."

"Nope."

Romy scanned through the list of songs and artists. About a third of the way into the list of songs, she saw her mother's name beside the note: ALL SONGS.

Her head swung up and she glared so fiercely that the student who'd started all of this stepped back. "Can I have my clipboard back?" she asked tentatively.

Climbing to her feet, Romy gave her a withering look. "I'll just return it myself, if you don't mind." Her tone said she didn't care if the girl minded or not; she'd have to pry that board from Romy's cold, dead hand.

Stalking across the dining hall to where Tyndall held court, Romy did her best to calm her temper. Confronting Tyndall in a froth wouldn't do any good. She highly doubted confronting Tyndall would do *anything*, but she couldn't just sit there in silence. Mercury, Summer, and Katelyn had all abandoned their meals to join her. As Romy approached, she scanned the faces near Tyndall, relieved when Julie wasn't one of them.

One of Tyndall's buddies leaned over to her leader as Romy walked over, whispering something in her ear. Tyndall straightened, a strained fake smile on her face. Stopping just inside of Tyndall's personal space, Romy stared at her. She held up the clipboard. "What's this?"

"Some pieces of paper attached to a clipboard," Tyndall said sweetly, her saccharine voice so cloying Romy thought she'd contract diabetes. The wordless 'duh' in her tone made Romy wish she could shake Tyndall until her teeth rattled. Especially when she saw one of the other girls with Tyndall snicker.

"Why is my mother's entire song catalog included on this list?" Romy knew that a few of Monet's hits could be considered questionable, but her entire song list? Her early stuff was pure pop confection.

"We're just making sure the impressionable minds of the students here at Verona Prep aren't exposed to lewd lyrics or overly sexualized imagery in what should be a very wholesome evening." She smiled a tiger's smile—all teeth and no feeling. "I'm just exercising my God-given right to stand against what I believe is wrong."

"While trying to control what everyone else thinks?" Mercury countered, coming up beside Romy. "If you had your way, we'd all be learning about Creationism in science class."

Romy got the idea that this was an old argument between the pair. Rather than let it head off in another direction, she pulled the focus back on the list. "So you're trying to ban songs you don't like? What about the other kids that attend Verona? The ones that might actually want to dance to any of these?"

"Then they can set up a protest of their own. It's not my fault they're too lazy to organize around their beliefs," Tyndall sniffed dismissively.

"Or maybe they're actually trying to mind their own business and get an education," Summer responded, flipping back her long hair. "Not everyone has such copious amounts of free time to worry about the state of people's souls, Tyndall." She walked back to her dinner, shaking her head.

"Why are you making it a point to target my mother?" Romy asked, holding up the clipboard again. "She's the only one you singularly excluded like that."

"We've already seen what kind of influence she has over young people," Tyndall said, pushing her shoulders back and puffing up in some kind of weird white girl threat display. She raked her gaze over Romy as if she was Exhibit A. "Right, Romy?"

At Tyndall's words, cold fury swept through Romy. So that was how she wanted to play it, huh? Forcing her clenched fists open, she propped her hands on her hips. "Got something to say to my face, T?"

Tyndall frowned. Mercury muttered, "Oh, damn," under her breath; Romy only heard her roommate because she was standing right next to her.

The other girl shrugged. "I think I just did."

Romy sucked in a deep breath, feeling the rage build inside of her like a wildfire burning out of control. She opened her mouth to speak, then saw Julie enter the dining hall, her camera bag slung across her body. Letting out the breath slowly, Romy reevaluated what she wanted to do. Much as she would like to yank hanks of Tyndall's glossy hair out by the roots, that actually wasn't going to solve anything and would probably just make things worse.

Instead of lunging across the empty space between them, Romy straightened to her full height and said, "I feel really bad for you. It must be so exhausting minding everyone else's business for them. Makes me kind of wonder the kind of shit you're trying *not* to think about." She turned around and began to walk away. "And as for the gay thing, it's like Shakespeare said—'methinks she doth protest too much,'" Romy threw over her shoulder.

She heard the sudden intake of multiple breaths as she turned back around, as well as Mercury's bark of delighted laughter. Romy glanced at Julie, who wore a worried expression while she watched the confrontation between the two girls. Romy debated about walking over to her to say hello when she felt something hit the back of her head. Hard.

An orange rolled past her boots.

She'd been concussed by fruit.

Romy thought she felt a cold stream of juice roll down the base of skull. It just made her angrier. Spinning around, she saw the horrified gaze of Tyndall Sutcliffe shift between the fruit on the floor and Romy's face. The girl looked like she'd even surprised herself with her fruity assault.

Reaching over, Romy scooped up someone's abandoned plate of nachos and launched it at Tyndall. She heard Mercury's laughter ring out like a bell, followed by her saying, "You just tried to smite her with citrus."

The resulting shouts of "Food Fight!" drowned out anything else Romy might have said.

# CHAPTER TWELVE

Julie checked her reflection in the mirror for the hundredth time in five minutes. She still had a spot of time before her parents arrived on campus for Parents' Weekend. She felt like she was going to vomit all over her canvas Keds. She ignored her gurgling stomach, knowing that even if she could eat, the food wouldn't sit well. This always happened when she got anxious—it felt like the acid in her stomach was burning a hole through her body.

She sat on her bed and fidgeted. Her mother had phoned a few days ago and said they had a surprise for Julie. No matter how much she'd harangued her mother, the woman still refused to tell her what the surprise entailed. Julie assumed this meant her mom and dad were coming in for Verona's parents' weekend. She'd been ecstatic—her mother hadn't been sure they could get away with her father's schedule being what it was. It meant the world to Julie that they would actually come and visit her in Connecticut. She wouldn't tell her mother, but she still missed home.

She missed her mother's voice and her father's arms around her. She missed her bed and Fluffles. To have some of that again, even if it was for a brief time, was almost too good to think about.

But she was worried too. This was the first time since she'd begun talking to Pastor Laurence that she'd be in the same room with her parents. What if they could tell there was something different about her? What if they couldn't?

Looking back in the mirror, Julie noticed the shine on her forehead. Leaning over to the desk, she swiped a couple of tissues and blotted at the sweat beading her skin. When had it gotten so hot in her room? Was she coming down with something? She had a sour taste at the back of her mouth and stomach was doing its best impression of a knotted bunch of curly fries. What was wrong with her? These were her parents, not the Spanish Inquisition.

Although the Spanish Inquisition might be easier to deal with.

It couldn't be the Spanish Inquisition though—nobody expected them.

Shaking her head in despair, Julie plopped down on her bed and immediately bounded up, straightening the wrinkles she'd made in the comforter. Everything needed to look perfect when her parents arrived. As much as she might hope this was just a chance for them to visit her and see how she was getting on, she didn't fool herself.

This was also an inspection.

Julie stopped in front of the mirror again, wiping her palms on the sensible khaki pants she wore. She'd paired it with a light blue polo shirt and navy cardigan. She made a face at herself in the mirror. This wasn't her, not at all. The ponytail she wore at the base of her neck to keep her wild mane of hair out of her face was the only thing about her that looked remotely familiar. She'd much rather have on her favorite pair of worn out jeans and battered sneakers or an old pair of worn-in cowboy boots, but that would embarrass her parents and Julie knew better than to embarrass them in a public setting.

Shuddering at her image in the mirror, Julie turned away. Mirror Julie was a different person, a fake Julie her parents wanted her to be, not the real her. All she needed was a pearl necklace and some fancy diamond stud earrings and she might as well drive to the country club and pick up her membership since she'd clearly given up on everything she'd ever wanted. Her sister Karen's words came back to her.

She could be a Christian and follow her heart.

The knock at her door cut through the still air like the crack of a gunshot. She jumped, glancing around her room wildly, looking for an escape route. Julie swallowed, once again wiping her damp palms on her khakis. She gave herself one last look in the mirror, the watery smile she wore wavering on her pale face. She tried for something better and managed an expression that didn't look like a rictus. Good enough

She turned away to get the door, already counting down the hours in her head before her parents would leave to go back to the hotel and Julie could retreat her dorm room again. With a sigh, she paused with her hand on the doorknob. These were her parents, after all—her family. How could she miss them and dread seeing them at the same time?

Was it normal to want to sneak out the window and hide in a fallout shelter, eating canned beans left over from 1962, until her family left the state?

With a deep breath, Julie twisted the knob. The door opened to reveal...a complete stranger. A young man, perhaps a few years older than Julie, stood in the hall. He was well dressed in a button down twill shirt, a v-neck sweater over it and charcoal grey tailored pants. His dark hair was slicked back from the angular bones of his face, displaying sapphire eyes that sparkled like gems in a jeweler's case. He looked like a soap opera actor—too rugged and good-looking to be real, all wrapped in a conservative sweater. Julie's mother would take to him like a cat to nip.

"Can I help you?" she asked cautiously, holding the door so it was only half-open.

"Hello, I'm Ferris McConnell." He gave her a smile that could have lit up all of Chicago with the power of its gleam.

Raising one eyebrow, she gave him a scathing look. "And?" she prompted, not sure why he expected her to know that name.

He began to laugh. "Am I to infer that your parents did not mention me coming by to visit you?"

"Got it in one," she snipped, crossing her arms over her chest. "Care to explain?"

"Can I come in and sit down first?" He smiled his charming smile.

Julie stepped out in the hall and shut the door behind her. Who the heck was this guy? She didn't know him and she sure wasn't going to invite him into her room—just the two of them. Her mother would have kittens if word got back to her that she'd entertained a young man in her room without supervision.

"Um, no," she answered as if he were dim, no longer caring about being nice. "I don't know you, I don't know why you're here, and I do not know your intentions towards me. We'll talk in the lounge. Come on."

The lounge had a few families already gathered in it, sharing the space with the Saturday morning television watchers. Julie led Ferris to two unoccupied chairs in the back corner. Once they were seated, she gestured for him to begin.

"I like a woman who asserts herself," he began, giving her another of his winning smiles. Julie resisted her mighty need to gag. "Your father and my father are friends. Mine's helping yours with his campaign for Senate. Your mom figured we should meet since I go to Stanbury."

Julie narrowed her eyes in suspicion. Stanbury was the private college the next town over. "What year are you?"

"Freshman." He rubbed the back of his neck with a broad hand. "My dad said your parents weren't able to make it here this weekend and that you might be lonely. Your mom suggested to mine that I come introduce myself and cheer you up. I figured it couldn't hurt to get to know a pretty girl that my parents approve of, so I said sure."

"How did you know I was pretty?" Julie had never seen him before.

He leaned back in his chair, blue gaze locked on her face. "Your mom sent a picture when she sent along your address and phone number."

Julie felt physically ill. She eyed Ferris' expensive footwear, briefly entertaining how they'd look covered in puke. Her mother had basically set her up on some kind of political blind date *without telling her about it*. She felt a little like a medieval princess being bartered for some kind of political alliance. She didn't know whether to laugh or scream.

She plastered on a pleasant smile. Ever since her mother had read that it took seven muscles to smile and forty-two to frown, she'd nagged at Julie to smile. Resting bitchface was for people who didn't care about wrinkles. "So I guess you're the surprise my mother mentioned."

Ferris held up his hands. "Guilty as charged."

Yeah, he thought he was adorable. All Julie wanted to do was stab him with a fork. She was going to have a long phone call with her mother when this day was over.

"I hate that you ca—" she began, hoping to get him to leave without offending him. He already knew she didn't have any other plans.

"Julie!" Tyndall's joyous shriek echoed throughout Cap's lounge. Julie saw one grandmother wince at the noise. Ferris jerked in his chair.

"Hi Tyndall," she said quietly, feeling the day spiraling out of her control. "What are you up to?"

"Oh my gosh, I can't believe I found you! I figured you'd already be off with your parents." Tyndall, wearing a navy skirt, lace collared shirt and grey sweater, eyed Ferris with suspicion. "I don't remember you having a brother."

Julie wanted to weep softly into her elbow while swanning gracefully over the arm of her chair, but thought that might draw even more unwanted attention to herself. The universe clearly hated her this morning. "This is Ferris McConnell—he's a friend of the family. My parents weren't able to make it so he came in their place. He goes to school at Stanbury."

Tyndall stuck out her hand. "I'm Tyndall Sutcliffe of the Texas Sutcliffes." Julie nearly lost control over her facial muscles at that. "And McConnell. As in Royce McConnell the senator from Iowa?"

Ferris smiled. "The same."

As Tyndall cooed over the senator's son, Julie tried to muster the will to care. Everything hit her all at once: her parents' absence, the letdown of her "surprise", Ferris himself, and Tyndall's inevitable appearance. All things Julie didn't want.

What *did* she want though? Chewing on the inside of her cheek, Julie let her mind wander and made a list.

Quiet.

Her camera.

A cheeseburger.

A nap in a sunbeam. She wondered if she might be part cat.

Romy.

Julie sat bolt upright, breath catching in her chest. Where had that last one come from? Romy Montoya was an impossibility, a mistake. Arms wrapping around her middle, she leaned forward, hunching around the pain that radiated out from her core.

"You feeling okay, Julie?" Tyndall asked.

Shaking her head, Julie managed to get out, "I'm not feeling so good. I think I'm going to go upstairs and lie down for a bit." She stood, managing to give Ferris a smile with effort. "I'm so sorry you came all this way for nothing."

"I wouldn't say nothing," Tyndall interjected, eyes sparkling as she turned to Ferris. "I'm happy to keep you company until Julie is feeling better. My parents couldn't make the trip this year."

Tyndall frowned, suddenly sad. It made Julie feel bad for the girl. She'd gathered in the past month or so of knowing her that Tyndall's family didn't contact her very often and that she didn't get home much. Her parents were very busy with her father's ministry and the syndication of his Sunday services.

"We'll check in on you later," Ferris offered, standing up to see her off.

"Oh, that's not necessary," Julie protested.

"Don't be silly!" Tyndall gave her a brittle smile. "Of course it's necessary!"

Nodding weakly, Julie scuttled toward the stairs, knowing it was useless to protest further. Once Tyndall made up her mind, it would take an act of God to change it. She just vowed not to be anywhere near her room when they came by. She'd just say she was sleeping and missed them. She should probably feel guiltier than she did about lying, but Julie couldn't stand to be around them right now. It was self-preservation; surely God would understand that.

Locking the bedroom door behind her, Julie breathed a sigh of relief. She was in her room, away from unwanted visitors and prying eyes. First order of business was to ditch the country club outfit. She slid into her well-worn jeans with the hole in the knee, a baggy Northwestern sweatshirt—Karen's alma mater—and her tennis shoes. Much better. That strangling sensation she'd fought since putting on that cardigan subsided with each piece of clothing she changed.

She thought about calling her mother, and discarded the idea almost instantly. Her mother would be angry that she had ignored Ferris, and Julie wasn't sure she could remain calm in the face of everything she wanted to say. Whenever Julie got angry, her eyes filled up with tears and her voice grew thick. Her mother always lectured her to be less emotional, to talk to her only when she could be rational and controlled. Right now, Julie didn't want to be controlled or rational. She *was* angry and she wanted to express it.

She paced, feeling her room shrink with every step. She needed to get out of here, to walk in the woods, to be in open space. If she stayed in her room, Julie would drive herself crazy.

She didn't want to risk going down the stairs—she might run into someone she knew or worse, Tyndall and Ferris if they hadn't already left for wherever they were going. Hopefully somewhere very far away. Katmandu was supposed to be lovely.

On her next turn around the room, her gaze strayed to the window and the huge maple outside of it.

Throwing up the sash, Julie leaned her head out for a better look. A limb ran right up to her windowsill—it would sometimes rub against the glass when the wind was right. It was a nice, thick branch that looked sturdy enough to hold her weight. The quad was fairly empty as most students had dragged their parents into town for lunch. She stood a good chance of sneaking out so long as the tree limb held.

Taking a deep breath, she slung her camera bag across her body. She'd risk it.

Julie shoved her desk out of the way and climbed up onto the sill. Reaching out and up, she snagged the higher branch, testing to see if it would break. It held. Easing out, she put her feet on the lower branch. This one was thinner, not as strong. She moved quickly, shoving away from her window. The limb she stood on creaked alarmingly but didn't snap. Julie hurried along to reach the thicker part, then the trunk, where she began to lower herself slowly to the ground.

Free. She was free.

# CHAPTER THIRTEEN

Romy lounged on her bed, watching Mercury finish getting ready for lunch with her folks. They were driving in from NYC for Parents' Weekend at Verona. Romy was more than a little excited to meet Will Tyrell Highbrook in person. Mercury had made her vow not to geek out too much on the man, but Romy had made no promises.

"Are you sure you don't want to come to lunch with us?" her roommate asked, folding the scarf she wore to bed to protect her hair and setting it beneath her pillow. "I feel bad just leaving you here all alone."

"It's fine, Merc." Monet had called earlier in the week to tell Romy she wouldn't be able to make it to Verona that weekend; her press tour and performance schedule didn't allow a large enough window to make it enjoyable for either of them. Romy assured her mom it was fine. Monet would come another weekend when the town and the campus weren't packed with people and they'd hang out then. "I'm just going to work on some music, maybe take a walk. You go enjoy some time with your family."

Mercury leveled an assessing look at her. "Why do I feel like you are up to something?"

"I am shocked and offended by that statement," Romy said, hands flat against her heart. "If I had pearls, I'd be clutching them. See, this is me. Clutching pearls."

"Hmmmm."

"Pearls! Clutching!"

Mercury laughed, lobbing a pillow at Romy's head. Romy caught it and sent it back. "Fine, fine. I'll leave you be. Maybe you'll actually work on your English project!"

"I'll have you know that I've read all of the stories assigned to me and I am halfway done with my part of the presentation," Romy sniffed haughtily.

"Good for you. Thank goodness mine's over with."

Romy shuddered. Poor Mercury had been paired with Tyndall who ran their group like a gulag. "You guys did a good job," she offered.

Mercury snorted. "We didn't have a choice. Tyndall would have flayed the skin from our bones if we dared not deliver an A. I know you'll find this hard to believe, but we argued. A lot."

Grinning at her roommate, Romy said, "I can imagine. Doesn't sound like fun."

"I don't know, yelling back at Tyndall may yet prove to be a very satisfying pastime. Maybe I can figure out how to make it my senior project." Romy's roommate gave a snarl and said, "I really don't like that girl."

"Never would have guessed, Merc."

"She's just so sneaky!" Mercury paced the room, movements sharp and short. "She's a sometimen'."

"A what?"

"Just something me and my friends in New York say. It's when a person acts nice to your face sometimes but then tears you down behind your back. Sometimes nice, sometimes not, you know." Mercury shook her head, twists shuddering. "Tyndall is one those. She acts all righteous, but she'll cut a bitch down just as soon as her back is turned. And she's the type that always seems to get away with it."

"What, like Christian?"

"No, like white." Mercury sniffed in disdain. "If I tried to pull half of what that girl did, you can bet I'd be out on my black butt faster than you could say 'Aunt Jemimah.'"

Romy sighed. She understood some of where Mercury was coming from. Monet was Puerto Rican and Romy's father was Korean. She certainly couldn't pass for white, but the casual racism she faced was more of the "Where are you from?" or "Are you Chinese?" variety rather than the "shopping while black" or "driving while black" type that some of her friends in L.A. got.

"Yeah," Romy said, "I can see that."

"I heard she's going to start up a no-dating petition for same sex couples on campus," Mercury told her, gaze coming to rest on Romy's face. "Something about it not being fair to the straight couples who can't have their boyfriends over to visit after hours. I think she's trying to bait you."

Now it was Romy's turn to snort with laughter. "Or date me. Which, no thanks." She thought briefly of Julie, then put her out of her mind. *Straight girl, no point.* "She does realize that gays and bisexuals can't have their significant others over either after lights out? It's not like there's some lesbian cabal that's teaching people how to Apparate themselves into their girlfriends' dorm rooms with the sole purpose of pissing off straight people."

"There's not?" Mercury quipped, trying to sound disappointed. "And here I was, all ready to sign up."

Romy chucked a throw pillow at her. "You just want to learn to Apparate. Admit it."

The pillow caught Mercury on the shoulder. She tucked it under her arm and sat down on her bed. "Who wouldn't? Think of the time you'd save. And bonus points for the use of the word cabal. I feel that is very SAT-worthy."

Smiling at her roommate, Romy lay back down. "I don't even understand how a petition like that is supposed to work. Is there going to be a sign-up sheet where you list your sexuality so they know who to monitor? Doesn't seem likely this is something that can be enforced."

"She'll find a way," Mercury muttered darkly. "That girl is the devil's own hellspawn."

A knock at their door derailed the rest of their conversation. Mercury answered it, revealing her parents and her younger brother and sister. As they all shuffled inside the dorm room—suddenly very small thanks to the addition of four more people—Romy put her laptop and headphones in her messenger bag in anticipation of a hasty exit. She did not want to horn in on her roommate's family time. When she finished packing, she slung the bag over her shoulder and turned to face the Highbrooks.

Mercury handled the intros. "Mom, Dad, Ceres, Cosmo—this is my roommate, Romy Montoya."

Romy shook everyone's hand, unable to resist smiling shyly at Mr. Highbrook. "I am a huge fan," she gushed. "I love how your special highlighted the contributions of female scientists that were left out of the original. Thank you for that."

Mr. Highbrook's eyebrows rose in surprise, but then he smiled. "Are you going to pursue a degree in a STEM field?"

Romy shook her head. "Music, just like my mom probably. But I like to read about the stars and planets."

Ceres whispered something to her mother, who frowned. Mrs. Highbrook was a tall, imposing woman with dark skin and eyes just like Mercury's. She wore the hell out of her dark green cashmere sweater and grey pants, looking too refined and elegant to be standing in a tiny dorm room.

"I am not going to ask her that," Mrs. Highbrook said clearly. Ceres blushed. "If you want to know, you can ask her yourself."

Ceres was twelve, though tall for her age. She straightened, cheeks still flushed, and looked Romy right in the eyes. Romy felt a little upset that a twelve year old stood as tall as she did. So unfair. "I was wondering," Ceres began, voice cracking. She cleared her throat and tried again. "I was wondering if I could get your and your mom's autographs?"

Romy blinked, startled. It took her a few moments to find words. "I'll see what I can do, but I think I can swing it." Ceres broke into a wide smile and it was like watching the sun appear from behind a cloud. Romy grinned back, then asked, "I get why you'd want my mom's autograph, but why mine? I'm not famous or anything."

"Not yet," Ceres told her confidently, "but you will be. Your music is really good." Romy gave her a surprised look. "As soon as Mercury told me who her roommate was, I subscribed to your YouTube channel. I really like your cover of 'I Will Wait.' You're going to be really famous."

Romy didn't know quite what to say. This was the first time she'd ever been asked for an autograph for her talent and not just because of who her mother was. She felt warmth suffuse her chest. "Can I give you a hug?" she asked, needing some outlet to show Ceres just how much her words meant to her and what a compliment it was.

Now it was Ceres' turn to look shocked. "Um, sure?"

Romy enfolded her in a hug and gave her an extra squeeze. "Thank you," she whispered. "And I'll see if I can come up with something special for you from me and Mom." Ceres squealed in happiness. Romy let go and took a step toward the door.

"I don't want to keep you guys from your visit." Turning to Mr. and Mrs. Highbrook and Cosmo, she said, "It was very nice to meet you all. Merc, I'll catch up with you later."

"Are you sure you don't want to join us for lunch?" Mrs. Highbrook asked.

"Mom, I already asked her," Mercury sighed, rolling her eyes when she thought her mom wasn't looking.

"I'm good, Mrs. Highbrook, thank you. I've got some studying I need to catch up on anyway. Good-bye!"

Romy hurtled down the stairs, practically floating from Ceres' request. She got tons of comments on her channel feed, but this was somehow different. Better. Was this how her mother felt when a fan came up to her and gushed all over her about what her music meant to them? If so, Romy could totally understand why her mom toured and gave interviews and did outreach. Not only did giving back make you feel good, but the ego boost was pretty nice too.

She hit the doors, shivering a little at the bite in the air. She wore her heavier fall jacket, but the temperature difference between L.A. and Connecticut was still marked. Romy knew she'd need to get one heckuva winter coat if she had any hope of surviving the winter without whining the entire season.

Crossing the quad, Romy skirted the sidewalk, content to crash through the fallen leaves off to the side. As she came up on the huge maple at the corner of Cap Hall, she noticed the rustle of branches above her. The maple still had a good chunk of its leaves left, though there were drifts beginning to accumulate at the base of the tree, so Romy couldn't get a good view from where she stood. There was no wind to speak of, and the rustling was too large to be a squirrel. She walked closer, curious as to what might be making such a racket.

Peering up, Romy caught a glimpse of jeans and sneakers. Someone was climbing down the tree. Edging nearer still, she cast about and saw the open window with the branch butting up against it. As she moved, she got a better look at the person shimmying their way down the trunk. She stared up with wide eyes, not believing what she was seeing.

"Julie?" When the blonde looked down, a horrified expression on her face, Romy asked, "Did the front door do something to personally offend you?"

# CHAPTER FOURTEEN

Julie risked a glance down as she clung to the trunk of the tree, bark scraping along her cheek. Terrific. Just great. She was hoping to get away unseen, and who should show up but the very last person she wanted to run into: Romy Freakin' Montoya. Why could she not catch a break?

"Go away," she whispered angrily, going back to making her slow way to the ground.

"Seriously though," Romy said, ignoring Julie's order, "what are you doing?"

"Brokering a peace talk in the Middle East. What does it look like I'm doing?" Irritated at the interruption, Julie didn't bother keeping her sarcasm to herself.

A short bark of laughter made her look down. Romy had clapped a hand over her mouth, but Julie could see her cheeks puffed up behind it. She was smiling. Julie forced her gaze back to the task at hand, reminding herself that she did not find Romy Montoya completely adorable. Nope, no sir, she did *not*.

"It looks like you're sneaking out of your dorm room," Romy answered, taking her hand away from her mouth. "But that wouldn't make any sense because Julie Cranston would never do something against the rules and there's a perfectly good working set of stairs and a door that would enable her to leave without the risk of breaking her neck." Julie saw Romy tilt her head back, surveying Julie with glittering eyes. "Unless there's a reason why you don't want anyone to see you leave?"

Julie leapt the last few feet, her shoes thumping against the hard packed ground. She staggered, but righted her balance without Romy's offered hand. She didn't want Romy touching her. That fell under Julie's list of Very Bad Things That Must Not Occur Ever.

"That's none of your business." Julie heard the front door of Cap open. Tyndall's voice wafted out. "Rats!"

Romy's gaze slid to the front of Cap Hall and then back to Julie, reading the situation in an eye blink. "Come on," she said, grabbing Julie's arm just above the elbow and hauling her around the side of the building away from the door.

Julie went with her, stumbling over the roots hidden by cascades of autumn leaves. Eventually she found her footing and took off, shaking her arm free of Romy and heading for the copse of trees behind Cap Hall. She didn't wait to see if Romy followed. Instead she ran, camera bag bouncing against her hip, the nippy air ripping though her hair and making her ears throb from the cold. It felt good to run like this. Hysterical laughter bubbled up in the back of her throat.

Romy ran in her wake, the rustle of leaves loud behind them. Julie didn't stop until she hit the stand of trees; then she spun and peered out into the quad. There was no sign of Tyndall. Julie figured she and Ferris must have turned the other way toward the visitor's parking lot if they were going to head off campus for some food. She leaned her hands on her knees, gulping in air. Romy leaned against a nearby tree, hardly winded. Irritation rose inside of her; of course Romy would be in better shape than she was. Like the girl wasn't already perfect enough.

She stifled that thought ruthlessly.

"Care to tell me why you're avoiding Tyndall?" Romy's voice held amusement as well as curiosity. "I mean, not that I blame you, but you've always seemed pretty cool with her."

Julie straightened and checked her camera bag, positioning it so it fell comfortably against her hip once more. "It's a long story."

Romy gestured around the trees. "I've got nowhere else to be. I was just going to work on our Lit project and maybe head to the music room." She shrugged. "Lay it on me."

Julie sighed, waging an inner battle. She should go; she knew that. It was safer to avoid Romy Montoya's company altogether rather than be tempted by what she could never allow herself to have. At the same time, she was tired and lonely and Romy was *here*, so amazingly present that it did things to Julie's thinking. Made her believe things were possible that weren't. Made her not care about who Romy's mother was, made Julie not care about who her *own* mother was.

She walked deeper into the trees. Romy followed, combat boots moving softly through the dry grass. "My parents couldn't make it for the weekend. I hadn't really expected them to come, but then my mom told me they had a surprise for me, so I thought maybe they'd be making the trip from Kansas after all." Julie pushed a pine branch out of the way, holding it so it didn't swing back and slap Romy in the face. "Imagine my shock when a strange guy knocks at my door and says my parents sent him."

"What, like a blind date delivered direct to your door?" Romy sounded horrified. Julie turned to look at her. "So they didn't even warn you to expect him?"

Julie shook her head. "Nope."

"Rude."

Her laugh took Julie by surprise, but when she saw the way Romy's face split into a wide grin, she vowed to do it again. "Yeah, exactly. And he tried to get me to let him into my room before even introducing himself!"

"Creepy much?" Romy nodded her head. "Obviously you didn't let him in."

"We went down to the dorm lounge. He explained that my dad is a friend of his dad and since my parents couldn't make it, they asked him to come and cheer me up. Make sure I didn't feel lonely." Julie glanced at Romy out of the corner of her eye. She stomped through the leaves beside Julie, cheeks tinted a soft rose. Julie clenched her hands into fists to keep from reaching out and seeing how soft and warm Romy's skin felt beneath her fingertips.

"So why the need to sneak out?" Romy ducked beneath a low hanging limb.

With a grimace, Julie answered, "Tyndall appeared."

"Ah." Romy paused. "You know, she completely weaseled out of clean-up duty after the food fight she helped start. Had one of her friends take the fall for throwing that orange at my head."

Julie nodded. She'd heard all about it from Grace, the one Tyndall had managed to strong arm into saying Tyndall hadn't been the one to throw the fruit, saying that Mercury must have been mistaken. All of the other girls involved in the petition had to attend the mandatory punishment, but not Tyndall. Julie didn't like that one bit, but didn't know what she could do about it.

"Yep. Anyway, I saw my opportunity and I took it. Tyndall seemed more interested in Ferris anyway, and I certainly didn't want to be stuck with him. I said I had a stomach ache and went upstairs to my room." Goodness, when she said it aloud, she sounded like a horrible person.

"And the shimmy down the tree was to avoid them seeing you when you decided you didn't want to be trapped in your room," Romy guessed.

Hanging her head, Julie muttered, "I'm a rotten person, aren't I?"

"Maybe a little," Romy answered, nudging Julie in the side with her elbow. When Julie looked up, Romy had her index and thumb up, maybe a half an inch of space between them. "Wee." She grinned. "I'm kidding! You might be as close to a saint as it is possible to get." She paused, glancing at Julie shyly from under her lashes. "But I have to admit, it's kind of nice to see you with your halo askew."

Julie swatted playfully at Romy's shoulder, a warm feeling gathering low in her belly. "I am not an angel!" *Far from it.*

"Could have fooled me," Romy murmured before turning her head to gaze out at the trees.

Julie cleared her throat. "So what about you? Where's your mom?"

Romy gave Julie a look that seemed to say she knew what Julie was doing by changing the subject but was content to let her have her way. For now, anyway. Julie felt a shiver slide along her spine at the briefly dangerous glint in Romy's hazel eyes.

"Mom couldn't get away from her press tour for the new album," she said in an airy voice, expression easy. She looked like her mother's absence didn't bother her at all. Maybe she was just more used to absentee parenting than Julie. "Which is probably better anyway. She said she'd come visit when it isn't so crowded. We won't have to worry about people gawking at her." Romy shrugged one slim shoulder. "We'll enjoy our time together more that way."

Biting her lip, Julie considered. That wasn't the answer or the reaction she expected. Romy surprised her with how level-headed and grounded she was, despite the stories that came out of L.A. Julie wondered how much of what the public knew about Romy— and to an extent, Monet—came from made up articles in the tabloids. Romy certainly didn't seem like a spoiled wild-child ready to go off on a tantrum any time she didn't get her way.

Romy's voice pulled Julie out of her thoughts. "So are you out to take some more pictures?"

One hand tightening around the strap of her bag, Julie nodded. "Since the leaves are turning, I thought I'd do some nature shots."

"Want company?"

Julie froze in place. What was Romy offering exactly? And did Julie want to accept any of it? She knew she shouldn't; she should just turn around and march back to her room like the straight girl she tried so hard to be, but the strength just wasn't in her today. She wanted, oh how she wanted. Even if it was just for a half an hour, Julie wanted to bask in the sunlight of Romy's presence. Closing her eyes, she braced herself to say the one word that would consign her to a temporary heaven and damn her to hell at the same time.

"Sorry, what I meant was that I was just going to study and stuff, I could do that here while you did your photography stuff, never mind, I shouldn't have asked, but you just seemed like you didn't want to be alone and I tho—" Romy babbled, eyes wild and wide as if she couldn't believe she'd just said that.

"Yes."

A whispered answer was the best she could do, but it seemed good enough for Romy. Her smile spread across her brown face like honey down a comb, thick and sweet. "Okay then," Romy whispered back.

♪ ♪ ♪

That afternoon was the best time Julie had had since coming to Verona Prep, possibly in her whole life. She discovered that Romy had a wickedly sharp sense of humor. Her stories of hanging out with her friends in L.A. or weird things she saw out there were always good for a laugh, and Julie found herself laughing plenty. As Julie wandered the nearby woods in search of the perfect shot, Romy spread her jacket on the ground and dug out her notes on Poe. She sat in the middle of a patch of sun, the light gilding her dark hair and turning the red streaks to crimson flames.

As she wandered, Julie let herself think about her parents. They'd be disappointed in her for not going out with Ferris; she knew that just as surely as she knew the sun would come up every morning. They'd had a purpose for sending her to Verona Prep. Ferris hadn't shown up at her doorstep by accident, just as her mother playing coy about a surprise hadn't been one either.

Julie feared she knew why her mother wanted her aware of Ferris and his proximity. Julie was a good age to start dating—soon to be eighteen—and Ferris was a great catch. He came from another conservative family, his father had political clout, and he was a good looking, clean cut, Christian boy. Too bad Julie didn't want anything to do with him. She felt too much like a prize at the end of video game.

She turned to go back to the small clearing, crossing over a small stream littered with smooth stones. Nothing was inspiring her; nothing touched her enough to make her want to capture it with her camera's lens. Her insides were in knots; as nice as this afternoon interlude was, it couldn't last. Julie would call her mother and be reminded of what good girls did and didn't do. She wished that she could just stay in this moment forever, never having to go back to the world that waited beyond the trees. Just her and Romy.

No. It couldn't happen. That was the dream of all dreams—beyond dreams, really. It was a wish, and Julie knew just how rarely they were granted.

She stopped as she neared the spot where Romy sat, eyes arrested by the girl in the clearing. Romy sprawled on her stomach, pen in her teeth as she read a passage in a book she'd brought with her. A furrow wrinkled the space between her dark brows. Her legs were up in the air, bent at the knee. She leaned on her elbows, long fingers of one hand braced against the pages to hold the book open.

Romy didn't know Julie was there. She was so much herself in that moment, so rooted and grounded while Julie felt like she would just slip off the edge of the world if she didn't find something to hold on to. How did Romy do it? How was she brave enough to let the world see who she really was? How did it come so easy for her?

Julie slipped the camera in front of her eye, viewfinder full of Romy's face. She'd loaded her long lens so she was able to perfectly capture the play of light and shadow along her cheekbones, the glitter of her eyes beneath lowered lids, the fracturing of sunlight through long lashes. Romy looked carved of copper and bronze, divine in some way that Julie didn't fully understand. She glowed from the inside out, that special fire only she commanded. Julie wondered if she'd get scorched if she stayed too long at Romy's side.

She wanted to find out.

Romy glanced up, as though feeling Julie's gaze on her. Julie snapped a couple more shots before lowering her camera. As she approached Romy, she heard people coming along the path that would lead them to their spot. And just like that, Julie's bubble burst, the magic inside of it evaporating like steam in cold air. She was foolish to think this—whatever this was—could last beyond this day, this afternoon, this hour. The real world would always pull her back.

"Get anything good?" Romy called with a wave.

Julie shrugged tiredly, feeling a thousand years old. "I'll let you know."

# CHAPTER FIFTEEN

Romy stood against the wall of Carmichael gym, arms crossed in front of her chest and wearing a disgusted expression. The music was atrocious. Mercury stood beside her, grinning.

"This must be like hell for you," her roommate said, bumping Romy with her shoulder.

Romy didn't bother answering, just let her gaze roam around the room. A few groups of girls danced at the edges of the gym's floor, but so far the center remained empty. No one was brave enough—or drunk enough—to risk having all eyes on them. Almost every student at Verona Prep had come to this dance— Verona's version of Homecoming—but most of the students appeared more interested in socializing than dancing.

To be fair, Romy doubted there'd be a lot of drinking at a Verona event. She was used to the parties in L.A., where everyone either showed up hammered or became so as the night went on. Romy had never imbibed, had never wanted to, but this mixer made her wonder if she should make an exception.

"Thanks for being so nice to Ceres," Mercury said. "I told my mom to tell her to not bother you."

Romy put her hand on her roommate's shoulder. "Your sister is a sweetheart and I'm happy to help. In fact, I'm trying to score her some backstage passes to Mom's Madison Square Garden show. If your mom would be okay with it, of course." Romy had mad respect for Mrs. Highbrook, especially since she was pretty sure the woman could snap her spine over her knee without breaking a sweat. Though the woman was tall and slender, she carried herself like she knew a hundred ways to kill a man with her pinky finger.

"Holy crap, really?!" Mercury burst out. Romy shushed her when heads started to turn in their direction. "If you can, that would be amazing. Ceres would flip out!" She pulled Romy into her shoulder for a tight squeeze. "I won't say anything if you promise to tell me one thing."

Romy leaned away from her roommate, eyebrow raised eloquently. "What's that?"

"What is your mom thinking about when she's performing on stage? She looks so scary when she's up there marching around."

Romy leaned against the wall, shoulders flat, hips pushed out. She snickered. "Yeah, she told me once that she just thinks 'Murder' and imagines she's stomping on critics."

"Well, it works."

"I find it's an important life skill to cultivate." She nodded in commiseration with her roommate. Mercury wasn't looking at her though; she was watching the entrance with a disgusted look on her face.

"Never thought she'd show up," Mercury muttered, staring at the door.

Romy turned her head to see who Mercury meant and froze. Tyndall Sutcliffe entered the gym with two girls Romy didn't recognize and Julie Cranston. Romy felt like all the air had been punched out of her lungs. Julie had her hair pulled up in some kind of high twist, exposing the long, creamy column of her neck. She wore a cute, conservative purple dress and yet another pair of those ridiculous ballet flats. Romy wondered how it was even fair for someone to look so effortlessly lovely.

"Why not?" Romy asked absently, too busy staring at Julie to pay too much attention.

"Because every time Verona has tried to do something enjoyable, Tyndall Sutcliffe has to go and ruin it. She's a ruiner." Mercury gestured expansively at the gym. "You know this dance used to be co-ed, right?"

Romy raised her eyebrows, giving her roommate a sidelong glance. "I did not."

"Yep," Mercury practically snarled. "Until Tyndall and her Go God squad decided to protest the decision to allow guys from Wittenburg to come. Rather than risk parents getting involved and calling the school, the administration caved even though it'd been a tradition for freakin' decades." Mercury sent a glare Tyndall's way.

Wittenburg was the all-male counterpart to Verona Prep. "Why do you care so much about whether some other school can come to a dance or not?"

Romy practically felt Mercury's emphatic eye roll. "Guys, Romy. You may be happy with the pickings around here, but those of us who only swing one way like a little eye candy once in a while to break up the monotony of all the boobs."

"That's the name of my new band," she said, looking back at Julie who had stopped next to Tyndall and another group of students that Romy vaguely recognized. "Monotony of the Boobs."

"I'd buy their album."

Romy turned back to her roommate with a grin. "Sorry for the lack of—what did you call it—eye candy?" She cocked her head. "You said Tyndall ruins everything. What else has she done?"

Mercury went on to list a number of student protests that were all led or organized by Tyndall and her Bible group. Anything that appeared inclusive seemed to raise the girl's ire. She'd been mobilizing since she first started at Verona.

"She sounds like a peach," Romy noted.

Mercury nodded. "She puts the fun in fundamentalism," she said drily. "Now you see why it's weird that she's here."

"Maybe she took a night off from saving all of us heathens from our baser impulses to drink bad punch and listen to horrible music?"

Shrugging, Mercury stepped away from the wall. "Doubt it." She waved at a group of people from Montag Hall who ventured out onto the gym floor to dance. "I'm going to go have some fun."

"Make good choices," Romy called after her.

"I always do!"

Romy saw Julie break away from Tyndall's group and head over to the snack table. She remembered the strangeness of their encounter in the maple tree, and how Julie had rushed away after Romy had sat down at the library table and been handed a tampon as a writing implement. Everything rational told Romy to leave her alone, to find someone else, someone who might actually like her. Romy really wished she could listen to that rational voice. But Julie was in her orbit, a star falling to earth, and all Romy had to do was reach out her hand to catch her.

How could she resist?

She walked over to Julie, coming up beside her when she was certain there was no one else around to overhear. "I don't see any Oreos," she whispered.

Julie jerked away in surprise. She turned her head quickly, eyes huge, the pupil nearly drowning out the blue of her iris. Romy froze, unable to stop staring. Her brain screamed at her, telling her she was only five seconds away from making everything weird and awkward, but Romy was mesmerized, like a bird before a snake. She managed to snap out of it only when Julie cut her eyes away to see if anyone had noticed them speaking.

Reminding herself that blue was not a good color for her, Romy sucked in a deep breath. *Play it cool. Don't screw this up.* "Clearly whoever set out this spread was seriously lacking."

As opening lines went, it wasn't terrible, but it certainly wasn't Shakespeare either. Still, Julie hadn't run screaming for the hinterlands or insulted Romy's mom, so she was taking it as a good sign.

"I'm more interested in the chips this time," Julie murmured, a small smile on her face.

Oh, how Romy wanted to lick that smile to see how those lips tasted. *Not good.* She changed the subject quickly. "How did those pictures turn out?" Romy picked up a napkin so she looked like she was getting food and not chatting up a straight girl who came from a family with Jesus issues. When Julie looked at her quizzically, Romy reminded her. "A few days ago. The ones you took from the other day?"

Julie flushed daintily, a wash of pinky-peach across her cheeks. She cleared her throat. "I haven't really gotten a chance to look at them yet."

"Oh. Well, I hope they turned out okay."

Julie tilted her head up, lips curled in a smile. That smile did things to Romy's insides, things she didn't want to think about. *This was such a bad idea.*

"If any of them turn out okay, I'll send them to you." Julie stared up at Romy.

Romy forgot how to word. She blinked stupidly at Julie until her brain finally engaged with a grinding of mental gears. "You would?" she stammered, thanking whoever controlled the universe that breathing was an autonomic function, otherwise she'd have passed out at Julie's feet by now. When Julie nodded shyly, Romy said, "I'd like that."

The strains of Monet's latest chart topper issued from the speakers. Every head in the gym swiveled in Romy's direction. Normally didn't mind all eyes on her; she'd grown used to it living out in L.A. But right now, tonight, it was unbearable—it was like sandpaper rubbing across an open wound. She wanted to march over the DJ and feed him his headphones. No one moved.

Romy held up her hand and waved weakly. That seemed to break the spell. Groups of students whooped and headed for the dance floor. She saw Mercury and her crowd head out to the center of the gym. The dance beat kicked in and more students streamed out. Romy sighed with relief.

At least until Tyndall stomped over to Julie. "Is she bothering you?" she asked with poisoned sweetness.

"I was just getting some chips," Julie said softly, holding up her napkin.

"Come on, Julie." Tyndall pulled on Julie's arm, dragging her away from the refreshment table. "There are some friends I wanted to introduce you to."

Romy took a step forward, hand out to grab at Julie's wrist. She didn't care what Tyndall said about her, but the way she hauled Julie around made her blood burn. You didn't treat a friend like that. Even Roz at her worst wouldn't have jerked Romy around like a dog on a lead. Romy stopped though when she saw Julie shake her head quickly, blue eyes huge in her pale face.

Clenching her teeth, Romy dropped her hand. She watched as Tyndall hauled Julie back to their table, leaving a trail of broken potato chips in her wake. After watching a minute longer, Romy spun on her heel. She definitely needed some fresh air.

♪ ♪ ♪

Romy trudged across campus beside Mercury, mind on nothing. The dance had ended—finally—and her roommate had found her sitting on the wide, shallow stairs that led up into the gym. Romy hadn't been able to set foot back inside, even after she saw Julie leave with Tyndall and the rest of the God Squad.

She really wished she had better control over her body. Specifically her heartbeat, which always seemed to approach warp speed whenever she was within a ten-foot radius of the pretty blonde. Stupid heartbeat.

Mercury interrupted her thoughts with, "You're pining."

Romy came back from her fugue state with a well-thought out, "Huh?"

"You. Are. Pining." Mercury shook her head. "It'd be kind of sweet if it wasn't so, you know, *pathetic*."

"Gee, thanks. Good to know I'm pathetic." Romy bumped her roommate with a bony hip. "Easy for you to joke about it. I suppose you've never been in unrequited like before?"

Snorting, Mercury nudged her roommate with an elbow. "Please, Romy. Everyone's been in unrequited like before. You don't have the corner of the market on it just because of who your mama is."

Cocking a brow at her, Romy straightened and said in her best British accent, "Who are you who are so wise in the ways of science?"

"I feel like I should know that reference," Mercury answered, giving her an odd look.

Romy shrugged. "Probably not. It's Monty Python and the Holy Grail."

"Oh, that one." Mercury sighed. "My dad loves them. I don't get what's so funny about it though." She pursed her full lips, surveying her roommate critically. "What are you going to do about this Julie situation?"

Shrugging, Romy stuck her hands in the pockets of her jeans. "Pine, I guess. She's straight. Her dad believes in electroshocking gay teens to make *them* straight. Pretty sure she'd rather douse herself with gasoline and set herself on fire rather than get involved with me, even if she were interested. Which she's not." She looked up at the stars. "What else am I supposed to do?"

"A girl doesn't just hang around with someone she hates, Romy." Mercury bumped Romy with her shoulder. "Just ask her how she feels. I think you might be surprised." She paused, giving her roommate an arch look. "At the very least, you could wind up with a new friend."

"I have enough friends, thanks," Romy scoffed. Her blood ran like ice in her veins at the thought of talking to Julie about *that*.

"Never took you for a wuss, Montoya. Talk. To. Her." Mercury shoved her roommate in the direction of the large tree that stood near the side of one of Cap Hall. Its branches spread out thickly, nearly touching the windows of the upper floors.

It was the same tree Julie had climbed down only a few days earlier.

Romy lurched to a stop, gaze transfixed. From this angle, she could see Julie Cranston through the open blinds. She sat on her bed, a pen gripped between her lips like the world's luckiest cigarette, laptop open in front of her. Her bedroom window was half-open, letting in the chill night air, but it didn't seem to be bothering the blonde, even though Romy shivered in her hoodie.

She felt her heartbeat stutter in that annoying way it did whenever Julie was around. The blonde dropped her chin as she stared at something on her laptop screen. Her hair was pulled up in a messy bun, escaped strands forming a wispy halo around her head.

"I'll just leave you to it then, Montoya," Mercury whispered before racing away in the direction of their shared dorm room.

"I am going to kill that girl," Romy muttered to no one in particular. She felt like a creep watching Julie in the darkness beneath the tree outside her window, but she couldn't help it. Julie's beauty shone like the sun, beating back the black of night outside her window. Not even the moon could shine as brightly as Julie did. Her eyes glistened more brilliantly than the stars above.

Cursing herself for an idiot, Romy boosted herself up the trunk of the tree to grasp the closest branch and haul herself up for a better look. This was crazy. So crazy. But Romy couldn't help herself, couldn't stop the pull of Julie even if she'd wanted to try. Julie was still absorbed in her computer screen, her fingers curved along her full cheek. Romy sighed before she could stop herself, wondering how soft Julie's skin felt against that hand, whether her cheek was silk or satin smooth. She wanted to reach out and touch it for herself. She was suddenly very jealous of the gloves that might cover those hands.

Blinking, Romy touched her own fingers against her cheek, mimicking Julie's position. Oh, she had it bad, no doubt about it. As she watched, Julie's bubblegum pink mouth turned down in a scowl, pale brows bunching up with displeasure. The petulant expression did nothing to diminish the beautiful shine of her eyes, as though all of summer had been captured in her cloudless blue-sky gaze.

Romy inched along the branch to get closer to the window for a better look. Yep, she'd crossed into full-on creeper mode. She wondered what the Verona Prep's student handbook had to say about stalking. Probably nothing good, even if the stalker could wax rhapsodic about how angelic the stalkee's voice sounded whenever she sighed.

Getting closer meant that Romy could finally catch a glimpse of what was on the screen that seemed to be vexing Julie so much. She nearly fell out of the tree when she saw her face on the large display. It was one of the pictures taken from that day when she'd been up in the tree near the chapel on the far side of campus. Julie stared at Romy's picture so intently that Romy didn't know if she liked what she saw or wanted to set it on fire with the power of her mind.

"Romy," Julie sighed, brow furrowed as if the word caused her pain. She rubbed her temples. "Why does it have to be Romy?"

Romy couldn't stop the delighted grin that stretched across her face, nor did she particularly want to. Julie Cranston was thinking about her? Enough to wish she wasn't maybe? Did that mean what Romy thought it meant—hoped it meant?

Edging closer to the window, Romy was sure her eyes must be as wide as saucers—no, dinner plates. Or maybe those giant round serving trays that were always used at formal banquets. As she watched from her spot on the branch, Julie reached out to touch the image's cheek—Romy's cheek—with her fingertips. The look of open longing on Julie's face sent a sharp pain through Romy's chest.

Romy staggered, nearly falling out of the tree with an undignified squawk. The branches shook wildly, leaves rustling, as she grabbed onto the limb she sat on in an effort to avoid plunging to the ground.

Julie spun around, wearing a frightened expression, and left the bed. She'd taken off the dress she wore to the dance and was now clad in fluffy pajama bottoms and an oversized sweatshirt. Slowly she leaned out the window, eyes narrowed as she peered into the darkness. "Is someone there?" Julie asked, voice a suspicious whisper.

Reluctantly, Romy edged forward on hands and knees, at least as far as the branch allowed. The limb narrowed the closer it got to Julie's window. She heard Julie gasp as she came into clearer view. "Hi Julie. It's…ah…me."

"What the H-E-double hockey sticks are you doing out there?" Julie shoved the window open wider so she could lean out farther. "Are you drunk or something?" she asked dubiously.

"What is with you and always accusing me of being drunk? Jeez! It's like you want me to be my own traveling Alcoholics Anonymous group! I'm straightedge for God's sake! I don't *do* stuff like that."

"Then why are you sitting in a tree?!" Julie's voice sounded exasperated.

Romy felt the sly grin cross her face. After the drunk comment, Romy really wanted to tease Julie, if only to get a little of her own back. "Because I want to engage in some K-I-S-S-I-N-G. Care to join me?"

Julie's face flushed brightly, then paled. She watched as Julie's mouth opened and closed wordlessly, as if her vocabulary had just up and left the country. *Ta, dears, we're off to lovely Puerto Vallarta, send you a postcard! Love, Words.*

Unfortunately, Julie hired someone to drag her vocab back after a brief hiatus, all 'Nope, sorry pardners, you're coming back to the ranch with me.' Julie's fists clenched down by her sides and she leaned forward so that her head was completely outside of the window frame. "So you were spying on me?" Then she went pale, her gaze darting to her laptop and the large image of Romy still displayed on it.

"Oh *no*. You didn't . . .you weren't . . . watching me, were you?" Her gaze shifted to the floor and Romy could make out the blush that crept across her neck and up her face as she realized everything that she'd just admitted.

Romy waggled her eyebrows at her, knowing that Julie probably couldn't make out her expression in the gloom. "If it's any consolation to you, I'm not really all that attached to my name. I can be someone else. Especially if it means I get to hang out with you." Romy gave Julie her best smile.

"Huh?' Julie's brows wrinkled and Romy thought how nice it would be to press her lips to the bunched flesh.

"You asked why it had to be Romy. If you want, you can call me whatever you like."

She glanced away, suddenly feeling overwhelmed. It was easy to be flip when Julie wasn't staring at her with eyes that seemed to hold the whole world and all its mysteries. But here in the dark, just the two of them, only separated by a few feet of empty space, it didn't feel easy at all. "You'd be worth the change," she said, voice huskier than she meant it to be.

She heard Julie draw in a surprised breath and when Romy looked over at her, she held a hand pressed against her chest, fingers drawn tight in a fist. Her eyes were impossibly wide, shocked, as though she'd never thought to hear anyone say something like that to her.

It felt like a giant had just squeezed Romy's heart to a pulp without bothering to remove it from her chest. It *ached* at the thought that Julie didn't see herself as anything other than perfectly amazing. She moved forward on the branch, trying to get closer, to touch this girl who didn't see herself as the miracle she was.

The branch dipped alarmingly. Romy squeaked, scrabbling at the bark for purchase and wondering how she were going to explain her broken neck to her mother. 'Sorry Mom, but I took the kissing in a tree thing way too literally.' Yeah, her mother would kill her if the fall didn't do it first.

A warm hand grabbed her upper arm and yanked her hard, while another slid under her armpit. "Get in here before you kill yourself, you idiot," Julie hissed in her ear as she hauled Romy through her dorm room window.

Romy wound up with her ass on the windowsill, back pressed against Julie's soft chest, hands clutching at Julie's shoulders. For a few moments the only noise was the sound of her gasping breaths and the rustling of the tree limb as it slowly went back to stillness.

"You're pretty strong," Romy rasped out, voice filled with admiration. She began to wiggle her way into a less precarious position—one where her legs didn't jut out into empty space.

Julie helped drag her over the sill, holding on to Romy until she found her feet. Romy sank into the feeling of being held, of Julie's arms around her waist, leaning back into the girl until Julie pulled away after a few moments. Romy twisted her neck to look at her, and saw the red blush burning in Julie's cheeks, flames beneath her skin.

"Yeah, well, you're not exactly heavy. Don't you eat?" Julie took a few steps away, arms huddled close to her body, hands grasping her elbows tightly.

Romy shrugged. "I was vegan—I went back to being vegetarian when I left California. And it's hard for me to put on weight—don't know why." She stared at the room, taking in the décor and the little touches that were uniquely Julie.

A comforter done in primarily yellow, grey, and white covered the twin bed. A few throw pillows in complementary colors sat against the wall on the long side of the bed, making it look more like a couch. The walls were mostly blank. There was a bulletin board that held a copy of Julie's schedule, campus info, and small items like tickets. Two large collage frames full of pictures were the only other items hanging on the wall. It was a neat room, tidy and prim, nothing like Romy and Mercury's which looked like a Crayola bomb and a suitcase full of shoes had detonated in it.

"Thanks for grabbing me," she said, turning her body to finish her perusal of the room. "I'd hate to go splat just as I find out you like me."

"I *don't* like you!" Julie protested, head whipping up to properly glare at her.

Romy leaned her butt against the edge of Julie's desk and crossed her arms in front of her chest. "Really." She jerked her chin in the direction of the laptop sitting on Julie's bed.

"You shouldn't be lurking in the shadows watching people when they don't know you're there!" Julie put her hands on her hips, head jutting forward in anger. "I could probably get you thrown out for peeping or something."

"But you won't." Romy uncrossed her arms to lean her hands, palms flat, against the top of the desk. "And even if you did, it would be totally worth it."

Julie stared at her, horrified. "You *want* to get kicked out of Verona?"

Shaking her head, Romy explained, "Not at all. But *if* I did, I would still think it was worth it to hear that you've been thinking about me."

"You are impo—"

"I think about you all the time too."

Julie froze at her words, mouth still open. Her lips moved but no sound came out for what seemed like forever.

Julie spoke into the silence. "You . . . you do?"

Romy closed her eyes, nodding. God, the hope in Julie's voice, married with disbelief. Like she'd never considered Romy could possibly be going through the same thing. It did something to Romy's insides, made them swirl and jump. Romy felt like she could laugh hysterically or throw up at any moment.

It. Was. *Awesome.*

When she opened her eyes again, Julie was standing in front of her, an arm's reach away. She hadn't heard her move. Romy gave her a shy smile. "Yeah."

"You like me?" Julie's lips were curved up at the edges, the barest hint of a smile, but her blue eyes were alight with an inner joy and fire Romy had never seen before. She thought that Julie could never be more beautiful than this moment. She wanted to lean forward and press a kiss to the corner of Julie's mouth, to feel her breath mingling with Julie's.

"Yeah," Romy said again, breathless and tight, like something had coiled up in the back of her throat. "A lot."

She stretched out a hand, palm up and open, not sure Julie would accept it. Julie's blue gaze caught her, pulled Romy into her like a planet's gravity, and Romy couldn't be sure of where she began and Julie ended. She wanted to mix their molecules together, to become an infinite being made of two hearts and two souls and countless dreams and all the damn stars in the universe.

Julie slid her hand into Romy's, their palms pressed together, warm and soft. Romy raised her other hand to touch the apple of Julie's cheek, flushed now the most delicate of peaches. Her thumb tip rested just below Julie's lower lashes, and with great care she slowly pulled Julie into her body.

And then, very gently, as if Julie was the most delicate of spun sugar confections, Romy lowered her mouth to Julie's and pressed a simple kiss to her curved lips. Just the barest pressure, the hint of a kiss really, with the promise of more, but, for now, Romy felt like she'd been given everything in the world.

Julie didn't pull away; in fact, she stepped in closer, molding herself along the slim lines of Romy's body, the lids of her eyes sweeping down to shutter the blue gaze in darkness. For a moment they stood there in the stillness of Julie's room, two people entwined, lips, hands, and hearts touching. Romy stroked Julie's cheek with her thumb one more time before breaking away to tilt her head and stare at the other girl.

Julie's eyes cracked open slowly with the effort to return to the ordinary boundaries of her room. She blinked dazedly for a moment before letting out a sigh. Romy lowered her hand from Julie's face only to grasp about until she found the girl's other hand where it was braced against the desk. She set her hand atop it and gave it a gentle squeeze.

"You really like me," Julie said, something like wonder in her voice.

When Romy's voice came, it was as dry and cracked as a sunbaked streambed in a drought. "A lot," Romy agreed. "Want me to swear on the," she turned her head to find something in the room worth swearing on before catching a glimpse of the fat white moon rising in the sky above the trees on the campus lawn, "moon?"

Julie made a face which Romy caught sight of out of the corner of her eye. "What's wrong with the moon?" she asked, nudging Julie's side.

Taking a step away from the desk, Julie squeezed into the free space between the head of the bed and the edge of the desk so she could get a panoramic view of the night sky through her window. Romy followed, not wanting to crowd Julie, but wanting very much to be close to her.

"The moon has phases. I don't want to be a phase with you." Julie's eyes were wide and guileless, her face falling into serious lines. "Never swear by the moon unless you plan to break it."

God, Romy wanted to kiss her again. This time with tongue.

Lots of tongue.

"Then what should I swear by?" Romy asked instead, coming to stand behind Julie so she could look out the window with her.

Julie cocked her head so she that was watching Romy's face. "Don't swear on anything."

When Romy opened her mouth, she pressed a finger to her lips. "Or swear on yourself—give me your word."

Romy kissed the finger pressed against her lips lightly just to get a glimpse of the subtle curl of Julie's mouth when she smiled. "Then I swear," she answered once Julie lowered her hand. "On everything I am and ever hope to be."

Julie made a humming noise in the back of her throat and turned her head to continue gazing out the window. Romy leaned against her, chest to her back, chin lowered to rest on Julie's shoulder. They stood there quietly for a few moments, until Romy had to ask the question she most needed an answer to.

"Can I ask you something that may sound stupid?" When Julie nodded, Romy took a deep breath and said, "I, uh, kinda thought you were, um, straight."

Julie stiffened, the muscles beneath Romy's chin locking up tight. "Why would you think that? And that wasn't actually a question."

Romy lifted her chin from Julie's shoulder, grabbing her hand and pulling her over onto the rug in the center of the room. They sat, facing each other, Romy keeping hold of Julie's hand in a loose grip. Julie could pull away if she wanted to. When Julie's hand stayed where it was, Romy gave it a squeeze.

"I just figured, with your folks being who they were and all." Romy shrugged. "And you always seemed scared to be in the same room with me. Which I guess now makes a sort of sense." She tucked a stray blonde hair behind Julie's ear, grateful for the chance to touch her again. "If I hadn't looked at your laptop when I was checking on you—"

"Don't you mean stalking me?"

Romy rubbed the top of Julie's hand with her thumb. "Stalking is such an ugly word. I prefer obsessively shadowing."

Julie snickered before growing serious once more. "You're right."

"Thank you, of course I am. About what exactly?"

"I was trying to avoid you. I didn't want to feel this." Julie stared at the patterned rug beneath her feet. "I was trying not to like you."

Romy found herself grinning, unable to stop it. It was like there was a balloon filled with happiness inside of her, steadily inflating until she felt like she would burst with it. "Did it work?" she asked just because she felt like being a little bit of a brat.

Julie's head snapped up, a sour look on her face. "No. Although I'm beginning to regret it."

Romy pulled her hand away, tucking it around her other one. "Is it really so bad? Liking me, I mean?" Romy watched Julie from under her fall of bangs, suddenly feeling the giddy balloon inside her deflate.

Julie's blue eyes widened. White teeth, the front one just the tiniest bit crooked, bit into a plump pink lip. "No."

Romy relaxed, only to tense up at Julie's next words. "And yes."

"Oh." She looked down at her hands resting in her lap. She'd bitten her thumbnail down to the quick again. Her cuticle had a snag on it, so she began to pick at it, needing something to hold her attention. That balloon inside of her now felt like it was going to choke her.

"You have to understand, Romy," Julie began in a soft voice, "my family would not be okay with this. Not in a million years. And not just because of who your mom is or who you are, but because of who *I* am."

"It's okay, Julie." Romy didn't look up at her, didn't want to. She was sorry she'd ever climbed up that stupid tree. "You don't have to explain." Putting her hands flat on the floor, Romy pushed herself to her feet.

Or would have, except that Julie put her hands over hers and held them down. "But I'm glad you're here now." She flushed deeper and ducked her head. "And I'm happy it's you."

Then Julie surged up to press her mouth to Romy's and all thoughts of parents and balloons and trees and anything else happening on the planet Earth completely left her mind because Julie was kissing her and it was *fantastic.* Not that Romy had a huge level of experience to compare this kiss to—just a few questionable make out sessions with friends while they all tried to figure their shit out, and that disastrous Whit thing—but this was definitely the best kiss in the history of ever.

The kiss was a study in contrasts: Julie's lips were soft but her teeth were hard; her hands cold, but her mouth warm. There was pressure and gentleness all at the same time, and all Romy wanted was for this magic never to stop because she very well might die.

Julie was kissing her and it was better than she'd ever thought possible.

Julie opened her mouth on a sigh and Romy pressed forward this time, moving her hands to rest on Julie's shoulders. Romy inhaled the clean scent of Julie. She smelled like jasmine and citrus, the smell of her body wash and shampoo and perfume and *Julie* combining to make Romy's head swim in the best way.

A knock at the door and then a hand trying the knob broke them apart. Julie sprang away so quickly that Romy could have believed she'd erupted into flames. Both of them stared at each other in shock and then looked at the door.

"Julie, I need to talk to you!" Tyndall's usual loud voice came from the other side of the door.

*Crap*, Romy mouthed and hurried over to the open window, Julie right behind her.

"Be there in a second," Julie called as Romy boosted herself up on the windowsill. "Be careful," she whispered, face next to Romy's.

Pausing, Romy reached out to touch Julie's cheek. "I'll see you again, right? This isn't it for us?"

Julie nodded, gaze darting to her door then back to Romy's face. "Yes. I do want to see you again."

Romy kissed her again. "What time tomorrow?"

"Julie, what's taking you so long?" Tyndall asked. Loudly. She was liable to wake up the entire floor.

"Go!" Julie tried to shove Romy along.

Grabbing her hand, Romy said, "Not until you swear you'll meet me tomorrow."

Julie looked at the door again. "Yes, yes, fine! Now go before she catches you in here!"

Romy wasn't going anywhere until Julie agreed to a time. She had to see her again, finish talking about what they'd discovered about each other tonight. "What time?" she insisted.

Julie rolled her eyes. "Nine at the coffee shop. Tyndall's already in class then. Now get going!"

Taking Julie's face in both hands, Romy told her, "I don't want to leave you. It sucks to be away from you when I just found out that you like me. I'm afraid you'll j—"

Julie cut her off. "I don't want you to leave either, but you have to! Tyndall is going to get a battering ram if I don't let her in right this second!"

"Fine. Good night." Romy kissed Julie on the cheek one last time.

"You can't sit here saying good night to me until the sun rises. We'll both get in trouble. Get moving." But Julie leaned in and kissed Romy on the mouth.

Romy pushed off from the window and grabbed the closest branch, lowering herself back down to earth with an easy grace. She stopped when her feet met solid ground and looked up one last time. Julie had her head sticking out of the window, staring down at her. She waved once, then disappeared back into her room.

Snatching up her messenger bag from the spot next to the tree where she'd left it, Romy ran all the way back to Montag Hall, certain she wouldn't sleep at all until she could see Julie again.

# CHAPTER SIXTEEN

As soon as she saw Romy make it to the ground, Julie closed her window and hurriedly put on her bathrobe. "Coming!" she called. She slapped her laptop closed.

Julie unlocked the door to find her friend glaring at her, arms folded across her chest. "What took you so long?" Tyndall asked, brushing past Julie to enter her dorm room. "What were you up to in here?"

Closing the door again, Julie walked over to her bed and sat down. "Suspicious much? I was in the middle of undressing, Tyndall. Sheesh."

She tried to stay calm as the girl leaned over the desk to look out the window. "What are you looking out there for?" Romy would be long gone, right? She wouldn't linger, wouldn't risk getting caught. She was too smart for that.

Tyndall didn't answer at first, just gazed at the ground below with narrowed eyes. "Tyndall?" Julie snapped her fingers to get her friend's attention. "What are you doing here?"

She turned around. "What's going on between you and Romy Montoya?"

*She knows.* Julie felt her guts lock up, but did her best to keep her expression blandly curious and nothing else. Nothing good could ever come of Tyndall finding out the way Julie felt about Romy.

"Uh, nothing," Julie told her in the most bored voice she possessed. "She's a classmate."

"You were talking to her at the dance. I *saw* you." Tyndall smiled triumphantly, as if she finally had caught Julie doing something horrible, like drowning puppies or arming a nuclear warhead.

"I talked to lots of people at the dance, Tyndall. What's the big deal? She was getting punch while I was getting something to eat. We spoke. We have classes together and we are in a group project together. It's not like I can avoid her." She got up from the bed and walked to the door. "Why are you acting like we were plotting the overthrow of a third world country?"

"I just don't see why you are being so nice to her. Have you heard the things her mother has said about yours?" Tyndall countered, sporting what looked very close to a sneer.

Julie had had enough. She and Romy were not their mothers; her mother's feud was not hers. She opened the door to her room and gestured for Tyndall to leave. "I don't know what your problem is, T, but I'm very tired and I still have studying to do. So if you've finished of accusing me of—what exactly is it that I'm supposed to have done?—then I have homework to finish."

Tyndall gaped at her for a second and Julie allowed herself a tiny inner smile at finally being able to shut the girl up through sheer surprise. Raising her eyebrows, Julie looked from Tyndall to the door pointedly.

After a few moments of quiet, Tyndall bit her lip and looked down at the floor. "I'm sorry, Julie." She reached up to tug at a stray strand of hair nervously. "I didn't mean to come off like you'd done anything wrong."

Julie couldn't help but feel bad. The way her friend's shoulders just slumped, as if she didn't even have the energy left to stay upright, got to her. Tyndall was always a bundle of energy, a person who came on strong, with more than a lion's share worth of pride. To see her tired and dejected like this almost made Julie forget how angry she was.

Almost.

"Well, you did."

Tyndall sighed. "I just want you to be careful, that's all. Your mom and dad are worried about you up here all alone—I'm supposed to keep an eye on you. Romy Montoya isn't someone you want to spend any time around, group project or not."

Julie gave Tyndall what she hoped was a lighthearted smile, although it felt more like a grimace than an actual happy expression. "I'm fine, Tyndall, really."

"I'd just feel better if you came to our Bible study group on Wednesdays, that's all."

"Tyndall, I'm with you guys every day. Why does a Wednesday evening matter?" She crossed her arms over her chest. She was not willing to give up her talks with Pastor Laurence yet. "Besides, I prefer to go to the chapel and pray on Wednesdays."

Tyndall crossed the floor of Julie's dorm room to come and stand in front of her. She stopped in front of Julie and stared into her eyes. Julie felt like a frog on a dissection tray for a moment, like something to be cut up and examined, disposable. It made her feel cold all over. She tucked her hands into the pockets of her robe and met her friend's stare with a level one of her own.

"Well, if you change your mind, you know where we are. We've been working on some things that I know you and your mother would love." Tyndall finally lowered her gaze when Julie refused to back down. She put her hand on Julie's sleeve. "Just be careful around Romy Montoya. People get ideas and then rumors start, and, well, you really wouldn't want something like that to get out, would you?" The unspoken threat of what something like that could do to her father's senate campaign floated beneath her concern.

Blowing out an exasperated breath, Julie began, "I'm just being civil to her and trying to be respectful. In case you hadn't noticed, the school has a pretty stringent policy on hate speech and treating others with respect. I'm just following the rules so I don't embarrass my parents while I'm here."

Hopefully that would be enough to satisfy Tyndall. "Are you done? Because I'm pretty tired." Julie bit back a yawn.

Tyndall watched her for a few moments more, before nodding slightly. "Yeah, okay. We'll talk more about this tomorrow at breakfast, okay? Get some sleep, Julie."

"Night, Tyndall." She leaned against the door frame and watched her friend walk upstairs to her floor before finally closing her own door and leaning against it.

*That was too close.* Julie pressed trembling fingers to her lips, unable to get the feel of Romy's mouth on hers out of her head. She was going to be in so much trouble for this. Julie found that she cared very little about what trouble might come from all of this. All that mattered to her was Romy.

Nine o'clock in the morning couldn't come fast enough.

# ACT TWO



*These violent delights have violent ends*
*And in their triumph die, like fire and powder,*
*Which as they kiss consume...*

*Romeo and Juliet, Act III, Scene VI*

## CHAPTER SEVENTEEN

Romy woke up as soon as the sun crested the horizon, heart thundering in her chest like a Preakness Stakes winner crossing the finish line. She'd barely been able to get to sleep last night, rambling about her moment with Julie to Mercury well after her roommate had drifted off to sleep. Romy had managed a few fitful hours, full of pleasant dreams of Julie's soft lips and luminous blue eyes. She bounded out of bed, heading for the floor bathroom to get ready for her coffee date.

She took her time getting ready, futzing with her hair and trying to pick out the best outfit possible. There wasn't much she could do about her uniform, but she added a black vest and purple skinny tie along with a pair of grey Chucks.

And then she sat on the bed with two hours to kill before meeting up with Julie. Worry came to keep her company. What if Julie didn't show up this morning? What if Romy had imagined the whole thing the night before? What if it was all some hallucination brought on by bad tofu?

"If you're going to sigh like a hurricane you need to take that mess outside," Mercury muttered sleepily, hair wrapped in green silk and face pressed against her pillow. "Because I've got another hour before I need to be awake."

"Sorry, Merc." Romy collected her bag and headed for the cafeteria where she could fret without disturbing her roommate.

At this hour, the cafeteria was sparsely populated. Romy grabbed an apple and fixed herself a bowl of oatmeal with almond milk before finding a seat at a table by the window. As she ate absently, Romy thought about last night. About Julie.

She wasn't an idiot. This was going to be complicated in a major way. Just because Julie liked her and she liked Julie didn't resolve anything. As much as Julie might think she wanted whatever they had between them, Romy didn't know if Julie would be able to go through with it, especially not if her parents disapproved. Romy had been out as bi since middle school. She knew how hard it could be—and she came from a liberal, accepting household. Julie trying to date a girl would be infinitely harder.

Would they start something together only to have Julie pull back at the last minute, leaving her alone? Did Romy want to risk the heartbreak that came with that?

She stared out at the cloudy, autumn morning unfolding before her eyes and tried to slow her brain. She was really getting ahead of herself. Julie hadn't even shown up for coffee yet; Romy needed to chill out with the dire predictions of doom and eventual breakups. She blamed English lit class and Poe for her dark mood. Stupid dead lovers.

The cafeteria began to fill up as more people arrived to grab breakfast before their first class of the day. Romy checked the time—it was half past eight. She supposed she could head to the coffee shop and grab a table and wait for Julie; she didn't have class until ten today.

Romy found a table tucked away in the back that would allow them a little bit of privacy. It wasn't perfect but it was the best she could do without faking a fire alarm to get everyone out of there. Setting her phone on the table in case Julie texted, Romy settled in to wait, a cup of coffee warming her hands.

Julie walked into the café fifteen minutes early, gaze scanning the room. Romy lifted her chin to catch the other girl's attention. Julie bit her lip and glanced quickly around the room before hurrying over to join Romy.

"I wasn't sure what you would want to drink, so I didn't order anything for you yet. What would you like?" Romy asked.

"I can't stay," Julie whispered, gaze still darting around the room as though expecting ninja assassins to jump out at her at any moment.

"Why not?" Romy tried not to sound upset, but her words came out sounding sharper than she meant them to.

Julie slid into the empty chair across from her, leaning forward so she could whisper, "You know why, Romy."

"Who's here that's going to care?" At Julie's frown, she amended, "Okay, besides your rather overly invested friend, Tyndall, that is—who seriously needs to get a life or a hobby or something. I hear lanyard weaving is nice and relaxing. Rosalyn said they even let her do it in rehab. We can just lie and say we're studying." Romy scanned the café just to make sure Tyndall hadn't popped in at the reference to her. Romy often suspected Tyndall was diabolically inclined, so maybe saying her name caused her to appear in puff of smoke and brimstone, like a demon of old. Nothing about Tyndall would surprise her at this point.

A soft chuckle from across the table surprised her. When Romy looked over at Julie, she saw she was trying to hide an enormous smile behind her hand. Romy's heart grew wings and lodged somewhere in the back of her throat at the sight.

Quiet settled over their table like a dusting of snow, but it wasn't uncomfortable. They stared at each other. Romy stared at Julie's face, imagining what it would be like to touch every part of it: the soft fullness of her cheeks, the hard bridge of her nose, the pale arch of her eyebrows, the bow of her candy pink upper lip, the spiky fringe of her eyelashes. She wanted to feel all of the different textures of Julie, to memorize the way she felt beneath her fingertips.

"So what should we do now?" Julie asked, eyes wide and breathing a little uneven. Not enough to be obvious, but Romy could probably write a thesis on the habits and reactions of Julie Cranston.

Romy looked at her thoughtfully, tapping a long finger to her chin. "What would you like to do?"

The grin that slid across Julie's face was positively wicked. Romy felt her breath catch in her throat, words and the way they worked shoved right out of her head by a wave of desire. She clenched her hands on her thighs so she didn't just reach across and grab Julie's face and kiss her right there in front of the whole café.

"Let's get out of here," Julie whispered as she checked the room from the corner of her eyes.

Romy was on her feet in an instant. She didn't need to be told twice.

♪ ♪ ♪

Romy cursed herself throughout her Physics class. She'd spent part of her free hours in the afternoon of the previous day with Julie, finding places to be alone just so they could talk and learn about each other without the worry of being seen or interrupted. They'd texted each other before curfew. Romy had almost suggested meeting for coffee again that morning, but worried she might be pushing her luck.

It was wonderful.

It was terrifying.

Romy didn't plan to develop feelings for Julie this fast, but it happened like an avalanche—a pebble sliding down in slow hops before the entire mountainside followed behind in a speeding flurry of white. She knew people would scoff at her feelings, knew all the admonitions and warnings and dismissals she would hear.

None of it mattered. None of it ever could. She'd set her heart on Julie Cranston. There was no help for it now.

It was difficult to part from Julie, even if it was for such necessary things as classes and eating and sleeping. Pesky little sundries that took her away from Julie's company. Still, those boring life requirements kept Romy out of trouble; the risk of being seen with Julie tempering Romy's need to tempt fate by being seen too often together in public.

In private, however…

Romy did her best to focus on school, but it was becoming more and more difficult as classes and homework and friends and clubs began to eat away at all her free time. And after Monet's latest salvo with Julie's mother hit the entertainment news, Romy felt attacked from all sides. Roz had sent her another text about the tweets that were coming from Verona. Romy was still trying to discover who was snapping pictures of her, but everyone carried a phone on campus. She had no way of knowing when one might be pointed at her.

It was a lot like living in L.A. The thought did not comfort her.

It was right before lunch when a group of freshmen caught up with Romy and Mercury as they were walking to the library. At first, it seemed like all they wanted was a quick chat—one girl had been following Romy's YouTube channel for years—and Romy figured there was no harm in it. But then the questions had begun, impertinent and unaware and so shockingly personal that Mercury cast Romy a pitying look before heading to the library on her own to get work done. It looked like it was going to take a while.

"So, you're gay, right?" The girl who asked the question cocked her head, resembling nothing so much as a confused bird. "Is that why you dress like a guy sometimes?"

Romy thought she might have sprained something in the effort it took not to roll her eyes. She knew she should be used to overly personal questions about things that weren't anybody else's business—it came with being the daughter of a pop star—but sometimes it really got on her nerves. Like today. Still, she supposed if the questions were meant with good intent and the people asking them were legitimately trying to correct their ignorance and overcome their preconceived notions, then Romy could live with it.

Mostly.

"I'm bisexual. I feel attraction for and am attracted to both guys and girls." Romy put on her best dry and boring scholar's voice before continuing. "When I date a guy, it doesn't mean I'm straight and when I date a girl it doesn't mean I'm a lesbian. And I dress the way I do because it's comfortable and I like it. I'm not trying to dress like a guy and I don't want to be one. I am quite happy with my body and the way it looks." She gave a little smile at the student's confused expression. "And if people don't like it, well, that's their problem. I don't really see what the big deal is."

Romy noticed that Julie had come up to the small group that had gathered to listen to what Romy had to say. Romy knew that many of her fellow students were more than a little curious about her, and not just because her mother was Monet. She was honestly surprised it had taken someone this long to ask her about the way she identified, especially since most of the entertainment news sites had reported her sexuality incorrectly.

"Gotta go, guys," Romy told them, throwing a smile and a wave. "I have to study."

She walked in the direction of the library, steps lazy. It was a gorgeous autumn day, the breeze carrying a chill, but the sun shone bright in a cloudless blue sky. She paused to look up at a few birds flying above her. She could feel Julie following some distance behind her. She knelt down to check her boot's lace and allow Julie to catch up.

"Meet in the music building. Practice room eight," Romy told her when she passed.

"Okay," Julie murmured, not even breaking stride.

Romy sent a text to Mercury that she wouldn't be making it to the library, that she was heading to the music rooms to work out some stuff. Her roommate was used to her behavior by now, and understood when Romy needed to get things out of her system in songs and instrument practice. She felt a little bad about bailing on their study session, but she wanted—no, needed—to spend time with Julie. Romy felt bewitched but she wasn't complaining.

She got to the practice room first, divesting herself of her jacket, gloves, and messenger bag before seating herself at the piano. Lifting the lid, Romy gently placed her fingertips on the keys and took a deep, centering breath. Then she began.

It was Lecuona's *Mazurka Glissando*, one of her favorite pieces to play, in part because her piano teacher had been such a bastard about it that, when she'd finally mastered the glissandos, Romy felt like she could accomplish anything. She'd played it at one of her recitals and it was a classical piece that she still loved to play.

The sound of the notes washed over her in a familiar wave and Romy was gone, pulled under by the music. It swept through her like a riptide, dragging her into that headspace she needed to compose her own music, to scribble her feelings down into notes and clefs and beats. This was her magic, a way for her to reshape and make sense of the world.

She came back to herself some indeterminate time later, feeling scrubbed clean. Romy's fingers stilled on the keys. She breathed out a sigh.

"That was amazing," Julie said.

Romy turned her head slowly, still caught up in her musical headspace. Her girlfriend stood just inside the doorway, shoulder propped against the closed practice room door, books and bag still in hand. When Romy gave her a questioning look, Julie smiled and stepped further into the room. "I didn't want to disturb you by moving around too much. I wanted to hear you play."

Romy got up, walked over to Julie, and took her bag and coat from her. "Thanks. It's just something I warm up with sometimes." She felt her face heat, suddenly bashful. Normally she loved praise and compliments on her playing and music—she lived for stuff like that. But hearing Julie say it, well, it meant *more* coming from her. Romy wanted her to like her music, wanted Julie to be impressed with her playing.

Romy realized that she knew very little about Julie. Guiding her over to a chair, she asked, "Do you play any instruments?"

"I took violin for a couple of years when I was younger, but I hated it. I just could never get the hang of it." She shrugged, rubbing her arms as if chilled. "But I did sing in the church choir back home." Smiling wistfully, Julie glanced up at Romy. "I always loved the Christmas service at my old church. It was so much fun to sing there."

"You don't sing anymore?" Romy set Julie's things down before grabbing another chair and dragging it over so she could sit beside her. The practice rooms were sound proof—with so many kids practicing so many different instruments and songs, it just made sense. It also made talks with a secret girlfriend much less likely to be overheard.

Julie shook her head. "No, not really. I can sing, I guess, but I choose not to."

Romy cocked her head, not understanding. Choose to *not* sing? For her, that would be like choosing not to breathe. "Why not?"

Pausing, Julie looked down at the palms of her hands, sitting in her lap. "Don't know. I sing when I'm happy, I guess."

Romy frowned, but chose to say nothing, especially when Julie ducked her head and let her hair hide her face. That was Julie's tell when she felt uncomfortable. Romy subsided, unwilling to waste the little time they had with old grief. "I get it," she whispered, reaching over to squeeze her hand.

"So tell me something about you," Julie said, changing the subject so fast that Romy blinked in surprise.

"What do you want to know?"

Thinking for a moment, Julie asked, "Your first kiss?"

"What about it?" Romy played with a stray thread on her sweater. She didn't think it was a good idea to talk about previous relationships, even if relationship's duration could be clocked with an egg timer.

"Who was it with?" Julie stared at her with wide, curious blue eyes.

"A guy named Whit. Short for Whitford." Romy rolled her eyes. They'd dated for a few months, nothing serious—hung out with friends, some kissing, maybe the odd grope or four. "His dad was a D-list actor. I think he wanted to date me to boost his profile."

Julie gasped, as if something like that was really surprising. "That's horrible!"

"That's Hollywood." Truth was Romy had wanted to see what dating was like. She'd used him as much as he'd used her. Still, him inviting her to the Fall Ball at their school and then ditching her to go make out with Gretchen Iberkowski was a dick move.

"How old were you?"

"Fifteen." Romy tilted her head to stare at Julie. "How about you? What was your first kiss like?" When Julie hesitated, Romy's heart pounded harder in her chest. She didn't know whether from terror or excitement. "It wasn't me, was it? I wasn't your first kiss?"

Julie waved her hand and chuckled. "No! I'm Christian, Romy, not celibate." Romy snorted. "It was with Greg Risher." Julie ducked her head, almost sounding embarrassed when she spoke. "He was on the football team—a receiver, I think. We both wanted to know what it was like, so he kissed me behind the bleachers after practice. He hadn't kissed anyone either and was embarrassed about it."

"Were you a cheerleader?" Romy asked, certain that was the case.

"Yes." She smacked Romy lightly on the shoulder. "Don't you dare make fun."

"Wouldn't dream of it," she assured Julie, although the idea of Julie in those short skirts did something funny to her breathing.

"Anyway, it was a terrible kiss. He stuck his tongue down my throat and I nearly gagged." Romy saw Julie's neck and cheek turn red with her flush.

She reached out her hand and put it against Julie's neck. Julie looked up, startled, then smiled. "So did you always know you were bisexual?" she asked.

Romy considered. "I guess so, I just never knew what to call it until I got older. But I think people can get too hung up on labels that they miss the important things. I like people. People are important to me." *You're important to me.*

Julie leaned back in her chair, one eyebrow arched. "So you don't like labels, huh?"

"I don't know," Romy told Julie, leaning forward so that they were practically nose-to-nose. "In this case, I wouldn't mind being labeled as Julie-sexual."

Julie pursed her lips in that way that meant she was quietly pleased. "Oh, ah," she said, a blush creeping across her peaches and cream complexion once more, "that's a pretty good label."

"I like it," Romy said, trying for nonchalance, but she was positive her giant grin gave away her real feelings on the subject. She closed the distance between them to kiss Julie on the mouth.

# CHAPTER EIGHTEEN

"Hi, Mom," Julie chirped into her phone, feeling like nothing could touch her. Since the night she'd finally confessed her feelings to Romy, Julie had been living in a fog of joy. She and Romy fit somehow. Julie didn't want to question it; she wanted to enjoy it. The last two weeks had been a blissful haze of stolen glances, secret meetings, and sneaking in and out of each other's rooms. Julie had never felt more alive than when she was with Romy.

Her parents could never find out.

"How are you doing?" she asked her mother, banishing thoughts of Romy to the back of her brain.

"Just fine, honey. How's school going?"

"Really well," she enthused, probably sounding more excited about Verona than she ever had before. "I feel like I'm finally settling in, making friends and all that." Julie grinned, unable to keep the smile from her face.

"Anything noteworthy coming up?" Her mother's voice was mellow, relaxed.

"I've got a group project in English lit next week. And a math quiz on Friday." She wracked her brain to see if she missed something. "That's about it."

"The group project is the one you have with Monet's daughter, correct?"

Julie's good mood evaporated like early morning fog before the sun. She had deliberately left out that detail in previous conversations with her mother and had asked her sisters to keep that fact quiet. She didn't think they'd said anything, but somehow her mother had found out anyway.

"Yes," Julie began, feeling dread chill her limbs. "She's in my group. We were assigned by the teacher."

"Mmmmhmmm."

Julie gulped. She recognized that humming acknowledgement. That was the 'Mom is disappointed in you' sound.

"Who told you?"

"Tyndall's mother mentioned it in passing."

Julie rolled her eyes, secure in the knowledge that at least her mother couldn't see her through the phone. Of course Tyndall had told her mother about Romy, and of course, Tyndall's mother had told Julie's. It was like a nightmare game of verbal tag.

"I'm a little disappointed that you didn't think it important enough to tell me you would be associating with that woman's daughter."

Julie clenched the phone so tightly that her knuckles turned white and her fingers ached. "I wouldn't call it associating with her, Mom," she said carefully, not wanting to anger her mother. "It's just a class project." It was just a class project; what happened outside of class was something her mother didn't need to know about.

"It still would have been nice to know, Julie." The rebuke in her mother's tone was painful.

"I'm sorry, Mom. I didn't think it was that important," she offered, dejected.

"Sweetie, it's not up to you to determine what is or is not important. Leave that to the adults." Her mother's tone was just shy of condescending.

Julie knew it would do her no good to get into an argument with her mother. She never won, and it would only aggravate the woman. Swallowing down her upset, she simply said, "I'm sorry, Mom. I'll do better next time." Her voice sounded dull, almost robotic, to her ears.

"Of course." Her mother made a clicking noise with her tongue and teeth, her signal that a subject change was coming hard and fast. "How did you like Ferris? Tyndall mentioned to her mother that you didn't get to spend much time with him." There was a faint disapproving tone to her voice.

"Yes, I ended up catching a stomach bug. I didn't want to make anyone else sick so I just came back to my room." Julie paused, wondering how far to push it. Adding regret to her voice, she continued, "I hate that he came all the way here for nothing."

"Have you called him to tell him so?" Her mother was a stickler for manners.

Rats. Julie should have stopped with the stomach flu. "I don't have his number," she said weakly, already knowing where her mother would take this.

"Oh, Julie." The despair in her mother's voice was completely out of proportion to the situation at hand. She hadn't slaughtered his family in a tragic chainsaw accident, she just hadn't gotten his phone number. Her mother's sigh seemed to come from the depths of her soul. "I have it right here."

Of course. Of course she did. Julie wished she could be surprised.

Dutifully she took down the number her mother rattled off, already knowing that her mother would be in touch with Ferris' mother to make sure Julie called him. "Got it."

"And you'll use it," her mother reminded her.

"Yes, ma'am." Julie felt her eyes prickle with unwanted tears of frustration. A scream clawed at the back of her throat, begging to be loosed. Even hundreds of miles away, her parents still controlled her life. What hope did she have with Romy?

Julie listened absently as her mother rambled on, talking about her father's campaign and the doings of the ladies at church. She told Julie about her sisters and what they'd been up to, as if Julie didn't talk to them herself at least once a week. Julie didn't bother paying attention to the words, just made noises of interest and acquiescence, her mind distracted by thoughts of Romy. What if her parents found out about them? Were these fleeting moments of happiness worth all of the risk she was taking? Julie didn't know anymore, and it enraged her. One phone call with her mother and she was calling everything she felt for Romy into question.

It was a relief when her mother said good-bye.

𝄞 𝄞 𝄞

Julie fluffed her hair one last time and applied a simple coat of berry-colored lip gloss before snagging her purse from the end of the bed and leaving her room. She'd decided to go with a denim skirt, patterned tights, and a soft green cashmere sweater for her date with Ferris. She'd only applied some mascara and powder, since this was a pointless exercise. She had no interest in catching Ferris as a boyfriend, despite her mother's wishes. This date kept her folks off her back, allowing her to focus on the person she actually cared about. If she had to keep it up once a month—or less, if she could swing it—then so be it. She could put up with a free meal and some boring conversation.

Romy was worth it.

Her call to Ferris had been blissfully brief, just her apology for his last visit, and his invitation to try again. Julie had deliberately kept the date from Romy, hoping she would never find out. She still worried about getting caught, but then she saw Romy and Julie realized it didn't matter. She wasn't willing to give Romy up just yet. She felt too good.

The residence hall lounge was nearly full when Julie made her way downstairs. It was nearly dinnertime. Students milled about, waiting for others to join them before setting out for the cafeteria.

As she stepped into the lounge, Julie noticed that Tyndall sat with several students in a group of chairs pulled away from the main body of the room. Julie hurried past, hoping her friend didn't notice her. She did not want a night of both Tyndall and Ferris, and she didn't trust her not to invite herself along. Julie already dreaded her date with Ferris enough.

She stepped quickly through the front doors. Checking her watch, Julie saw that she still had a few minutes before Ferris was supposed to pick her up. Buttoning up her coat, she settled herself on the low stone wall next to the front steps of Cap Hall and waited.

"You didn't reply to my texts about going off campus to grab some dinner," came a soft voice from behind her. Julie turned to find Romy standing at the far end of the wall, hands tucked in the pockets of her jacket. Her hazel eyes darted over the quad, the walkways, and the students passing them by. She never looked at Julie directly. It was like talking to the wind. "You look amazing." Julie saw Romy's throat work on a swallow. "I'm guessing it's not for me though."

Her heart plummeted to her feet. Julie hadn't wanted to upset Romy so she'd said nothing about Ferris. They were still relatively new in their—relationship? Was that what this was? Either way, Julie didn't think telling Romy that she was going out on a date with a guy she didn't have the slightest interest in was necessary.

Julie felt a slow flush creep up her neck at Romy's words. "Tyndall's just in the lounge. What if she saw you?" she whispered, trying to get Romy to leave before Ferris showed up.

Romy snorted. "The only way that girl would notice me was if I was on fire and she held a tank of gasoline." Julie looked over her shoulder to see that Romy had leaned one hip against the stone wall. "You're avoiding the question."

"I didn't hear one." Julie picked at her tights absently, needing something to keep her hands busy.

"So are you going to tell me where you're going?" Romy asked, voice still soft.

"I have a d—," she began, voice dying as Ferris took that moment to pull his car up to the curb. He put the car in Park before stepping out to come fetch her.

"I'm sorry, Romy, I can't talk now. But I promise I'll call you as soon as I get home." Julie hurried to meet Ferris, hoping she wouldn't have to introduce them.

She glanced back, hoping for some kind of acknowledgment, but Romy had already turned around, vanishing back the way she'd come.

$$\text{𝄞 𝄞 𝄞}$$

"Thanks for dinner, Ferris," Julie told her "date" as they pulled up in front of Cap Hall. Her hand was already on the car's door handle, ready to have this night come to an end.

It hadn't been horrible, per se, but it hadn't been the ideal way she wanted to spend her evening. Ferris had taken her to a small, modestly priced restaurant in town. She'd ordered a salad with grilled chicken and made sure to keep the conversation going by asking him lots of questions about himself. Ferris didn't notice or mind that she wasn't contributing besides the odd head nod or murmured affirmative. If she'd been interested in a second date, his lack of interest would have been disheartening. Instead, it was a relief.

"Do you have to go inside right now?" Ferris turned the car off. Julie felt her stomach sink to somewhere around her ankles. "I was kind of hoping we could stay here and maybe talk or something."

*Shoot. Shooty shoot shoot shoot.* Julie didn't want to be rude, but she really didn't want to spend any more time than she already had with Ferris. "I do have a lot of studying tonight. Big test on Thursday." The lie came easy to her lips.

"I forgot how many tests they give you in high school." He leaned back in the leather seat and smiled at her. He was good looking in that conservative, young Republican sort of way, all neatly trimmed hair and clean-shaven jaw. "Still, a few minutes won't hurt."

Sighing, Julie clasped her purse in white-knuckled hands, resting it on her lap. If she was overtly rude to him, she had no doubt it would make it back to her parents and that would defeat the whole purpose of these dates. Ferris was supposed to be a distraction, not another problem. Giving him a tentative hint of a smile, she said, "I suppose not."

"I realize that I did most of the talking at dinner," he said, leaning closer to her in the darkness of the car. "Why don't you tell me something about yourself?"

*Well, nuts.* Julie wracked her brain for something innocuous to say, something that seemed personal but revealed nothing of who she was as a person. As she opened her mouth to answer his question, Ferris slid through the space separating them and pressed his lips to hers.

Julie shoved him backward, galvanized by the feeling of his slimy tongue invading her mouth. "I am *not* that kind of girl!" she told him angrily, hand groping for the door handle in the dim light filtering in from the lampposts.

Ferris leaned against his door, an unpleasant smirk on his face. "Oh come on, Julie. Everyone knows that the conservative kid is the wildest one of all."

"This one *isn't*," she snapped, indignation and offense warring inside of her.

He shrugged, unconcerned by her outburst. "Can't blame a guy for trying. You're pretty." He looked at her as if he was seeing her for the first time. "Geez, what is your problem? Will you chill out—it was just a kiss!"

"Your family—what would they say!"

Ferris gave her a condescending smirk. "You think that matters when it comes to getting some?" He laughed. "Probably half the high school students in my church have already cashed in their V-cards. Abstinence does *not* make the heart grow fonder, despite what adults say."

"Ugh. Good *night*, Ferris!" she sneered, yanking the passenger door open. She practically fell out of the car in her haste to get away from him. Slamming the door closed with all her strength, Julie breathed in the crisp New England air, hoping it would do something to calm the anger boiling inside of her.

"Good night, princess," Ferris said mockingly through the lowered passenger window. He hit the button to raise it as she glared at him through the glass. The car sped away, leaving her standing on the steps of Cap Hall, her insides a knot.

She wanted Romy. To see her, to talk to her. She pulled out her phone and sent a text as quickly as her shaking, stupid fingers would allow.

**JC: Back from date.**

It took Romy a few minutes to respond. As she waited, Julie trudged up the stairs to her room, stripped off her coat, and made the immediate decision to take a shower. She could still feel Ferris' disgusting tongue forcing its way into her mouth. Grabbing her basket of toiletries, she headed to the communal bathroom and took the hottest shower she could stand.

Bundled in her robe, blond hair wrapped in a towel to catch the drips, Julie returned to her room and her phone. Romy's response didn't fill her with encouragement.

**RM: That's nice.**

**JC: You're mad.**

**RM: Nope, quite sane. Can still tell a hawk from a handsaw.**

**JC: ???**

**RM: nm**

**JC: What's wrong?**

Julie pulled on a pair of fleece pajama pants and her sleep shirt while she waited for a response. She wouldn't blame Romy for being angry—if their positions were reversed, Julie doubted she would have enjoyed seeing Romy go out on a date with another person, even if that person didn't mean anything to her. But Romy had to understand that this couldn't be helped. If Julie wanted to keep Romy in her life, she had to keep her parents happy. She knew that if they caught even the faintest whiff of impropriety—and Julie knew that she and Romy would qualify as that in a *major* way—they'd yank Julie home so fast she'd likely leave a cartoon dust trail in her wake.

**RM: Maybe my mom was right.**

**JC: About what?**

Julie stared at her phone in shock. Romy had told her mother about her? Like, she actually talked to Monet? She tried not to feel nervous about what Romy had said; or worse—what her mother had.

**RM: This is getting complicated.**

No. No no no no. This was not happening to her. She'd just finally gotten something she had been telling herself for years she didn't want and it felt so right, so perfect. Julie couldn't give it up now.

**JC: Too complicated?**

**RM: idk. Maybe.**

Julie rubbed her hair dry frantically, feeling like the jaws of a giant mouth were slowly closing in around her, ready to swallow her whole. Was Romy trying to end things between them? The thought of it sent Julie into an anxiety-fueled panic. She threw on a hoodie and slapped a hat over her damp hair, shoved her feet into boots and shrugged back into her coat. Keys in pocket and phone in hand, Julie slipped out of her room and down to the front doors that led out to campus and Montag Hall

She was not going to get dumped via text message. If Romy wanted to end things between them, she could do it to her face.

Julie's phone pinged as another text from Romy came through.

**RM: It's just...**

**RM: I've spent years figuring out who I am**

**RM: And I'm proud of that person**

**RM: But this…**

**RM: with you…**

**RM: I have to hide**

**RM: Like I'm ashamed**

**RM: When I'm not**

**RM: I'm not ashamed of you**

**RM: I'm not ashamed of us**

**RM: But I think you might be ashamed of me.**

Julie didn't respond to that text, didn't know how to. The rage inside of her flared brighter, this time directed at herself. She hadn't meant to make Romy feel this way—it was the last thing she'd ever want to do. Romy was the best thing to come out of this whole stupid boarding school experience, and Julie wasn't willing to give her up so easily.

Her body turned to Montag Hall automatically. Her brain went somewhere else, not having to worry about the destination—Julie was a lodestone and Romy was True North. She'd find her anywhere. She rubbed the feeling of Ferris's lips on hers away with her coat sleeve, trying not to think about him. She'd do that later, but right now all she wanted to see was Romy's face.

Another ping from her phone, and Julie looked down, dread pooling in her stomach. What she saw made her bite her lip.

**RM: I've been thinking…**

Julie broke into a jog, fingers already typing out a one word message.

**JC: Don't.**

Julie didn't want them to be done, not yet, not like this. She wasn't ready to stick a knife in this burgeoning relationship and call it dead. Romy was important to her and she wasn't going to let her give up just because things seemed difficult.

It seemed like a blink and Julie stood in front of Romy's door. She knocked once, gaze darting around the hallway, but all the doors around her stayed closed.

# CHAPTER NINETEEN

Romy sprawled on her bed, headphones on and music loud. She'd set her phone off to the side of the bed after Julie's last text. She wasn't interested in anything Julie had to say right now. Seeing her get into the car with that guy had gutted Romy in a way that surprised her. She liked Julie. A lot. But now she wondered if it was too much, because feeling this bad wasn't a usual thing for her.

Maybe her mother had been right. Monet had warned her after the dance, when Romy had been giddy with the kiss and desperate to share the good news with someone, that Julie might not be ready for the kind of relationship Romy wanted. Maybe having any contact with Julie Cranston had been a bad idea. Romy was beginning to think there was no way what she had with Julie could end in anything but tears.

She meant what she'd said in text. Being with Julie was great, but if it meant feeling ashamed of who she was, of having to hide what they meant to each other forever, Romy wasn't so sure she could do it. It was bad enough to have Tyndall sniping at her every chance she got—when she wasn't outright ignoring Romy. Then there were the weirdo tweets: edits of every horrible DZN photo and rumor about her and her friends, paired with scenes of her walking around Verona's campus, and warnings to parents about her influence over their precious babies. Romy wasn't sure what she should do anymore.

She looked up as Mercury got up and opened the door. Her roommate stood a little to the side so Romy could see into the hall, an expression of surprise on her face. Julie Cranston stood there, miserable. Romy pulled off her headphones. "Is Romy in?" Julie asked.

Mercury blinked once, before opening the door wider. "Uh, yeah. Sure. Come on in. Romy, there's someone here to see you."

Julie stepped inside, closing the door behind her. Romy stared at her dumbly, words lost. Julie's hair was still wet from her shower and she looked to be wearing lounge pants. She appeared the picture of unhappiness—from the slump of her shoulders to the shadows in her eyes.

Romy's breath left her in a rush. Julie had never looked more beautiful. She felt her heart clench, the beat pounding in her chest, like a drummer still trying to find the rhythm.

"What are you doing here?" Romy's words were both question and accusation. Just because Julie made her stomach do somersaults didn't mean the hurt wasn't still there.

"I needed to see you," Julie told her. "It couldn't wait." She glanced over at Romy's roommate. Mercury sat at her desk, a textbook open in front of her, but she was instead staring intently at Julie. Julie gave Romy a pointed look, glancing back to Mercury. Romy sighed.

"Merc, could you, ah, give us a few minutes?" Romy asked her roommate.

"You're buying my coffee tomorrow morning," Mercury told her with a grin, gathering up her book and laptop and heading out of the room. "Make good choices," she admonished before closing the door behind her.

Romy rolled her eyes at her roommate's words, then scooted along her bed until her back was braced against the wall. "How was the date?" She tried for casual, but her words came out as something else entirely. Angry maybe, and more than a little bitter.

"Can I sit down?" Julie asked.

Romy waved at her desk chair. Julie crossed the room, removed Romy's black canvas messenger bag, and sat down. "Thank you."

Rubbing a hand over her eyes, Romy asked her question again. "What are you doing here, Julie? I would think you'd be worried about being spotted coming over here so late." She couldn't keep the edge from her voice and realized she really didn't want to. Yeah, she was furious.

"I needed to talk to you. To see you." Julie watched her hands as they twisted themselves into pretzel shapes in her lap.

"Why?" Romy's voice cracked. She coughed and asked again. "Why?" Romy cursed silently at the quaver in her voice. She hadn't wanted Julie to hear that.

"Because I like *you*. And I'm sorry that it wasn't you I was on the date with."

Romy turned her head so she wasn't looking directly at Julie. The wall beside her head was totally fascinating. Yep, completely enthralling and her interest had nothing to do with the spiking burn of tears in her eyes. Clearing her throat again, she asked, "So why weren't you?"

Sighing, she said, "Hi, I'm Julie Cranston. Perhaps you've heard of my parents?"

Romy's mouth twitched before she could stop it. She did love it when Julie was a smartass, in part because she did it so infrequently. "I get why you can't take me to freakin' prom, Julie. I just don't get why you're suddenly dating douchebags."

"Because it's the only way to keep you!" Julie burst out, tears standing unshed in her blue eyes.

Romy's jaw dropped, transfixed both by Julie's words and by the sapphire sheen of her gaze. There were oceans in Julie's eyes, deep enough to drown in and Romy realized she didn't want to be saved.

Instead of saying anything, Romy slid to the edge of the bed. She pulled Julie over to her, long fingers buried in the damp hair at the nape of Julie's neck. Romy lowered her lips to Julie's, sealing their mouths together in a kiss that spoke of her affection and longing and hope for the girl pressed against her. Julie gasped in surprise before returning the kiss with enthusiasm.

It was several moments before they parted. Julie's lips were kiss-swollen and red, her cheeks flushed adorably. Romy ran a gentle hand down the side of Julie's neck, urging her to sit beside Romy on the bed. Julie arranged herself, her body a warm comfort against Romy's side. She twined their fingers together. Romy dropped her head to rest the side of her face against Julie's shoulder.

"I'm not ashamed of you," Julie whispered. "And I'm sorry if I make you feel like there's anything in you that you need to be ashamed of." Romy felt Julie place a kiss in her dark hair before continuing. "I'm ashamed—of myself. Of what I have to do and what I have to pretend to be when it's the last thing I want to do. I want to be able to hold hands with you, to go to dinner with you, to kiss you in the middle of the quad and not care who might be snapping pictures or tweeting about it. I want the world to know you're mine."

Julie pulled away a bit, forcing Romy to look up at her. "But I can't do any of that. If my parents found out about you, about me, about *us*, they'd yank me out of here and never let me see you again. And my sisters—I don't know. I might not get to see them again. I love them, Romy. They're my best friends. Maybe I'm being selfish, but I don't want any of that to happen. I want you with me any way I can have you. I know it's super selfish of me to even ask that of you, but I can't help it."

Romy stared at Julie for a long moment, considering. Was Romy any less selfish in what she wanted? She wanted Julie to suddenly be out and proud, to defy everything she'd been raised with, to go against—not just her parents—the entire foundation her life had been built on. And she wanted her to do it basically overnight. It wasn't fair to ask Julie to do something like that, or to try to force her to do it before she was ready. Love didn't work that way.

Love…

Oh *shit.*

Romy took Julie's face in her hands, palms pressed lightly against her flushed skin. "It's okay, Julie. I don't want to lose you either." Her thumbs brushed lightly against the apples of Julie's cheeks. "We can work around everything so we can stay together. It may not be perfect, but it's worth it." She paused, biting her lip before meeting Julie's watery gaze. "You're worth it. You're worth *everything.*"

Julie leaned forward so fast their foreheads nearly cracked together and captured Romy's lips. Romy let out a startled squeak. Then all she could do was kiss back.

Julie kissed Romy as though she were air and Julie was suffocating, like Romy was an oasis and she was dying of thirst. Julie was a fire beneath her skin, lighting Romy up inside and turning her to liquid warmth. Romy never wanted Julie to stop kissing her. This was right and good and now the world was perfect, the two of them at its center.

Romy watched Julie pull away slowly before running the back of her hand over Romy's cheek. Romy's eyes slipped closed to relish the sensation of that soft hand lying against her skin. She would give up everything for the feel of Julie's touch on her bare skin, so warm and smooth. They both sat in silence for some moments, letting their racing hearts slow to a normal beat once more. Romy didn't have words to describe everything she felt.

Romy pulled Julie down so they lay on her bed, legs and hands entwined. She took a deep breath, inhaling the scent of Julie's fruity shampoo and the floral undertones of her body wash. Pressing her lips to Julie's hair, Romy closed her eyes and sent up a silent plea to whatever god was listening. *Let me have this. Please. Let me have her.*

"The date was horrible, by the way," Julie told Romy as she snuggled against her side.

"Good," Romy said, tightening her arms around Julie and feeling mollified.

# CHAPTER TWENTY

"There's someone I want you to meet," Julie whispered to Romy in the hall one Wednesday after English class. "Meet me in that stand of trees by the chapel after classes are done for the day."

She was glad that Romy kept her gaze straight ahead since Tyndall was in the hallway and their group project on Poe had ended. Julie would have no need to talk to Romy again without raising Tyndall's suspicions. Romy simply nodded once and left. Julie heaved a sigh of relief, feeling the strain of their secret relationship keenly. It wasn't right that she had to act this way. She wanted to shout how happy she was from the rooftops. But she couldn't, not if she wanted to keep seeing her.

It seemed an interminable wait until classes ended for the day. Julie raced back to Cap Hall to dump her books and grab her camera bag, feeling her heart pound inside of her chest. *Ro-my. Ro-my. RO-my. Ro-MY.* Her footfalls matched her heartbeat as she pelted up the stairs to her dorm room, thoughts of time with Romy fueling her steps.

She slipped into her most comfortable jeans and favorite boots, strewing her uniform around the room in her haste to change.

Camera bag over her shoulder, she yanked open her door only to come face-to-face with Tyndall, her hand upraised to knock.

Julie jerked back, instinctively closing the door halfway to give her cover from Tyndall. "Oh, uh, hey T."

Tyndall's eyes narrowed suspiciously. "Where are you off to in such a hurry?"

Shaking her head in feigned confusion, Julie decided playing dumb was the way to go. "Nowhere special. Just wanted to get some shots while the light is still good."

Raising one eyebrow, Tyndall crossed her arms over her chest. "Julie, why won't you come to my Bible study?"

She managed to keep from groaning in frustration, but just barely. "We've been over this, Tyndall." Julie leaned against the edge of her door, blocking Tyndall's view into her room with her body. "I like praying by myself in the school chapel. It's got nothing to do with you or the Bible group."

"That's a non-denominational church, you know."

Oh, how Julie wanted to roll her eyes, but that would only antagonize Tyndall and then Julie would get an earful from her mother. "I do know that, but I like it all the same. God doesn't care where you pray anyway." She smiled, hoping to soothe her friend.

Tyndall made a sour face. "That Pastor Laurence has some rather broad ideas of what's acceptable," she warned, imparting the news as though she spoke of barbarians gathering for war. "I don't like him."

Thank goodness Tyndall didn't know about the old church Julie had once attended back home. That pastor would have given her fits. Still, Julie needed to get going and a prolonged argument with Tyndall over religious expression just meant Romy had to wait longer in the cold for her.

Julie inched past her friend, closing her door firmly behind her. "You're entitled to your opinion," she answered. "Just like I'm entitled to mine. I like the quiet of the chapel for my prayers."

Tyndall glanced at her feet. When she next spoke, her voice was tentative, more unsure than Julie had ever heard. "Julie, did I do something wrong?"

Those words pulled Julie's thoughts away from Romy. "What? No, why would you think that?"

Tyndall lifted her head, expression uncertain. "It's just . . .," she shrugged helplessly, "I thought we'd be doing more stuff together. Every time I try though, you say you're busy."

Julie paused in her hurry, guilt pulling at her. "We eat together almost every day. And we study together and hang out on the weekends." She wasn't sure what else Tyndall wanted from her.

"Yes, but you seem distracted lately, like your mind is a million miles away. You're always running off to do something. Is it me? Did I do something?"

"No, gosh Tyndall. Of course not! I just have a lot going on, that's all." Julie tried her best to soothe her friend. "I'm sorry, I didn't realize."

"I just have all of these ideas for projects we could get going," Tyndall said, flapping her hands in frustration. "And you don't seem very interested."

Julie bit her lip, torn. She hadn't meant to hurt Tyndall's feelings, and she wanted to make things up to her, but Romy was waiting for her. She couldn't afford to get dragged into a long conversation with Tyndall at the moment. She needed to get going.

Putting a hand on Tyndall's shoulder, she said, "I'm sorry if I've made you think I'm upset with you. I'm not, I promise. I've got a lot on my mind." *Understatement.*

"And I promise I'll be better about spending time with you." Julie held back a wince, physically pained at having to bargain away time that could be spent with Romy, but Tyndall was hurting. She'd always struck Julie as someone who was desperately lonely, despite the brave face she put on it. Tyndall wanted to fit in so badly, she'd created her own social group to make it happen. "And if it makes you feel better, I'll come to your Bible study before the semester is over."

The girl's face lit up like a tree at Christmas. "You will?" She clapped her hands in front of her face, a huge grin splitting her pale lips. "Oh, you'll have so much fun, Jules!' Julie sighed at the despised nickname but didn't bother correcting Tyndall. "When?"

"I'll let you know," Julie told her, already turning to go. "See you later!" She rushed back down the stairs, in too much of a hurry to worry about Tyndall any longer.

Romy waited for her, one shoulder propped against a tree along the path that led to the stone church on the campus grounds. "So who did you want me to meet?" she called when Julie appeared. "An Ent?"

"A what?"

"Never mind." Romy leaned in to kiss Julie's cheek, but Julie flinched away. A flash of hurt crossed Romy's mobile features, but she said nothing except, "I forget you're not a fantasy nerd."

"Come on," Julie said, grabbing Romy's hand and pulling her along, hoping that would make up for the snub of a moment ago.

"Unhand me, woman," Romy laughed, tripping along behind her. Julie grinned, glad that she hadn't done any lasting harm.

Pushing open the door to the chapel, Julie stepped inside. She saw Pastor Laurence sitting with his head bowed in the first pew at the front of the chapel. Romy followed behind her, eyes wide as she took in the stained glass and general quiet charm of the place. "This is where you come to pray?" she whispered as they moved down the center aisle.

Julie nodded, pleased that Romy appreciated it. "You don't have to whisper," she told her.

"I totally have to whisper," Romy shot back. "God is watching."

"He's doing that all the time." Julie saw the glitter in Romy's eyes and cut her off before she could say anything. "This is the person I wanted you to meet."

Pastor Laurence stood up from the pew and extended his hand. Romy stopped short, head tilted up so she could look into his face.

"I'm Pastor Laurence," he said, taking Romy's hand in his for a shake. "You must be Romy. Welcome."

"Um, hello," Romy said. Julie smiled; she'd never seen the usually brash young woman so tentative. "It's nice to meet you."

"It's a pleasure," Laurence greeted. "Julie has told me quite a bit about you."

Julie blushed as Romy turned her head to stare at her. "It was all good stuff," she assured Romy, who raised her eyebrows in an unspoken question.

"How long have you been working here?" Romy asked him.

"About five years. I had my own congregation before this, but left that church when the governing body decided a change more in-line with their beliefs was in order." Pastor Laurence gestured for them to follow as he led them to his office. He had a fire going in the grate and an electric kettle with mugs out on his sideboard. "Would you care for some tea?"

"Yes, please," Julie answered, grateful to be in a private space away from prying eyes. This room felt safe.

Romy looked at Julie as though for guidance, then shrugged. "Sure. Tea would be great." Julie stifled a giggle—she knew Romy would rather drink anything other than tea, which she referred to as *gross leaf juice*.

They settled into chairs as Pastor Laurence fetched cups. Julie passed one to Romy, then took her own. Romy took a sip, managed to not make a horrible face, and said, "I feel a little out of the loop. I'm not entirely sure why Julie wanted me to meet you." She turned to Julie and smiled softly. "No offense."

Julie took her hand, squeezing Romy's cold fingers in hers while she tried to explain why this meeting was so important to her. "I know you sometimes don't understand why my religion is so important to me," she began.

Romy said, "Julie, I don't need to understand why. If it's important to you, then that's enough for me. I'd never make you change that."

"I know." Julie smiled shyly at her girlfriend. "But Pastor Laurence was sort of instrumental in me even being with you." Biting her lower lip, she continued, feeling a sudden burn in her chest as her emotions surged. "That's why I wanted you two to meet."

Romy's eyes went wider, and she stared at Laurence with wonder. "She talked to you? About me?"

The pastor nodded. "She never mentioned you by name, but yes, Julie was struggling with her feelings and came to me for counsel."

Setting the mug down, Romy pierced him with a doubtful look. "And you were okay with it?"

"I was." He paused, and then clarified. "I *am*." Settling behind his desk, he folded his hands on top of the blotter. "I can understand how you can think I wouldn't be supportive, but I subscribe to the belief that God is love. And wherever there is love, so there he is."

Pastor Laurence looked at Julie fondly, and she found herself smiling at him. He said, "I don't think anything can ever be solved with hate."

Romy picked up her mug, turning it slowly in her hands. Julie watched her, noting the thoughtful frown she wore, the furrow between her brows. She wondered what Romy was thinking. Had Pastor Laurence somehow offended her? That wasn't what Julie wanted.

Then Romy raised her mug in salute to Pastor Laurence. "Pastor Laurence, you've just said something with which I wholeheartedly agree." Then she drained her gross leaf juice with barely a grimace.

𝄞 𝄞 𝄞

Julie was pulling on her pajama pants when someone knocked at her door. Glancing down she saw that her clock read ten forty-five, nearly time for curfew. Romy wouldn't cut things this close—or if she did, she'd be knocking on Julie's window.

"Who is it?" she called, wrapping her robe around her body.

"It's me." Tyndall.

Frowning, Julie opened the door and let Tyndall inside of her room. Her gut churned with unease. What could Tyndall want so late at night? The feeling only grew when she got a good look at her friend's face. Tyndall was pale and shaking.

"What's wrong?" Julie asked, reaching out for her shoulder.

Tyndall jerked away from her grasp before Julie could make contact. "You were with *her*."

"What?" Julie felt her body grow cold at the anger in Tyndall's voice. "Who?"

Tyndall spun around, a furious snarl twisting her face. "I *saw* you!"

Doing her best to stay calm, Julie stood beneath her friend's basilisk gaze and didn't flinch away. "Who did you see me with?" she demanded.

"Romy Montoya!" Tyndall practically shouted. "How could you?"

Keeping her voice level, Julie asked, "How could I what?" She swallowed with effort. "What are you talking about?"

Tyndall's hands clenched into fists, and she flushed an ugly shade of crimson. "Don't think I haven't noticed how chummy you are with her, Julie." She glared accusingly at Julie, as though daring her to deny it.

"When have I been chummy with her?" Julie's throat closed in fear, but she held on to her composure. "During our group project? I had to be nice to her—my grade depended on it." Mrs. Escalus had dinged Tyndall's grade on her group project after getting the group's feedback on their project participation. "We've talked about this before!"

"You were walking back with her. You were holding hands!"

Julie laughed. "Oh, Tyndall, stop it." She covered her mouth with her hand as though she were trying to stifle further laughter. Inside she quailed. "You're imagining things! I ran into Romy on my way back from the chapel."

She hoped she'd guessed right as to when Tyndall saw them. Julie had thought they were far enough out that no one would notice them, but Julie reminded herself that she and Romy needed to be more careful in future. Who knew when someone might be watching.

But for right now, Julie knew she had to be convincing.

"And you walked back with her? What was she doing out that way?" The accusatory whine in Tyndall's voice had faded somewhat. Julie took that as a good sign.

Julie threw up her hands in faked frustration. "How should I know? She came out of the woods near the path when I was about halfway back. She asked about my holiday plans. I saw no harm in walking back with her. But holding hands?" She shook her head. "I think you've been studying too hard."

Julie walked over and pushed Tyndall toward her desk chair. "Be honest with me now, T," she said, seriously. "Were you following me?"

Tyndall glanced up at Julie out of tangled, sweaty bangs. "No." Julie scowled at her. "Not exactly," she amended.

"Okay, that's beyond the pale, Tyndall." Julie funneled her fear into anger. She needed to go on the offensive, to derail Tyndall's suspicions before her snooping ruined everything. "I don't know what friendship means to you, but, to me, stalking is *not* okay. If there's something you want to know, just ask me."

Tyndall looked chastised. Julie kept her gaze firm even though she was sure her knees were knocking together. Nervous sweat made her heavy hair stick to the back of her neck. Tyndall didn't say anything right away, so Julie prompted her. "Tyndall?"

She stood, shoulders slumped. Julie relaxed infinitesimally. "I understand," Tyndall mumbled. Julie exhaled in relief.

"But answer me one thing, and be honest. Is there something going on between you and Romy Montoya?" Tyndall's eyes pleaded with her.

Julie smiled coolly, even as her heartbeat thundered in her chest. She met Tyndall's gaze with a steady one of her own, rehearsing the lie inside her head before shaping it on her tongue. Then in a voice that didn't waver, she said, "No, Tyndall. There is nothing going on between me and Romy Montoya."

Tyndall stared into her eyes, searching for something in them. What she found in them, Julie didn't know. Tyndall nodded shortly, before saying, "Sorry, Julie. Good night."

"Night, Tyndall," Julie said, opening the door so the other girl could return to her own room, and then closed it behind her.

Breathing out a sigh of relief, Julie rested her forehead against the closed door and uttered a prayer for forgiveness into the silence.

# CHAPTER TWENTY-ONE

It was their last night at Verona Prep before Romy left for the holidays. Julie was leaving the day after, traveling back to Kansas to spend the holidays with her family. Romy knew she wouldn't hear from Julie over the break, so she would have to make tonight last her for nearly a month without the sight of Julie's face or the sound of her voice.

The thought of her absence, even for a month, in Romy's life was not an appealing one.

Romy had planned a surprise for their last night together before the holidays. Mercury had left earlier that afternoon. Romy had sent a text to Julie telling her to come by Montag Hall at six that evening; the dorm party would be in full swing and she would be lost among the throngs of people. All of the residence halls were throwing their own holiday/end of semester parties, so Tyndall would be busy at Cap Hall.

Romy had the best pizza place in town on speed dial, order already placed. And she had Julie's gift ready too. Now she waited for Julie to knock. She adjusted her shirt one more time and tried not to feel nervous.

It wasn't working.

At five minutes of six there came a faint knock at the door. Romy pounced, flinging it open to find Julie standing in the hallway, face flushed adorably pink from the cold. Ushering her inside, Romy wiped sweaty palms on her jeans.

"Hi." She swung the door closed once Julie stepped inside, flipping the lock with a click.

"Hey," Julie answered as she shrugged out of her coat, hat, and scarf. Romy took them from her and dumped them on her desk chair.

"Did anyone notice you?" Romy asked.

Shaking her head, Julie said, "No, it was just like you said. Everyone was too busy celebrating to notice. Same thing over at Cap. Even Tyndall was having too good a time to notice."

"Are you sure she won't miss you?"

Julie shrugged. "I might have mentioned that I was feeling a little sick and would probably go to bed early." She gave Romy a vibrant grin, her white, even teeth biting lightly into her lower lip. Romy wanted to kiss her so badly.

What was stopping her? Romy leaned over and pressed her mouth to Julie's. She heard the other girl gasp in surprise before their lips met fully. It was a sweet kiss, not too long or deep; just enough to get both of their hearts beating faster.

"Happy Christmas, Julie."

Julie pulled away, clearing her throat nervously in that way that Romy found so cute. "You too." She tilted her head to one side, surveying Romy like she'd just had an unpleasant thought. "Do you and your mom actually celebrate Christmas?"

Romy laughed. "Sure we do! Why wouldn't we?"

Julie looked down, playing with the bottom of her sweater. "I don't know, I just thought since she went to the Enlightenment Center. . ." She trailed off, uncomfortable.

Romy took Julie's hand in hers and led her to her bed so they could sit down. "Yeah, we celebrate, and it's okay to ask. You didn't offend me. We always have at least one tree decorated in blue and silver though. Mom calls it our Hanukah bush." She pulled her socked feet up on the bed and sat cross-legged across from Julie. "We don't do anything big anymore—not like we used to. Mom used to have a turkey and stuffing, the whole bit, but now we usually just order Chinese or Thai and watch movies together."

Romy looked over at Julie, noting how tense she still seemed. "What about you? What's Christmas like at your place?"

Looking down at her hands, Julie sighed. "We all get up and go to church in the morning. Then we head home to start preparing dinner. Or we go to one of Dad's friends' houses."

Smiling sadly, Julie raised her head to look at Romy, and Romy felt like someone had just wrapped her heart in a fist and squeezed. "I remember our Christmases before Dad's political career took off. Mom would make these amazing waffles with three different fruit compotes for all of us for breakfast while we opened presents. Then we'd go to our old church—it was great. I really miss it. Then we'd go home and Mom would be in the kitchen all day—with our help—and make the best turkey and ham for dinner. It was a real feast—mashed potatoes, carrots, Brussel sprouts, homemade rolls. Everything was delicious. Grandma and Grandpa would come over, along with the rest of the family in town and we'd just eat and talk and laugh until people started falling asleep."

"It was perfect."

"Why isn't it like that anymore?" Romy asked, voice hushed in the sudden stillness. She took one of Julie's hands in hers, rubbing a circle on the back of it with her thumb.

Julie wrapped her long fingers around Romy's hand, giving it a squeeze. "Mom started helping Dad more and more with his campaigns. They started inviting his manager and staff to dinner. Mom stopped cooking and ordered catered food. It's a strategy session rather than a holiday." Julie sighed. "My sisters and I keep making our favorite foods, but it isn't the same as it was." She took a breath, collecting herself. "There *is* one good thing. My sisters and I always make a big pan of brownies and eat them while they're still hot while watching Elf on Christmas night. We stay up late and talk too."

"Sounds like you miss it."

"I miss a lot of things." Julie glanced out of the corner of her eye, gaze catching Romy off guard. "I'm going to miss you," she told her, a sweet smile on her face.

Romy felt the blush creep up her neck into her cheeks, face flushed and warm. "Me too." Shyly, she said, "I, um, got you something. For Christmas."

Julie's face brightened, blue eyes glowing like twin stars. "You did?" She sounded beyond pleased. Romy felt her heart swell almost to bursting inside of her chest. Was it possible to die from happiness? Romy might be close to finding out.

"Yeah, I did." She reached over and grabbed her guitar from beside the bed and settled it on her lap. A quick check to make sure it was still in tune, then she began to play the song she wrote for Julie, back before they started…whatever this was they were doing.

Romy's fingers faltered over the chords at first, tentative and searching. But then she settled, the music flowing through her like a wave, beating inside her like a second heartbeat, and Romy sang. The words came pouring forth like water from a spring. She couldn't look at Julie as she sang; instead, Romy kept her eyes closed, focusing only on the sound of the music. She'd done her best to capture the essence of Julie in words and notes, in chords and chorus.

After only a few minutes, Romy's voice died away along with the last notes of the song. Placing her hand flat on the guitar, she stilled the strings and opened her eyes. Julie sat on the bed, looking shell-shocked. Her blue eyes were wide, glossy with tears—as Romy watched, one escaped to slide down her creamy cheek. Her lips were parted slightly, as if she wanted to say something but had forgotten the words.

Romy watched her from beneath lowered lids, a lead weight pressing down on her chest, making it hard to breathe. She'd uploaded countless original songs to her YouTube channel, she'd sung for friends and family. But now, here in this room, Romy felt like she was singing for the first time, singing the most important song for the only audience that mattered.

"That was," Julie began, but her voice cracked and broke. She cleared her throat and began again. "That was…incredible. It was the most beautiful thing I've ever heard." Another tear fell. Julie wiped it away with the back of one hand.

Now Romy looked up, hazel eyes locking with blue. "It's you." She set a gentle hand on Julie's knee. "It's beautiful because it's you. How I see you."

Romy suddenly had her arms full of soft, warm girl. She managed to slide her guitar out of the way before it was crushed to splinters between the two of them. With that impediment out of the way, Julie clung tighter because her arms around Romy's neck made it increasingly hard to breathe.

Wrapping her arms around Julie, Romy didn't care if she passed out from lack of air. Julie was holding onto her as if she was the only thing anchoring her to earth and Romy was not about to complain. Julie sniffled, sounding suspiciously like she was crying, and all the joy Romy felt drained away.

"Hey," Romy whispered, "hey there. Why are you crying?" She pushed Julie away a bit so she could look at her.

Julie blinked, eyes wet. "How can you make me feel like I'm the most amazing person in the world?"

Romy grinned. Softly, she answered, "Because you are." She dropped her forehead to Julie's.

Julie closed her eyes, arms draped loosely over Romy's shoulders. "I'm sorry. I didn't get you anything."

Romy lifted Julie's chin with one finger, tilting her head until she could lean down at the proper angle and press their lips together. The kiss was gentle, another offering. Julie's mouth opened under hers, hot and sweet. Slowly Romy pulled away.

"You just did," she told her, a happy smile on her face. "You're the only gift I could ever want."

Julie chuckled softly. "You're pretty smooth, Romy Montoya. Has anyone ever told you that?"

"You're the first. And you'll be the last." Romy leaned into Julie, pulling her close.

Looking pensive, Julie searched her face for something—Romy didn't know what. "Why are you so nice to me?" she asked at last.

"Because I'm Romy and you're Julie." She held Julie tighter. "And we belong together."

Before Julie could respond to that, Romy's phone rang. Checking the number, she announced, "That would be the pizza. Be back in a sec." She grabbed her wallet from her desk and said, "Go ahead and start up a movie. We're having a celebration." She gave Julie a happy wave before disappearing out the door.

As she trooped down the stairs, the noise of the party echoing in her ears, Romy couldn't fight the grin that spread across her lips. Monet could buy her a car, a house, a small island country, and none of it could compare to the look in Julie's eyes when Romy finished playing her song for her.

Romy couldn't wait to send Julie a copy of it on Christmas Day. She only wished she could be there to see Julie's face once more while she listened to it.

# CHAPTER TWENTY-TWO

It was only her second week back from winter break and Romy was already heartily sick of the cold, the wet, and the snow. It was hard to sneak around to a secret date at her girlfriend's dorm when she left tracks a blind man could follow, not to mention the mess she made in hallways, stairs, and dorm floors with her damp and muddy boots. Romy was officially over the Northeast. It could suck it.

She had managed to get back into the swing of the spring term relatively easily. Her classes hadn't changed, except for a few electives. Romy had missed Julie over break, but it was good practice in patience. This semester's workload was going to be hard on both of them, and Romy knew there wouldn't be a lot of time left over for dates and snuggles and makeouts. They'd just have to make do.

Romy and Mercury slid into their seats, coffee cups clutched in their fists as Mrs. Escalus closed the door. They'd just made it. Sharing a grin with her roommate, Romy began to unpack the items she'd need for English. She risked a glance over at Julie, sitting beside Tyndall as usual. Julie tapped one end of her pen absently against her notebook, lost in thought. Tyndall caught Romy's glance and threw her a hard glare. Romy quickly looked away. No need to rile Tyndall up and make things that much harder for Julie.

Mrs. Escalus was halfway through her introductory spiel on Henry James when the door opened to reveal the assistant Dean and another school functionary. Romy, along with the rest of the class, immediately sat up straighter, attention caught by the deviation from their regular schedule. The Dean beckoned for the instructor to join them outside in the hall, and when she was gone, the class erupted into hushed whispers.

"What do you think this is about?" Romy asked Merc, one elbow braced on her desk, chin on her fist.

Mercury shrugged. "No idea." She watched the door, curiosity bright in her golden-brown eyes.

Mrs. Escalus returned after only a few minutes, expression neutral. "When I call your name, please take your school bag and proceed into the hallway to see Dean Burns."

She called the first name—it looked like they were going row by row rather than by alphabetical order, which meant that Romy would be going before Mercury—and then continued with her lecture. Romy's gaze kept sliding over to the closed door, wondering what was going on out in the hallway. It looked like most of the other students were doing the same thing as she was. When she looked over at Mercury, she saw she was doodling abstract shapes in the margins of her notebook.

The first student returned, clutching her backpack to her chest, face pale. What the heck was going on? Why were they asking them to bring their bags with them? Were they doing a search, or was it in case they had to be removed from the room after the talk in the hall? None of it made sense—nothing like this had ever happened at her old school.

Finally, it was Romy's turn. Mercury gave her a surreptitious thumbs-up as she stood up, bag in hand. She couldn't help another quick glance at Julie, hoping to catch her eye, but Julie's gaze stayed locked on her desk. Tyndall, however, was watching Romy cross to the door with an unwholesome amount of glee on her face. Frowning, she stepped into the hallway.

Dean Burns nodded to the other woman who sat in a chair behind a desk that had been pulled into the hallway. "If you'll hand Ms. Yeung your bag, Romy, we can get this over with quickly."

"What's going on?" Romy asked, fingers tightening around the shoulder strap of her messenger bag. "Why are you searching through everyone's stuff?"

"I'm afraid that we have reason to believe there is someone holding drugs at this school. We're asking all students to empty their bags and submit to a search. Those that do not will be dealt with accordingly."

Romy swallowed. This didn't make any sense, and it felt like her class was being singled out—she didn't see any other classrooms being searched on this hall. "This sounds like a violation of our rights," she hedged, unsure what the right decision was in this situation.

She knew she had nothing to hide—Romy didn't take drugs or drink. But this whole situation sat wrong with her. She wanted to protest, wanted to take a stand. Then she remembered the lawsuit and the reminder her mother had given her before she'd left L.A.—she needed to stay out of trouble. Romy imagined that staging some kind of one-person protest by refusing to submit to a bag search would not meet her mother's definition of staying out of trouble.

Romy handed over her bag with a sour look. The Dean nodded at her, then proceeded to watch as each item was removed from her bag, one at a time, and set on the desk. After a few moments of silence, the Dean asked her, "Is there anything in your bag that you feel we should know about?"

Romy blinked, unsure what he was referring to. "I mean, I have a tampon in there, if that is likely to make you uncomfortable," she told him in an even voice, folding her arms across her chest. "Otherwise, no." What, did he think she was a drug mule?

"What's this?" the woman who was emptying her bag asked, holding up a single dose pack of Extra Strength Tylenol. It was unopened.

"Um, exactly what it says on the packet," Romy said, unable to keep her voice from sounding snide. This was fucking *stupid*. "In case I get a headache." *Like the one you people are giving me right now.*

The woman frowned and set the offending packet off to the side. Once the bag was emptied, all pockets checked, she upended the bag and shoved her hand inside, searching for any compartments she might have missed. She shook the bag once, twice, and then, apparently satisfied, handed the bag back to the Dean.

"Thank you, Ms. Montoya. You may gather your things." He gestured to the contents of Romy's messenger bag now spread out all over the desk.

"Gee, thanks," she said, shoving everything into her bag with a sweep of her arm. "Pretty sure this is not kosher, so I'm going to be giving my mother's lawyer a call after class." Making sure she had everything, Romy turned and stomped back into the classroom.

"You're up," she whispered to Mercury as she flung herself into her seat, arms crossed over her chest in an Olympic-grade sulk, glaring at her lap.

Romy felt someone looking at her, so she turned her scowl outward. Julie had glanced over, a question in her eyes, but it was Tyndall who caught Romy's attention. She looked like a black cat had just walked over her grave, all huge eyes, pale lips, and quivering mouth. What did she have to be nervous about? Romy doubted Tyndall had anything harder than an Advil in her bag. Tyndall caught her looking and whirled around to face forward in her seat, nibbling on her thumbnail.

Romy caught Julie's attention again and cut her eyes over to Tyndall. Julie shrugged with the shoulder closest to Romy. She didn't know what her friend's problem was either.

The door opened and the assistant Dean strode to Mrs. Escalus's desk, the picture of iron control. He spoke a few words, too low for Romy to have a hope of hearing what he was saying. She gritted her teeth in frustration. The next student in her row got up and left the room at Mrs. Escalus's wave, but Mercury never came back in.

What was going on?

"Where's Mercury?" Romy stood up and asked, gaze lifting from her roommate's empty chair.

"That is none of your concern, young lady," the man said, condescending and dismissive. Oh, Romy was going to make his life miserable—it would be her new hobby. She did her best not to enjoy the thought, but failed.

"I'm her roommate," she said, not backing down. To hell with keeping the peace, to hell with that dumb lawsuit, to hell with what people who didn't know her thought about her. She knew who she was and she didn't give a shit over who might be judging or laughing at her. This was *Mercury*. "So it is my concern."

Mrs. Escalus leaned forward to whisper something in the Dean's ear. After a moment of consideration, he said, "I will check and see if she wishes to speak to you." He stepped out into the hallway again, this time only gone a few moments.

"You can come into the hallway, Miss Montoya, for a few minutes."

Romy bit back an inelegant snort. She risked one last look at Julie to find she was staring at Romy with worry in her cornflower blue eyes. Throwing what she hoped was a reassuring grin in her general direction, Romy left the room, feeling the eyes of all of the students following her.

When Romy stepped into the hall, she froze. Mercury sat on the floor, back braced against the wall, tears streaming down her brown cheeks. Glancing at the woman who'd searched her bags, Romy crossed to her roommate and knelt before her.

"What's going on, Merc?"

"They found drugs in my bag. I don't know how it got there." Mercury watched Romy through eyes that threatened to spill tears once more. "It's not mine!"

"What?!" Romy exploded. "Of course it's not yours!" If Mercury even smoked dope, Romy would have known, even if she didn't toke up in the room. She knew what pot smelled like—Rosalyn was an experimental girl—and she would have smelled it on Mercury. "How did they get in your bag?"

"That's what I'd like to know!"

Dean Burns interrupted them. "Miss Highbrook, if you'll follow me, please. Dean Prince would like to speak with you." He turned to Romy. "Miss Montoya, I suggest you return to class."

Romy's gaze jumped between the assistant Dean and her roommate. "I'll head to the Dean's office after class and wait for you."

Mercury smiled weakly, wiping wetness from her face. "Thanks, Romy."

♪ ♪ ♪

Romy paced the interior of the Dean's office, probably freaking out the woman's secretary, but she didn't especially care. Mercury was behind closed doors and had been for nearly two hours. The Dean's secretary had tried to get rid of her several times, but Romy refused. Verona Prep would need a crowbar to pry her out of that office before she knew what was going on with Mercury.

Romy was on what must have been her nine hundred and twenty-third circuit of the room when the interoffice phone buzzed on the secretary's desk. Romy's head came up, curious and not the least bit ashamed about eavesdropping.

"The Dean would like to speak with you," the secretary said, directing Romy toward the closed door that led to Dean Prince's inner chambers.

Romy stalked over to the door that opened to reveal Dean Prince. She beckoned Romy inside a small sitting area separated from what must be the Dean's office by yet another door. There were so many stupid doors in this place that Romy wouldn't have been surprised to open one and find herself in freaking Narnia.

"Please have a seat."

Romy selected the loveseat closest to the back wall of the office and sat, waiting to find out what Dean Prince wanted. She didn't have to wait long.

"I wanted to speak to you about your roommate, Romy."

"Is she okay? What going to happen to her?" Romy burst out, unable to contain herself.

The Dean held up a calming hand. "That still remains to be seen. Verona has been in contact with her parents and they've been made aware of the situation." She leaned back in the chair. "But this is a very serious charge that she's facing, and it comes with significant consequences. So I have to ask you, are you sure there isn't anything you'd like to tell me?"

Romy didn't engage her brain, just started spewing. "There's no way that stuff is Mercury's. I don't know how it got into her bag or whatever, but she's never even smoked regular cigarettes around me and she's never come back to the room smelling like dope before. It can't be hers."

"I'm inclined to agree with you," Dean Prince said, giving Romy a significant look. "This is Mercury's third year here at Verona Prep and I will admit that this is quite out of the ordinary for her. She's always been an excellent student, embodying the principles of Verona for as long as she's been here."

It took Romy a few moments to understand what Dean Prince was implying. She blamed it on the ridiculousness of the situation that she hadn't clued in sooner. Slowly, Romy said, "So, what you're getting at is that you think the drugs were mine?" Romy didn't know whether to laugh or scream.

"I'm simply offering you the opportunity to tell me anything you would like to at this time." The Dean sat upright in her chair, so frosty Romy was surprised there weren't snowflakes swirling in the air around her.

"The drugs aren't mine either," she gritted out, feeling anger bubble up inside of her. Her mom had sent her away from home to get a good education and a fair shake, to not be hounded by her mother's fame or suspected just because she was the child of a music star. And yet, here she was, having to defend herself because, of course the pot *had* to be hers. "I don't drink or do drugs. I'm straightedge."

Dean Prince frowned at the term, as if she didn't believe Romy. Romy just stared back at her, jaw set mulishly. She was so pissed off she nearly couldn't stand it, sitting in this poshly decorated sitting room while being accused of something she didn't do.

"May I ask how you knew which classroom to search?" Romy asked instead, digging her fingers into the denim covering her thighs to control her anger. "I didn't see any of the other classes on the hall being searched."

Meeting Romy's eyes calmly, the Dean answered. "They were to be searched after yours. The office received an anonymous tip about questionable activity regarding the possession and sale of drug paraphernalia. As you know, it is in the student handbook that students are required to report violations to the code of conduct here at Verona Prep. We have a phone number that allows students to remain anonymous."

*And this has all the makings of a nice little witch hunt.* Romy knew she was being fed the party line and didn't like it one bit. This reeked of bullshit—so anyone could report another student anonymously and the accused never got a chance to confront her accuser? There was something seriously wrong with that, right there.

"Are you sure there's nothing you'd like to say?" the Dean prompted once more.

"I told you. The drugs aren't Mercury's and they aren't mine!" She sat with her arms crossed in front of her chest.

Sighing, Dean Prince shook her head. "Mercury has already agreed to a room search. Will you agree as well?"

Romy shrugged, the rage that filled her very close to busting loose. She wanted to call her mother as soon as she got out of this room. Her mother would know what to do. "Sure. But I want to be there."

"Of course," the Dean said, getting to her feet in a gracefully fluid motion that made Romy momentarily jealous. "If you'll follow me."

"Can I talk to Mercury?"

"She's speaking with her parents right now. But she'll be returning to your room as soon as she is finished. You can wait for her there."

Romy followed Dean Prince out, teeth grinding together. She waited while the assistant Dean was paged. It took a few minutes for both Dean Burns and another female functionary to arrive at Dean Prince's office, and then the four of them set off for Romy and Mercury's room at Montag Hall. Romy pulled out her phone on the walk to the residence hall and texted both her mother and Beverly, giving them a brief rundown of what had happened in the last few hours.

Unlocking the door to her room, Romy gestured the assortment of campus officials inside. Romy stood just inside the door, arms crossed over her chest, the low froth of fury still churning in her stomach. Pointing to one side of the room, she said, "That's Mercury's side. What do you need me to do?"

"You can either wait in here," the assistant Dean told her, "or you can stay in the hall. However, if you do stay here, you can't touch anything."

Romy nodded, keeping her hands tucked beneath her elbows. "Not a problem." She leaned against the wall closest to the door and watched as the Dean and his assistant began to go through the room.

They were about fifteen minutes into their search when Romy's phone rang. Excusing herself, Romy stepped outside to have a little privacy for the call. It was her mother's PA, Beverly. "Your mother is in sound check but she told me to call you. We got your text— what the heck is going on up there? There was a drug bust?"

Romy filled her in on everything that had happened in as much detail as she could. Occasionally, Bev would ask for clarification or for Romy to repeat something; she could tell Bev was making notes as Romy spoke. When she finished, Beverly was silent.

"Bev? You still there?" Romy asked when the silence stretched out too long. She felt punch-drunk, so tired after reliving everything that she wanted to fall into bed. But there was the matter of the two people still rooting through her room to deal with.

"I'm here. Look, Romy, I'm going to call the lawyer as soon as I get off the phone with you. You might get a phone call from him, and I know you're going to get one from your mother as soon as she's free. Just hang tight. This all sounds really fishy to me." Romy heard Bev take a deep breath. "Is there anything else I should know?"

"I don't think so, but I'll text you if I think of something," Romy told the assistant.

"Okay, good. Don't say anything to anyone from this point on until you speak with the attorney, okay? If you have to, give whoever it is the firm's number. Hang in there, kid. Your mom will call as soon as she can."

"Will do," Romy said, feeling much better now that an adult she trusted was on the case. She was still angry at the insinuation that the drugs were hers, but at least now Romy felt she had a little bit of recourse available to her.

What this meant for Mercury, she had no idea.

The search of the room was nearly finished when Mercury arrived in the company of Dean Prince. Her roommate looked beyond upset: eyes red and puffy until they were nearly slits in a face gone ashen with worry and fear. All of her makeup had smeared and her clothes were tearstained. Mercury looked like she hadn't slept in months. Romy immediately folded her roommate into a hug.

They followed Dean Prince into their room, which now felt crowded with five people in it. Assistant Dean Burns said, "We're just wrapping up, but there's no sign of either drugs or paraphernalia. There's only been what we found in the bag."

The Dean beckoned the two underlings into the hallway, leaving Romy and Mercury alone in her room. "How are you doing?" Romy asked her.

"My parents are on their way." Mercury sniffed, wiping her nose on the sleeve of her Kelly green sweater. "I'm being expelled."

"What? No. You can't be expelled!"

"Technically, I suppose it's not expulsion. We pay too much money to come to this place for it to be that. Expelled is such a poor people word." There was bitterness in Mercury's usual sunny voice. "We say, *regrettably required to pursue my education goals elsewhere*." She laughed mirthlessly. "Which is just the fancy white people way of saying, 'Girl, bye.'"

Romy couldn't stop a snicker, so glad to have Mercury back with her—even if only for a short time—that she ached. "We can fight this."

Mercury shook her head. "No, Romy. We can't."

# CHAPTER TWENTY-THREE

Tyndall grabbed Julie's elbow as soon as class was over and dragged her down to the bathroom at the end of the hall. She flung Julie through the door, following her, ducking her head to make sure no one else was in a stall to overhear them. Julie stared at her friend as if she'd been taken over by an alien, book bag cradled in her arms like a baby.

"What are you doing?" Julie asked, slinging her bag over one shoulder to free up her hands.

Tyndall was actually wringing her hands, eyes darting around the room wildly, unable to focus on one particular thing. A sudden spike of fear speared Julie through her chest. She'd never seen Tyndall this upset. She put her hands on her friend's shoulders and said, "Breathe, T. Just breathe."

Tyndall's green gaze locked with Julie's blue, and slowly she nodded. As Julie began to demonstrate the *breathe in-hold-breathe out* rhythm, Tyndall mimicked her pace. After a few minutes of this, she seemed to calm, clenched fists loosening so that her hands lay relaxed against her sides. Carefully, fearing Tyndall would descend into another panic attack with the loss of contact, Julie removed her hands.

"You okay now?"

Tyndall nodded, a little too emphatically to make Julie completely confident with her response. "Yeah, I think so."

"You sure?" Julie didn't want to push, but Tyndall still looked far from okay.

"Can I ask you something and have you answer honestly?" Tyndall's voice was soft, almost regretful.

"Yes, of course," Julie answered, startled at the seriousness of her friend's tone. "Sure."

Taking a breath, Tyndall straightened and said, "Okay—" but stopped as soon as the bathroom door opened. She spun, snarling at the intruder, "Find somewhere else to pee! Can't you see we are trying to have a conversation here?"

Julie could do nothing but blink as the poor girl scurried way, probably in fear for her life. She drew back in surprise. "Um…Tyndall? This is kind of a public bathroom."

Tyndall shook her head. "Sorry." She collected herself once more, but the momentary vulnerability was gone. She asked, "Do you think God sees it as a sin if you do a bad thing for the right reason? Like for the greater good?"

Eyeing Tyndall carefully, the way someone considers an unstable landmine, Julie answered, "I think it would depend on what that bad thing was. I mean, killing someone is pretty bad. Is that the kind of thing you mean?" Julie had no idea what Tyndall was getting at.

"No, not like that." Tyndall's voice rose in frustration. "I'm just wondering, if you did something that breaks one of the Commandments, but you did it to bring people closer to His glory, would that be forgivable?"

"I think it would be, if you really regretted it," Julie answered, worried now. "Tyndall, what are you talking about? What did you do?"

Tyndall froze, as if finally aware that she was babbling. She glanced from Julie to the floor and then back up again. "Never mind, it was just a question."

"No, T," Julie put her hand on Tyndall's arm. "It wasn't *just* a question." What had Tyndall done?

"I said, forget it," Tyndall snapped, jerking away from Julie's grip on her. "It's not important anyway."

Julie tried again. "Look, you know you can talk to me about anything, right? I'm here any time you need an ear."

Tyndall paused at the door to the bathroom and turned around to face Julie. She looked torn for a moment, the victim of some internal argument. Then her face cleared and she smiled. It was strained, but still a real smile that actually reached her eyes. Julie hadn't realized how long it had been since she'd seen it. Why was Tyndall always so unhappy?

"Thanks, Julie," she said, sounding sincere. "I know." Tyndall sighed deeply. "I just have a lot to think about, but I promise I'll talk to you if I need to." She turned to leave, but threw her last words over her shoulder. "And thanks again. Sorry for the freakout."

Julie watched her leave, feeling her heartbeat beginning to slow back to normal. She walked to one of the sinks and washed her hands, and then splashed cold water on her face. Nothing made sense. Why had they all been pulled out of class for a bag search? What was the Dean looking for and why was it just her class? Why had Mercury and Romy left class? And what was bothering Tyndall? She'd been jumpy all through English and now in the bathroom—it didn't make sense. Unless...

Did Tyndall have something to do with what had happened?

Julie chewed at her lower lip, considering the events of the last hour. Something was going on, and she needed to find out what. Pulling her phone out of her bag, she sent a quick text to Romy asking if everything was okay. She tried not to worry when she didn't get an immediate response. Romy would call or text when she got the chance, she had to believe that.

When Julie finally left the bathroom, the halls were abuzz with gossip and speculation. It had taken hardly any time for word to spread about the bag searches and Mercury and Romy leaving class. Texts were sent to those in other buildings, tweets were flying, and Facebook status updates sounded in the faint beeps of everyone's phones. The atmosphere in the halls made it feel like the day before a school holiday.

Julie felt sick. A few students she knew tried to stop her to ask what had happened, but Julie pushed away from them. There was no way she could go to class, not when there was this air of gleeful celebration, not when she had no idea what was going on with Romy and her roommate. She walked as fast as she could back to her dorm room to wait for word.

# CHAPTER TWENTY-FOUR

Romy followed Mercury over to her side of the room, words failing her. Mercury began pulling out the suitcases she had stored under her bed and left them open in the middle of the room. Romy went to shut the door, only to have the Associate Dean shake his head.

"Can I at least just leave it cracked?" she asked, giving the man her best pleading look. "I don't want people poking their heads in while I help Mercury pack."

Dean Burns nodded once, face softening. Romy whispered, "Thank you," feeling her throat close with emotion. At least she didn't have to fake being near tears—they were already close to the surface. Romy was going to miss Mercury like crazy.

"My mother is going to kill me," Mercury muttered. "That's it, bye-bye Mercury, nice knowing you. You can ask for me at the cemetery. I'm sure my parents have a lovely plot picked out and a headstone ordered with my name on it!"

Romy watched her roommate open her wardrobe and begin yanking out drawers, which she carried over to the suitcases and emptied into them. Romy knelt down and tried to straighten out the clothing to make it easier to pack but Mercury waved her away with an empty drawer.

"Don't bother. It's not like I'm going to be alive long enough to wear anything once my parents get here." She shoved the drawer back into the dresser and grabbed another one. "I can't believe this is happening."

Romy got up and put an arm around Mercury. Her roommate dropped her head to Romy's shoulder and heaved out a sigh that seemed to come from the depths of her soul. Romy could feel Mercury start to shake and then felt wetness on the collar of her shirt.

Romy's heart convulsed painfully in her chest. Here was her best friend being expelled from school, and she was powerless to do anything about it. Romy knew Mercury didn't do drugs—she'd shared a room with her for months and could testify that she'd never witnessed a single incident of either using or selling. The hardest drug either of them kept on hand in their room was Pepto Bismol, or maybe Extra-strength Tylenol.

But that didn't matter. The school had found a dime bag of weed in Mercury's book bag. In the middle of class.

"This is bullshit," Romy told her friend, sinking to the floor so they could both sit down. "Complete and total bullshit."

Mercury lifted her head from Romy's shoulder, wiping away tears. "No arguments there." With a sniffle, Mercury began to sift absently through the items in her suitcase. "You know that stuff wasn't mine, don't you?" She sounded nervous, like she was worried Romy would believe the worst about her.

Romy nudged Mercury in the side and gave her a bracing grin. "Please, girl. You're more straightedge than I am! I know that crap wasn't yours." She lowered her voice and said, "But the big question is, since it wasn't yours, then whose was it?"

"And how did it end up in my bag?" Mercury began to nibble on her full lower lip.

Nodding, Romy tapped her fingers on one knee. "This doesn't make any sense though. If someone toked, they wouldn't want to just dump their stuff without the hope of getting it back. And it's not like this school does random drug searches or anything like that."

"How did Dean Burns know to ask me to empty my bag?" Mercury blurted out, eyes wide as she turned to stare at Romy.

Romy smacked her forehead with her palm. "I'm an idiot. Of course, it was a setup. Someone wanted you to get caught with that stuff on you."

Mercury nodded slowly, as if the pieces were finally starting to come together so that the puzzle made sense. "Someone planted it on me."

The two of them sat there in the center of their dorm room, staring at each other for a few long moments. Finally, Romy broke the silence. "Why do I feel like I've suddenly stumbled into an episode of CSI?"

"Because we're being ridiculous," Mercury said, but she sounded unsure. "Aren't we?"

Shaking her head, Romy answered, "I don't think so. We know that stuff wasn't yours. And then there's the sudden search in class today—like the school knew they'd find something. It makes sense if you figure someone had to tip them off that it would be in there. Which means someone had to plan to plant it on you." Romy's voice rose in volume with her excitement.

Mercury clapped a hand over Romy's mouth and shushed her with a look. They waited a moment to see if the Assistant Dean would pop his head in; when he didn't Mercury asked, "Who hates me that much to go through all that trouble though?"

"And were you really the target?" Romy eyed the messenger bag slung over the back of her roommate's chair. "Our bags are almost identical."

Mercury tugged on one of her twists. "Now you're being paranoid." But she sounded even more uncertain.

Holding up an index finger, Romy countered, "Just because you're paranoid doesn't mean that someone is not out to get you."

"That doesn't even make sense." Mercury pushed herself up to her feet, trudging back over to the half-empty wardrobe to continue with her packing. "It's not like it matters anyway. I'm expelled, Romy. That's it, I'm done, goodbye, hasta la vista, toodles, later, ta."

"But what if I can prove that this was all a frame up?" Romy hopped to her feet as well, grabbing a notebook from her desk.

"What, like in the next half hour? Not even David Caruso is that good." Mercury dumped another drawer full of t-shirts and socks into the suitcase. "He needs forty-four minutes."

"Wow. I finally met one of the five people that actually watched CSI: Miami. I feel like I just met a unicorn." Romy ignored the finger gesture from her roommate and went on. "So we need a list of suspects." She tapped the eraser of the pencil lightly against the pad.

"My mom watched it," Mercury grumped. "You know, the mother that's going to show up here and promptly kill me and bury my body where it will never be discovered because the woman took copious notes on how not to get caught committing a murder because she watched it on CSI!"

Laughter escaped Romy's lips as she fell over onto her bed. She couldn't help it—Merc looked so funny standing there with her arms full of furniture, head thrust forward, and screaming about a mediocre crime procedural while packing after being expelled. It was surreal. Romy knew that no one would ever believe her if she told them.

A splutter came from Mercury and then she burst out laughing too. The empty drawer she held dropped to the ground with a thump. She threw herself in the direction of Romy's bed, landing half-on and half-off it, draping herself over her roommate's legs.

"I'm going to miss you," Romy told her, throwing an arm across her eyes.

Mercury's giggles quieted. "I'm going to miss you too."

Romy felt her friend squeeze her legs in a tight embrace. Pushing herself into a sit, Romy stared down at Mercury, settling a hand on her head. Mercury shoulders shuddered as if she were shaking or fighting back sobs.

Trying to lighten the mood, Romy nudged her shoulder. "List of suspects. Go!"

Sitting up, Mercury rubbed at suspiciously bright eyes. Romy pretended not to notice. After a soft sniffle, Mercury finally answered. "If it's someone who could have it out for both of us, only one name comes to mind." She pushed herself up and continued with her packing.

"Starts with T and ends with -yndall?"

"You know it," Mercury agreed with a nod. She finished emptying out the wardrobe and tried to close her suitcase. "Get your narrow ass over here and sit on this thing so I can zip it up."

Romy did as she was told, dropping onto a sit on top of the overstuffed suitcase. "Okay, let's go over where you were with your bag since last night." She shifted her weight, trying to get the corners to meet so Mercury could get the zipper around the suitcase's curve. "Recount your steps."

"I had, ugh," she grunted as she forced the zipper to close, "math study group after dinner last night. Lean over this way, will you?" Mercury shoved down on the opposite corner, tucking in a scarf that was sticking out of one end. "Good. And then I went to the library for a couple of hours to work on my lit paper." With a sigh, she leaned back on her palms, suitcase finally closed.

"Did you ever leave your bag alone?" Romy asked her.

"I don't think so," Mercury said, moving on to her next suitcase. "Then I came back here and packed up what I'd need for the morning's classes. And then I went to bathroom to get ready for bed."

"And I was in here the whole time so it wasn't like anybody snuck in without us knowing." Romy nibbled on her lower lip and got up off the suitcase to sit back on her bed. "Okay, so what about the morning?"

"We went to grab coffee." Mercury folded up a pair of jeans and dropped them in her second suitcase.

"Yeah, I put our stuff down at the table while you saved our place in line." Romy stared at Mercury, mouth agape. "We left our bags at the table."

"We left our bags at the table," Mercury repeated in a hushed voice. And then, louder, "We left our fucking bags *alone* at the table!"

Romy glanced at the partially open door to her room, but the Associate Dean didn't poke his head in. Mercury walked around her suitcases on the floor to sit on the bed beside Romy. Tapping the pencil against the pad, Romy asked, "Do you remember seeing anyone hanging around our table?"

Mercury shook her head, lips pursed in thought. "Not really."

Pulling one knee up to her chest, Romy rested her cheek against it, thinking. "Hey, wasn't Clarice von Bueren hanging around our table when we got back? Any idea what she wanted?"

Nodding thoughtfully, her roommate said in a distant voice, "Yeah, I think she was. Said she had to talk to me about the chess club's next meeting or something." She plucked at her bottom lip. "She's a freshman—new to the club."

"Huh. So what did she have to ask?"

Mercury tilted her head in thought. "Nothing. She ended up checking her watch and saying she had to go, that she'd catch up with me later. I didn't think anything weird about it at the time, but now that I remember it, she was acting odd. Jumpy. Nervous." With a deep breath, she said, "No way, she's way too timid to do something like that. I think she'd have a heart attack if you looked at her wrong."

"That's a place to start though," Romy said. "I wonder if she knows Tyndall?"

"You think Tyndall somehow put her up to this?" Mercury looked skeptical. "I think you might be assigning a little too much power to the girl. Don't get me wrong, I don't like her, but I don't think she's a criminal mastermind either."

A knock sounded at the door, followed by the entrance of Mercury's mother and father. "Hi, Mr. and Mrs. Highbrook,"

Romy said, feeling guilty and awkward. She wanted to stay and support her friend, but also felt out of place. Maybe she should offer to go? She wasn't sure what to do in these kinds of situations.

"Hi Romy. How are you?" Mr. Highbrook asked. Mercury's mother just stared at her daughter in tight-lipped fury.

"Been better, sir," Romy told him honestly. "But I guess that's true all around."

Mr. Highbrook nodded, looking nothing like the genial man he usually appeared to be on his television specials. "That's true." He sighed, glancing at his daughter. "Would you mind giving us the room for a bit?"

With a quick nod, Romy got up and grabbed her laptop and headphones, stuffing both in her messenger bag. She stopped at the door, hand on the knob. "Mr. and Mrs. Highbrook, you may not want to hear this, but I just wanted to say that I know those drugs weren't Mercury's and I think someone did this deliberately." Gaze focused on Mercury, she said, "Text me before you leave so I can say goodbye." Then Romy ducked out the door, both sad and grateful to be out of that room.

She ambled away from Montag Hall, tucking her hands into the overlong sleeves of her coat. It was a sunny afternoon, which helped alleviate the icy chill from the breeze that blew through naked tree branches. Romy wandered, messenger back slung across her shoulder in a cross-body carry, not having a destination in mind. Normally, she'd hang out in the coffee shop on campus, but that place felt tainted to her now.

As she walked the grounds, Romy let her mind rove, hoping she'd think of something that would help her roommate. Clarice von Bueren. Romy knew nothing about the girl other than what Mercury had just told her. She was a freshman and had no classes or clubs with Romy; their lives intersected not at all. It made sense for Tyndall to use her as a mule because there was no connection between them. But why would Tyndall even bother framing either Romy or Mercury for drugs? That was what made no sense to

Romy—who would want to go to this much trouble just to get back at someone they didn't like?

At the very least, Romy knew what her next step had to be. She needed to find out if Clarice could be connected to Tyndall in any way—a class, an afterschool club, a study group, church, anything. If they did know each other, then Romy could figure out the best way of finding out if Clarice had anything to do with the dope in Mercury's book bag.

Without even realizing it, Romy found herself standing in front of the broad stone steps of Cap Hall. Julie's dorm. Pulling her phone from the back pocket of her black skinny jeans, she checked the time. It was still early enough before dinner that it wouldn't look weird for her to be going to see Julie.

Romy stopped in front of Julie's door and knocked. At least with her bag and laptop, it would look like she was there for something schoolwork related.

The door opened a fraction and Julie's blue eye peeped out through the gap. "Romy?"

Romy rubbed the back of her hair, fluffing the shorter strands at the base of her skull. "Hey, yeah. Can I come in?"

Julie opened the door wide and ushered her in before closing and locking it. Hustling over to the desk, she slapped her laptop closed before turning back around. "How's Mercury doing?"

Shrugging, Romy set down the messenger bag. "As well as can be expected, I guess. Her parents came so I'm giving them some space while Merc finishes packing."

"I'm so sorry."

"Me too." Romy met Julie's blue gaze. "Look, I need to ask you a favor."

A hesitant expression crossed her face, but all Julie said was, "Okay."

Romy leaned forward, earnest. "Do you know a Clarice von Bueren? She's a freshman."

Julie considered for a moment, before nodding her head. "Yeah, I met her the first day of classes. She sometimes eats breakfast with me and Tyndall. Why?"

Sighing, Romy flopped into a sit on the middle of the carpet. "Just trying to figure something out." She paused, picking at a seam on her jeans, trying to think of a subtle way to ask, before deciding that since she was barely on a first name basis with subtlety at the best of times, it was stupid to try. "Are you friends with her?"

Romy watched as Julie sat down cross-legged in front of her. She put a hand on Romy's knee, giving it a gentle squeeze. "I wouldn't call us friends. I think she's actually closer to Tyndall." She paused, head ducking down shyly before coming back up to meet Romy's eyes. "Is this about Mercury?"

"Yeah, it is." She hated to drag Julie into this, but she needed answers. She sighed and launched into an explanation of what she and Mercury had figured out about the coffee shop and the possible set up.

"Do you want me to talk to her? See if she knows anything?"

"Would you?" Romy brightened; Julie continued to be amazing. "That would be great." She scooted forward so she was closer to Julie. "I'll owe you one."

Julie grinned, making Romy's heartbeat gallop in her chest. God, Julie looked so incredibly hot when she grinned like that, wicked and knowing, with just a hint of mischief dancing in her narrowed blue eyes. She'd never wanted to kiss Julie more than at this very second.

Julie leaned in so she could whisper in Romy's ear, sending a shiver through her body at Julie's warm breath against her earlobe. "I can't wait to collect."

Oh, *hell*. Like Julie needed to be any hotter. Romy felt her gut tighten, a shudder rolling through her body at the dark promise in those words. Romy couldn't wait for her to collect either, not when she sounded like that. Instead of saying anything else, she turned her head and pressed her mouth into the join where Julie's jaw met her neck. Kissing her gently, Romy felt Julie stiffen against her mouth before letting out a sigh and relaxing into Romy's body.

Romy's hands found Julie's waist, pulling the girl closer to her. Julie moved, sliding over until she sat in Romy's lap, a warm, welcome weight. Her arms slid over Romy's shoulders, hands dangling against her back as Romy wrapped her arms around Julie's middle, pressing her close, mouth to mouth, chest to chest, and hip to hip.

The kiss was going somewhere deeper, darker, less innocent than they'd ever gone before. Julie's mouth opened beneath Romy's, her breath rushing out in a sigh. Romy had never felt anything like this before in her life, this focus on another person, of wanting to be with her so badly she ached with it. Being close to Julie wasn't enough; she needed to be closer, to be one.

Julie broke the kiss with a gasp. "Your butt is ringing," she whispered, breathless.

Romy cursed silently. Stupid phone. Julie tried to lift her arms and slide away, but Romy held her. She wasn't ready to let her go just yet, wanting to feel her closeness for a little while longer. She wiggled a bit to get her phone free, pulling it out of her back pocket.

"It's Mercury," Romy said. "I told her to text me when she was ready to leave so I can say goodbye."

Now Julie did get up. Romy let her go reluctantly. "You'd better get moving then," she said. Her cheeks were flushed the most delicious shade of pink. Romy wished she had more time to spend with her, but her roommate was leaving. She had to go.

"I'll see what I can find out about Clarice." Julie climbed to her feet, then offered Romy a hand up.

When she stood, Romy pressed her forehead to Julie's.

"I wish I could stay," Romy said, as Julie rested easy in the circle of her arms.

"Me too," Julie agreed. "But you need to see Mercury, so get going." She pushed Romy in the direction of her door. "Unless you want to use the window?"

"For old time's sake?" Romy grinned. "Maybe some other time." She leaned over and gave Julie a quick peck on the lips. "I'll text you later."

"K."

Romy left quickly, heading toward the small parking lot closest to Montag Hall. Mercury's parents were just finishing loading their daughter's things into their SUV, with Mercury carrying down the last of her stuff from the room. Romy took the box from her friend and walked with her over to the car.

"Julie knows Clarice. She's going to see what she can find out," she told her roommate. "And then I'll figure out what to do next."

Mercury gave her a concerned look. "Romy, don't do anything too wild. I don't want you to get kicked out too." She glanced over at where her parents were waiting for her. "I'll be fine. My parents have already found me a private tutor to make sure I stay current while we look at schools for next term." She gave Romy a shaky smile.

Romy threw an arm around her friend's shoulders. "You're coming back, Mercury. I'll figure out a way to prove that stuff wasn't yours."

Mercury gave Romy a fierce hug. "I don't care about that," she whispered into her roommate's ear. "You and I know I didn't do it and that's enough for me. Just don't let Tyndall win. You have to stay. For the both of us."

"Love you, Merc."

"Love you too, Romy."

Mercury took the cardboard box out of Romy's hand and began to walk to her family's car. "You'd better email and text me!" she called as she pulled open the back door.

"You know it!" Romy yelled back, giving her a wave.

She stood in the parking lot, waving, until the car had disappeared around the curve of the road. With a heavy sigh, Romy turned and marched up the stairs to her now-single dorm room.

# ACT THREE

*"Thus with a kiss I die."*

>Romeo and Juliet, *Act V, Scene III*

*"No."*

>Romeo and Juliet, *Act IV, Scene III*

# CHAPTER TWENTY-FIVE

The next few days passed by Romy in a blur of faces and voices that made little impression on her. As she went through the motions of going to classes and doing homework, Romy's mind was busy working out the problem of Mercury, Clarice van Bueren, and how Tyndall might fit into it.

She'd had a talk with her mother's legal counsel, who'd advised Romy of her rights. While it made Romy feel a bit better to know what could and could not be expected of her, the talk didn't get her any closer to clearing Mercury's name. If only she had something concrete on Tyndall, something she could take to the Dean. She would have had Mercury back before dinner.

Romy kept in touch with Mercury every day. It sounded like she was doing okay—as well as could be expected, really—and was taking some time to figure out where she would go to school next. Her parents had believed her when she'd told them the drugs weren't hers, and they had hired a private tutor to make sure she stayed on top of her studies. Romy hoped that she'd have something concrete to prove Mercury's innocence before too long.

So when Julie texted her to meet at her room after class because she'd convinced Clarice to speak with them, Romy nearly whooped with hope. The rest of her classes dragged on interminably; it seemed like a century before Romy was free to make her way to Julie's dorm. She practically ran all the way to Cap Hall to meet up with Julie.

Clarice van Bueren stood up as soon as Romy stepped through Julie's door. The freshman paled, going whiter than bleached linen when she saw her, but Julie nodded encouragingly. Romy didn't know what Clarice thought she was going to do to her to make her so nervous—stab her with a ballpoint pen? Defenestration from only the second floor? Romy tried to appear as non-threatening as possible. She needed Clarice on her side if she had any hope of getting Mercury reinstated.

"Hi," Romy greeted, giving a little wave. "Clarice, right?" She tried to sound casual, like she just dropped by Julie Cranston's dorm room every day, which, granted, she did, but not for this particular reason. Romy usually visited Julie for much more pleasant reasons.

Clarice nodded, still pale but looking less likely to expire on the spot. Romy gave the freshman what she hoped was a bracing smile. "Cool. I'm Romy Montoya."

She caught Clarice's gaze flick over to the messenger bag currently resting against her hip. Romy thought she saw Clarice's eyes widen, so she decided to push things a bit—to see what would happen and how Clarice might react in this situation. Reaching over, Romy pulled the strap over her head and dumped the bag with a muffled *whump* onto the bed right beside Clarice.

"Mind if I set that down?" she asked, not really caring about the answer so much as the freshman's reaction to the bag. "It's super heavy."

"S-sure," Clarice managed to sputter out, gaze jumping around Julie's dorm room so she didn't have to look at Romy.

Flopping on the floor in the middle of the room, Romy glanced over at the freshman. "I don't know what you heard about me," she said with a small grin, "but I don't usually sacrifice people to the devil or anything weird like that. And my mother most certainly does not bathe in the blood of virgins to gain eternal youth. She just has a really good personal trainer."

She received a tentative smile from Clarice after an initial look of surprise. Romy nudged the freshman's foot gently with her elbow before subsiding back onto the carpet.

Julie's soft voice filled the silence. "Clarice, I was hoping you'd tell Romy what you told me." Romy watched as Julie set a comforting hand on Clarice's knee. "You know, about the favor Tyndall asked of you."

Clarice looked from Julie to Romy and back again. Romy pushed herself up into a loose sitting position, weight resting on her hands behind her. She tilted her head so she could look at both girls.

With a nervous clearing of her throat, Clarice began to speak. She stared at her hands sitting loosely in her lap as she said, "Those weren't Mercury's drugs."

"I kind of figured that out," Romy said as kindly as she could. "Can you tell me how you know that though?"

In halting words, Clarice told them the whole story: how she'd been having problems making friends and missing her family terribly; how Tyndall had invited her to the prayer group; how she'd had taken a genuine interest in the struggling freshman. The entire time Clarice spoke, Julie patted the shaking girl's shoulder while Romy listened intently.

"So when Tyndall asked me to do her a little favor, I figured I owed it to her, you know? She was my friend—I *wanted* to do something for her, considering everything she'd done for me." Now Clarice met Romy's eyes, a tortured expression on her face. "I didn't know what was in that baggie she gave me. All she told me was to drop it into your backpack, Romy, and not get caught." She hung her head. "So I did."

"You had to know something was wrong, though," Julie said softly. "You don't get warned not to get caught for no reason."

Romy saw the girl's shoulders begin to shake and took pity on her. "It was that morning in the café, wasn't it?" she asked. When Clarice nodded, misery in every line of her, she said, "But you didn't put it in the right bag."

The freshman nodded again. When she looked up once more, Romy saw the wash of unshed tears in Clarice's brown eyes. "Your bags looked too much alike. I didn't know whose was whose. But I knew I couldn't wait to figure it out. Tyndall told me it had to be that day. So I guessed."

Raising her hands in a pleading gesture, Clarice begged, "I had no idea that drugs were in that package. I didn't think anything bad would happen—I just wanted to help out a friend." Clarice bit her lip before continuing. "Then I heard about Mercury and the drug search and I felt horrible."

"If you knew the dope wasn't Mercury's, why didn't you come forward?" Romy did the best she could to keep the anger out of her voice. She didn't do a good job.

Clarice sniffled. Julie handed the freshman a box of tissues. She grabbed one, dabbing delicately at her eyes. "I wanted to," she told Romy, "I planned on it. But when I told Tyndall what I wanted to do, she told me that it would be me who would be expelled. She said the drugs would never lead back to her—and that nobody would believe me if I told them what really happened."

Wiping at her red nose, the freshman continued. "I couldn't risk it. My parents would never speak to me again if I got kicked out. And Tyndall, well, she told me she'd make sure I never got in anywhere else." Wiping at her streaming eyes, she finished with slumped shoulders and a desolate, "So I kept quiet."

Romy blinked, trying to make sense of Clarice's words. Did the girl really think Tyndall wielded that much power in the real world? Is that what all the students around here thought? Romy highly doubted Tyndall was a mastermind with connections at every private school along the eastern seaboard—she was just a small-time bully who enjoyed using her bit of power to make people's lives miserable. She wasn't freakin' Lex Luthor. Julie's voice brought Romy back to the conversation.

"What changed your mind?" she asked, placing a comforting hand on Clarice's shoulder.

The freshman gave Julie a watery smile. "I can't do this anymore." She shrugged. "I haven't been sleeping well and my stomach has been tied in knots since all this happened. I can't focus. And I tanked a math test the day you talked to me that first time about all this."

She fidgeted, her fingers plucking at each other from her place in her lap. "I guess I'm just lousy at keeping secrets." Clarice gave Julie a shy smile. "I knew I wanted to tell someone, but I didn't know how."

Romy stifled the surge of jealousy that raced through her at the way Clarice was looking at her girlfriend. The freshman was probably just grateful to get the secret off her chest and out in the open, but she was looking at Julie with such adoration, it made Romy's teeth ache.

Though that could be because she was clenching her teeth really hard.

"Would you be willing to go to the Dean with what you know?" Romy asked, keeping a tight rein on her temper. She did her best to put herself in Clarice's shoes—being scared and manipulated by a boarding school sociopath on her first time away from home—but it wasn't easy. Mercury had been thrown out of school because of this girl, had been embarrassed, and could have been arrested. Mercury could have gone to jail. Romy couldn't let go of that so easily.

"The Dean?" Clarice's voice was a squeak of fear. She swallowed, a nervous bob of her throat. "I don't know if I can do something like that."

Julie gave Romy a warning look when she caught her rolling her eyes. *I'll handle it*, Julie mouthed from behind Clarice, where the freshman couldn't see. Romy gave a brief nod to show she understood, conveying with her eyes how little patience she had left for Clarice's timidity.

"I think you've been incredibly brave," Julie told Clarice, pulling her into a warm hug. Romy unclenched her jaw consciously—she had not even realized she was gritting her teeth again. "You've already done the really tough part," she continued, voice and expression glowing with approval. "You've spoken up! I think your parents would be very proud of you."

Clarice's face opened under Julie's words, like a flower unfurling and turning toward the sunlight. Romy didn't understand that need for approval—her mother had instilled in her a fierce independence from a young age—so this chick's need for affirmation for doing the right thing just seemed weird to her. But Julie seemed to understand it—almost identified with it even.

"But going to the Dean is different," Clarice began, "and Tyndall...," here the girl shuddered. "I don't know if I could go against her. What she said..."

Now Romy did speak. "You won't be the only one, Clarice," she told the freshman. "Julie and I will be with you when you go talk to the Dean."

Clarice turned her body so she faced Julie. "But Tyndall's your friend," she said, brows pulled low in puzzlement.

Julie's gaze met Romy's, and for a moment she looked very afraid. Then that spark of fear disappeared from those blue eyes, replaced by warmth and strength. Romy wanted to lean over and enfold Julie in the biggest hug of her entire life, but she held back. She'd save it for when they were finally alone.

"She is," Julie agreed. "But that doesn't mean I can just ignore it when she does something that's really wrong. My parents taught me better than that." She waited a beat and then continued. "Just like your parents taught you, I'm guessing."

"And what Tyndall used you to do was really *really* wrong," Romy reminded Clarice. "Like, galactic amounts of wrong." She gave Julie a cheeky grin.

"So what do you say, Clarice?" Julie asked, but not before giving Romy one of her secret smiles that made her insides heat like she'd swallowed fire. "Will you come to talk to the Dean with us?"

The freshman sat very still, teeth nibbling at her lower lip as she considered. After a few moments, she raised her head, fixing Julie with a determined stare. "Yes, I will."

It was well past curfew when Julie heard the scrabble of Romy's hands on her dorm windowsill. Julie got up and helped the other girl into her room before closing the window. The room was frigid from the night air, the radiator working overtime to try to combat the seeping cold. Julie was bundled in her robe and her coat while she waited for Romy.

"I don't think anyone saw me," she said as she blew on her fingers.

Julie took Romy's hands in hers and began to rub feeling back into them. "We should be quick, just in case."

"Yeah," Romy agreed. "So how do you want to handle this?"

"Tomorrow morning, you should go to the Dean first thing. I'll bring Clarice and a few of the others from the prayer group who agreed to tell their stories about Tyndall. While you all are in there, I'll go to class to keep an eye on Tyndall, make sure she's occupied."

"Sounds good."

"There's something else." Julie snagged her phone and pulled up Twitter. She showed Romy one of the pictures of her with an anti-gay message. "It seems she was behind these as well."

Romy took the phone from her, peering at it with wide eyes. "*She's* @jesussez?" She handed the phone back with a disbelieving look. "I don't believe this."

Julie nodded, feeling ten shades of horrible. That she'd been Tyndall's friend, that Romy had such things said about her, that Tyndall felt this much hatred toward someone she barely knew, that they all had to go through something like this. "From what Clarice and the other girls said, she asked her prayer group to take pictures of you on campus whenever they could and send them to her. She did the rest."

"But they knew what she was doing with them?" Romy's voice was low with rage.

Julie nodded. "Try not to be too angry with them," she said, hoping to calm her girlfriend down.

"My mom almost hired a bodyguard for me because she was afraid I had some kind of creepy stalker!" Romy realized she was getting loud and subsided. "Instead I had, what, like five of them?"

"They're going to tell the Dean about the pictures and the tweets. I think it qualifies as hate speech or harassment." That was a serious offense at Verona Prep. Tyndall could be put on probation. Julie thought it might do her friend some good to see how she hurt other people.

Romy didn't look the least bit mollified, but all she said was, "Fine, whatever. As long as Mercury gets to come back, that's all I care about." She smiled slowly, eyes bright when she looked at Julie. "Thanks for all of this. I know you didn't have to do it."

Julie felt her cheeks flush with warmth. Romy was staring at her like she was the only person on earth worth watching. Julie smiled and leaned forward for a kiss before she could stop and think about it.

Romy leaned in, cool lips meeting Julie's warm ones in a gentle kiss. Julie pulled back with a sigh. "What was that for?" Romy asked her.

"For being you." Julie smiled once more, though the fear-flutters in her belly were making it tight. There was no going back from what they were about to do. She knew it was the right thing, but turning in Tyndall was the scariest thing Julie had ever done. She had no idea what Tyndall would do when all of her misdeeds came out, and that was truly what frightened her.

Romy took Julie's face between her hands, her expression serious. "Are you sure you want to do this? I can handle Clarice and the others. You've done enough, Julie."

Covering Romy's hands with her own, Julie closed her eyes. "I'm sure," she whispered. Romy's palms were warm against her cheeks. "I can do this."

"I know you *can*," Romy said, voice so gentle that Julie's eyes filled with tears. "My point is you don't *have* to."

Opening her eyes, Julie gazed at Romy, mesmerized by her face. Red tipped black hair fell across a high forehead and into brown eyes flecked with green. Full lips, flat cheekbones, skin the color of sun-kissed suede, all of it beautiful, all of her wonderful. Romy was everything Julie had never known she wanted. She could do anything for her.

Julie stepped forward, folding Romy into a hug. This was what she'd wanted from her father and her family—the ability to make her own choices and Romy was handing it to her with both hands. It felt like the best gift of all.

She amended that. *Romy* was the best gift of all.

Romy's arms closed around her back, pulling Julie tighter into her body. She felt Romy's lips press into her hair. She closed her eyes once more, savoring the feel of Romy in her arms, of Romy holding her tightly.

"Julie?"

"I know I don't have to." Julie nuzzled into Romy's neck, wanting to be closer, to be one. "I want to."

# CHAPTER TWENTY-SIX

Romy was nervous as she waited in the antechamber of the Dean's office along with Clarice and Rose, Felicity, and Diane—the three girls Julie had managed to convince to report Tyndall's behavior in the prayer group. She smiled weakly at them. Romy had spent a lot more time than she ever wanted to in Dean-related activities this month. She hoped this was the last of it.

"Romy," Clarice began, biting her lower lip nervously, "do you think we're doing the right thing?"

Romy wished Julie were here. She was not cut out for this whole *being supportive to people she barely knew* thing, especially when said people were directly responsible for getting her roommate thrown out of school and making her life deeply unpleasant for the past couple of months. But she had to try, because if all these students started getting cold feet now, Mercury was never getting back into Verona Prep. Romy would be forced to do something drastic, possibly involving a llama, a desperate pact with dark powers, and some duct tape.

Pretending a confidence she didn't feel, Romy answered, "Yes, I do. I don't think any of us would be in this office if we didn't think so." She gave each girl a smile in turn. "Everything will work out okay, I promise."

The four of them returned shaky smiles just as the Dean's office door open. "Come inside, ladies," the older woman said, beckoning them inside.

Romy stood, allowing the others to go in ahead of her. It was in part to give her time to calm her nerves while insuring none of the girls decided to skedaddle at the last moment. You could never be too careful.

They settled in the chairs in front of the Dean's desk. "What brings all of you to my office today?"

Four heads swiveled in Romy's direction; four sets of eyes stared at her. Romy took a moment and thought of Julie, drawing strength from just the thought of her girlfriend. Julie had risked a lot to help Romy clear Mercury's name, and she wasn't going to let her down. She cleared her throat and began. "We've got some information about Tyndall Sutcliffe and the drugs you found in Mercury Highbrook's bag."

And with that, she began to explain.

# CHAPTER TWENTY-SEVEN

Julie waited outside the Dean's office, fingers clenched in the fabric of her sleeves, nerves making her fidget. She'd walked Tyndall over when she'd been summoned from class by the Dean, even though Julie knew it would be better if she had remained in class. Her guilt wouldn't let her stay behind. Now she had no choice but to wait.

Romy was behind closed doors with Tyndall and Clarice and a few other freshman girls who Tyndall had been bullying all year. Julie wanted to be in there too, supporting Romy, but they'd both agreed that it would be better for Julie if Tyndall had no idea how involved she'd been in clearing Mercury's name. Julie would be called on only if they needed her, and only then if there was no other way. Romy had been adamant about that, and Julie felt grateful. If Tyndall got angry with Julie, she could do a lot of damage with her hotline to Julie's mother.

Julie could admit to herself that she'd been glad of Romy's suggestion. She didn't want to go against Tyndall so openly, especially since it would mean conflict with her parents. So she waited outside and trusted Romy to handle it.

She felt like a coward though. Tyndall was her friend—Julie felt a responsibility to the people Tyndall had hurt—almost as much as she felt a responsibility to Tyndall herself. She knew Tyndall was deeply unhappy and she wanted to help her before Tyndall really hurt herself or her future.

Julie chewed on her thumbnail and stared at the closed door of the Dean's office, wondering for the zillionth time what was happening on the other side of the door. She didn't know what would happen to Tyndall after all of this. Maybe school community service? Some kind of volunteer hours? Academic probation? Julie knew Romy was hoping Mercury would be invited back—Julie did too—but what would that mean for Tyndall? A formal apology, maybe?

Tyndall wouldn't like it, that much Julie knew, but she'd help her get through it. She wasn't going to abandon her friend in her hour of need.

She dialed Karen's number while she waited. Julie was surprised when her sister picked up right away. "Hey Julie!"

"You sound out of breath."

"On my way to class. What's up?"

Julie bit her lip. There were so many things she wanted to say to her sister, so much she wanted to tell her. But now wasn't the time. "Just wanted to tell you I love you."

Karen drew in a deep breath and let it out, a gust that Julie heard over the phone. "What's wrong?"

"Nothing," Julie stammered.

"Julie," Karen said in her big sister voice.

Julie swallowed. Maybe she could tell her sister, just a little of what was happening. "There's something going on here with Tyndall—I told you about her. I can't tell you much, but it's pretty bad."

"Are you okay?" Now Karen sounded worried.

"I'm fine. It's just," Julie paused, unsure how to best express her thoughts, "sometimes to do the right thing, you have to make a choice."

Karen was quiet for a few minutes. Her next words made Julie's heart swell. "I trust you, Julie-bear. Whatever's going on, I know you'll make the right decision."

She didn't think it was possible to love her sister more in that moment. "I've got to go."

"I love you, Julie. Call me when you can talk more, okay?"

"I will. Bye."

Julie didn't know how long she sat there, freezing in the waiting room in front of the Dean's office. She wished she'd brought a sweater. The door opened and Romy came out, followed by Clarice and the others who'd come forward. Romy passed her without looking at her, but stopped at the door that led out of the building and muttered something to the others. They left, looking exhausted but relieved. Romy stepped over to Julie and dropped into the seat beside her. Neither of them said anything for a long moment.

Finally, Julie couldn't take it anymore. "How'd it go in there?" She tucked her arms around her body for warmth.

Romy shrugged off her jacket and passed it to her. Julie wriggled into it, snuggling into the warmth of Romy's body heat, comforted by the spicy scent of Romy embedded in the cloth. It calmed her jumping nerves.

"Have you been waiting here this whole time?" Romy asked her, lifting one foot to the chair and wrapping her hands around her knee.

Nodding, Julie told her, "I came with Tyndall—she asked me to wait for her."

"You want me to go and get you a coffee or something? It may still be awhile."

"I want you to tell me what's going on," Julie pressed, staring intently at Romy.

With a defeated sigh, Romy leaned her forehead against her upraised knee. "It's not looking good, Julie. The Dean sounded pretty pissed. I think she wants to make an example out of Tyndall."

"What do you mean, an example?" Julie felt her throat lock up with anxiety.

"She got another student *expelled* on a false drug offense. She's been caught practicing hate speech and harassing other students—you know there's a zero tolerance policy for that shit on campus. I don't think Tyndall's just going to walk away with a slap on the wrist and a lecture." Romy gave her a sad look.

"Oh my gosh," Julie breathed, hands flying up to her mouth, eyes wide. "I need to talk to the Dean. There's got to be something I can do, something I can say…" Fear galvanized her. She rose to her feet and crossed to the closed door of the Dean's office.

Make an example out of Tyndall? What did that mean? And what did that mean for Julie when Tyndall found out about her involvement?

"Julie," Romy began, then stopped, shaking her head. "I don't know if anything can be done." Her voice was muted, regretful. She tried to pull Julie back to the chairs, but Julie shrugged out of her hold.

"No." Julie turned around, tears gathering at the corners of her eyes. She blinked them away. "If I could just explain—I never thought it would get this far…" Julie trailed off, helplessly staring at the closed door.

"Julie," Romy repeated, placing a gentle hand on her shoulder.

Shaking off her touch, Julie rounded on her. "Why didn't you tell me something like this would happen?" Julie whisper-shouted. "I would never have gone through with it if I had known she'd be punished so harshly! She's going to flip out! And when she finds out I helped bring her down, she's going to tell my parents!"

Romy stared at her, a stunned expression on her face. As Julie watched, her expression hardened, turned distant. It was a look she'd never seen before on Romy. It frightened her a little, but not enough to calm down.

"What the hell did you think was going to happen to your friend, Julie? She's been harassing me for months, she's spouted horrible things about gays, bisexuals, and transgendered people in a school club meeting—a *Bible* club, at that—and she got an innocent girl kicked out over drugs *she* bought! Did you honestly think she was just going to be sent to bed without fucking dinner?" Romy took a breath. "And would you actually want them to?"

"It isn't fair though—she should get a warning or something!" Julie continued to protest, feeling like she was being pulled out to sea by an undertow of her own making.

Romy's eyes narrowed, dark brows drawing down in anger. "Did Mercury get a warning?"

Julie shook her head, feeling the edges of panic fluttering inside of her chest. She didn't think about what she was saying. "No, but that's different."

The silence that followed her words hit like a blow.

Romy spoke and Julie realized her terrible mistake. "How is it different, huh, Julie?" Romy crossed her arms over her chest and glared at her girlfriend. "Mercury didn't have even a single write up against her, just like Tyndall. She'd been a student here for the past two years—again, like Tyndall. She was an honor student, involved in clubs. Just. Like. Tyndall. Shouldn't she have likewise been given the benefit of the doubt instead of getting expelled?"

Romy pressed her lips into a thin line, eyes narrowing suspiciously. "Or is it because she's black that she doesn't deserve a fair shake?"

"I never said that!" Julie countered, horrified. She wasn't a racist! "I would *never* say that."

"It sounds to me like you just did." Romy checked her phone for messages before sliding it back into the pocket of her jeans. Romy's gaze rested on Julie, making her want to hide from that cold look on Romy's face. "Or is it only the Cranstons and their friends that are deserving of special treatment—what, the rules should only apply to other people?"

"You know I don't think that," Julie began, but her words slid away from her when she tried to argue with Romy. She could only stare down at her hands as she tried to come up with something better to say, something that wasn't inexcusable.

"Then what, Julie? Because it sure sounds like some privileged bullshit from where I'm standing."

"I'm not a racist!" At Julie's words, Romy's shoulders went tight, pulling up around her ears "I'm not! I'm dating *you*, aren't I?"

Romy met Julie's eyes with a green-brown gaze that swirled with anger. "I must be a great checklist item—you must tick off a lot of boxes with me," she said so softly Julie almost didn't hear her.

Julie's eyes went wide. "What are you talking about?" She had no idea what Romy had gotten so angry about, or why she was acting this way. What had she said that was so wrong? She wasn't a racist!

"I'm half Puerto Rican and half Korean." Romy counted off each point on her fingers. "I'm bisexual." She glared at Julie accusingly.

"I don't like you because of those things!" Julie protested. She held out her hand in a placating gesture, but Romy shook her head, her own arm slashing down in denial. "I like you in spite of them!"

*Crap.*

She hadn't meant for it to come out like that.

Romy reeled away from Julie as if she'd physically punched her.

Romy asked her next question in a quiet, broken voice. "Would you have done anything about your friend if you knew what the punishment for her might be? What the consequences to you might be? If you had thought about it, would you have helped?"

That voice did something to Julie's insides, made them seize up and twist, choking off her breath. She'd never heard Romy sound like that before. There was a question in her eyes, one that Julie wasn't sure if she could answer.

They stared at each other, long moments of silence stretching out like an empty highway between them. Finally, Romy lowered her gaze, one arm crossing her body as if trying to hold herself together.

"Never mind," she said. "Just forget I said anything."

"Romy, wait," Julie said, reaching out for her once more.

But Romy was gone, the door swinging shut behind her.

# CHAPTER TWENTY-EIGHT

Julie watched the closed doors—the one Romy had left through and the one Tyndall was currently behind—unsure of what she should do. She *wanted* to go after Romy, to fix the hurtful things she'd said to her girlfriend, to make whatever was wrong right again. What she felt like she *had* to do was wait and be there for Tyndall when she came out, however long that might be. She had to know Tyndall's punishment. She had to be prepared for damage control.

It was no choice at all, really. Julie waited, pacing out her frustration between the two doors. Romy's warm, prickly scent surrounded her, the comfort of the jacket a welcome one as the time passed. She had no idea how long she'd been waiting since all of this started.

The door to the Dean's office opened, showing Dean Prince with Tyndall huddled behind her in a chair. Tyndall wasn't facing Julie, but she could tell by the girl's hunched shoulders that things were not going well.

"Miss Cranston," the Dean began, lips quirked in a tired smile, "I appreciate your commitment to your friend—and I know she does too—but we're going to be here a bit longer. Why don't you return to your residence hall and Tyndall can contact you when we are finished?"

Julie looked over the Dean's shoulder. "T?" she asked. If Tyndall wanted her to stay, she would, regardless of what the Dean preferred.

At the nickname, Tyndall turned. Her eyes were red and swollen from crying, her cheeks blotchy. She looked utterly miserable. "It's okay, Julie," she sniffed. "I'll see you later."

Julie wanted to run in and give her a quick hug, but the Dean's presence at the door prevented her. She had to settle with asking, "Are you sure?"

Nodding, Tyndall said, "Yeah. Go on. I'll see you soon." She sounded more defeated than Julie had ever heard her.

Julie wanted to cry, but knew that wouldn't solve anything. She felt so completely helpless. So she put on her most supportive smile and simply said, "Okay. See you soon."

She headed out the door feeling two sets of eyes on her retreating back and tried not to think of the outcome of what was happening inside the Dean's office. Julie thought about going straight to Romy's room, but then decided against it. If Romy was still mad, it might be best to give her time and space to cool down. She would call or text when she was ready to talk to Julie again. Julie didn't want to be one of those overbearing people who constantly pressed herself into someone's space in order to make herself feel better.

She made her way back to Cap Hall and sat in the lounge, watching some mindless show on the television there. She only managed fifteen minutes before she knew she wouldn't be able to concentrate; the only cure for her nervousness was quiet. Trooping up the stairs, she gratefully let herself into her room and plopped down on the bed, not even bothering to remove her shoes or Romy's jacket. She pulled her laptop over, opened up her camera bag, and began to sift through photographs, trying to decide what she should download to her computer: She tried to put Tyndall's punishment, her argument with Romy, and Mercury's expulsion out of her mind. She stared at photos until her eyes grew heavy, at which point she set the computer and camera back on her desk before lying down.

She must have fallen asleep because she woke to a knock on her door. Bounding up, hoping it was Romy coming over to talk to her, Julie flung it open. Her eyes widened in surprise to find Tyndall slumped in the hallway, looking exhausted. Grabbing her hand, Julie tugged her friend into her room.

"What happened? What did the Dean say?"

Tyndall shook her head, hair falling into her face. Julie led her to her bed and pushed her to sit down. "Tyndall, are you okay?"

"I'm getting expelled." Tyndall sounded beaten, her voice lifeless.

"That's what the Dean decided?" She dropped down beside Tyndall.

Tyndall's fingers wound around each other, locking together in her lap. "I was just trying to do the right thing," she began, voice shaky. "I only meant to help you, that's all I was trying to do."

"Help me? What? Why?" Julie put her hand over Tyndall's, and asked, "What did you do?"

"I bought some dope from a guy in town and had one of the girls from prayer group put it in Romy's bag. Or at least, it was supposed to be Romy's, but the idiot got the bags confused and put the stuff in Mercury's bag instead." Shaking off Julie's hand, Tyndall rubbed at raw, red eyes. "And then I called in the tip about the drugs."

Julie pulled away, horrified that Romy had been right. Deep down, she'd kept hoping against hope that there had been some mistake. That Clarice had been playing a cruel joke. "Why would you do something like that?"

Tyndall tossed her hair back in frustration. "I told you, Julie, I was trying to help you—I saw how you were with Romy. It wasn't right."

"But you were framing someone!" Julie shook her head, realizing something. "Is that what you were talking about that day in the bathroom?" When Tyndall didn't answer, she continued, "You *knew* it was wrong! That's why you asked me that! Tyndall, I wouldn't have wanted you to do something like that, no matter the reason."

Tyndall glance up, tears in her eyes. "I know. It's just . . ." she stopped, looking at Julie curiously. Then she studied her hands. "I really messed up."

Julie gave her a hug. "You did," she told her, unable to remain mad at Tyndall when she looked so miserable. After a few moments, Julie released her and sat back. "Did the Dean already call—"

"Have you always had that jacket?" Tyndall interrupted, not looking up from her feet.

Julie plucked at a sleeve, feeling like a field mouse trapped in a raptor's glare. Trust Tyndall to notice the jacket. She couldn't believe she'd forgotten to take it off when she got back to her dorm. She blamed it on the warmth of Romy enveloping her, comforting her. It was like a wearable security blanket, and it had lulled her into a sense of safety.

Julie should have remembered that nothing between her and Romy was safe.

"You look beat, Tyndall," Julie said, changing the subject, her growing panic making her nerves tingle beneath her skin. "Can I get you anything?"

Tyndall's gaze dropped to the floor and she rubbed at her upper arms. "A soda would be good," she said, voice barely above a whisper. "Anything not Diet."

Julie stopped on her way to the mini fridge. She always kept a few cans of Diet Coke stockpiled in there. Turning around and grabbing a few bucks from her wallet, she walked to the door. "I'll get us something from the machines in the lounge. You want some chips or anything?"

Tyndall shook her head, clearly distracted by her thoughts. Julie couldn't blame her. "Just the soda," she told Julie, sitting carefully on the edge of the bed.

"Okay, be back in a sec."

Julie scuttled down the stairs that led to the lounge where the snack and drink machines lived. Verona Prep tried to stock healthy food options, but even they weren't foolish enough to deny late night study groups and cramming students their necessary caffeine and sugar fixes. Feeding a dollar into the machine, Julie selected a Dr. Pepper for Tyndall, then turned to the snack machine and got her a Rice Krispy Treat to go with it. Everyone loved Rice Krispy Treats.

Tyndall's suspicious question about the jacket came back to her, so Julie set her purchases on the closest table and shrugged out of Romy's coat. She'd just drop it behind her door and hope Tyndall would forget about it. She reached out to collect her stuff to go back upstairs when a tentative voice stopped her.

"Hi Julie."

It was Clarice. *Ugh.* Julie didn't want to be rude, but the timid freshman was the last person she wanted to see right now. She had more important things to worry about.

"Oh, hey Clarice." Julie couldn't muster the drive to put happiness in her voice. "What's up?"

Clarice looked to the side, embarrassed. Julie bit back a groan; she dearly hoped that this girl would grow out of her hesitancy sometime before the next millennium.

"I was just wondering if you knew what the Dean's decision was. You know, as far as Tyndall goes."

The freshman looked pale, fingers twisting themselves into knots as she fidgeted. With an almost audible sigh, Julie gave her an encouraging smile to try to get her to relax.

"I can't really say anything," she told Clarice, knowing that Tyndall wouldn't want her expulsion getting around the gossip mill at Verona Prep. It would happen soon enough, but Julie didn't want to help the news spread.

"Can you at least tell me if she's getting to stay at Verona?" Clarice asked, seemingly desperate for some information.

Shaking her head, Julie said, "Sorry, Clarice. I can't even tell you that." She gathered up her snacks and moved past the freshman. "Tyndall will let everyone know what happened with the Dean when she's ready to talk about it." She gave her a small smile. "But I'll let her know you asked about her."

Clarice caught Julie's arm as she crossed to the stairs. "Can you...," she trailed off for a moment, catching her lower lip between her teeth, "will you tell her that I hope she's okay?"

Julie nodded before moving away. She was surprised that Clarice genuinely seemed to want to be Tyndall's friend, even after everything that had happened. It gave her hope that not everyone would see Tyndall as a villain.

Although she supposed it didn't really matter since Tyndall wouldn't be at Verona Prep any longer. And Julie had been one of the people responsible for that. A weird mixture of pride and guilt filled her, along with a huge helping of fear. Julie was glad she'd helped Mercury, and terrified there would be consequences.

She finished trudging back up the stairs and fumbled to get the door open. Tyndall sat on the bed, fiddling with her cell phone. She didn't look up when Julie entered.

"I got you a snack," Julie said, dumping the jacket on the floor by the door, before handing Tyndall the soda.

Tyndall tucked her phone back into the pocket of her coat, and then stood up. She took the can that Julie held out for her, and then walked to the door. "Thanks. I should probably go and start packing. My mom's coming in tomorrow first thing."

"Tyndall?" Julie asked, turning her body to follow the girl's progress through the room. "Everything okay?"

Tyndall didn't look at her, hand grasping the doorknob. "Yeah, just really tired. Got a lot to do before the morning," she told her, voice muffled by the high collar of her coat. "I need to get started."

"I can help you, if you want," Julie offered.

"No, it's okay. You've done enough."

Julie thought there was an edge to Tyndall's voice, a harshness that wasn't present before. Something in her tone warned Julie not to press. "Okay," she said, watching as the girl opened the door and slipped through, closing it behind her.

Turning away, Julie noticed her desk. Her camera wasn't where she had left it.

Julie felt all of the color drain from her face as she rushed to her desk.

# CHAPTER TWENTY-NINE

Romy stalked around the confines of her room, wishing she could hit something. She loved Julie, she really did, but Julie just couldn't be that naïve, could she? To think that Tyndall would just weasel out of any kind of significant punishment after framing another student for drugs was ridiculous.

Wasn't it?

Raking a hand through her hair, Romy crossed to her desk. Her laptop sat on it, waiting for her. Music would help—it always did. Romy set everything up, pulled out her guitar, settled on the bed and began to play. She let her mind wander. She didn't know if she'd get anything useable out of this session, but Romy sometimes did her best work when she was trying to work things out in her head. She let her fingers move across the strings, let her voice rise and fall, let the magic of music take her where she needed to go.

It had hurt her, the panic that she'd seen in Julie's eyes when she had finally realized how much trouble Tyndall was going to be in. It hurt because it had been *Romy* that Tyndall had been harassing, it had been *Romy* that the stashed drugs had been meant to frame, it had been *Romy* that Tyndall had meant to get expelled, and it had been Romy's roommate, Mercury, who had been caught up in the middle of it all. Julie said she cared about Romy, but what she'd seen in the Dean's office said otherwise

Shouldn't Julie have been satisfied that Tyndall's reign of terror had been brought to an end? That Romy wouldn't have to worry about when another tweet would go up, or when another bogus drug search would be called? Shouldn't Julie have been glad that they wouldn't have to sneak around anymore since her so-called friend wouldn't be there to spy on every little thing the two of them did together?

Closing her eyes, Romy tried to let the hurt wash away under the notes she was playing. She knew it seemed like nothing got to her—she'd tried not to make a big deal out of the harassing videos that had popped up almost as soon as she started at Verona—but she wasn't made of marble. She had plenty of practice in hiding how she felt—growing up with the paparazzi always after a picture made it a survival skill. But that didn't mean she didn't feel the pressure and the anger, disappointment, and isolation of being singled out *again*, be it for her sexuality, her gender, or her race.

Tears gathered in her eyes, and instead of fighting them back, she let them fall. Fat drops slid down her cheeks to fall on her hands and on the strings and wood of her guitar. Her fingers still slid up the neck, still danced out a melody.

What *was* she doing with Julie anyway? Was all of this really worth it? Christmas had been nearly impossible to get through. Romy had wanted to be able to call and talk to her girlfriend, to send goofy messages, to text stupid pictures, to say she missed her. But with Julie's family, there was no way she could do any of that. It made for a very frustrating break.

And now, back at school, there was this whole shit-storm to deal with. Maybe being with Julie wasn't such a great idea. There was so much hiding, so much they both had to keep secret. Romy had always been encouraged to be herself, to figure out what she wanted and pursue it and not to be ashamed of who she was as she did it.

Except now, she felt like hiding was all she did.

Romy looked over to the empty bed on the other side of the room. God, she missed Mercury. She missed having someone to talk to, someone who knew her. She could really use a friend right now; Romy knew she could call Rosalyn or one of her L.A. friends, but the backstory she'd have to catch them up on would take the entire conversation and she couldn't out Julie. She was stuck.

With a sigh, Romy hit the Stop button on her recording and set aside the guitar. Leaning over the desk, she gazed out the window. The sun had set and mid-winter twilight was waning into true night, cold and dark. She should probably head to the cafeteria to get something to eat, but the thought of walking in the freezing cold and food just didn't appeal to her at all right now.

And she'd given Julie her favorite jacket. Terrific.

Her eyes widened. *She'd* given Julie her favorite *jacket.* Julie was wearing it. *Shitshitshitshit.*

Tyndall was going to notice something that obvious, especially since she'd been glaring at Romy all day in the Dean's office while she'd been wearing it. And it seemed like Julie had been too upset about Tyndall's impending expulsion to bother worrying about that fact, if she had even noticed it at all.

Romy grabbed her heavy coat, tucking her phone into the pocket, and ran out of her residence hall. Cap Hall was diagonal across the quad where the dorms clustered like children at recess. Slogging through the snow and slush, Romy moved as quickly as she could, cutting across snowbanks instead of sticking to the shoveled walks because they didn't follow the most direct route.

Her phone buzzed from the depths of her pockets. Fishing it out, Romy saw it was Mercury calling her. She didn't want to take the time to answer, but it was Mercury. She owed her. Slipping off one glove, she answered, "Hey Merc."

"I'm back in!" her roommate crowed, voice a high-pitched squeal of excitement.

Wincing, Romy held the phone away from her ear. "That's awesome news, Mercury!" she said.

"You haven't been cheating on me with another roommate, have you?" Mercury asked slyly. "My bed is still empty and available, right?

"Yep," Romy answered, "I've been keeping myself pure for you." She grinned, relief a warm feeling in her stomach. "No one could ever take your place. I knew you'd be back so I didn't even bother requesting someone new."

"And I'm sure you having a double room to yourself had nothing to do with it," Mercury scoffed.

Shrugging, even though her roommate wouldn't be able to see the gesture, Romy asked, "Your parents are okay with you coming back?"

"Well, we still have to discuss it," Mercury hedged, "and they are not happy with the school, but I think if I'm okay with coming back, they'd be okay too." She paused. "I'm pretty okay with coming back. I miss you and I really liked Verona."

"Your room awaits you," Romy told her, a grin on her face and in her voice. She heard what sounded like shouting on Mercury's end of the conversation.

"My mom's calling for me to come down to dinner. I'll call you so you know when to expect me. See you soon!"

"Bye, Merc!"

She was grateful that it hadn't been a long call; Romy had lost feeling in her fingers by the time she put the phone back in her pocket. She quickly slogged her way toward Cap Hall's front doors, plowing her way through the pockets of snow before making it to the partially cleared steps.

Julie's room was on the second floor. Romy took the stairs two at a time, wishing she could kick off her boots so she could move faster. She'd already stripped off her gloves, tucking them into her pockets. Romy rapped on Julie's closed door.

"Julie, it's me. Let me in," Romy said through the door.

No answer. There had been a light on in Julie's window when Romy had spoken to Mercury. She usually turned the lights out if she was out of the dorm. It was possible that she'd forgotten, but

Romy didn't think so. Something, some special kind of Julie-sense, told her that she was still in there.

"Come on, Julie," Romy pleaded, leaning her forehead against the painted wooden door, "please just open up and talk to me."

Pressing an ear to the flat surface, Romy strained to hear any movement from the other side. Nothing. She waited, breath held, hoping for some sound to filter through. *Come on, Julie.*

After several minutes, Romy sighed. She pressed hands flat against the door as if she could push through it and into Julie's room. She didn't want to leave, but she couldn't exactly camp out in front of her door. Julie wouldn't appreciate it and Romy really hated camping.

"I'm sorry," she whispered, feeling tears clog her sinuses. Damn, she hated to cry. Blinking them back, Romy straightened up and pulled herself together. She would go back to her dorm, make some decaf, and try to get a good night's sleep. Maybe in the morning Julie would be willing to talk to her again. Or maybe her dorm room would be struck by a meteor while she slept.

Either would be a win at this point.

She had just taken a step back when she heard the lock on the door click open. Julie had been in there after all! Romy waited, barely able to breathe, as the door slowly opened. A pale hand snaked out, holding Romy's jacket. Romy took a step forward, a hopeful smile crossing her face.

The fingers opened and the jacket fell to the floor of the hallway. Then the door shut. Romy could hear the lock clicking once again.

She stared stupidly at the closed door, then the jacket, and then back again. Romy felt like someone had just punched a hole in her chest big enough to drive a tank through. What had happened? Did this mean what she thought it meant?

"Julie?" Romy whispered, knowing Julie wouldn't hear her through the door even if she were listening.

Romy fell to her knees the way a tree fell in the forest: slowly and then all at once. Her kneecaps hit the carpet with a thump, hands in fists landing hard behind them. Slowly she reached out and gathered the jacket in her arms, holding it carefully. It still smelled faintly of Julie, and Romy had to fight the urge to bury her face in it and cry right there in the hallway.

She'd never known a hurt like this before. Romy thought she finally understood how people in love could go mad; if this is what it felt like, she could see the appeal in losing herself in a red sea of insanity. It had to be better than this hollow ache at the very core of her.

Carefully, feeling like she might break apart if she moved wrong, Romy climbed to her feet. Thank God no one had come down the hallway to find her like this. She stared at Julie's closed door for a long moment, wondering if she should try one last time to get her to open the door. Then she glanced at the jacket in her hand.

Romy had Julie's answer.

"I love you," Romy whispered, knowing Julie couldn't hear her through the white door. But she said it anyway because she needed to hear it for herself.

Turning, Romy made her painful way down the stairs, out the front door of the residence hall, and back to Montag Hall.

# CHAPTER THIRTY

Romy lay on her bed in the darkness, curled around a pillow. The digital clock's red numbers showed it was almost one in the morning. She'd been awake for hours, staring into the empty dark of her room, feeling like she'd lost something vital. She wondered if this was how amputees felt with the phantom pain of a missing limb—like a part of you was lost but also inexplicably there. Romy thought that if she just reached out her hand, Julie might just be there, waiting to grasp it.

She wasn't though. And she likely never would be again.

Romy had finished crying before she'd crossed the quad to get to back to Montag Hall. Now she just felt numb, the hurt buried beneath an emptiness that seemed to stretch to infinity inside her. She'd pushed herself to climb up the stairs to her dorm room, forced herself to brush her teeth, wash her face, and put on her flannel pajama pants and an old Salt-n-Pepa t-shirt she'd stolen from her mother years ago. Then she'd locked herself in her empty room and crawled into bed, hoping for sleep.

That had been ages ago. Still sleep wouldn't come. Romy's mind bounced from thought to thought with only one thing in common between them all: Julie. For the first time, Romy wished she had something stronger than water in her desktop refrigerator, wished she'd had any experience with alcohol at all. She thought that beer or liquor would help her sleep, or at least get so unconscious that she wouldn't replay her encounters with Julie like some kind of morbid relationship greatest hits collection.

She wished Mercury were here—at least then she'd have somebody to bother with her problems. But it was just her, alone in her room, feeling like she'd been abandoned by everyone important to her.

Yeah, Romy was deep into her pity party. She had to admit there was something dramatic and satisfying about staring at the wall in a dark room, wondering if the person she was missing so terribly might be thinking of her. It was like pushing at a bruise to see if it still hurt and being surprised when it did.

Something had happened, that much Romy knew. She didn't know what, but it had to be more than their little tiff in Dean Prince's office. Tyndall had been expelled, but Julie couldn't be too surprised about that. There had to be something else. Had Tyndall somehow made a connection between the two of them? Had the jacket been the giveaway? Surely Julie could figure out a way to explain that.

With Julie not talking to her, it was unlikely she'd find out any time soon.

Romy thought for a moment about calling her mom. Monet was on a short break from touring so she'd probably be home. It was still a decent hour in Hell-A. Maybe her mother would be able to shed some light on why Julie might be acting this way, or have some suggestions for how to get Julie to talk to her. Her mother wouldn't be thrilled, but her mother had handled worse and Romy needed someone to talk to.

Fumbling blindly, Romy slapped at her desk, feeling for her cell phone. She could at least send a text to see if her mother was free for a call. If she were, Romy would take it as a sign from the universe that she should talk about her failure with Julie.

Before Romy could punch in more than two numbers there came a faint knock at her door. Dropping the phone in surprise, Romy froze, half-sitting up in bed. That couldn't have been a knock on the door, not at this hour. Curfew was in effect. No one was supposed to be out of their room, except to go to the bathroom. Had somebody gotten the wrong room? It was possible, but unlikely this late in the year.

The knock came again, this time a bit more insistent. Romy got out of her bed, shivering a little at the cold air against her bare arms. The old coil heater beneath the window clanked as it came on. There were two settings, as far as Romy could tell—boiling hot, making the room feel like a beige lobster pot, or completely off, leaving the room an icy tundra.

Padding to the door, Romy put her ear to it, feeling goosebumps rise along the flesh of her exposed arms. "Who is it?"

"Romy? Can we talk?"

It was Julie's voice. What the hell was she doing here at this time of night? She could get in serious trouble if the RA caught her out of bed, let alone in a completely different residence hall. Romy opened the door quickly and yanked Julie inside before anyone woke up and discovered her in the hallway.

"What are you doing here?" Romy whispered, pulling her deeper into her room

She could feel Julie shaking beneath her hands. She was only wearing a sweater, jeans, and sneakers. She didn't have a coat, hat, or gloves. Julie's skin was ice cold, her eyes dazed.

"Jeez, you're freezing!" Romy ushered Julie over to her bed, shoving her into a sit and wrapping the spare blanket folded at the foot of it around Julie's shoulders. "Where's your coat?"

"Coat?" Julie blinked, looking down in confusion. "I . . . don't remember having it."

Romy peered into Julie's eyes. She looked stunned, eyes razed clean like those pictures of nuclear mushroom clouds that detonated in the desert. The blue of her eyes was muted, dimmed, as if someone had snuffed out the light behind them. Romy tightened her grip on Julie's shoulders, fingers digging into the blanket. Julie just sat, still staring into emptiness.

"Julie, what's wrong? What happened?" Then in a lower voice, Romy pleaded, "You're scaring me."

Romy knelt in front of her, taking Julie's hands in hers to rub some warmth back into them. She murmured soft things, nothing urgent, just a string of nonsense sentences meant to soothe. Slowly, Julie seemed to come back to awareness, blinking owlishly in the dim light of the digital clock. Her body straightened a little, coming out of its slump though her shoulders were still rounded as if she were supporting a heavy weight. Her eyes focused on Romy's hands on hers.

Remembering the scene at Julie's door, Romy pulled her hands away. Julie stopped her, clutching tightly at her hands so Romy couldn't pull away.

"Please," she whispered. "Don't leave me."

Romy shuddered, heart throbbing a heavy bass beat like one of her mother's song remixes. She was more scared than she'd ever been before. Julie still wasn't talking, wasn't making sense, but she held onto Romy's hands like they were a lifeline and she was drowning.

"I'm not going anywhere," Romy told her, voice low and comforting. She pushed up, noticing how the fear in Julie's eyes flared cerulean bright when she thought Romy might leave. She sat down next to Julie on her bed, their hands still gnarled together like tree roots.

Julie fell into her with a sigh. Extricating one of her hands from the jumble, Romy wrapped her arm around Julie's shoulders and held her close. She could feel the shivers that shook Julie's body, whether from cold or upset Romy wasn't sure. She just rubbed her palm up and down Julie's back, trying to soothe the girl and get her to a place where she could talk.

It was several minutes before Julie's trembling subsided. With a soft sigh, Julie pushed herself away from Romy's shoulder, wiping at her red eyes with the sleeve of her sweater. Romy reached across her to her desk and handed Julie the box of tissues.

"Thanks," Julie said in a whisper.

"Not a problem." Romy waited, strangling the need to ask what was wrong yet again. Patience was not something she was good at, but patience was what Julie needed from her right now. She didn't press further. She just had to wait until Julie was ready to talk, as much as that might drive her crazy.

Romy knew she had a talent for words. Her mother would probably insist that she'd never been at a loss for them. Romy was quick to anger and spout off, and just as quick to forgive. Romy didn't hold onto things, didn't let bad feelings fester. Get it out in the open, deal with it, and move on from it—that was how she handled herself. But Romy had learned that Julie wasn't like that. Julie internalized, fretted about things, tortured herself with how she could have done things differently or better to avoid whatever unfortunate situation she was caught up in. It was never just *explode and get over it* with Julie.

Romy waited and tried to show silent support for whatever Julie was processing. Julie would tell her eventually.

"I'm sorry about earlier. When you, ah, came by to see me." Romy watched Julie's throat work as she swallowed. "I didn't mean to hurt you. What I did—it wasn't fair to you."

Romy felt tears gather in her eyes at Julie's apology. "Don't worry about it," she whispered into Julie's hair, throat so tight it was a wonder her voice worked at all.

"No." Julie shook her head, pushing away a little so she was looking into Romy's eyes. Had Julie's eyes always been so incredibly blue? It was like a piece of sky had been stolen and set into Julie's eyes for safekeeping. "No, I don't want to be *that* person. I am going to worry about it because what I did was wrong. Just because I'm your girlfriend doesn't mean I should be allowed to get away with doing cruddy things to you."

"I forgave you the moment you did it," Romy countered.

Julie's soft, tremulous smile was the most amazing thing Romy had ever had the grace to see. It made her heart swell and jump inside of her chest, a dance of muscle. "Thank you," she said, "but I still need to apologize." She bumped her shoulder into Romy's. "I'm sorry."

"It's okay," Romy assured Julie. "I got over it." She bit her lip, catching it between white teeth. "But can you tell me what brought it on? What happened?"

"Tyndall looked through the photos on my camera." Julie's voice was harsh, raspy from crying.

Romy blinked. "I'm going to assume that's bad."

Julie made a noise between a scoff and a snort. "Yeah, you could say that. It was full of pictures of you, the ones I hadn't downloaded to my computer to edit. The ones from Christmas. In your room. No one was ever supposed to see them."

"Is it that bad?" Romy asked. They were just pictures after all.

Julie straightened enough so she could look in Romy's eyes. And the look she gave her conveyed, quite clearly, that she thought Romy might have sustained a traumatic brain injury sometime in the last thirty seconds. "Tyndall was already suspicious of us. I didn't tell you before but she accused me of being *friendly* with you before we left on holiday break." She ducked her head, cheeks blushing a gentle rose. "And there were a lot of pictures of you. Some of when you were sleeping."

"Oh." Romy felt the heat of a flush flood her cheeks with color, but she couldn't completely hide the grin that spread across her face like honey. Julie took secret photos of her? And what did she mean by a lot?

*Focus, Montoya!* This was not the time to be all gooey and crap. Julie needed her to be serious, not all gushy and lovey-dovey.

But damn how she wanted to be.

"Okay, that could be kind of a bad thing," Romy conceded, forcing her face back into a worried expression more suited to the discussion they were having. "How did Tyndall get access to your camera?"

"I was an idiot, that's how." Julie flopped backwards onto Romy's bed, hands over her eyes. "I was upset after our fight in Dean Prince's office. I just needed to figure out what I was feeling. So I started scrolling through the photos on my camera's memory card. I must have fallen asleep, so I didn't put my camera back in the bag as I usually do. When Tyndall knocked on my door, she woke me up." Julie sighed. "She came over right after she got done with the Dean. She was supposed to call first, to let me know that she was coming over so I could be ready, but she didn't. She was really upset."

"I bet. Mercury called and told me that the Dean called her parents. And that Tyndall got expelled."

Julie nodded her head, swallowing heavily. When she spoke again, her voice was thick with gathering tears once more. "Yeah, Tyndall told me about the Dean's judgment. And she was just so unhappy and scared and I felt so bad for her. I asked if I could do anything and she asked me for a soda. So I went to the lounge to get her something to drink and I…I left her alone in my room with my camera."

"Crap." Romy stared at Julie's face, waiting for her to continue, even though she already knew what happened.

"I never thought," she began, and the shattered look on her face made Romy's stomach plummet.

"Oh, no," Romy breathed, fingers wrapping tight around Julie's hand.

Shaking her head, Julie stared down at her hands. "While I was gone, she must have looked at my pictures. When I got back from downstairs, she just grabbed the drink and left. I thought it was because she was upset, but then I noticed that my camera was in a different spot from before and I didn't remember moving it."

Romy took several deep breaths in an effort to stay calm. When she thought she could speak without a waver in her voice, she said, "Okay, so she looked through some of the shots on your camera." Another bracing breath. "How much do you think she saw?"

She waited while Julie considered. "I don't know. But I'm pretty sure what she saw was enough."

Romy felt like she was standing on a small patch of ground surrounded by quicksand. One wrong step and she'd be dragged under. She didn't want to frighten Julie any more than she already was, but everything she could think to say wasn't exactly helpful. "What do you think she's going to do?" was all she could think to ask.

"She already did it," Julie said, voice dull, almost lifeless.

"What, Julie? What did she do?" Romy wanted to shake her, to get Julie to respond, but that wouldn't help. She counted backward from one hundred, focusing on keeping her breathing even and calm. Both of them having a panic attack or simultaneous nervous breakdowns wouldn't solve their problems.

It took Julie a few minutes to answer and when she did, her voice sounded very small and far away. "She must have taken pictures of what was on my camera with her phone. She sent them to my parents."

"Jesus take the wheel," Romy blurted out, then wrapped Julie in an enveloping hug. She could feel her tremble even beneath all of the blankets she'd piled on top of her to warm her up. Julie's arms wrapped around Romy's body, pulling her in tight to her body. Romy felt a weight—one she hadn't even realized she'd been carrying—suddenly fall away at Julie's touch. It was like a reconnection or a regeneration.

They were together. They would figure out the rest.

But now that Julie had started, it seemed like she couldn't stop the words that welled up and spilled from her lips. It was like speaking what happened out loud had broken down a wall that had been inside of her and she was in no hurry to build it back up again.

"My parents know." Julie's voice was strangely calm and quiet. Romy gripped her tighter. "Tyndall called them and told them about me." Her throat worked on a swallow. "About how I like girls."

She raised her eyes to stare into Romy's. "How I feel about you."

Romy was struck silent at the emotion in Julie's blue eyes. There was fear there, certainly, but beyond that there was warmth and kindness.

And love.

Romy felt like she'd been given an electric shock. Everything tingled: the roots of her hair, the pads of her fingers, the soles of her feet. The hair on her arms stood on end. Heat filled her—not the blazing flames of a California wildfire run amok, but rather the comforting hearth blaze in a stone fireplace, a sweet, even heat that chased away the chill that had held her heart in frozen claws earlier in the day.

"Julie, I…"

"I love you, Romy Montoya," Julie said, stampeding over what Romy was planning on saying. "And I'm terrified and worried and a thousand other things that if I think about too long I'm liable to freak out, but one thing that hasn't changed is the way I feel about you.

"I love you."

Romy's heart was going to burst from happiness, right there in her chest. It was going to burst and she was going to die, but it would be so worth it, just to have heard those words. Julie loved her. She loved her and she wasn't going to deny it.

"I don't expect you to say it back to me—that's not why I told you. I just needed to say it out loud, needed you to hear it, so you know…so you know how important you are to me. So you know that you're the piece I've been looking for, the only thing I think I've ever wanted in my entire life. I've found you and I'm afraid I'm going to have to let you go."

Romy clutched at Julie's shoulders beneath the heavy blanket. "You can let me go all you want," she told Julie, feeling the tightness in her chest that came from holding back tears for too long. "That doesn't mean I won't be holding on to you." She pressed her forehead to Julie's. "I love you too."

"God, Romy. What are we going to do?" Julie's voice quivered and broke on the last word.

Romy enfolded her girlfriend in another hug, a choked sob escaping her lips before she could stop it. What would this mean for Julie? For her? The Cranstons were conservatives and Julie had mentioned already that they weren't open to anything deviant—her words, not Julie's, not anymore.

"What did they say?" Romy asked softly, breath feathering Julie's hair.

"They're coming here. As soon as they can get a flight out in the morning." Julie sniffled, and Romy felt tears soaking the collar of her shirt. Julie's shoulders shuddered beneath her hands. "I've never heard my father so furious."

"We can talk to them, make them understand…" Romy started, but Julie's mirthless laugh stopped anything else. She took a deep breath and said in a low voice, "You could file for emancipation. Strike out on your own. I could help you."

"I couldn't do that," Julie told her, pulling the blanket tighter around her. "My sisters…they'd never speak to me again."

Helping with the adjustments, Romy whispered, "We could run away."

"Where would we go?" Julie asked. "The moon?"

"Where would you want to go?"

Julie closed her eyes, head heavy on Romy's shoulder. "Someplace warm," she said around a huge yawn. "I miss warm."

"We'll go to an island. Someplace where the sand looks like snow, the water is the same blue as the sky, and the horizon just stretches out endlessly in front of us. Fiji or someplace like that."

"I like that, it sounds nice," Julie murmured. Romy stroked her hair, gentle fingers weaving carefully through thick blond strands.

"Fiji it is," Romy said. She leaned back until they were both supine, head on her pillow and Julie a cocooned bundle of warmth beside her on the bed.

"I don't know what's going to happen."

Romy held her tighter, feeling Julie cling to her just as hard. Julie shuddered intermittently still, shivers ripping through her body and Romy wondered if Julie would just fly apart if not for Romy's arms around her. "It will be okay, Julie." Pressing her lips to the top of her girlfriend's head, Romy kept up a steady whisper of "It will be okay."

It had to be.

# CHAPTER THIRTY-ONE

Julie woke slowly to a pounding headache that always came from too much crying, and eyes glued shut from dried tears. She didn't move at first as she tried to understand why she was lying in a bed that wasn't hers. Romy's breathing was deep and even behind her, her arm resting across Julie's waist. Julie lifted a hand to rub the grit from her eyes, not wanting to wake up Romy. She basked in the quiet of the morning, the warmth of Romy's slim body next to hers, the weight of Romy's arm and the comforting presence of her molded against her back.

It felt right, like this was where Julie belonged.

Her thoughts drifted back to the phone call from her parents of the night before. Her father had been furious, her mother disappointed. Julie had thought about lying, about telling them that Tyndall had doctored the screen shots of Julie's blog in Photoshop as some kind of stupid joke, but then she'd decided against it. Her parents wouldn't have believed the lie anyway, and Julie wasn't going to lie about the girl she loved. Romy deserved better than that.

Julie deserved better than that.

But her parents weren't going to stop with late night phone calls. She expected them to be on the first plane out of the Kansas City airport so they could come corral her and set her back on the path of righteousness. They probably already had her registered at one of those camps. Julie tried not think about *that*.

Julie was jolted out of her thoughts by Romy's lazy yawn and her arms tightening their hold around Julie. "Good morning," Romy mumbled, still half-asleep.

Turning her head, Julie took in the sight of her girlfriend first thing in the morning. They'd fallen asleep fully clothed—well, Romy had been in her pajamas before Julie had shown up—and this was the first time they had spent the night together. It gave Julie a little thrill to wake up beside Romy, one more thing that just felt right.

Romy's short hair was a mess of flyaways and cowlicks that stood up in curlicues and commas. Her dark eyes were half-open, glaring at the sun through heavy lids, as if wanting to scold it for being up so early. The coppery skin of her face sported creases from the pillow's case.

She looked, in short, adorable.

"Morning," Julie replied softly, not wanting to break the spell that was the two of them wrapped around each other, limbs heavy and entwined like climbing ivy.

"Mmph." Romy made a noise, hand raised to cover her mouth. "Ugh, let me brush my teeth before I kill you with my morning breath." The words were muffled against the palm of her hand.

Julie pulled Romy's hand down and away from her face. "I don't care about your morning breath. I have it too." Romy's rose-colored lips quirked up in a smile, white teeth a flash almost as bright as the sunlight gleaming buttery yellow outside the window. "They cancel each other out."

"I can't imagine your morning breath being that bad. It probably smells like gumdrops and chocolate cake and rainbows." Romy lay back, fingers playing with the ends of Julie's blond hair.

"You make me sound like a Disney princess," Julie scoffed, poking Romy in the arm.

"If the baby birds that braid your hair fit...." Romy smiled widely, eyes crinkling at the corners.

"I am going to smother you with a pillow if you don't shut up," Julie warned.

"Okay, okay," Romy said, admitting defeat with raised hands. "No more references about your utter perfection as a human being."

"Smothering imminent in three...two...o—"

Julie was cut off from her countdown when Romy leaned up and kissed her. Julie startled for a moment before relaxing into the feeling of Romy's chapped lips on hers, the soft, delicious pressure of their mouths meeting, the silken caress of tongues, the clack of teeth. Usually Romy was the one to push things, but this time Julie was the one to deepen her kiss, it was Julie's hands that roamed over Romy's skin, it was Julie's desire to be as close as possible that pressed them chest to chest and hip to hip.

Romy pulled away after a few minutes. Her breathing was harsh, a series of pants, and her hands pressed at Julie's shoulders. "Dear God, girl, you are going to kill me," she muttered, hazel eyes meeting Julie's blue.

She pulled Julie back down for one last lazy kiss. "But what a way to go," Romy whispered into the shell of Julie's ear.

Julie grinned, snuggling against Romy, nose pressed against the skin of her neck as her head rested against her shoulder. "I could stay here like this all day," she said.

And she wanted to; she wanted to ignore the outside world and just lay wrapped in Romy's arms watching the world rot away around them. Hundreds of years in the future, some poor archeology student would dig up this residence hall and find their skeletons, still arm in arm, bones fused together like two parentheses, the hearts that beat for each other long ago consigned to dust. Someone would look down on their remains, finger bones slotted neatly together like locks and keys, and know that theirs had been a love beyond what even death could steal.

But she couldn't stay here, not today and certainly not forever. Julie might not know when they were coming, but her parents *were* coming. She wanted to be ready for the storm of arguments and recriminations that they would have ready. Julie knew that there was nothing she could do to prepare herself for the confrontation—it didn't matter that she knew every scripture verse her father would throw at her, using his Bible like a bludgeon. It didn't matter that she could describe the look of weathered disappointment down to the last detail and line that her mother would wear like armor. When she faced her parents with who she truly was, no preparation would be enough.

It didn't mean she wouldn't fight though.

"What do you want to do today?" Romy asked into the comfortable silence that buoyed them. She sounded hesitant, like she didn't want to upset Julie. It made her smile.

"A whole lot of nothing." Julie sighed and pushed herself up, leaning on one palm. She scratched at her hair, sure that it was a messy blonde cloud around her head. Well, she had never done the walk of shame before and she likely would never get the opportunity again. "But I know that's not actually possible."

Romy frowned, serious as she looked at Julie. "You can hide out here for the day. I can go grab us some breakfast and coffee and we can just spend the day lazing around and watching stupid YouTube cat videos. It'll be fun."

Julie didn't know when it had happened, but something had changed in her overnight. Whether it was for better or worse, she couldn't say, not yet anyway. As much as she'd like to hang out and do a whole lot of nothing with Romy, there was one thing she really needed to do.

"I need to talk to Tyndall."

Romy looked away, her jaw working to bite back words. But all she said was, "Okay."

"Are you sure you don't want me to come in with you?" Romy asked as they made their way across the quad back to Cap Hall. "I don't have to go to music theory."

Julie shook her head, the end of the hat she'd borrowed from Romy bobbing wildly. She was also in an extra coat of Romy's since she hadn't worn anything even close to weather-appropriate gear last night when she'd walked to see her. She still had her sneakers since none of Romy's snow boots fit her.

"No, you are going to class. I am not having the responsibility of you flunking out of music theory on my conscience."

Romy rolled her eyes. "You do realize I've been writing music since pretty much before I could crawl, right? It's highly doubtful I'm going to fail out of music theory over one missed class." Romy nudged her with her hip.

Smiling, Julie said, "I know, I get it. You're a prodigy. A musical super genius." She pursed her lips as Romy shot her an amused look. "But you still need to go to class."

"Don't wanna," Romy whined, giving Julie her best puppy eyes.

Julie sighed. "You really do not want to be anywhere near Tyndall right now," she told her girlfriend. "I don't even want to be anywhere near Tyndall right now, but I need to know why she did it." When Romy opened her mouth to protest, Julie held up a hand and said, "Seriously, Romy, it'll be better if it's just me."

Romy shut her mouth, but Julie could tell by the stern look she got that she wasn't going to let this drop. They walked on in silence. Julie took Romy's gloved hand in hers.

"You don't have to do this alone," Romy offered one last time as Cap Hall came into view. She pulled Julie a little closer into the shelter of her body.

"I know," she told her. "And that's what makes it awesome and less scary." Julie's face turned serious. "But I want to talk to Tyndall alone. There's a lot we have to say to each other."

Romy nodded, gaze slanting away from Julie to take in the residence hall in front of them. "Just…promise me you'll text me when you're done, okay? I want to know how it goes."

Julie nodded. "Sure thing." She shoved Romy's shoulder to get her moving. "Now hurry or you're going to be late."

"Can I kiss you?" Romy asked.

Julie's head snapped around on her neck, blue eyes wide and staring. "What did you just say?"

"Can." Romy leaned forward in increments to punctuate each word. "I. Kiss." She ended up very close—practically nose to nose—with Julie. "You."

Julie didn't move away, which she thought was a huge step forward for her. But she couldn't stop glancing around. Most everyone looked lost in their own struggle to get somewhere covered; the allure of snowball fights had ended after the first few feet of snow had fallen. Now everyone seemed to be focused on getting somewhere warm and dry.

"Here?" she couldn't help but ask.

Romy's sigh brushed across Julie's cheek. "Yes, here."

Julie hesitated. She wanted to, she really did, but it was so public…

Romy's snort of laughter brought Julie out of her thoughts. "Look, it was just going to be a chaste little peck. I wasn't planning on sticking my tongue down your throat or grabbing your ass in front of an audience. Despite what the gossip pages say, I am *not* into exhibitionism."

Julie stared into Romy's warm hazel eyes. They were so close she could almost count the golden flecks in them. Everyone always had plenty to say about beautiful blue eyes, but Julie didn't think she'd ever seen a pair of eyes as pretty as Romy's. They were warm like a fire, something comforting and lively, never still, always changing.

"Okay," Julie said, and closed the distance between them.

It was a quick kiss, a press of lips and little else. But Romy took Julie's hands in hers and held them as she leaned up to meet Julie.

Romy's lips were soft and tasted like mint from the lip balm she wore. Julie didn't mind the waxy taste. She thought she heard a few cheers, but she didn't care.

Romy pulled away after a moment with a crooked smile on her face. "Don't forget to text me when you're done." She turned away, only letting Julie's hands go when the distance between them became too much. Julie thought she saw a passerby snap a photo with her phone, but couldn't be sure.

"I won't forget," Julie told her. With a wave, she said, "Go be brilliant!" Then she turned and finished the walk to Cap Hall and Tyndall's room.

Tyndall lived on the third floor of the old red brick residence hall. She didn't have a single room like Julie did, but Tyndall may as well have—she had a tendency to make her roommate feel so uncomfortable that she spent as little time in the room as possible, thus making it feel like a single. Julie wondered how Tess—the mysterious roommate—felt about Tyndall's expulsion.

Julie took a deep breath as she approached the half-open door. Her anger and fear from last night had settled somewhat. She suspected this was just a reprieve, a lull in the mounting anxiety of her parents' eventual arrival. If she thought about it too much, Julie suspected she'd be terrified, so she was doing her best not to think about it.

She focused on Tyndall. On finding out why she had snooped in Julie's private photos. Focus on what was going on in Tyndall's admittedly labyrinthine mind. Distraction it may be, but it was important to get answers to her questions.

Julie heard the sounds of furniture being moved and the heavy breaths of effort as she approached the door. Knocking, she stuck her head in to find Tyndall wrestling with her desk, struggling to pull it out of its tight spot against the wall. She looked up with a sour expression at the knock.

Tyndall's expression only curdled more when she saw Julie in her doorway. "What do you want?" she practically snarled, going back to her assault on the desk.

Julie stepped inside. The room was a mess. Clothes were scattered everywhere, suitcases lay open like gaping mouths, waiting to be filled. Books were strewn about the room. Her bed was unmade, comforter half on and half off the bed.

She closed the door behind her. Tyndall may have outed her to her parents but that didn't mean Julie wanted the entire third floor knowing her business. "I came to ask you why you did it."

Tyndall grunted, not looking at Julie as she crawled beneath her desk to retrieve her power strip. "Did what?"

"Why'd you go through my camera?" Julie leaned one shoulder against the wall, arms crossed over her chest. She was still wearing Romy's coat and hat; she could have stopped by her room to change, but it had felt proper somehow, showing up in her girlfriend's clothes to confront Tyndall.

Tyndall crawled out from beneath the desk, power strip dangling from her hand and an expression of disgust on her face. Her eyes swept over Julie, taking in the Beaker hat she sported, the coat that wasn't hers, and yesterday's clothes.

"I don't know what you're talking about," she replied, so coolly ice wouldn't melt in her mouth.

Julie raised an eyebrow. Really? She was going to do this, just stand there and lie to her face? "Do you ever get tired of being the biggest hoofbag on the planet, Tyndall?" she asked, just as casually.

"That's good, coming from an abomination like you!" Tyndall snapped, squaring off.

Julie didn't want to fight with Tyndall, God knew, she really and truly did not. That didn't mean she wouldn't. The one thing the girl hadn't thought of was now that Julie's secret was out, what more did she have to lose? It wasn't as though Tyndall had anything left to hurt her with.

"You know, it's got to be completely exhausting," Julie began, taking a step away from her spot against the bedroom wall, "policing everybody else's morals so you don't have the energy to deal with your own crap."

"Nice language, Julie. Did you pick that up from your girlfriend?" Tyndall's eyes glittered with malice.

Julie snorted on a laugh. "I don't need Romy's help to call trash out, Tyndall." She cocked her head. "What *is* your problem? I've been wondering what made you so angry ever since I got here."

"I'm not the one who's a disgusting homosexual!"

Julie looked at Tyndall, standing in her room with fists clenched, cheeks flushed, hate spilling from her mouth and her eyes. Julie simply shook her head. She felt sorry for her, she truly did. It didn't excuse her hateful words or her hurtful behavior though. "I don't get it. I don't get *you*. Why did you send my personal photos to my parents? What did that get you? You're still expelled—you still have to go back to Texas and face your folks. So can you just tell me why you did it?"

"You have to ask why?" Tyndall shouted, incredulous that Julie had even asked her that question. "Are you blind? Or just an idiot?"

Julie blinked, taken by surprise at the anger in Tyndall's voice. She took a step backwards, brows drawing down in confusion. What was she talking about?

"I tried to help you. I saw how you were struggling with your sexuality. I knew God was testing you." Tyndall's green gaze swept over Julie, lip curled up in a sneer. "How many times did I ask—no, *beg*—you to come to Bible study. I wanted to help!"

Tyndall took a step closer, but Julie refused to back up any more. She wasn't going to let this person, this stranger, bully her like she'd bullied the freshmen around her. Julie wasn't one of her prayer group punching bags.

"But you didn't want my help. Instead, you spent your time with *her*, with that…"

"You really want to think about the next thing coming out of your mouth, Tyndall," Julie warned.

Tyndall stared at her stunned. "You're still defending her! She's done nothing but drag you away from your Lord. What are your parents supposed to do with someone like you?"

"They're supposed to *love* me. It's kind of what parents *do*." Julie felt her hold on her temper fraying. "And what happens between me and my parents is absolutely none of your concern! You had no right to invade my privacy like that!"

Tyndall practically screeched at her. Her face flushed an ugly red and tears stood in her eyes, making them glassy. She looked like she was going to pop out of her own skin. "And you had no right to throw my friendship over for that skank!"

Julie blinked, realization hitting her like a hammer to the back of the skull. Was Tyndall jealous? Was that what all this was about?

"Tyndall, you were my friend." She looked at the girl with a mix of pity and horror. "But I love Romy. And that was no one's business but mine. I am not a project for you to fix or another soul for you to save. If you were actually my friend you would have known that!" Fury bubbling up inside of her like water in a hot kettle.

"How could you choose her?" Tyndall whispered. She swallowed thickly. "I would have listened to you. We could have prayed together, asked God for help. You don't have to be this way."

Julie felt like her insides were boiling.

"This is who I am, Tyndall. I'm not doing anything to deliberately hurt my parents or anyone else. And even if I was, it is none of your business!"

"None of my business? You made it my business when you decided to take up with that whore's daughter!"

Julie's hand flew on its own. Her palm met Tyndall's cheek with a sharp crack. "You will not speak about Romy that way," Julie snarled.

She felt hot and icy by turns, her breath gusting out of her in harsh gasps like she'd just run a race. Tyndall stared at her as if she had grown horns and fangs and carried a pitchfork, her hand pressed to her reddening cheek. Julie was shocked at her actions, but not sorry for them. She would not listen to this person badmouth the person Julie loved.

Tyndall just continued to gape at her in horror, mouth half-open in shock. Julie knew this opportunity wouldn't last long, so she needed to take advantage of it—Tyndall at a loss for words was a rare thing indeed.

"Look, Tyndall, I'm sorry for whatever is going on with you. But you are out of control here. You were bullying people, lying about them, making their lives miserable. And however mad you are about what happened in the Dean's office—which *you* started by planting drugs in an innocent student's bag—you had no right to go through my camera and forward what you found to my parents." She swallowed, throat so tight it was hard to get words out. "I can forgive you, but I will never forget this."

Julie turned to leave, but stopped at the threshold to the door. Before opening it, she said, "I feel sorry for you."

She was halfway across the quad when the shakes hit her. She'd needed to walk, to relieve some of the anger from her confrontation with Tyndall. Julie stopped, afraid her knees were going to give out on her and send her sprawling to the snowy ground. Taking deep breaths of the frigid air, she gave herself a few minutes to calm down. Her heart was pumping so hard, she was afraid it might decide to escape from the confinement of her chest and burst forth like one of those gross little Alien things.

Keeping her breathing steady, Julie felt her heartbeat return to something approaching normal. The sweat on her back had dried for the most part, and she was beginning to feel the cold even through Romy's heavy jacket. Exhaustion rolled over her in a heavy wave and she swayed on her feet. While spending the night in Romy's room had been just this side of wonderful, Julie hadn't slept well, anxious dreams waking her throughout the night. Combined with the stress of the last twenty-four hours, Julie thought she could just curl up under a tree and sleep for a week.

And she still had to deal with her parents when they arrived.

Pulling out her phone as she walked back to Cap Hall, she sent a text to Romy.

**Heading back to my room to take a nap. Talk w/ Tyndall went about as well as expected. Love you. Come by when classes are done.**

She pocketed her phone, not expecting an answer since Romy was in class. It took all her remaining energy to walk up the stairs to her floor and drag herself down the hall to her room. Without even bothering to take off her sneakers, Julie fell onto her bed, already asleep before her head hit the pillow.

# CHAPTER THIRTY-TWO

Romy tapped her pen against her notebook absently, gaze trained on the snowy landscape outside the classroom's window. She really shouldn't have bothered coming to class today—she wasn't able to concentrate on anything other than Julie and the impending arrival of her parents. Romy was surprised at how calm Julie was, but she had a feeling it wasn't going to last for much longer.

Romy felt her phone vibrate in her pocket, and surreptitiously slid it out to check. Someone had tagged Romy and Julie in an Instagram post. With a quick glance at her teacher, she swiped the app and checked notifications. There it was—a mid-distance shot of her and Julie, holding each other's hands and smiling. It had been right after the kiss on the quad this morning. At least the amateur photographer hadn't tagged Julie's name to the picture. That was a small miracle.

But Romy had no doubt that this photo would be all over the gossip outlets by tomorrow morning—if it even took that long. And then their secret would be officially out of the bag. Romy felt like her stomach had suddenly turned to lead. It was not as big a deal to her—her mother may not be thrilled, but she'd accept it with relative ease—but Romy knew that Julie's parents would be a different story. Not that Tyndall hadn't already primed the pump by sharing Julie's private photographs…

Another buzz, this time indicating a message from Julie. Romy pressed two fingers to her lips, remembering the heat of Julie's mouth on hers. She read the text, a slow smile stretching across her face. Julie wanted her to come to her room after class. As much as they had to talk about, as much as Romy was worried about what could happen when Julie's parents arrived, she still felt hopeful. The worst was over—Julie's parents knew about her liking girls. The rest they could figure out as it came to them.

Putting her phone back in her pocket, Romy did her best to concentrate on what her teacher was telling her.

$$ \text{\textomega} \quad \text{\textomega} \quad \text{\textomega} $$

Romy practically flew to Julie's room, pausing once to check her messages. As she had suspected, the Instagram photo of her and Julie was being passed around and forwarded and commented on, and all other manner of things that Romy had been expecting. Julie's face was partially obscured by her hair, so there was some speculation already about who she was, but Romy knew that wouldn't last long. She supposed that it didn't matter much— Julie's parents already knew about them, thanks to Tyndall.

Before heading into the residence hall, Romy called her mother. Might as well warn her of what was coming. She was hoping just to leave a voicemail—cowardly as that was—but Monet surprised her by picking up after three rings.

"Hello, kiddo. What's going on?"

"Hi Mom," Romy began, biting at her lower lip. Now that her mother was on the phone, words deserted her. "I, uh, kind of need to tell you something."

There was a long pause. "Does this something have to do with you looking longingly into the eyes of one Julie Cranston?"

"You saw the picture."

"I saw the picture." She heard her mother take a deep breath and wondered just how upset she was. Monet had excellent control over her voice.

"Okay, so yeah, we've, um, been dating." When her mother didn't say anything, Romy went in a rush. "I know you didn't think it was a good idea to spend time with her and I know I told you that I'd be careful and I'm really sorry, but she's amazing, Mom, and I just—"

"Do her parents know?" Monet interrupted, cutting off Romy's babbling the way an executioner cut off heads.

Romy shifted from foot to foot. It wasn't like her mother could actually see her, and yet that tone made Romy feel like she was six years old again and had just gotten in trouble for breaking one of the crystal figurines Monet collected.

"Yeah, uh, now they do. A so-called friend just revenge-outed her." Romy found herself gazing up at Julie's window. "Her 'rents are on their way up here now."

"I thought you were smarter than this, Romy." Monet's voice was low, disappointed.

Romy's heart seized up in her chest. She'd never heard her mother sound like that before, never felt the sharp edge of her disapproval and disappointment. It throbbed inside of her, a wound that she couldn't see, but felt regardless. "We tried to keep it a secret," she whispered into the phone.

Monet sighed. "Things like this never stay secret. You *know* that. What did you think was going to happen when this all came out?"

Blinking back tears, Romy tried to answer, but no sound came out of her mouth. Swallowing, she began again. "We hadn't thought that far, I guess."

"Clearly." That one word held such censure that Romy cringed. "Look, I've got a plane to catch. I'll see you soon."

"Wait," Romy practically yelled before her mother could hang up. "You're coming here?"

"Of course I am," Monet said, voice even. "Try not to get in any more trouble until I arrive." She hung up.

Romy stared dully at her phone for a long moment, unable to reconcile the phone conversation with reality. Her mother was coming here. And so were the Cranstons.

She had to warn Julie.

Romy broke into a run, feeling like everything was spiraling out of her control. She hadn't thought everything would get this crazy, this fast. She pounded up the stairs, heart thudding dully in her chest and banged on Julie's door.

No answer.

"Julie!" Romy shouted, hoping that she was just passed out asleep and hadn't heard the knock. "Open up!"

The door across the hall opened up. Romy continued her assault on the door until she heard her name being called.

"What?" Romy snarled, whirling around.

The student standing behind her blanched. "Um," she began, clearly taken aback by Romy's ferocious response. "Some guy came and got her."

Frowning, she asked the girl, "What did he look like?"

"Maybe our age, a little older." She shrugged. "Julie didn't seem to want to go with him at first, but then he said something and she got her coat. They left, I don't know, ten minutes ago."

It was probably Ferris, as he was the only young man she could think of that Julie even knew up here. Julie's parents probably wanted her firmly in hand with someone they trusted before their plane even landed. Romy's stomach twisted at the thought of Julie with Ferris. "Did you hear what he said to her? Any of it?"

"I don't know. Something about a camp. Maybe?" The girl shook her head. "I don't know."

Romy froze, veins pumping ice to her heart. Camp. There was only one kind of camp that mattered when some parents found out their kid was gay. Conversion camp. And the Cranstons supported conversion camps. They probably already had one in mind.

Oh sweet Jesus. *No.*

She held a piece of paper out to Romy. "He said Julie wanted to give this to you."

Romy stared at the envelope for a moment before taking it out of the girl's hand. "Thanks," she said. "Sorry I snapped at you."

She just shrugged and returned to her room. Romy swallowed, gazing nervously at the letter. She was afraid to open it. She didn't want to know what it said.

What if it was goodbye? What was Romy supposed to do then?

With trembling fingers, Romy unfolded the small piece of paper. Taking a deep breath, she began to read Julie's frantic scrawl.

*Romy,*

*I love you. I'm sorry.*

*Julie*

Romy slid down the wall, resting her head on her knees. She didn't know what to do, how to help Julie. She had told Julie she'd never let her go, but how was she supposed to hang on when Julie was being yanked away from her?

She pounced on her phone as it buzzed, not even bothering to look at who it was. Fumbling it out of her pocket, she checked the notification with a desperate hope it was Julie—that somehow she'd managed to find a way to contact her. But it was Mercury, sending her a text.

**MH: On our way to Verona. Parents are meeting with the Dean to get me back in. See you at our room!**

Romy stared at the message, the inkling of a plan beginning to form in her brain. She pulled herself together as best she could and headed back to Tag Hall, typing a message to Mercury all the while.

**RM: Something horrible has happened. I need your help.**

# CHAPTER THIRTY-THREE

The car was cold. Or maybe it was Julie herself, huddled in the passenger seat of Ferris' car as he drove her to the hotel where her parents would meet her when they landed. They'd sent Ferris to collect her—she supposed they were worried that she'd run away and had sent him to keep an eye on her. Her chest felt carved of ice, her heart frozen in her chest. She couldn't feel her hands, or her feet inside of her boots. She felt like one of those ice sculptures that were always at her father's fundraising dinners.

Verona Prep disappeared behind her. Julie pressed her face against the icy glass of the window, straining her neck for one last look at it, at the place where she'd been happy. Tears burned in her eyes, making her blink rapidly. Her breath frosted the glass as she pressed her forehead against it, wondering when the pain would stop. Right now trying to breathe without Romy was nearly impossible—what would it be like to have her ripped out of her heart? Julie wondered if she'd die—it certainly felt like she was dying in the car that sped away from the girl she loved—or if she'd just get used to the ache and the absence, like a limb that's been amputated.

In medicine, the infection was cut out so the rest of the body could survive. She knew that her parents were trying to help her, trying to save her soul. They thought her love for Romy was like that: an infection. Trouble was, Julie didn't think that. She didn't want Romy cut away from her. And if it meant she'd die, well, Julie was beginning to think she could handle that.

A tear slipped down her cheek. With how cold she felt, Julie expected it to freeze halfway down her face. When it splashed on the back of her hand, she jerked in surprise. She pulled her knees up to her chest so she could wrap her arms around them.

"Get your shoes off the seat," Ferris said, watching her out of the corner of his eye. "You'll scuff the leather."

The ice inside her cracked and melted beneath the heat of her sudden anger. Julie thought of how Romy would respond and the flames inside of her body leapt higher. "Hey Ferris," Julie said, channeling her girlfriend for all she was worth, "go fuck yourself."

Ferris pursed his lips, wearing a disgusted expression. Julie choked out a bitter laugh. She'd never said the f-word before, but thought if ever she was going to drop it, now might as well be the time. Keeping her feet right where they were, she glared at him as he drove them along the dark highway.

"I suppose your gutter-trash girlfriend taught you such language," he said, risking a glance at her before returning his gaze to the road. "I wonder what else she taught you?"

The suggestion in his voice made her physically ill. "Don't you dare talk about her." Julie surprised herself with the snarl in her voice.

She heard Ferris sigh. Oh, was she being difficult? Too bad. She didn't care. Her parents couldn't even be *bothered* to pick her up themselves; they'd just sent their special little errand boy to collect her like she was a package and not a person, in the hope of avoiding a scandal.

"You're being ridiculous," he scoffed, easing off the gas as the road grew icy. "But your parents are sending you to a place that will get you sorted."

Biting down on her lip so hard she drew blood, Julie swallowed her squeak of fear. Her parents were sending her to a Christian reprogramming camp—the ones where they prayed the gay away, or worse. The idea terrified her. She'd kept who she was inside for so long, had been so afraid of what she was. She'd tried prayer and quiet meditation, she'd tried daily affirmations and reading the Bible, she'd tried ignoring what she wanted, she'd even sacrificed her happiness on the altar of "normal," and none of it had been able to change who she was and what she wanted.

She liked girls. She loved Romy. Now that she knew that, she didn't want to go back to hiding. She didn't want to be fixed.

She wasn't broken.

Julie's eyes flooded with tears, not of pain but of relief. She *wasn't* broken. The thought resonated inside her soul, a tuning fork striking true. It vibrated inside her, filling all of the jagged, empty spaces that Julie hadn't even realized were there. Finally, she felt whole. *She wasn't broken.*

She was gay. And there was nothing wrong with that, despite what her family thought.

"Stop the car," Julie said quietly. She knew she couldn't stay. She couldn't possibly go to the hotel to meet up with her parents.

"Are you kidding me?" He gaped at her. "No."

"I'm serious. Stop the car. I'll walk back." The click of her seatbelt releasing echoed like a shot through the quiet car.

"I'm taking to you to the hotel so you can wait for your parents, Julie. Now put your seatbelt back on." He turned his head, eyes flashing in the lights from a passing car.

"Stop the car, Ferris!" she screamed, slamming the side of her fist against the window.

"So you can run back to your Sorta-Rican slut?" He shook his head. "I don't think so."

Julie's heart beat a tribal rhythm in her chest as fear clutched at her with razor-sharp claws. "You're kidnapping me!" Sweat rolled down her back. Her legs trembled, her whole body bowing up with tension.

"Stop being so melodramatic. This is for your own good."

"The hell it is," Julie snarled, Romy's androgynous beauty flaring to life in her memories. The way Romy tilted her head to examine something she wanted to learn more about, how her dark hair hung over her forehead to get into her eyes. The way she nibbled on her thumbnail absently when working on math homework. She'd captured those habits and countless others in her photographs, in vivid color and in stark black and white. The way Romy squinted her eyes when she smiled at Julie—a special smile reserved only for her. That smile made Julie feel like she was being born again, fresh and clean with limitless potential in front of her. She'd die to see that smile one more time, to feel that way one more time.

Ferris was still talking, a litany of her sins. "You're just lucky your parents even want to deal with you after the crap you pulled. You're a Christian, Jules." Goodness, how she hated that nickname. "Being a homo is a choice. You were raised to know better. Was this some kind of crazy rebellious phase to see if your parents would forgive you? Some kind of cry for attention?"

This was it then. This is what her life was going to be like from now on. A constant reminder of all the ways she'd failed and betrayed her father and mother. It wouldn't matter what she did in future—how much she prayed, how sorry she was, how much penance and good works she performed. She'd sinned in the worst possible way in the eyes of her parents. She'd fallen from grace. Her love for Romy would hang over her head like the Sword of Damocles.

Was this what Lucifer felt like, when he fell? Was this what it was like to burn for eternity?

The empty pit in her stomach opened into a black chasm. Julie knew that she couldn't take years of it, this repudiation of who she was. She could barely stand five minutes of it.

While Ferris continued his screed on her behavior, Julie lunged to the side. She grabbed the steering wheel, her hands next to his. Ferris shouted. Julie yanked the wheel hard to the right. He struggled, shoving Julie away. She held on tightly, pulling on the wheel, forcing them over the side.

The car slid off the road. Ferris tried to brake, but the car hit a patch of ice, going into a spin. Julie saw his eyes go wide, and then there was nothing but the cold and the dark.

CHAPTER THIRTY-FOUR


Romy paced the common room of Tag Hall, an endless circuit of steps. *Julie was gone.* Another loop. *Julie was gone.* The words didn't make sense. They'd had so little time together. How could she be gone? This didn't happen in this time, in this country. This happened in old books and period costume dramas, not today.

She wanted to hurt something as badly as she hurt. Someone had pried open her ribs and rooted around inside of her until they'd found her heart and crushed it in their fist. The hurt left her breathless. It swamped her in waves, like a boat in a hurricane fighting against the next crest. Romy stalked her angry circle as a way to manage it. If she stopped, she thought she'd die. Like a shark swimming to keep breathing, she had to keep moving or she'd feel everything all at once and Romy didn't think she could handle it.

Julie. Her parents were going to put her in one of those conversion camps. Romy had heard the stories about those camps, about gay kids sent to them to be reprogrammed by aversion therapy, abuse, even electrical shocks. Vomit rose in the back of her throat. The thought of Julie at one of those places, the thought that her parents supported them, that they would willingly send their own daughter to one made her sick.

Romy ran to the wastebasket in the corner of the room, dropping to her knees in a slide. She stuck her head in the bucket and heaved out her lunch. Hot tears leaked down her face as she choked and coughed out her fear and impotent rage. She sobbed once, head hanging low over the trashcan.

"Here." A hand holding a tissue appeared in her periphery.

Romy took it and wiped her nose and mouth. When she felt like she wasn't going to hurl anymore, she glanced up at her roommate. "Thanks. Merc."

Mercury shrugged, then knelt at Romy's side. Romy felt her roommate's gentle hand on her back, rubbing small, slow circles between her shoulder blades. "You gonna be okay?"

Romy closed her eyes as more tears threatened. Tears were useless. They didn't solve anything. What she needed now was a plan. She shook her head, letting out a croaked, "No."

Mercury forced Romy to her feet, then over to one of the overstuffed couches. She pushed Romy down. When she tried to stand up, Mercury glared at her. Romy slumped back, exhausted, and watched as her roommate walked to the vending machines and got two sodas. She came back and handed Romy the Diet Coke.

"You know I don't drink this shit," Romy said, as she took the can from her friend.

"Shut up and drink it. You need it." Mercury cracked open her own can and took a swig.

"You know, contrary to your belief, Diet Coke does not actually fix everything." But Romy opened up her own can just as Mercury told her.

Mercury swallowed, then turned her head so she could survey Romy through her dark curls. "Duh. But it gives you something to focus on, which you totally needed. You were pretty scary there, Romes."

Romy ducked her head. "How long were you watching?"

"Long enough."

Romy closed her eyes, holding the cool can to her temple. "I don't know what to do, Merc. They're going to destroy her." Her nose clogged with the tears she refused to shed. Her throat hurt from holding back her screams so she could talk in a normal voice.

Mercury opened her mouth to say something but Romy flinched before she could. "Please don't tell me I'm being overdramatic or that it might not be that bad, Merc. Not now."

Her friend reached out and put her hand on Romy's knee, giving it an encouraging squeeze. Romy heard her take a deep breath. "Okay." Romy took a sip of the Diet Coke. It tasted terrible, but she kept drinking it because she didn't want her roommate yelling at her. Mercury asked, "So, what do we do?"

Romy startled, giving her friend the side-eye. "What do you mean, what do we do? Ferris is probably taking Julie to her parents' hotel room right now. Not much I can do."

Mercury stuck out her lips in a disbelieving pout. "What, you're just giving up on her? Is this the same person who figured out a way to prove Tyndall was a lying, racist asshat to get me back into Verona even when everyone said it wasn't worth it, including me?" She took a swallow of her soda and nudged Romy's side. "And second, I didn't say you. I said we. Pay attention."

Romy nearly choked on her Diet Coke. "Mercury, I—"

"You love her, don't you?" Mercury wore an expression on her dark face almost as serious as the day she'd been thrown out of Verona Prep.

"Like I love the sun." Romy swallowed thickly, feeling the heat of tears gather once more in her eyes. "Like life itself."

Mercury nodded. "Right." She smiled hugely. "So let's figure out how to get your girl back."

♪ ♪ ♪

Romy stamped her booted feet on the steps of Tag Hall, trying to keep warm. She could have just waited for the Uber driver inside where it was warm, but Romy felt the walls closing in around her. She needed space, to feel like she was doing something more than just sitting and waiting. At least out here she was standing and waiting.

Romy thumbed through her phone while she waited for Mercury to grab her coat and join her. The best plan they'd come up with was to head to the hotel where Julie's parents were staying and try to get in and talk to Julie. Romy wasn't sure what she could do yet—they didn't teach Mission Impossible infiltration stuff at Verona—but at least it was something.

Her phone jangled at her; a text message just came through. Romy exited out of her game and pulled up her texts. There were a few from Roz that she hadn't answered yet and a new one from a number she didn't recognize. Romy eyed it warily for a moment. She guarded her number zealously, so she rarely got unknown number texts. Reluctantly, she opened it.

**It's Gabrielle**.

Romy stared at the screen for a second, brain working slowly. Then it clicked. Gabrielle from the group project. They hadn't been in touch much since their lit project ended. Why would she be texting Romy now?

**There's a girl on my floor who volunteers at the hospital.**

Okay, good for her. What did this have to do with anything?

**There's been a car accident. A bad one.**

Romy heard a roaring in her ears. Her hands went numb. The beeping of the text notifications echoed relentlessly in her head. Her brain only processed one word: No.

**Julie was in the car.**

Romy didn't hear her phone clatter to the ground. She didn't realize she'd climbed the stairs to the building or crashed through the front door of Tag Hall. She didn't even realize she was screaming until she heard her own voice shouting, "Mercury! We need to go! Now!"

♪ ♪ ♪

The hospital parking lot was a mess of slush and cars and lights. Romy chewed on her thumbnail as their Uber driver navigated them over to a safe section of sidewalk to let her and Mercury out. Romy took off toward the main entrance as soon as her boots hit the snow. She heard Mercury cursing and sliding behind her.

Passing through the automatic doors, Romy slowed, looking around. There was an information desk just inside. Pulling her hat down lower over her hair, Romy walked over, trying to calm her breathing. She needed to keep it together, at least until she knew Julie was okay.

"I'm here to see Julie Cranston, please," she said, hoping that the Cranstons hadn't arrived yet. Romy knew that if they were already here, she'd have no hope of seeing Julie again.

"Let me see if she's in a room yet." The woman tapped at her keyboard. "She's in 439. But she's not allowed visitors."

Romy opened her mouth to protest, but Mercury stepped in smoothly. "We understand. We're friends of hers from school. Is there a waiting room on that floor so we can have the nurse give us updates and so we can wait for her parents?"

The woman smiled benignly. "Of course, dear." She pointed down the hall. "Take the elevator to the fourth floor. There's a small waiting area right across from the nurses' station. You can go up there."

Mercury shot Romy a smug look. "Thank you so much, ma'am. Have a good night."

"You too, girls."

"Oh," Romy blurted, remembering the other occupant in the car. "I think there was someone else in the car with Julie. Is he okay?"

"I'm afraid I can't release details to non-family members."

Romy swallowed. That didn't sound good. "Okay, thanks."

When they stood before the elevator, waiting for the doors to open, Mercury said, "See what honey gets you? Politeness works."

Sticking her hands deep in the pockets of her jacket to keep from fidgeting, Romy answered drily, "I stand in awe of your prowess. Teach me the ways of your people, sensei."

Mercury nudged her into the elevator with her elbow. Romy entered and hit the button for the fourth floor. The doors closed and suddenly the space was too close, too warm. She yanked her hat off, feeling like she was going to pass out from the sudden overwhelming heat and closeness of the compartment. What was wrong with her? She'd never been claustrophobic before.

"Take it easy, Romes," Mercury said softly, setting a gentle hand on her shoulder. Romy flinched but didn't move away, suddenly aware of the rasping breaths that sawed in and out of her. Was this a panic attack? Was this what Julie felt like when her parents had found out about them?

Nodding to show she heard, Romy fought to bring herself under control. Mercury kept up a steady stream of blather, all of it meaningless words but helpful nonetheless. She closed her eyes and centered herself, pulling herself together and winding the ends tight. She needed to keep it together for a little while longer. When the doors finally opened on the correct floor, Romy was back in control of herself.

"439," she murmured, stalking out of the elevator. She'd learned long ago that if you acted as though you belonged somewhere most people would go along with it. She didn't hesitate getting off the elevator and she didn't look around for directions. She didn't stop at the nurses' station, just walked right by as if she'd been there a thousand times before and knew exactly where she was going. Mercury peeled off at the waiting area while Romy continued without her.

Without a backward glance, she slipped into the half open door of room 439. And froze.

Pastor Laurence sat in the chair beside Julie's hospital bed, holding her pale hand.

# CHAPTER THIRTY-FIVE

"Pastor Laurence?" Romy whispered, closing the door softly. "What are you doing here?"

The man looked up with a tired smile. "Hello, Romy." The room was dimly lit and warm. The faint scent of antiseptic pervaded everything. There was the soft thrum of the mechanics of the bed and the hushed sounds from out in the hall, but otherwise the room was eerily silent. No beeping. No buzzing. Nothing like what she was used to in movies. Romy didn't know whether to be worried or relieved.

Romy's breath locked up in her lungs. Julie lay on the bed, pale and still as an icy pond. Her golden lashes rested against her skin, the only color on her face, except for the bruising on her temple and forehead. Even her lips looked bloodless. Romy's hand flew to her mouth, too slow to stifle the strangled moan that slipped out.

"She'll be okay, Romy," Pastor Laurence said, rising to his feet and walking over to her. "She's got a broken ankle and a concussion. They'll probably keep her a night or two for observation." He winked. "I overheard the nurses talking when they brought her up."

"How did you get here so fast?" she asked, gaze glued to Julie. She took a step forward and then stopped, suddenly unsure. What if Julie didn't want her here?

Pastor Laurence pushed her closer, ushering her to his abandoned chair beside the bed. "I sit with patients, read to them, minister to them—whatever they need. When Julie was brought in I thought it would be a good idea to sit with her in case she woke up. I didn't want her to find herself in a strange room all alone."

Romy stumbled into the seat, ripping her eyes away from Julie long enough to stare into the pastor's lined and tired face. "Maybe I shouldn't…" she began.

"She'll want you here when she wakes up," he soothed. "Trust me."

Nodding, Romy lowered her gaze back to Julie's face. Carefully she reached out to take the hand that sat so still on the cover, the hand without the IV line. Cradling it in both of her hands, Romy let out a choked sob, all the worry of the past few hours crashing over her. She trembled, her body shaking like a tree in a wind storm. Pressing her lips to Julie's cool hand, Romy closed her eyes against the warmth of her tears. "I'm here, Julie. I'm right here."

She didn't know how long she stayed bent over, elbows planted on the mattress beside Julie's body, clutching her hand. All Romy could do was mouth silent pleas, bargains, and threats to whatever might be listening. For the first time in her life, Romy wished her mother had taken her to a real church so she didn't feel like such a fraud praying to God. Eventually, the stress of the day wore her down and she dozed.

"R-romy?"

Romy's head snapped up, eyes popping open blearily. "Julie?" Blue eyes blinked dazedly up at her. "Julie! Oh thank God, you're awake." Romy leaned over and gently brushed the blond hair from her forehead and pressed a gentle kiss there.

Julie raised her free hand, then stopped when she saw the IV tube running from the top of her hand. "Wha-what happened?"

"You were in a car accident," Pastor Laurence supplied from his spot near the door.

Julie's eyes went wide. Romy felt the shudder that ran through her and wrapped the girl in her arms. "It's okay. You're okay," she told her.

"I remember grabbing the wheel and yanking it away from Ferris," Julie whispered, another shiver tearing through her. "The car ran off the road."

"You grabbed the wheel?" Pastor Laurence asked, stepping closer. "Why would you do something like that?"

Romy gave Julie's shoulder a careful squeeze. Julie exhaled shakily, blue eyes wet with sudden tears. "My parents—they found out about," here she glanced at Romy. She gave Julie a bracing smile and squeezed her good hand even as her heart split in two. Pastor Laurence nodded once. "They're sending me to one of those pray-the-gay-away camps."

"Conversion?" he asked, an unreadable look on his face.

Julie nodded, wincing when it hurt her head. "Ferris came to get me." She looked up, a haunted expression on her face. "Is he okay?"

"He's in surgery, but he'll be fine," Pastor Laurence told her.

Julie wilted in relief, subsiding back into the pillows. "Thank God," she whispered.

Romy leaned in, desperate to be close to Julie, and murmured, "I'm not going to let them take you."

"You may not have a choice," Pastor Laurence told her.

Julie gasped as Romy's grip tightened convulsively. Romy released the injured girl, afraid her unconscious reactions would cause her more pain. She shifted on the bed so she could face the pastor. "They take her over my dead body." She felt her phone vibrate in her jacket pocket but ignored it. "She's gay, not mentally ill or sick. It's not something that can be changed—it's not something that *needs* to be changed. What they're going to put her through is torture."

His expression turned sad, then thoughtful. "They're her parents, Romy. And Julie is still seventeen."

"I'll be eighteen in less than two months," Julie spoke up, but her voice sounded tentative and frightened. Romy wanted to scream with frustration. How could nobody understand?

"Julie," Pastor Laurence said, spearing her with an intense gaze, "is this what you want?"

Romy heard footsteps coming down the hall—a good number of them. She turned to Julie, catching the terrified look in her eyes. She grabbed her hand.

"I want to be with Romy," Julie said firmly, fear melting away into determination. "I'm gay. I don't want to go to a camp that tells me I shouldn't be who I am. That who I am is wrong. I deserve to be happy being who I am."

Romy felt Julie tighten her grip on her hand, and she leaned down to kiss her cheek. "I love you," she whispered.

The door flew open. Julie jerked in Romy's arms, face going paler—something that Romy hadn't thought possible.

"What are *you* doing in here?" the woman who must be Julie's mother exclaimed. Loudly.

"Get away from my daughter!" Julie's father yelled, his face flushing crimson.

"Go, Romy," Julie whispered to her, clutching her hand once more before letting go.

"I told you, I'm not leaving you," Romy told her, trying to grab Julie's hand again. Julie had hidden it under the covers, damn it.

"It will just be worse if you stay," Julie said, looking deep into Romy's eyes. "Please. I don't want them to say horrible things to you."

"But it's okay if they say them to you?"

"They love me," Julie insisted. "I can make them listen." But Romy didn't see any glimmer of hope in her eyes. "But not with you here."

Romy ground her teeth together. Julie was trying to protect *her*, which was lovable but ridiculous. Romy wasn't the one in a hospital bed with a concussion. Romy wasn't the one about to get shipped off to a place she didn't want to go. She wanted to stay at Julie's side, help fight for her. But Julie wanted her to go. Romy didn't know what she should do.

The choice was taken from her. One of the men who came in with Julie's parents grabbed her upper arm just above the elbow and yanked her off the bed. "You need to leave," he said, forcibly dragging her away from Julie at a hand signal from Mr. Cranston.

"Let go of me!" Romy snarled, struggling to free herself. She saw Pastor Laurence talking calmly with Julie's mother while Julie pleaded with her father. Then Cranston's security guard shoved her at the door, and into the approaching nurse.

The nurse staggered a bit, then recovered with an angry look on her face. She was a plush woman with dark skin and hair, her eyes bright with surprise. "That's enough of this noise!" she snapped, getting everyone's attention. She wheeled in her diagnostic cart, the instruments rattling angrily in her stead. "Everyone out!"

"We're her parents," Julie's mother began, only to be cut off by the nurse.

"I don't care if you are the Queen of England, lady, if you're upsetting my patient or preventing me from doing my job, you can wait outside. Now move!"

Romy scuttled out, turning her head for one last look at Julie. She'd sagged back in bed, wearing an expression of relief.

"I'd like to post a bodyguard outside the room to make sure no one who shouldn't be here gets in," Julie's father told the nurse as he walked past. Romy paused just outside the door to listen.

The nurse shook her head emphatically. "No sir. Not going to happen."

Cranston blustered, clearly surprised by her answer. "It's for her protection."

"If that's the case, then you need to file the appropriate paperwork with the police and they will handle security," she said briskly, busying herself with latex gloves. "Otherwise, you are endangering the safety, care, and privacy of other patients on this floor. Nobody—I don't care who they are—is allowed to do that on my floor."

Romy wanted to cheer. She made a note to have her mother buy this woman her own private island. She deserved it for taking care of Julie.

"Now out. All of you. Julie's parents can come back in when I'm finished, but that's all. The rest of you can wait in the lobby waiting room." She turned to Pastor Laurence. "Thanks, Peter, for staying with her."

"I'll pray for you, Julie," he said as he left, nodding to the nurse.

Romy hurried away before she could run afoul of the Cranstons. She didn't feel up for a shouting match and she knew that if she did try to talk to them they'd likely take their anger out on Julie and that was the last thing Romy wanted. She grabbed Mercury and headed for the bank of elevators.

"I texted you—did you not get it?" her roommate asked as they waited in charged silence.

Romy flinched. She wasn't ready to talk. She felt raw in places that shouldn't be that way. Like she was one exposed wire, arcing and sparking, in danger of electrocuting anyone who touched her. She tried to pull the broken parts of herself together. "I did, but didn't get a chance to look at it."

"Was it bad?" Mercury turned mournful eyes to Romy.

She sighed, shoulders slumping in defeat. She was at a loss for how to help Julie. How to help herself. "They're going to send her away, I know it, and there is literally nothing I can do about it."

Mercury pulled her in for a hug, wrapping her arms around Romy tightly. Romy leaned into the embrace, grateful for the support. What she wouldn't give to have her mom here right now. Her mom gave the best hugs.

The doors opened. Mercury and Romy stepped inside. Merc kept her arm around Romy's shoulders, shoring her up. It felt like a long way back down to the main hospital waiting room. When the doors opened, Romy stepped out and stretched. "I think I'm just going to get a bit of air. To clear my head."

Nodding, Mercury pulled a bankcard from her pocket. "Sure thing. I can go grab us some coffee or something."

Romy shared a smile with her, a genuine one, what felt like the first of the night. "Thanks, Merc. You're the bestest roommate ever."

"I expect cookies. And a commemorative plaque."

"Duly noted." Romy gave her roommate another tired smile before separating to walk to the front of the hospital's main entrance. She stared at her feet, noting how ragged the laces of her boots had gotten, barely noticing the automatic doors opening to spit her out under the patient pick-up and drop-off overhang.

Camera flashes. Lights. News cameras. People shouting her name.

Romy staggered beneath the onslaught of sight and sound. She stared, dazed and bewildered as reporters shouted questions in her face.

"Were you in the car with Julie Cranston and Ferris McConnell, Romy?"

"Are you a friend of Julie's?"

"What about the picture of you and Julie?"

"Are you dating Miss Cranston?"

"Are you dating Mr. McConnell?"

"Were you admitted to the hospital?"

All of the questions bled together into a cacophony that threatened to scramble what remained of Romy's brain. Where had all these reporters come from? How did they even know she was here? Then she realized that word must have leaked about Julie's car accident. They were here for her and her parents, desperate to get a story. If Romy had just stayed inside, they never would have seen her. She cursed her distraction that had given the newshounds a story no one wanted.

"No comment," came a deep voice to her right and then she was shepherded gently back through the doors of the hospital by Pastor Laurence.

Ushering her inside, he led her to a small chapel out of the way from prying eyes. He settled her in a pew before crouching in front of her in the narrow space between the pews. They were alone. Unless you counted God, which Romy didn't.

She wiped at her wet eyes, only half-aware that she'd started crying at some point. She wished she could rewind the day, stop time and unspool it all over again, only this time weaving the threads of events properly, so that she and Julie could be together. So that her parents never found out.

"Romy." Pastor Laurence had his hands on her shoulders. He shook her, gently. "Romy!"

She shoved him away, unable to stand anyone touching her. "Yeah, yeah. I hear you." Her voice was a sullen croak.

"I have an idea for how to help Julie," he murmured.

Her head snapped up, like a dog hearing her master's footsteps on the other side of the door. "What?" she breathed, barely daring to hope.

"I haven't worked it all out but I think there's a way to get her out of the hospital. Do you trust me?"

Romy looked at him, really looked at him. He was craggy and careworn, but his eyes were kind. She remembered the first time she'd met him, when Julie had introduced them. Romy hadn't thought much about it at the time, too newly in love to focus on anything else, but now she thought she saw what it was that drew Julie to this man, and why she trusted him.

If Julie could bring herself to trust him, could Romy do any less?

She nodded. "What do you need me to do?" The exhaustion and hopelessness that dogged her steps just a few minutes ago vanished like morning fog.

He pressed a key into her hand. "Wait for me at the chapel at Verona. You remember where it is?" At her nod, he continued. "That key will let you inside. I'll bring Julie to you."

"Is it safe for her to be out of the hospital?" Romy asked, folding her fingers around the key. She felt the teeth bite into her skin and clenched her fist around it. The pain grounded her.

"No less safe than her staying here," he countered. "Are you serious about this, Romy? Because this is Julie's life we're talking about. This isn't a game. She's still a minor. *You're* still a minor. Her parents are going to fight you for her."

Romy shook her head. "They aren't fighting me for her," she corrected. She didn't own Julie; she didn't want to. Julie was hers, but only so much as she was Julie's. You couldn't own someone's heart anyway—you could only borrow it for a while. If you were lucky, that while turned into forever. "They're fighting *her* for her."

"Then get ready because you've both got a big one coming."

Romy grinned wolfishly, the beginnings of an idea taking shape in her mind. She reached for her cell phone. "That's fine," she answered. "I never liked fighting fair anyway."

# CHAPTER THIRTY-SIX

Julie passed a hand over her eyes as the nurse finally managed to get her mom and dad to leave the room without using a crowbar.

"Thank you," she managed after a moment.

The nurse gave her a broad smile, sympathy shining in her warm brown eyes. "I'm Rhonda and I'm the night nurse. Brigit will be coming on in the morning to replace me, but I'm here until six a.m. Now, how are you feeling?"

Julie answered the questions about her pain, about who the president was, and what year it was; she let Rhonda take her vitals, and accepted her help getting more comfortable. Her ankle throbbed every time she moved, so she tried to keep still as much as she could.

"Was that your girlfriend?" Rhonda asked as she unhooked the blood pressure cuff.

Julie felt the shy smile curve her lips. "Yes."

"She's cute." Rhonda winked at her.

"I think so." She grinned back.

"I'm guessing your folks aren't too happy about her." The nurse tucked everything back in her cart before typing a note in the computer.

Julie's smiled faded. "I think that's an understatement." If she hadn't been so fuzzy headed from the accident, she'd be a lot more frightened, but right now it was just one more thing piled on top of a day full of them.

Rhonda patted her arm gently. "They'll come around."

Choking on a laugh too bitter for her years, Julie answered, "You don't know my parents."

"But I know *parents*." Rhonda moved the table with the water pitcher and cup closer to Julie. "I've seen them hold their babies as they come out of the womb addicted to drugs, I've seen them hug their kids during chemo, I've watched them say goodbye to their children because of disease and accidents and violence. You're alive, hon. It may take them some time, but they'll come to realize how lucky they are."

Julie leaned her head back on the pillow, staring up at the ceiling, brain foggy. Maybe Rhonda was right, but it didn't help her right now. Her parents had seen Romy with her. They weren't going to be reasonable about that any time soon. In their church being gay was a sin, was unnatural. And now, so was Julie.

"Should I let them in now or do you need a few minutes?" Rhonda asked.

Sighing, Julie braced herself. She wished she had a few more minutes. Who was she kidding? She wished she had a few more years. But that wasn't possible, not after Tyndall and everything that had happened since. "You can let them in." It wasn't like things were going to get any better if she waited.

"Hit the call button," here Rhonda put the phone receiver looking device next to her hand, "if you need anything. I'll be back in to check on you shortly, okay?"

Julie nodded, not trusting herself to speak. Tears waited. She'd held them back so far, but Julie wasn't sure how long that would last. She didn't want to cry in front of her parents.

Rhonda opened the door for Julie's mother and father who were crowded outside in the hall, and Julie tried not to feel like a Christian getting ready to face the lions of the Coliseum.

It was past eleven, but Julie couldn't relax. Her whole body was one giant knot of tension. Her muscles ached with the strain of staying still, of keeping quiet. The entire time her parents railed at her, she felt like a rabbit frozen before a diving owl. Julie hadn't been able to get a word in as her parents informed her of their disappointment in her and their plans to correct her behavior. Her mother cried, big fat salty drops that smudged her perfect makeup. Her father held himself stiffly apart, barely contributing anything but monosyllables. His disapproval was palpable. Clearly, he didn't want to be in the same room with her. Eventually, he turned around to face the windows and told her mother to deal with her.

Julie felt like another item on his docket that he didn't want to waste precious time on. It hurt but it wasn't exactly surprising.

"I knew sending you here was a bad idea!" Her mother threw her hands up in frustration. "An all-girls private school. What were we thinking?!"

Julie stared at her mother in astonishment. "Wait, you knew I was gay?"

"Of course we didn't!" her mother snapped. "But these all-girls schools are hotbeds for experimentation. Your father and I should have known you wouldn't be able to resist the temptation to act on your sinful urges, that you aren't strong enough. You couldn't help yourself—without someone to watch over you, it was bound to happen. And that…girl—"

"Romy." Julie spoke through gritted teeth, jaw tight and aching around all the words she wanted to say. "Her name is Romy."

"Oh, it doesn't matter what her name is! She's the daughter of that godless woman!"

"They're not godless—they both attend the Enlightenment Center. I think they're Buddhist." Once the words were out of her mouth, Julie realized how ridiculous they sounded. She blamed the medication.

"Oh please, that's no better than a cult, Julie. They may as well be Scientologists! Or Catholics!" Her mother lowered her voice with effort, straightening her blouse with a jerk of her hand. "Clearly she took advantage of your weakness, clouding your mind, your judgment, your morals—your upbringing!"

"Romy didn't do any of that!" Julie snapped, frustrated beyond her ability to stay quiet in the face of her mother's anger. "She's not to blame for any of this! It was me—I was the one who wanted to be with her. Me!" Julie paused for breath, lungs heaving as if she'd just run a sprint in gym class. "And if you knew it was such a bad idea to send me here, then why did you? I never asked to come here—it wasn't my idea. That decision is all on you and Dad!"

Julie watched her mother's eyes open wide with shock. She'd never talked back to her parents, never raised her voice to them. It wasn't *done*. Good girls didn't get angry, they didn't backtalk their folks and they certainly didn't argue in raised voices. They were respectful, accepted what they were told, and said please and thank you. Julie was sick of being that narrow definition of what a *good girl* was. At Verona Prep, she'd seen a lot of variation on the good girl theme and *all* of them were valid. She realized she'd seen it at her school in Kansas too, but she hadn't recognized it until she'd gotten space away from her parents' narrow definition of what good meant.

"We trusted you'd be able to control yourself," her mother snipped, fury overwhelming the shock in her eyes. "If not for your own future then at least for your father's! You knew what was at stake and you willfully chose to ignore it, instead throwing yourself at the daughter of that tart!"

Julie reeled back at the venom in her mother's words. Of course, it was all about her father and *his* future, nothing about hers. Julie felt alternately hollowed out and filled with rage. Rage won.

"I didn't choose it!" Julie yelled her mother, the words nearly strangling to death in her throat. "Do you really think I'd choose to be gay knowing how you all feel about it? I *am* gay—I was born this way! And whether you like it or not, I love Romy!

"God knows, I fought against who I am, and I've tried not to be this way. I tried to stay away from Romy, I tried praying, I tried to be who you wanted me to be. And I can't do it! Romy means everything to me—can't you understand that? Did you ever, even just once, feel like that? For Dad? Because it feels like I can't breathe, like I'll never be whole again if I'm not with her! Why is it so hard for you and Dad to understand that?"

Her mother slapped her. Hard, right across the cheek. Julie's hand flew up to her face, mouth pressed in a thin line with shock. Her mother had *slapped* her. In all of her seventeen years, her mother had never laid a hand on her in anger. Her mom looked like she had surprised herself, staring down at her shaking hand with a shocked expression on her face.

Then her eyes hardened, like cut gemstones. "You will not speak like that to me, young lady!"

Julie looked into her mother's eyes and saw tears glistening there. She didn't know if they were tears of anger, regret, sadness that she had a gay daughter, or if it was because something that she'd said got through to her. "Mama," she whispered. "I didn't do any of this to make you and Daddy unhappy."

Her mother's face softened for a moment, giving Julie a glimpse of the mother she knew, the mother of kissed boo-boos, of homemade chocolate chip cookies, of bagged lunches and afternoons spent riding horses on the trails near her house. The mother before the conservative suits and bobbed haircuts, the mother who didn't mind dirty kids running through the house to run and splash in the sprinklers outside.

Her father put his hand on her arm, and Julie saw her mother blink. A shutter closed over the window of her eyes, and that old mother was gone, lost beneath the successful politician's wife veneer that had usurped her. Biting her lip to keep from crying at the loss, Julie stared at her hands, waiting for whatever came next.

"I'll be keeping your phone and your clothes in case that…girl…" she said, her lip curling, "tries to get in contact with you. You are forbidden from having any contact with her from this moment on, Julie."

"Mom—"

"You've given us no choice, Julie. I'm not going to have my daughter's soul in hell just because of a bad choice she made back in high school!"

While her mother excoriated her, Julie hung her head, doing her best to hold back her tears. Only Rhonda stopping in on her rounds deterred her parents from continuing.

Her mom and dad had finally left the hospital to check into their hotel. Again her father had wanted to post one of his security people outside of her door, and the floor nurses once again shut him down. It wasn't as though Julie could really go anywhere anyway, not with her ankle. Not unless she invented a set of jetpack powered crutches.

She should probably look into that. She had the time.

Slowly, Julie unclenched her fingers from their stranglehold on the blanket. The bones ached with cold. She flexed her hands and tried to rub away the chill. She'd gotten a reprieve from conversion camp, but only until her ankle healed. As soon as she was released from the hospital, she'd be on a plane home to Kansas for recovery.

She would not be allowed to see Romy again.

Julie curled up as much as her tubes and ankle allowed and prayed. She hadn't wanted any of this to happen. She hadn't come to Verona to fall in love with Romy. But she had and she didn't want to give that up. But now she couldn't see a way to stop anything.

Julie prayed.

And Pastor Laurence opened her door. In his arms he had a blanket and what looked like a coat and…were those winter boots?

"What are you doing?" Julie asked, struggling to sit up straighter. Her heart beat faster in her chest. Her ankle throbbed in time to it, but she ignored it.

"Do you want to get out of here?" he whispered, closing the door quietly behind him.

"Yes."

"Do you want to see Romy?"

She nodded desperately. "Yes!"

He dumped his armful of outerwear in the chair by her bed and set about taking out her IV. Julie held still until he was done, Band-Aid firmly attached to the back of her hand before struggling into the bulky coat he handed her. It came down to her calves. She managed to get on one of the boots, but the other wouldn't fit over her cast.

"You could get in trouble for this, for helping me," Julie managed to whisper as she struggled with shaking hands to put on the knit hat.

"I'll worry about that," he said. "Right now, you're checking yourself out of the hospital—against your doctor's wishes—and we're getting you someplace safe."

"With Romy," Julie reiterated.

"With Romy," Pastor Laurence said with a small smile. He wrapped Julie up in a big blanket before swooping her up in his arms.

Julie knew what she was doing was selfish. Pastor Laurence would get in trouble. So would the nurses and the hospital. She didn't care, not right now. She'd feel bad later, after her parents shipped her off to a place where she could regret all of her choices. She knew her parents weren't going to let her go, not without a fight. They'd make who she was disappear.

What kind of life waited for her anyway? Not one she wanted. And if she couldn't live as she wanted, then what was the point of anything? Just a daily slog of meaninglessness, one sundown to another, strung endlessly together? A half-life with nothing approaching joy or truth, the glimmering light of the stars reserved for those lucky enough to chase their dreams?

Better this. Better a brief glimmer of magic, of light and love, of hope that things could be different than the brutal, crushing emptiness of never being allowed to have it at all. So she'd go now. To Romy.

She gave a little squawk as he lifted her, gritting her teeth as her ankle dangled. It wasn't an ideal way to go, but Julie had to admit it was faster than a wheelchair. And Pastor Laurence was really strong.

They hurried past the unmanned nurse's station, all of them out on rounds. Julie would have liked to say goodbye to Rhonda, but the thought passed as quickly as they passed the empty station. After a swift elevator ride to the first floor, Pastor Laurence took her out a side exit near the closed cafeteria. His car was warm and waiting as she slid inside and buckled herself in. Julie shifted uncomfortably, the pain from her ankle manageable. Her head still hurt when she stayed upright too long, but she could handle all of it if it meant she got to see Romy one more time.

She had no illusions that she'd be able to avoid her family, no illusions that she wouldn't pay for sneaking away from the hospital. But if it meant she got to talk to Romy, it would be worth any price. Julie wanted to see her one last time, even if it was just to say goodbye.

## CHAPTER THIRTY-SEVEN


Romy hadn't wasted the hours in the church.

She made a quick stop at Montag, to upload the song she had written for Julie's Christmas present to YouTube. Her idea to get Julie to stay required some major attention, and Romy thought she had just the thing. This time, she included a special introduction of the song.

"So I wrote this song a couple months back for the person I had a huge crush on at the time. I hadn't thought I'd ever get to play it for her, but it turns out, I was wrong. I played it for her as her Christmas present after we'd started dating. It was supposed to be something only she would hear, but I just found out her parents are yanking her out of school to send her to some camp that says it can fix gay kids.

"I'm not sure if I'll ever see her again or if she'll even want to see me after this is all over." Romy's voice broke, and she bit the inside of her cheek to keep from breaking down completely. The web camera swam before her eyes.

"I'm putting this song out here so that everyone will know how I feel about her. So that everyone will know we existed and that we loved each other."

She smiled, and stared into the camera. "I'm Romy Montoya and I love you, Julie Cranston. I always will."

She fed that, along with the video recording of the song she'd done for Julie's gift, up to her YouTube channel and sent out the notification that new content was loaded to her site. That notification then fed out to her Twitter and Tumblr followers, and everyone who followed her on Instagram.

Romy opened a group message on her phone to Rosalyn, Antimone, Shawna, and a few of her other close friends back in L.A. They all had huge social media presences and she knew they'd be happy to help her get the word out there. She needed maximum visibility in a minimum amount of time.

**RM: Huge favor to ask you guys. Pls blast this link to all ur followers ASAP. Rly IMPORTANT!!!!**

She added the link to the song on her YouTube channel and hit Send.

And waited.

And prayed.

Romy didn't have to wait long. A few minutes later, her phone pinged. Rosalyn, of course, was the first to reply.

**R0z: OMGGGGGG!!!!11! So that's Y U were such a sad panda at xmas! Best thing you've evah written! Blasting it now! Calling in the cavalry 4 this 1, Romes. Lemme know what else u need, k? <3**

Shawna responded next with a "**Done and done! Go get ur girl!**"

Antimone followed almost immediately with "**Started #freejulie. <3 U!**"

Romy wished she could ask her mom to retweet it to her followers, but thought that might be pushing things considering Monet was flying halfway across the country to deal with the fallout from that Instagram. She'd just have to rely on her friends to get the word out and hope it was enough.

Still, there was one more thing she could do. Romy didn't like sharing photos without the other party's permission, but somehow she thought Julie wouldn't mind in this instance. Thumbing through her phone, Romy found what she was looking for: one of the rare selfies that Julie had allowed of the two of them, wrapped in each other's arms on Romy's bed. Julie was wearing a bemused expression as she and Romy smiled for the camera.

With shaking fingers, Romy hit the share icon and loaded it up to her Twitter, Tumblr, and Instagram. She added the caption, *Cuddles with the girl I love.* **#freejulie #lovewins**.

Then she called her mother.

It was the hardest phone call she'd had to make. Monet had quite enough on her plate as it was and Romy was already in a metric asston of trouble from the Instagram photo, but she needed all the help she could get. Her mother took a few minutes to respond to her question, a fact that made Romy nervous. Her mother was pretty smart—likely, she already suspected Romy was in hot water up to her eyeballs. She amended her estimate of the trouble she was in to *several* metric asstons. But at the end of the conversation, her mother agreed to help.

It only took a few more minutes for the notifications, likes, and favorites to start rolling in. A symphony of pings broke the silence of Romy's bedroom, but by then she was already on the phone with the DZN and too busy to pay attention.

She had more calls to make.

♪ ♪ ♪

Romy was almost positive her mother was going to kill her, but she didn't dwell on it. She paced and obsessively checked her phone. Julie's Song, as the internet had dubbed it, had gotten nearly two million views in less than an hour. Twitter was in an uproar— **#freejulie** was trending in the US. A few reporters on entertainment and social sites had already been in contact with her, asking about Julie and what was going on with her. News of Julie's accident had hit, but the cause was still being determined. Romy kept mum about that part, but she answered questions about her secret relationship with Julie as best she could. One article had already gone online with the headline of 'Star Crossed Lovers.'

But Romy needed more. Julie didn't have time to fight a court battle right now. Romy was relying on a different court, a court where she held the advantage: the court of public opinion.

She neared the last pew before the lectern, eyes on the stone floor beneath her feet. Romy felt the cold radiating up through the soles of her boots. She wondered if they turned the heat down during times when the church wasn't holding services. She wrapped her arms around her body, wishing that she'd asked Mercury to bring her a heavier coat.

The front doors of the church opened. Pastor Laurence carried a bundled up Julie inside the sanctuary and set her on the pew closest to the back. The man's face was red, and he straightened up with a twinge, pressing a hand to his back, but otherwise, he appeared fine.

Romy didn't realize she broke into a run at the sight of Julie in his arms; one minute she was at the front of the church, the next she knelt next to her girlfriend, lifting her bad leg up onto the pew. Julie's smile was strained with pain, but Romy thought she'd never looked more radiant, horrible deerstalker hat and all. Romy leaned up and kissed her lightly on her chapped lips.

"You're really rocking the deer stand chic look," she whispered in Julie's ear as she moved away.

Her words had the desired effect: Julie's bright laughter rang out in the quiet of the church. Romy's heart swelled inside of her chest at the sound. She'd do anything to hear it every day of her life.

Romy's phone chirped at her. Another notification. As she pulled it from her pocket to check, Julie leaned over to see what she was looking at on the screen. "What's going on?" she asked, blond hair brushing against Romy's cheek. "What's #freejulie?" Blue eyes narrowed, Julie stared at her. "Romy, what did you do?"

Sudden fear made Romy's stomach churn. Would Julie be angry? Romy hadn't given it much thought at the time, so desperate to keep her from being sent away, but now she wondered if she'd done the right thing. She'd just outed Julie to the world. Without her explicit consent. That might have been a kind of dick move.

"I posted the song I wrote for you on YouTube. It, um, may have taken off. A bit." Romy tried her best to look contrite. And cute. But mostly contrite.

"Define 'a bit.' My parents took my phone." Julie held out her hand for the device. Romy passed it over sheepishly. As she scrolled through the phone, her eyes widened a little more with each swipe. "Oh. My. Gosh. Romy Montoya, what on earth is all this?!"

"If you want to go the full Mom route, you need to use my middle name." Romy reached out tentatively to touch Julie's hand, needing the physical connection and reassurance desperately. She didn't know if Julie would brush her off. It might kill her if she did. "Are you mad?" *Please don't be mad.*

Julie clutched Romy's hand like a lifeline. "Mad? It's got over three million hits!" She shook her head. "I can't believe you'd do something like this for me!"

Gripping Julie's shoulders, Romy glared into her eyes. "I'm selfish, Julie. You think I want to be in a world without you in it? Without your smile? Without your eyes or voice? You think that would be easy for me, Julie? Jesus Christ, I'm in love with you!"

Romy took Julie's face in her hands, forcing her to meet her gaze, needing her to understand. She needed Julie the way she needed air or water or music. "I would do anything for you," Romy told her. "Your parents want to make you disappear—they want to make *us* disappear. This was the only way I could think of to stop that. We're in this together, Julie. Just because things are hard, that doesn't mean I've given up. Or that you should."

Julie threw her arms around Romy's neck with a sob, kissing her with a passion like never before. The coat and blanket she wore made it hard to hold her tightly, and the way she had to sit because of her ankle made everything awkward, but Romy didn't care about any of it. All that mattered was this moment, here in the chapel, with Julie's warm body pressed against hers. They were alive and together. That was all she wanted.

Finally, Julie broke the kiss, dropping her head into the join of Romy's neck. "You know how people say you can't learn to love someone else until you've learned to love yourself?" Julie asked her, face buried in Romy's shoulder.

"Yeah." Romy held Julie tight, willing them into one body, one soul.

Julie pulled away so she could look into Romy's face. "They're full of shit."

Romy laughed before she could stop herself, surprised and delighted to hear Julie say such a crass word. "You think?"

Julie nodded once, emphatically. "Yeah. Because I was never taught how to love myself, not really, not all of me. I was only taught to hide who I was." She smiled then, an expression both sweet and fleeting. "But God, do I love you." She pressed a kiss to Romy's jaw.

"I love you so much, it made me forget that I should hate myself."

Romy's eyes filled with tears. She tried blinking them back, but they fell anyway. How was it possible for her heart to feel so heavy and so light all at the same time? Was this what bittersweet actually meant? Tightening her arms around the girl she loved, Romy closed her eyes and focused on this moment. She licked away the few tears that made it to the corner of her mouth. They held the taste of joy mixed with sadness, and she squeezed Julie just a bit tighter, wanting to hang on to the fragile peace suspended between them.

Then her phone chimed. Mercury.

"I've got to take this," Romy said, pulling her phone out of Julie's grasp. She saw Julie nod and wipe away her own tears. "Hey Merc."

"They're starting to show up at the gates. They aren't allowed beyond that though." Someone shouted something on Mercury's end of the line. With a sigh, Mercury said, "You know I love you girl, but I just got unexpelled. I'd like to wait at least a week before committing a felony."

"I wasn't planning on doing anything that required shovels, lye, or wood chippers," Romy assured her.

"I don't even want to know," Mercury muttered.

"Oh come on, don't tell me you've never thought of it," Romy said.

"Yeah, comments like that one make me want to sleep with one eye open."

Romy could hear the grin in Mercury's voice. "I totally wouldn't murder you. You're a good roommate."

"Thanks for that enthusiastic reference."

"We're on our way." She ended the call and turned to Pastor Laurence. "Give us a ride?"

He stepped out of the alcove by the door where he'd waited while they'd had their reunion. Julie looked between the two of them, confusion furrowing her lovely brow. "Where are we going now?"

Romy pulled her girlfriend in close for another hug, hopefully not their last. "Julie, my love, how do you feel about press conferences?"

# CHAPTER THIRTY-EIGHT

Julie accepted Romy and Pastor Laurence's help navigating over the ice and snow covered ground at the front of the school. Mercury had ducked back into the pastor's car to get warm while she and Romy stood just outside the gates surrounded by press.

People shouted. Flashes blinded her. Her ankle and leg ached, she was cold and tired, but Romy held her up and that counted for a lot. Romy pulled her into the circle of her arms, helping her keep weight off her bad leg. More shouts and flashes. "What did you do?" Julie whispered, still confused even after Romy had tried briefing her in the car.

"Made it so you can't just disappear. Now smile for the cameras."

"Romy! Julie!" came the cries from the assembled reporters. Julie scanned the crowd and saw local news crews, cameras, and even a DZN member in the throng at the gates. "Were you in the car accident together?"

Romy answered smoothly and confidently, and Julie couldn't help but gape at her girlfriend, amazed. She was a natural with the press but then Julie shouldn't have been surprised. Romy had been famous since the day she was born. "No, we were not, but that was only because Julie's parents found out about our relationship. As you all know, they support the belief that homosexuality is a choice and a sin, and they support camps that try to turn young people straight. They were planning to send Julie to one to "fix" her before word of our relationship went public."

Julie looked beyond the line of press and saw a sleek black car pull up. She stiffened in Romy's arms as she watched Monet get out of the car. She didn't know whether to be scared or delighted. On the one hand, it wasn't her parents—though she suspected they were on their way now that cameras were rolling—on the other, she was meeting her girlfriend's mother under less than ideal circumstances.

A man in a Saville Row suit stepped out after Monet and walked alongside her, offering her his arm to help her over the uncertain ground. They skirted the edge of the crowd, staying half-concealed in the shadows cast by the cameras' lights.

"How does your mother feel about your relationship with Julie, considering she and Mrs. Cranston are battling it out in the press over the morals in her music?" one reporter shouted.

"Julie and I are not our parents," Romy said simply. "We love each other and want to be together and if our families can't get behind that then it's their problem." Julie watched Romy turn her head in her mother's direction. The impish grin that crossed her face made Julie want to kiss her. "But if you really want to know how she feels about it, I guess you can ask her yourselves."

The crowd of reporters went crazy. Monet shook her head, obviously familiar enough with her daughter's antics not to be too upset at being revealed. She stepped up beside them, the man standing just behind her.

"My daughter is free to love whomever she wants," Monet answered as more flashes went off. She turned her head in Julie's direction and gave her a megawatt star smile. "It's nice to finally meet you, Julie. Romy's told me a lot about you."

Julie blanched. "She has?"

Monet nodded. Before Julie could say anything more, a reporter shouted another question. "Julie, how did your parents take the news? Is it true you tried to kill yourself when they found out about you and Romy?"

Romy squeezed her hand as Julie flailed about for an answer. She'd been desperate when she'd grabbed the wheel from Ferris, in a dark place certainly, but she wasn't sure if she'd wanted to die. She just knew she didn't want to go to that camp. She knew she didn't want to leave Romy.

"The Bible tells us suicide is a sin," she began, choosing her words carefully, "and I've always thought it so. But after discovering and accepting my feelings for Romy, I can understand now why some people in a situation like mine might turn to it as a solution. They feel like there is no other path to take. I did not mean to cause the accident and I certainly regret my actions that led to it, but I do not regret falling in love with Romy." She looked at the girl who'd changed everything about her life. "She's the best thing that ever happened to me."

"Julie, what about your parents? How will this change your father's campaign?"

Another car pulled up, fishtailing on the slushy pavement as it came to a stop. Julie watched her mother and father tumble out. They still looked polished and presentable, though their eyes were tired. She wondered if they'd gotten any sleep. She imagined they'd been up dealing with the fallout from her accident and subsequent stay in the hospital when the news of the press conference came to them.

"Hang on, babe," Romy whispered in her ear. Julie pressed closer to her, shivering.

"That's enough," her father bellowed, making his way through the packed snow. Her mother trailed in his wake like a sled after dogs.

Julie felt Monet step closer to her daughter and, by extension, her. It made her feel a bit better as her father bore down on them, his face no longer the calm mask that he presented to the public.

"This is a circus! An absolute circus!" Her father stalked over to them, gesturing at the crowd of people, most of them with cameras. "I can't believe you would do this to me, Julie, to our family. We didn't want our personal life dragged out into the open for media consumption…"

"Oh, but it's okay if you do it to my mother?" Romy snapped. Julie squeezed her arm. Monet spoke quietly with the man to her right.

"Your mother is a public figure—she opens herself up to that kind of thing." He stepped closer to Romy, eyes narrowed in frustration and anger.

Romy took another step to meet him, so they were standing practically toe-to-toe. "So are you, Mr. Cranston. You are running for public office and your wife picked a very public fight with my mother. It would seem you're just as much a public figure as my mom although not nearly as popular."

Julie swallowed nervously, gaze shifting between her father and her girlfriend. Romy's face was a study in anger—lowered brows, narrowed eyes, flared nostrils, curled lip. Her father's face was still lobster-red, and his voice was hoarse from shouting. He towered over Romy, trying to intimidate the girl with his greater size and bulk. He actually looked a little ridiculous.

For her part, Romy looked like she gave zero fucks about anything to do with David Cranston, going head to head with him, refusing to be cowed. She tilted her head up a fraction, a mocking smile playing around her lips.

"Smile for the cameras, Mr. Cranston," Romy whispered, giving him a slow, wide grin.

Julie saw her father's mouth thin, lips pressed tightly together. He ignored Romy, gaze sliding to meet Julie's. "Get in the car."

Here it was. She could go with her parents. Or she could stay with Romy.

Julie had expected her decision to be hard to make.

It wasn't.

"No," she told him with a shake of her head.

"Get in the car, Julie. I've had enough of this nonsense!"

Julie's mother wrung her hands and said, "Calm down, David."

"Do you know what she's done?" he snapped, indicating Romy with a jerk of his head. "This girl has poisoned your mind, Julie. This rebellious phase of yours is over. I might still be able to salvage something, but only if you come with us right this instant."

"I'm not going anywhere," Julie said, hoping her voice sounded more confident than she felt. Standing up to her father's anger and disappointment was the most difficult thing she'd done up to this point. "Whatever you want to say to me can be said in front of Romy."

Her father blew out a frustrated breath. "Be reasonable—"

"And Romy isn't just some kind of rebellious phase," Julie continued, talking over him so she could finish what she wanted to say. "I love her and she loves me." More flashes, more pictures taken of this moment.

"You have no idea what you're talking about. You're seventeen years old, Julie, you have no idea what love means," he scoffed.

"Mr. Cranston, Mrs. Cranston, I don't think we can dismiss this quite so easily," Monet offered, giving Julie a bracing smile. She reached out and took her daughter's hand. "I think they've made it pretty clear how certain they are in what they feel." Now she gave Romy a dubious look, as if to say she would pay later for this little stunt.

"No one asked for your opinion," Julie's father ground out, disgust in his eyes as he barely looked at Monet.

Monet shrugged as if his response came as no surprise to her. Romy opened her mouth to say something, but Monet shook her head, urging quiet. Julie understood. As much as Romy loved her, and as much as Julie appreciated her willingness to fight for her— sometimes when she wasn't even sure she wanted to fight for herself—this was something between Julie and her parents.

"You come with us now, Julie, or you don't come back at all." Her father crossed his arms over his chest and gave her a hard look. Her mother whispered something to him, but he shook his head. He wasn't interested in listening.

She swallowed, mouth desperately dry. If she went with her father, it meant giving up Romy, giving up who she really was. It meant pretending to be something she wasn't for the rest of her life. "No, Dad, not unless you accept that Romy and I are together."

Her father's face went pale, and Julie saw his hands clench into fists at his side. "Absolutely not."

"Then I'm not going with you."

"You're still a minor, Julie. I'm still your father."

"I can file for emancipation." She didn't want to but she would. Julie would figure out a way to have a relationship with her sisters. She wasn't going to give them up without a fight.

"With what money? How do you plan to get a lawyer?"

"In that, I can help," Monet offered, voice deadly quiet. "My foundation for at-risk LGBTQ plus youth is more than willing to offer legal counsel and I am more than happy to cover her expenses. Julie, may I introduce Lyndon Sanderson, the lawyer for the Rainbow Youth Coalition."

The man nodded. "It's a pleasure, Miss Cranston." Romy grinned so wide it looked like her face was going to split in half.

Julie felt her eyes fill with the hot burn of tears that she refused to let fall, part relief, part sadness. She'd cried enough for today. She locked gazes with her father and saw no give there. He would never bend. She was on her own. Julie's father glanced at Romy once more, his lip curling in disgust when he saw her arm around Julie's waist.

"Very well." Her father drew himself up to his full height, looking like he was going to begin one of his campaign speeches. "If you want to be independent, consider yourself an adult. We'll no longer pay for your tuition or anything else. When you are willing to admit that your actions are wrong, the door will be open to you." His expression was cool, distant. "But not until then."

"Jeanine," he said, dismissing Julie entirely as he turned to her mother, "we're leaving."

Then he turned around and walked back to the car.

More flashes went off. Julie felt frozen in place, as though she had lost the ability to move or control her limbs. All she could do was watch her father's retreating back disappear through the door of the car. She could swear all of her blood rushed somewhere around her feet—the door swam in her vision.

Her mother was slower to follow. She looked back at Julie several times, her feet dragging in the snow. Julie mouthed an *I love you* to her.

She waited in agony until her mother gave her one last tremulous smile and mouthed *I love you* back.

Julie suspected her mother would have something to say to her father when the cameras weren't rolling.

♪ ♪ ♪

The next day was a flurry of activity. More interviews, a talk with Dean Prince about appropriate behavior—and probation for holding a press conference after curfew—Julie's visit to the hospital to get the all clear, and talks with the lawyer took up most of the daylight hours. Mercury and her parents had joined them for dinner at the hotel, but Julie had insisted on returning to school even after Monet had offered to pay for a hotel room. Monet sent them back to Verona in her rented Maybach with the order to get some sleep.

Romy grabbed her hand as they watched the car pull away. "So we're taking the elevator to your room, right?" she asked as the taillights disappeared around a curve. She gestured at Julie's crutches.

"We're going to get in so much trouble," Julie said, fighting back a grin.

Romy shrugged. "Eh, I just faced down your father. I'm not afraid of an RA."

Julie tugged her closer. "About that." She looked down at her feet, unable to think of the words to express what she was feeling. "Thank you," was all she could manage.

Romy set their course up the steps of Cap and to Julie's room. "I meant everything I said," she said lightly as she helped Julie navigate the stairs.

Julie swallowed, unable to say anything else. It wasn't until they were safely inside her room, door locked, and coats discarded on the desk chair that Julie finally found the words she needed.

"I can't believe you did all that. For me." Julie watched as Romy toed off her boots before she padded to the bed in her socked feet.

Romy beckoned her over with a lazy hand. "I'd do anything for you. I hope you know that after all this."

Julie leaned her crutches against the desk and hobbled to her, grateful to be warm and snuggled tight against Romy's lean body. She wrapped her arms around Romy's waist and breathed in deeply, feeling like a ship that had just pulled up its anchor and now floated unmoored on a great, dark sea.

"I do." She pulled her head back so she could look at Romy's face. "Just like I'd do anything for you." She kissed Romy's mouth, light and brief. "I'd die for you, Romy Teresa Montoya."

Romy ran a hand over Julie's hair, expression fond and happy. "I think there's been enough talk of dying," she said, leaning up to nip at Julie's earlobe. "How's about you live for me instead, Julie Veronica Cranston?"

Julie stared into the depths of Romy's hazel eyes and smiled broadly, finally at peace.

Yes, she could do that.

*FIN*

# ABOUT THE AUTHOR

Jeanette Battista is the award winning and Amazon best selling young adult author of The Moon Series, Long Black Veil, and The Demon's Gate series. She received her MA in English literature with a concentration in medieval studies. She loves words, weapons, and epic fantasy. She believes Tolkien's Lord of the Rings should be classified as a gateway drug. She was a technical writer and project manager before leaving the private sector to write what the voices in her head tell her fulltime. She believes raisins are the devil's mischief and that brownies should never have nuts in them. She lives and works in North Carolina.

www.ingramcontent.com/pod-product-compliance
Lightning Source LLC
Chambersburg PA
CBHW031022120726
47905CB00007B/2012